JEFFREY FORLOINES

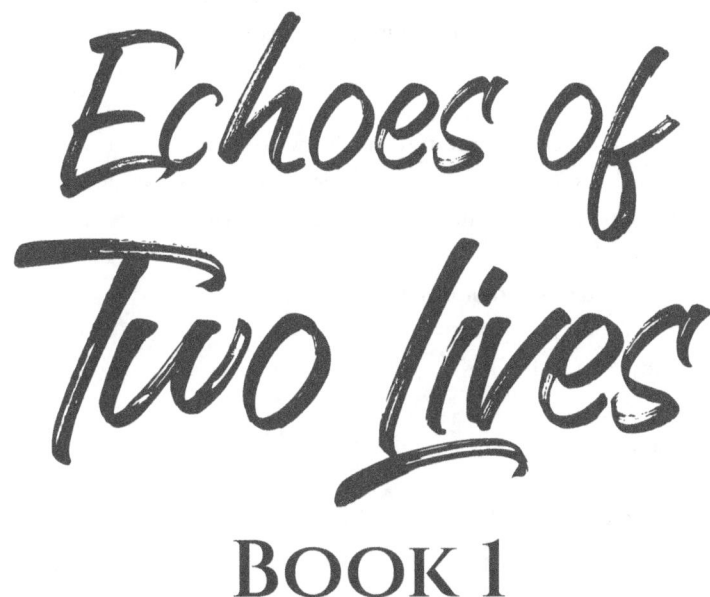

Echoes of Two Lives

BOOK 1

WHAT WOULD YOU DO WITH A SECOND LIFE?

First edition 2023.

ISBN (Paperback): 979-8-9891964-0-1
ISBN (Ebook): 979-8-9891964-1-8

Content Warning. This book contains material dealing with: Mention of self-harm, suicide, or suicidal thoughts; stalking or harassment; mention/ insinuation of sexual violence; mental Illness/mental abuse; violence/abuse; murder.

To my wife, Emma, who has supported me in all my crazy endeavors! I love you!

To my children: Abigail, Kelsey, Brooke, Gus, Mattie, and Amber.

To my Mom, Dad, Chip, Patty, and Cindy.
Thank you to Lauren!

The Last Day

I stood on the streets of Baltimore, a city once filled with life and vibrancy, now consumed by the dark shadows of war. The sounds of chaos filled the air, mingling with the distant echoes of explosions and the piercing wails of sirens. Buildings, once proud and grand, now stood as crumbling remnants of a time gone by, their facades scarred by the ravages of conflict.

As an Army combat medic, my purpose was clear amidst this backdrop of turmoil. I wore my uniform with a mix of determination and trepidation, knowing that the lives of my fellow soldiers and the civilians caught in this war's grip rested in my hands. The weight of my medical bag pressed against my shoulder, a constant reminder of the responsibility I carried. The streets were a labyrinth of chaos, filled with the wounded and disoriented. Smoke billowed from the wreckage of buildings, obscuring the once-familiar landmarks that now served as haunting reminders of the destruction that had befallen this city. People, desperate and afraid, rushed past me, seeking safety amidst the mayhem.

I moved with a sense of urgency, my training kicking in, as I scanned the surroundings for anyone in need of immediate medical attention. Blood-stained streets bore witness to the countless lives forever altered by the brutality of war. I kneeled beside the wounded, my hands working swiftly to administer first aid, to staunch bleeding, and to provide comfort in the midst of chaos.

The cries of pain and anguish filled the air, mingling with pleas for help. I did my best to drown out the cacophony, to focus on the task at hand. Every life mattered, and in this tumultuous environment, time became both my ally and my enemy. Each decision carried the weight of consequences, and the line between life and death blurred with every heartbeat. I witnessed the strength and resilience of the human spirit, even in the face of unimaginable horrors. Soldiers fought with unwavering determination, camaraderie provided vital support in the midst of tumult. Civilians banded together, supporting one another with acts of kindness and selflessness that defied the darkness that surrounded us.

Amidst the turmoil, moments of solace and humanity emerged. A child's tearful gaze met mine, and I offered a reassuring smile, a glimmer of hope amidst the devastation. A comrade's voice echoed through the chaos, reminding me that we were in this together, that our shared mission was greater than the individual trials we faced.

As I moved from one wounded soul to another, the weight of their pain and suffering became etched in my memory. The scars I carried were not only physical but emotional, a reminder of the sacrifices made in the pursuit of peace and protection. My purpose remained unwavering—to heal, to comfort, and to preserve life.

Once I had tended to all the wounded I could, I stayed as low as possible, peering from the side of the building I had taken shelter against. There was shooting close by me, but I couldn't tell where it was coming from. My fellas were all in tactical combat positions in various places around me. I tried my best to keep an eye on all of them.

"I'm getting too old for this shit," I mumbled, going back to hiding behind the corner of the building again. I *was* getting too old for this. Just two years ago, if you had told me I'd be a combat medic in the Army, I would have laughed at the very thought. I was thirty years old, after all. Unfortunately, the world had gone to hell so quickly. The politicians had finally passed a "gun ban," banning all guns of any sort for civilians. There was a lot of civil unrest when this happened, and a lot of people were killed when the government went after people's guns. When the smoke cleared, and the "wrong" people were in charge of the country, the drug cartels started to move in from the south, disguised as immigrants. We were pretty much letting *everyone* in. When the cartels rose to power, the police and military had a hard time trying to contain them once they were inside our borders. Our enemies abroad took advantage of this, knowing the civilians didn't have any weapons, which had always deterred them in the past. Now the military was busy fighting with the cartels, too busy to notice where the new danger was coming from. After the initial invasion, the military started to draft *"all available personnel"* to fight. I was a computer guy, and a volunteer EMT, so I got drafted to be a combat medic in the Army.

Two long years now, and all I could think about was the last time I had a milkshake. Chocolate, vanilla—either would have done it for me. Food was practically a luxury now—even though we held the Midwest of the United States, Texas, and a lot of the South. The Northeast was completely under enemy control.

My soldiers were not just comrades, they were like my own children. I felt a deep sense of responsibility and care for each and every one of them. Their well-being became my highest priority, and I would stop at nothing to ensure their safety. I listened to their fears, their worries, and their hopes, offering a reassuring voice and a comforting touch. I treated their wounds, both physical and emotional, with the utmost care, providing respite in the face of pain and uncertainty. There were only five of us left in our unit, and it was starting to get really depressing. It made sleeping nearly impossible, as I struggled to get the faces of the dead out of my head. I was sure all of us were suffering from PTSD in some form.

Just as a parent watches over their children, I monitored their health and well-being. I ensured they received proper nutrition, reminding them to eat and drink amidst the challenges of the battlefield. I tirelessly checked their vital signs, attuned to even the slightest changes that could signal trouble ahead. Their lives were intertwined with mine, and their survival was my driving force. I encouraged them when morale was low, lifting their spirits with words of encouragement and reminding them of their strength and resilience. I knew that in the darkest moments, a gentle smile or a reassuring hug could instill a renewed sense of purpose and determination. When the battles ceased and moments of respite arrived, I shared in their triumphs and sorrows, forming a bond that extended far beyond the battlefield. We laughed together, we cried together, and we shared the weight of the experiences we had endured. They became a part of my family, and I became a part of theirs. As I looked into their eyes, I saw the reflection of my own dedication and love. They were not just soldiers under my care; they were the embodiment of hope, resilience, and the unbreakable bond forged in the crucible of war.

I kneeled on the dusty ground, my heart racing with determination. My focus was singular—I needed to find the necessary medical supplies buried within my pack. With trembling hands, I unzipped the worn, olive-green bag, feeling the weight of responsibility settle upon my shoulders. My gloved fingers rummaged through the compartments, feeling the familiar texture of bandages, the cool touch of sterile gauze, and the reassuring weight of medical instruments. Each item held the potential to alleviate pain, to staunch bleeding, and to offer a glimmer of hope in the midst of despair. The smell of antiseptic filled the air as I pulled out a roll of bandages, its pristine whiteness contrasting against the grim backdrop of war. I mentally inventoried the supplies, ensuring I had everything I needed. A rush of relief washed over me as I discovered vials of life-saving medications tucked securely within a pouch.

With my pack organized and ready, I zipped it up, the sound cutting through the chaos like a brief moment of calm. I hoisted the pack onto my shoulders, feeling its weight settle against my back, a reminder of the responsibility I carried.

As I sat in the quiet solitude of the day, my mind filled with memories of my family. The weight of their absence pressed heavily on my heart, and I longed to be reunited with them once again. Pulling out a weathered photograph from my pocket, I gazed at the familiar faces captured within.

There she was, my beautiful wife Ella, with her strong and determined gaze. Her time in the United States Navy had shaped her into a resilient and courageous woman. I couldn't help but feel a sense of pride and admiration for her service to our country. But in the midst of war, I had convinced her to prioritize the safety and well-being of our child. In the photograph, our daughter, Katrina, was captured in a moment of happiness and innocence. Looking at her face, I couldn't help but marvel at how she had grown and changed over the years. To keep her safe, we had made the difficult decision to separate temporarily. Ella and Katrina found refuge in one of the makeshift forts, a place known as the "green zone."

"How are we looking, Doc?" Staff Sergeant Carl Hamilton asked As he sat down next to me, pulling me out of my thoughts. He was in charge now, after the death of First Sergeant Tannen, back in the town of Odenton, Maryland. Carl was probably six years younger than I was.

I turned to Carl, meeting his gaze with a weary expression. "Low on everything, Carl. If you fellas can manage not to get hurt anytime soon, we'd be okay," I replied, my voice tinged with a mix of frustration and concern. The constant scarcity of supplies had been a pressing issue, and we needed to find a solution before it jeopardized the well-being of the entire unit.

Carl let out a sigh, his eyes scanning the desolate surroundings as if searching for a glimmer of hope. His youthfulness contrasted with the harsh reality we faced, reminding me of the stark generational difference between us.

"Welp," he said quietly, his voice laced with a touch of resignation, "that's the general idea. We're gonna move farther into the city."

"You're the boss," I said, my tone flat and devoid of enthusiasm. While I respected Carl's authority, my reservations about the plan lingered. It was clear that our mission had lost its original purpose, and survival had become the sole focus. I couldn't help but question our motives and the sense of purpose that drove us forward.

"Sanderson," Carl whispered to Sally, the only female in the unit. She was a private, and assigned to stay close to "keep me safe." She was young, around nineteen, friendly, very girly-girl. Her middle name was Olive, so they called her "S-O-S." She stood before me with her long brown hair cascading out from under her helmet. Her determined brown eyes met mine, filled with a mix of resilience and vulnerability. It was evident that her helmet was a size too large, sitting precariously on her head, constantly in danger of slipping off. I couldn't help but admire her tenacity and courage, battling not only the enemy but also the practical challenges of ill-fitting gear. Her presence was a stark reminder that the battlefield did not discriminate. As my gaze lingered on Sally, I saw strength and determination etched on her face. The chaos of battle seemed to fade into the background for a moment as our eyes met, a silent acknowledgment passing between us as she crouched down next to us.

"Yeah, boss?"

"Keep Doc *safe*," he whispered.

Sally gave a determined nod, calling me "Doc," and whispered, "Stay close to me." I acknowledged her instructions, crouched down, and readied myself to move.

"Yeah, yeah," I replied, focused on the task at hand.

With a small smile, Sally turned to me and whispered, "Happy Birthday, Mark."

I chuckled, surprised that she remembered. In a heartwarming gesture, she reached into her bag and offered me half of a chocolate bar, apologizing for having eaten the other half to ensure it was "*safe to eat.*"

"You're very sweet, but you keep it," I insisted, closing her hand around the treat. "They're rare to come by."

Sally looked momentarily hurt, but she persisted, pleading for me to enjoy something on my birthday. Carl, who had overheard our conversation, couldn't contain his curiosity and asked if it was indeed my birthday. I confirmed it, laughing as he tried to calculate my age. "Thirty. The big 3-0," I revealed, amused by his attempt to figure out the age gap.

"Oldest by ..." Carl began, attempting to do the math.

"Yeah, that's great. Shut up and let's go," I said playfully, giving him a shove that elicited a chuckle from both of us.

Still holding the chocolate, Sally expressed her affection for me, considering me like a father figure. She insisted I take the gift, explaining that it would hurt her feelings if I refused. Her genuine care touched my heart, and I couldn't help but smile. Feeling the weight of Sally's puppy dog eyes and the sincerity in her gesture, I let out a sigh and accepted the chocolate she offered. "Thank you, Sally," I finally said, unable to resist her enthusiasm. Her face lit up with a huge smile, and she prepared to move out as we continued with our mission.

Taking a bite of the chocolate, I couldn't help but revel in the moment. It wasn't as heavenly as a chocolate shake from Ann's, but it was wonderful nonetheless. The taste of the chocolate brought a sense of comfort and delight, making the mission ahead feel a little less daunting.

As we forged ahead, my gaze was drawn to the sight of Private First Class Randy Trombley, affectionately known as "Cowboy," bounding towards us with his trademark infectious grin. He was known for his daring and sometimes reckless behavior, his cropped dark hair adding to his rugged appearance. His piercing dark eyes held a spark of intensity that matched his reputation on the battlefield. Despite the chaos and danger that surrounded us, Cowboy's presence was unmistakable, commanding attention with his charisma and boldness. He looked back at me and flashed me a smile, which was always unnerving. He was certain to do something stupid. Carl made a series of hand gestures, signaling the start of our movement.

"Here we go, Doc," Sally whispered, staying low but moving forward. "Stick to my six."

Private Roger Cordell, a young man in his early twenties, trailed behind us, his presence understated and his demeanor quiet. He was a reserved individual who seemed to keep to himself most of the time. Among our ranks, he had earned the nickname "Helen Keller," a moniker bestowed upon him by Carl due to his perceived obliviousness and lack of reaction.

While I understood the camaraderie and lighthearted banter that often emerged in the midst of chaos, I couldn't help but find the nickname slightly inappropriate. Admittedly, I did laugh when they referred to him by his nickname. Nevertheless, I respected Roger and saw beyond the surface-level jesting. He struck me as a decent person, unaffected by the taunting that surrounded him.

We moved with precision, navigating through the debris-strewn streets, our senses on high alert. Our mission was to scavenge for supplies, to gather what we could to sustain our weary group.

Cowboy was on point, as we made our way up the road, car to car, building to building. Sally looked back to check on me and gave me a quick smile. Her helmet tipped down, as always. She tipped it up, gave me another quick smile, and then the shooting started.

Sally and I sought refuge behind an aging Chevy Camaro parked in the middle of the desolate road, the remnants of a bygone era. The rusted metal provided limited protection, but it was better than being completely exposed in the open. Roger followed suit and sought cover beside us.

"Incoming fire!" I heard Carl yell, though I'm pretty sure everyone knew.

"No shit," Sally said in a low tone.

Beside me, Roger maintained his composed demeanor, his gaze focused and his movements calculated. Despite the chaos unfolding around us, he remained remarkably calm, displaying a stoicism that commanded respect. Sally scanned the surroundings with determined eyes, her grip on her weapon firm and steady.

I cautiously peered over the hood of the car, my heart pounding in my chest as I surveyed the chaotic scene unfolding before me. Cowboy sought cover behind a Jersey barrier on the left side of the road.

My gaze shifted to Carl, who had positioned himself strategically behind another vehicle, a mere hundred feet ahead of us to the right. His focused expression mirrored my own determination as we locked eyes for a brief moment, silently communicating our shared objective.

My M4 felt weighty in my hands as I steadied my aim, fixating on the source of the gunfire. The window of an old, dilapidated row home on the second floor revealed the enemy's position. Without hesitation, I squeezed the trigger, unleashing controlled bursts of gunfire towards the hostile threat.

The deafening sound of shots echoed through the war-torn streets, mingling with the cacophony of explosions and the shouts of my fellow soldiers. Dust and debris danced in the air as bullets tore through the crumbling walls, a testament to the violence that had consumed this once-thriving neighborhood.

"Right side, second floor!" My voice pierced through the chaos, carrying the urgency of the situation. The crack of my rifle echoed through the air, and for a brief moment, a sense of relief washed over me as I saw my shot find its mark. The enemy combatant slumped, his position no longer a threat to us. However, I knew all too well that our respite would be short-lived.

"You should stay down, Doc," Sally said, sounding concerned while taking aim at the windows and firing.

"Yeah, yeah."

As the shooting continued, I heard Cowboy yell out, "I'm hit!" My heart sank as Cowboy's cry pierced through the chaos.

"Of course he is." Sally's remark cut through the intensity of the moment, momentarily diverting my attention from Cowboy's condition. I turned to face her, catching a glimpse of her frustration and weariness in her eyes. The toll of war was etched across her face, mirroring the burdens we all carried.

"I need to focus on helping Cowboy right now," I replied, my voice laced with a mix of concern and determination. "We'll square him away, after. Right now, I've got to get to him. Can you see the bad guys?"

With a nod of agreement, Sally redirected her attention to looking out past the car. "Yep, straight up the street, behind the barrier in the road with the orange and black sign on it. Some may still be in the windows. It's *not* safe."

"Give me suppressing fire. I have to reach him," I said, prepping my bag and M4, ready to run out.

"Doc, I'm not sure that's such a good idea," Sally said. "You're our *only* medic, and this is the millionth time he's been shot doing something stupid."

"I still have to get to him, Sally," I insisted. "I won't leave *any* of you behind."

Sally frowned but nodded. She peeked her head over the car with Roger, and they started firing. "Go!" She laid down supressing fire, as did Roger and Carl.

I ran out towards the Jersey barrier, where Cowboy was lying, clutching his knee. His position was being pelted by bullets. I zig-zagged on my way to him, trying my best to avoid being hit. Some bullets started to come close.

I reached him a few moments later, handing him my M4 as I arrived.

"Just the knee?" I inquired, swiftly assessing his condition for any additional injuries before promptly tending to the wound, carefully applying a dressing and securing it with a bandage. "Yeah, man, hurts like a bitch!"

"I'm sure it does. You ever think about not being so goddamn stupid? You're literally gonna be the death of me."

"You've got nine lives, Doc."

"I'm not a fuckin' cat," I grunted, my voice laced with determination, as I slung Cowboy over my shoulder. The weight of his body pressed against me as bullets whizzed past us, each one a reminder that mortality was a very real threat.

Believe me, I can die.

The words echoed in my mind, a stark acknowledgment of the risks we faced every day on the battlefield. No amount of training or resilience could guarantee our survival. But in that moment, my focus remained steadfast on getting Cowboy and myself to safety, against all odds.

"Hang tight," I grunted, my voice firm and resolute, "and cover our six!" The words were a command, a call to action as we navigated the chaos, bullets raining down upon us.

With every passing moment, our distance from the danger grew, the shelter of cover drawing closer. I could feel the adrenaline coursing through my veins, a surge of energy that propelled me forward, defying the limitations of fatigue and pain.

JEFFREY FORLOINES

Suddenly, pain ripped through my body as a sharp, searing sensation tore through my back. The impact sent a jolt of electricity coursing through every fiber of my being. The world seemed to slow down, as if time itself were suspended in that agonizing moment.

I stumbled forward, my grip on Cowboy weakening as the weight of my own body became unbearable. The gravity of the situation hit me like a sudden onslaught, and I realized that I had been hit. My vision blurred, the world spinning in a disorienting dance of shapes and shadows. Each breath felt like a battle, as the pain intensified with every movement.

With each labored breath, I pressed on, my body screaming in protest. The world around me faded into a haze as I honed in on the singular goal of reaching a place of relative safety. My mind blocked out the gunfire and the chaos, channeling all my energy into the task at hand. The adrenaline coursing through my veins propelled me forward, defying the limitations of my broken body. My vision blurred with pain, but I refused to let it hinder me.

Finally, I reached a spot of relative cover, laying Cowboy down gently as the intensity of the situation washed over me. The pain in my back radiated through my entire being, overwhelming my senses.

"Doc's hit!" Sally's voice trembled with panic as she urgently reached out, pulling me to safety behind the car. Roger joined her, assisting in getting me to a secure spot. Carl quickly fell back to our position, where Cowboy was clutching his knee and cursing. I couldn't make out the words he was yelling, everything sounded muffled to me. My eyesight started to get blurry as Sally turned me to my side to apply dressings. Roger struggled with my vest to get it off of me, but eventually managed to do so. Sally had applied the battle dressings to the two holes in my back, putting a lot of pressure in an attempt to stop the bleeding.

"Hold this tight!" she yelled to Roger, while coming around to face me. "Doc, what else can I do?"

It was so hard to hear her. She took off her helmet and her long brown hair spilled around her shoulders. I shook my head and weakly said, "Put your helmet back on."

Sally ignored me. "What else can I do for you, Doc?"

I thought for a moment. I felt so tired. I didn't really hurt too much anymore. Everything around me seemed to be going in slow motion.

10

I cleared my throat. "Please, Sally, tell my wife, and my daughter, that I love them very, very much. Please tell them my last thoughts were of them."

"No, Doc, no!" She cried, tears streaming down her face. "You tell them that yourself!" She gripped my hand tightly. "You tell them that!"

Carl came up behind Sally, and I heard him whisper in her ear, "There's nothing we can do for him now."

"No! NO!" Sally yelled, getting on both knees to be closer to my face. "You hang on, Mark, you hear me? I'm right here!"

"Just promise me you'll tell them," I insisted. I felt so weak now, I just wanted to sleep. I'd feel so much better if I could sleep.

"I promise!" She started crying again, tightly gripping my hand.

The tears streaming down Sally's face was the last thing I ever saw, and her agonizing cries were the last thing I ever heard. The world faded into darkness, and my watch had ended.

Where Am I?

As I gradually regained consciousness, the beeping sound of a heart monitor resonated in my ears, instantly triggering a wave of disorientation. The familiarity of the sound and its association with hospitals brought a sense of unease. Blinking, I struggled to make sense of my surroundings. Everything appeared hazy, and my vision was blurred, making it difficult to discern where I was.

With effort, I managed to focus my gaze, and the fog in my mind began to clear. I found myself in a bed, slightly elevated to allow for a seated position. The rhythmic beeping sound persisted, originating from my right side, accompanied by the display of my vitals. I could vaguely make out the numbers indicating my blood pressure, which surprisingly seemed to be within a healthy range. It struck me as remarkable, as I hadn't experienced such optimal blood pressure since my teenage years.

Confusion engulfed me as I tried to piece together how I had ended up in this hospital bed. Flashes of fragmented memories flickered in my mind, hinting at a profound event or experience. A nagging thought began to surface—an unsettling realization that I might have passed away. Was this the afterlife I found myself in? Questions swirled in my mind, seeking answers that seemed elusive in the midst of my disorientation.

As the fragments of my memory started to coalesce, the events leading up to my current situation began to take shape. I remembered the intense firefight, the desperate attempt to protect Cowboy, and the searing pain as bullets pierced through my body. Sally's heartfelt words echoed in my mind, serving as a reminder of the risks I had taken and the potential sacrifices made.

The realization struck me that I must have been brought to the hospital just in time, with the dedicated efforts of those around me ensuring my survival. It felt like a genuine miracle to have made it this far. The question of how long I had been in this state lingered, leaving me with a sense of temporal disconnection.

Seeking some relief from the discomfort, I shifted in the bed, only to be met with an unexpected sharp pain emanating from both of my forearms. Confusion washed over me as I tried to make sense of the sensation. I distinctly recalled being shot in the lower part of my back, so it puzzled me why my forearms were now causing such agony. Curiosity mixed with a tinge of trepidation prompted me to examine my arms more closely.

As my gaze descended, I noticed the presence of bandages tightly wrapped around both of my forearms, obscuring the skin beneath. The realization dawned upon me that these bandages were likely a result of some additional injuries sustained during the chaos of the firefight. The pain in my forearms served as a stark reminder of the violence that had surrounded me, leaving visible marks even beyond the primary wound on my back.

The realization that I was unable to move my hand sent a surge of panic through me. My voice grew louder as desperation set in, repeating my plea for assistance. The distant noises seemed to grow fainter, and my calls went unanswered. It was as if I were trapped in a silent void, isolated and immobilized.

With growing frustration, I mustered all my strength and shouted once again, this time with a firmer resolve. "Is anyone there?" My voice reverberated through the room, filled with a mix of fear and determination. Yet, the silence persisted, amplifying my feelings of helplessness.

As I attempted to shift my hand, the reality of being strapped down to the bed became painfully evident. Panic surged within me, my mind racing with questions about why I was restrained and who was responsible for my current state.

A whirlwind of emotions swept over me, oscillating between frustration, confusion, and a growing sense of vulnerability. The uncertainty of my circumstances intensified, leaving me yearning for answers and desperately hoping that someone would soon respond to my pleas for help.

Shit!

A moment later, two nurses entered the room, their hurried footsteps echoing against the sterile walls. I observed their features, trying to make sense of their presence. They appeared American, which puzzled me. How could I be in an American hospital? Our area had been ravaged by conflict, and all the local hospitals were either destroyed or overrun.

Confusion washed over me as I struggled to reconcile this discrepancy. My mind raced with questions, seeking an explanation for this unexpected turn of events. Were they really nurses? Or were they part of the captors who had restrained me?

The nurses approached my bed, their expressions professional but devoid of warmth. Their eyes scanned the monitors, checking my vitals without acknowledging my presence. It was as if I were merely an object in their care, devoid of agency or voice.

I mustered the strength to speak, my voice trembling with a mix of apprehension and curiosity. "Where am I?" I managed to utter, hoping for some semblance of understanding.

The nurses exchanged a quick glance before one of them, a young woman with a stern expression, finally spoke. "You're in the hospital," she replied, her tone curt and businesslike.

Confusion deepened within me as her response failed to provide the clarity I sought. What kind of hospital was this? Who were these people? And most importantly, how did I end up here?

"He's awake! Quick, get Doctor Forsyth!" the one nurse said, swiftly coming to my bedside. Her eyes darted to the monitor, registering my awakening, and then returned to me, concern etched across her face. With a gentle touch to the side of my head, she said, "I'm Cindy. How are you feeling?"

But I was not easily deterred. My voice strained, I repeated my questions, my desperation growing. "Where am I?"

Cindy hesitated, taken aback by my insistence. However, instead of providing the answers I sought, she chose to acknowledge my wakefulness and brushed aside my inquiries, perhaps in an attempt to diffuse the tension in the room.

"You gave us quite a scare," she remarked, evading my questions and emphasizing the relief of my awakening.

Frustration welled up within me as I demanded answers. "Answer me! Where am I?"

Cindy's expression reflected her surprise at my aggressive tone, momentarily caught off guard by my persistence. She took a moment to compose herself before responding, her voice carrying a touch of caution.

"I told you already, I'm your nurse, Cindy," she replied, her tone measured, "you're at the hospital."

Seeking more information, I struggled against the restraints that bound me, the pain in my forearms serving as a painful reminder of my current state. I croaked out my next question, my voice strained with discomfort.

"How long have I been here?"

Cindy's response was curt, "About a week."

My heart sank at the realization of the lost time, fueling my growing unease. Seeking some semblance of familiarity and reassurance, I pressed on with my inquiries, desperate to find answers.

"Where's my unit?" I implored, hoping against hope for news of their safety and well-being.

"I understand that you're worried," she began, her voice calm and measured. "But you need to focus on your recovery right now. As for your unit, I don't have that information."

Her response did little to quell my rising anxiety. The uncertainty of my comrades' fate weighed heavily on my mind, and I could not simply dismiss their well-being.

"Please," I pleaded, my voice strained with emotion. "I need to know. Are they safe? Did they make it out?"

Cindy's expression softened, a hint of compassion shining through her professional façade. She reached out and gently placed a hand on my arm, offering a small measure of comfort.

"Right now, your focus should be on your recovery. The rest will have to wait."

"Am I the only one that got captured? Where are the others? Tell me!"

She leaned back, cocking her head. "Captured? What are you talking about? Who are the others? Why would you think that you've been captured?"

I pulled violently against my restraints, to no avail. "The restraints are a dead giveaway."

Nurse Cindy cocked her head, "Are you just messing with me?"

"No, why would I be messing you? Why else would I be here?" I answered, perplexed. "*Where* is the rest of my unit?"

I didn't immediately notice him, but a doctor had walked into the room. "I heard you were awake," he stated. "I'm Doctor Forsyth. How are you feeling?"

"You can forget it, I'm not telling you anything!" I responded defiantly.

He looked perplexed. "Calm down, William. I'm only here to help you."

Had he just called me William?

"If you want to help me, you can let me go." I stated firmly.

"I'm afraid I can't do that just yet."

"Then you're not here to help me."

"Are you in any pain?" Dr. Forsyth asked, trying to change the topic.

"Why do you care?" I retorted.

Dr. Forsyth approached my bedside. "It's my job to care for you. Why don't you just let me do my job? So, on a scale of zero to ten, zero being no pain at all, and ten being the worst pain of your life, how would you rate the pain in your forearms?"

I glared at him for a moment before reluctantly answering, "Maybe a five? Look, man, why are we worried about my forearms? Just take these straps off and let me go."

"We'll take care of that pain," he assured me, patting my hand gently and turning to the nurse. "Cindy, can you administer some pain medication for him?"

"Sure thing, Doctor," the nurse replied, swiftly exiting the room with her colleague.

"Were the other members of my unit captured too?" I asked, my concern for my comrades resurfacing.

"I'm sorry, William, I'm not following. What do you mean by *your unit* and *captured?*" Dr. Forsyth inquired.

I chuckled, convinced that this guy was trying to mess with my mind. "My military unit! What have you done with the others?"

The doctor genuinely appeared surprised, "What's the last thing you remember, William?"

That was the third time he had called me "*William*." The only reason I hadn't corrected him was that it was probably best if they didn't know my real identity.

"Getting shot in the back," I replied.

"Shot? Who shot you?" he asked, looking even more surprised.

I narrowed my eyes at him. "One of *your friends* did."

"One of *my* friends?" He chuckled. "I'm not sure what you're talking about."

"Yeah, from your army," I insisted.

"I'm not in the military," he said flatly. "Can you tell me your name?"

"Nope," I replied defiantly.

"Why not?"

I decided to stop answering his questions.

"Can you tell me about your time in the military?" he tried again.

I remained silent.

He sighed. "Okay then, can you at least tell me about being shot?"

I looked at him and said, "Shot. Twice. In the back."

"No, son," the doctor said calmly. "You were not shot at all."

"What kind of commie mind games is this? Okay, so if I wasn't shot, then why the hell am I here?"

"Are you telling me you don't remember what happened?" he asked.

"Of course I remember. I just told you! Your buddies shot me!"

"No, William," he said gently, "they brought you here because you attempted to kill yourself."

"I fucking attempted what? Suicide? Bruh, that's crazy! You're crazy!"

The doctor nodded, acknowledging my outburst. "Under those two bandages on your forearms are two long cuts, from your wrists up your arms," he explained, tracing his own forearm with his finger. "Cuts that *you* inflicted on yourself."

"I did not try to kill myself. You may have cut both of my arms to make it look that way for some reason, but I know what happened. We're starting to win, and you don't like it."

He raised an eyebrow. "William, what are you starting to win?"

"The war, of course. Do what you have to with me, but I'm not telling you shit."

He studied my face intently before speaking again. "There is no war going on right now."

I looked at him, bewildered. "Are you telling me the war's over?"

"I'm saying you were never in a war, nor were you in the military."

I sighed, realizing that this conversation was going nowhere fast. I had no idea what game they were playing or why they were orchestrating this elaborate hoax.

"Can't you at least tell me your name?" he asked.

I pondered his request for a moment. In the military, if caught, we were only required to provide our name, rank, and military ID number. "Fine. My name is Staff Sergeant Mark Fales, United States Army."

"Really?" he asked, showing genuine interest. "And ... *Mark* ... how old are you?"

"I'm not required to answer that."

"There can be no harm in you telling me your age, right?"

I considered his question. I supposed there was no harm in it, "I'm thirty."

"Thirty!" he exclaimed with a laugh. "Thirty years old?"

"Yeah, that's what I said."

The doctor reclined in his chair, pressing a button behind him, and retrieved a folder with a stack of papers. His eyes scanned the pages, searching for a specific piece of information. Just then, the nurse named Cindy entered the room, inquiring about the doctor's call.

"Did you call for me?" Cindy asked attentively.

"Yes, Cindy. I need you to stay here," replied Dr. Forsyth, as he extracted a pen from his pocket and jotted down some notes. Moments later, he returned to my bedside, ready to continue our conversation. "You mentioned your name is Mark, you're thirty years old, and a member of the United States Army?"

"I literally just said that," I responded, slightly frustrated.

The doctor motioned for Cindy to approach, whispering something to her before she left the room. Turning his attention back to me, he began speaking with a calm and reassuring tone. "Now, I want you to listen carefully. I'll explain why you're here, and then I'll provide evidence to support the truth."

"I'm all ears, Doc," I replied, my curiosity piqued.

"In this hospital, there is no record of a patient named Mark Fales. You didn't come from a war zone; rather, you came from your home in Linthicum, Maryland. There was no military unit, no guns, and no gunshot wounds on your body. Instead, you have bilateral cuts on your forearms, indicating a self-inflicted act. These deep cuts align with the intention of self-harm. One of your sisters discovered you in that state and, with the assistance of your other sister, applied pressure to the wounds until the ambulance arrived. The cuts on your forearms, I assure you, were self-inflicted. There are no gunshot wounds on your body."

As the doctor concluded his explanation, Cindy returned to the room, holding something in her hand.

My anger turned into a mixture of disbelief and amusement. "That's quite a story, Doc. I must admit, I'm entertained. You're really trying to make me believe I'm crazy."

"There's more to it, William," he persisted, glancing at Cindy, who handed him something. "Thank you, Cindy," he acknowledged curtly before refocusing his attention on me.

"Dude, stop calling me *William*! That's not my name!" I protested, "I told you my name was Mark Fales."

"Your *real* name is William Michael Fenwick, and you are not thirty years old," he asserted, passing me a small mirror.

I gave him a puzzled look before reluctantly gazing into the mirror. The reflection staring back at me … it couldn't be mine! I scrutinized it closely, feeling a sense of disbelief and confusion. I looked so young, so different. My eyes were blue, and my hair a lighter shade of brown … and more of it! There was no way that person in the mirror was me!

"You're sixteen years old, William. You go by *Wil*. You're a student at Andover High School. You live at home with your mother, father, and two sisters," the doctor revealed.

"This is some kind of trick mirror, right?" I exclaimed, flipping it over and searching for any signs of deception.

Cindy took the mirror from my grasp and leaned in as close as possible. She held the mirror so I could see her reflection and mine simultaneously. While her reflection was hers, mine … mine was unrecognizable. "That's you, William," she said softly. "That's what you look like."

Holy shit, maybe I am losing my mind.

With every ounce of strength I could muster, I attempted to break free from the straps. Dr. Forsyth and Cindy held me down, struggling to restrain me. "We need help in here!" the doctor called out towards the door. Within moments, three additional nurses, one of them male, rushed into the room. In my escalating panic, I should have anticipated what was coming next. The sharp pain that shot through my shoulder confirmed it—a needle to calm me down.

My Parents?

<hr/>

As my eyes fluttered open, I felt a wave of disorientation wash over me. It was as if a truck had plowed into me. What a fucking nightmare that was! Being young again, a different person entirely. Although I must admit, I was quite a handsome young dude. I had always wanted blue eyes, but I was stuck with hazel instead.

My vision remained hazy, yet I could discern a woman seated in a chair beside me, while a man stood behind her. A pulsating ache throbbed in my head, causing their forms to appear blurred and indistinct.

"Wil!" the woman exclaimed, wrapping her arms around me in a gentle hug. "We were so worried about you!"

It wasn't a figment of my imagination. The sound of someone calling me *Wil* echoed through my ears. Gradually, my blurred vision sharpened, revealing a woman in her late thirties or early forties. Her golden tresses flowed down to her shoulders, framing a pair of piercing blue eyes that locked on to mine with genuine concern.

"Who are you?" I blurted out abruptly, interrupting whatever she was about to say.

Her smile faltered, and surprise crept into her voice. "You ... you don't know who I am?" she asked, her tone filled with disbelief.

"Well ... no," I replied honestly, my confusion growing.

The woman cast a quick glance at the man standing behind her, who responded with an uncertain shrug. Refocusing her gaze on me, she continued to exude a sense of genuine concern. At that moment, the doctor reentered the room.

"Should I know who you are?" I asked, my voice devoid of emotion.

She looked at me thoughtfully for a moment, her expression a mix of shock and hurt. Pulling her chair closer to my bed, she spoke with a hint of sadness in her voice. "You're not joking, are you?" she said, her words laced with disbelief. "I'm *your* mother."

"It's as I told you, Mr. and Mrs. Fenwick," Dr. Forsyth began, addressing the couple. "He believes he's someone else, not your son. These things can happen when a patient experiences mental trauma, although I had hoped he would recognize you."

"What the actual fuck is going on here?" I exploded, completely losing my composure. I sat up in bed but felt the restraint of the shackles, my frustration boiling over. "Seriously! What the hell is happening?"

"Son, you were ... injured," the man tried to explain.

"Son? You're *not* my father!" I retorted, my voice filled with disbelief.

The man looked puzzled, clearly taken aback by my reaction. "No? Then who is? Why don't you tell me about yourself? Only what you want to share," he suggested calmly. The nurse, Cindy, walked into the room and positioned herself behind the doctor.

"Alright," I replied, my tone more composed as I shifted to a more comfortable position. "I have already stated this several times now—My name is Markus Leland Fales. I'm thirty years old. I have an identical twin brother named Viktor. I have two half-sisters, Denise and Susan. I'm married to Ella. We have a daughter named Katrina. I am currently serving as a combat medic in the United States Army." As I finished speaking, I studied the expressions on their faces, waiting for a reaction. It was clear that my story had left them shocked and perplexed.

Cindy interjected, breaking the silence. "I looked up the name you mentioned, Mark Fales. I even contacted the police. There is no record of a Mark Fales, Markus Leland Fales, or anything close, whatsoever. No criminal records, no Social Security Number, no driver's license ... nothing." The weight of her words hung in the air, further deepening the mystery surrounding my identity and the bizarre circumstances I found myself in.

I let my head fall back onto the pillow, overwhelmed by confusion and panic. "Doctor," I began, my lips trembling as I spoke. "This can't be happening."

Dr. Forsyth rubbed his chin, deep in thought, before responding. "William, you attempted to take your own life. It's possible that you're experiencing a mental breakdown, leading you to believe you are someone else. Perhaps it's a coping mechanism for the challenges you've been facing. I don't have all the answers, but I've contacted a psychiatrist who will be able to help."

"Doc, I haven't invented a new identity! I've lived a full thirty years with vivid memories of my entire life. I was present for the birth of my daughter, even cutting her cord myself. I was literally just in the middle of World War III. I can provide you with precise details. I'm telling the truth about who I am."

"I wish I could offer more assistance, William. Doctor Norris, the psychiatrist I mentioned, will be able to guide you through this. She can help unravel what's happening."

"I can't comprehend how my face appears so young. It's not even recognizable to me," I expressed, my voice filled with frustration.

"William … or whoever you may be, or think you are …" Dr. Forsyth paused, his eyes reflecting a mix of empathy and confusion. "I believe that you genuinely believe you are someone else. It's difficult for us to fully understand what you're going through, but we'll work together to find a resolution. You were a deeply troubled young man, but I assure you that you will receive the help you need."

"I truly believe that this is all a colossal misunderstanding. I just can't fathom how the *new face* aspect fits into it," I admitted, my mind grappling with the perplexing situation.

Dr. Forsyth glanced at the clock on the wall. "Doctor Norris should be arriving soon."

Turning to the man beside me, I asked, "And your name again?"

"Michael," he replied, furrowing his brow, "And your mother's name is Sarah."

Taking a deep breath, I let out a heavy sigh, hoping that the arrival of Dr. Norris would shed some light on the bewildering circumstances I found myself in.

* * *

I waited with bated breath, as seconds stretched into what felt like an eternity, until the psychiatrist, Dr. Norris, made her entrance. Prior to her arrival, I could hear hushed voices resonating through the hallway, building up a sense of anticipation. To my surprise, a young and striking woman entered the room. I had expected an older psychiatrist, but she couldn't have been more than twenty-six. As she approached me, a broad and infectious grin illuminated her face, revealing a set of pearly white teeth. "Hi, I'm Doctor Norris, the psychiatrist here at the hospital."

"Hello," I replied simply. The doctor had long brown hair tied back in a ponytail, and her vibrant green eyes scanned the notepad she carried with her.

"I understand you've been calling yourself '*Mark*' or '*Markus*'? Would you prefer me to address you by that name?"

"*Mark* is fine," I responded.

"Do you mind if I take a seat?" she asked, gently resting her hand on the back of a nearby chair.

"It's your place, Doc," I said with a hint of bitterness.

"Thank you!" She smiled again, her grin lighting up her face as she sat down. Immediately, she jotted something down on her notepad. "Now, Mark, I want you to know that this is a safe space for you. No one can harm you here, and you won't face any judgment. Everything you share with me is strictly confidential, just between you and me. Only a court order can compel me to disclose our conversations. The only exceptions are if you reveal plans to harm yourself or others. If there's anything I ask that makes you uncomfortable, you don't have to answer. Do you understand what I'm explaining to you?"

I sat up more in the bed, feeling a glimmer of hope in her words. "I understand."

"Can I get you anything? Maybe a glass of water?"

"If this isn't a military prison, and I'm not a prisoner, then prove it by removing these restraints," I challenged, my frustration evident in my voice.

Her smile faded a little, and a hint of sadness appeared on her face. "I wish I could, Mark, but we need to establish trust between us first. Is that alright? It's for your safety and mine. Considering what happened, we have to take precautions to ensure you won't harm yourself. If our sessions go well and progress is made, we might be able to remove the restraints during my visits, but we'll likely have to put them back on when I leave. It's part of the safety protocol." I wasn't thrilled with the options presented, as they didn't feel like true options to me. But I knew

I had to remain composed. Being argumentative and resistant wouldn't help my situation.

"Alright," I replied flatly. "I'll uphold my end of the deal if you promise to uphold yours."

"It's a deal, Mark," she said, her smile returning. "Now, I'm going to ask you a series of questions, and remember, if you're uncomfortable answering any of them, you don't have to. Okay?"

"Got it." I nodded.

"Good!" Dr. Norris made a note on her pad before proceeding. "What is your full birth name?"

"Markus Leland Fales."

She jotted down something on her notepad and moved on to the next question. "And how old are you, Mark?"

"I just turned thirty on June the first."

She smiled warmly. "Well, happy belated birthday, Mark!" She made another note on her pad. "Now, do you know today's date?"

I pondered for a moment. "Honestly, I don't. I'm not even sure how long I've been here. The last thing I remember was it was around my birthday."

Dr. Norris smiled and nodded. "Yes, being in the hospital can make the days blend together."

Her next question caught my attention. "Do you know who the president of the United States is?"

"Sure do. President George Simpson," I replied.

She paused and looked up from her notepad. "George Simpson?"

"Yeah, that's the one. The idiot," I added with a hint of disdain.

Dr. Norris seemed taken aback by my response and made a quick note on her pad. Her smile had faded, and I could sense a change in the atmosphere.

I realized what she was doing. "You're evaluating my alertness right now," I said, meeting her gaze. "These are the four questions used to assess orientation. You're checking if I know who I am, the current president, the date, and testing my situational awareness. Each correct answer earns me a point, and I need to be at least 'alert and oriented times three' to be considered mentally sound."

Dr. Norris put down her pen and looked at me with an intrigued expression. "How do you know that, Mark?"

I chuckled softly. "I'm a volunteer EMT, and as I mentioned, a combat medic in the Army."

Her eyes lit up with excitement. "Really?" she asked, a bit too eagerly.

"My guess is right now, you have me as *alert and oriented times zero*. Since y'all think I am this other fella, that would be strike one with the name question. I didn't know the date, so that was strike two. I will say, though, that most patients don't know the date, and you have to go to another question—it's not a very accurate question to determine someone's state of mind. By the look on your face, I answered wrong for the 'president of the United States' question, but I assure you, when I *left* wherever I was last, he *was* the president. Your last question will be about situational awareness, so let me just answer for you: I'm in the hospital, supposedly for attempted suicide, though I say someone shot me in the back, twice, while fighting in a battle in Baltimore City, saving *Cowboy*, per usual. That's strikes three and four. With my answers, and what Dr. Do-Nothing told you, and me believing this is a ruse by my enemies, you'll assume I'm crazy and need to be institutionalized."

Dr. Norris listened attentively as I explained my reasoning behind the evaluation questions. She maintained her amused expression, but I could sense a genuine curiosity in her eyes. After I finished speaking, she picked up her pen and began writing some notes.

"You're right, Mark," she admitted, still smiling. "That's exactly what I'm trying to assess with those questions. And I must say, you're very astute. Where did you learn about this evaluation?"

I sighed, feeling a mix of frustration and resignation. "As I *just* mentioned, Doc, I learned it from being a combat medic. It's part of my training, and I've used those questions many times."

Dr. Norris seemed momentarily taken aback. "I apologize, Mark. You did just tell me that, didn't you?" She chuckled softly, acknowledging her oversight.

I couldn't help but feel a sense of defeat as I realized the implications of our conversation. "So, I'm guessing this means it's not good enough to take off the restraints," I concluded, my voice tinged with disappointment.

Dr. Norris looked at me thoughtfully before putting her pad and pen down. She leaned over me, untying the first restraint, then the other. I smiled like a kid on Christmas, massaging my wrists. "I appreciate your honesty. I realize you could lie and just say you were not *Mark*' Let's keep being honest with each other, okay? I can't say when we'll be able to keep the restraints off permanently. If you look at it from my point of view, if I leave off the restraints and you try to hurt yourself, or worse, my career is over." I listened to Dr. Norris as she explained her decision to release the restraints and emphasized the importance of honesty in our interactions. Her words resonated with me, and I appreciated her trust, even though it seemed perplexing given my situation.

"Thank you, Doc," I replied sincerely, still feeling a mix of gratitude and confusion. "I understand the risks involved, and I will do my best to be honest with you. I can only share what I know and what I've experienced as Mark Fales. It's a bizarre and maddening situation for me, looking in the mirror and seeing a face that isn't my own."

Dr. Norris nodded empathetically, acknowledging the gravity of my predicament. "I can only imagine how distressing it must be for you. Rest assured, though, you are not in a prison or a prisoner of war. You are at BWMC in Glen Burnie, Maryland."

I nodded once more, my curiosity piqued by the mention of BWMC. "So close to Baltimore … BWMC? That hospital was seized at the onset of the conflict. I lived in this area for many years."

Dr. Norris couldn't help but chuckle softly, her amusement evident. "There is no war, Mark. In fact, there hasn't been one for quite some time."

I regarded her with a serious expression, my gaze unwavering. "What will it take for you to believe that I am who I claim to be?"

Leaning back in her chair, Dr. Norris crossed her arms, contemplating my question as her eyes drifted upwards, lost in thought. "That's an excellent question, Mark. If your words hold true, then you inhabited another existence, perhaps beyond our known reality. There is no record of you or Ella here, or anything resembling such an extraordinary occurrence. It would be nothing short of a miraculous phenomenon, possibly even evidence of life after death. This is the challenge I face."

Suddenly, a realization struck me, and I hadn't considered it from that perspective before. How could I dismiss my own experiences as mere delusions when they felt so vivid and real? "It does sound unbelievable," I admitted sadly, my voice filled with defeat and exhaustion. "I sound delusional, don't I? But I assure you, I am not fabricating an entire life. I lived it. I have memories, knowledge, and an identity."

Interrupting my despondency, Dr. Norris interjected, pulling me out of my self-pity. "I have a question for you, Mark."

With a sigh, I replied, "Sure, why not?"

"What will it take for me to convince you that you are, in fact, 'William Leland Fenwick'?"

Shrugging, I expressed my doubts. "I can't fathom any way you could persuade me of that. I possess no recollection of being William, nor any memories of individuals named Michael and Susan—"

"Sarah," Dr. Gellar corrected gently.

Perplexed, I responded, "What?"

"Your mother's name is *Sarah*," she clarified.

Realization washed over me as I remembered the correction. "Oh, right …"

"It's okay, Mark. This process will take time. We will navigate it together and strive to uncover the reality you seek."

I chuckled softly at her mention of time, a hint of nostalgia tugging at my heart. "I've had the same thought before."

Dr. Norris's response carried a somber truth. "None of us truly know when our time will come."

Silence enveloped the room as we exchanged glances, both lost in our own thoughts. Finally, breaking the quietude, I sought to establish a connection beyond our roles. "What's your name, Doc?" I inquired, genuine curiosity lacing my voice.

Dr. Norris seemed taken aback by the question, but her smile returned. "Mia. You can call me that if you prefer."

"Mia," I repeated, savoring the sound of her name. "Okay, I like that better. Mia, can you tell me what William was like?"

Mia shook her head regretfully. "Unfortunately, no. I haven't had the opportunity to speak with your parents or your sisters yet. It's my understanding that your sisters are on their way."

I nodded, understanding the limitations of her knowledge. "I see. Well, can I at least tell you all about Mark while we wait for my sisters to arrive?"

She nodded in affirmation, her curiosity evident. "Please do. I would love to hear about your life, your experiences. We have the time, and I'm here to listen."

With a heartfelt sigh, I prepared myself to recount the tale of Markus Fales. "Sure, Mia. I hope you have a lot of time, because I have thirty years' worth of stories to share."

Sisters

As I shared my life story with Mia, she listened attentively, jotting down notes and occasionally interjecting with questions or sharing a laugh. It was refreshing to have someone who genuinely cared and didn't rush me for answers. We developed a rapport, laughing and joking together as the conversation unfolded. Our cheerful moment was disrupted as a youthful and radiant woman, with her long, flowing blonde hair and captivating brown eyes, entered the room clad in a candy-striped ensemble. She approached Mia and whispered something, to which Mia nodded in response. Standing up, she turned to me with a warm smile. "Well, Mark, it was great talking to you!" she said, extending her hand towards me. "I'm going to meet with your parents and sisters now."

I shook her hand gently, feeling a mixture of gratitude and concern. "Please don't tell me that the restraints have to go back on," I pleaded, a touch of worry in my voice.

Mia's smile remained reassuring as she placed a hand on the shoulder of the young woman who had entered. "No, Mark. This is Crystal. She's what we call a *watcher*." she explained, introducing the young woman to me.

"So her role is to ensure I don't make any foolish decisions?" I chuckled.

"In a sense. She's here to take care of you," she replied.

"Sounds like a good plan," I replied, feeling a sense of ease in their presence. Mia had managed to create a comforting atmosphere, and even

Crystal's presence seemed reassuring now. Our laughter had lightened the mood considerably.

As Mia made her way out of the room, I playfully saluted her before turning my attention to Crystal. She seemed engrossed in the book she held, eager to dive into its contents. I could sense her preference for reading over idle chit-chat.

"Don't worry," I assured her, a hint of weariness creeping into my voice. "I won't cause you any trouble. I'm actually quite tired. I think I'll take a nap."

A gentle smile spread across Crystal's face. "That's perfectly fine. I'll be right here if you need anything."

Feeling a sense of security in her presence, I settled myself comfortably, ready to drift off into a much-needed rest. With Crystal by my side, I felt reassured that someone was watching over me.

I yawned and stretched; it felt good to have my arms freed. I snuggled my head into the pillow and closed my eyes. I let the weariness wash over me as I succumbed to sleep.

* * *

I blinked away the remnants of sleep, feeling a bit disoriented as I woke up to the knocking on the glass door. Rubbing my eyes, I noticed Crystal still close to the door, bookmarking her book and preparing to answer the knocking. As she slid the curtain and opened the door, I could hear faint whispers and see the silhouettes of a few people outside. Moments later, Crystal returned to the room.

"You have some visitors," she informed me, retrieving her book from the chair.

Curiosity sparked within me as I turned my gaze toward the doorway. Two young ladies stood there, both with blonde hair, but one had her hair neatly tied up in a ponytail while the other let her hair cascade freely down. They seemed to be in their late teens. The girl with her hair down entered the room first, while the other girl, whose eyes were red and puffy from crying, appeared visibly nervous.

As they stepped into the room, I raised myself up from the bed, sensing a blend of anticipation and unease. The profound impact of an event was clearly visible on the second girl's face.

"Hi, Wi—" the gal with her hair down started. "Hey, you!"

As the girl with her hair down began to greet me, her words halted abruptly, replaced by a surprised exclamation. Without hesitation, the tearful girl with the ponytail rushed towards me, her voice trembling with sobs as she embraced me tightly, seeking solace in the reunion. "Oh, Wil!" she wept into my ear, overflowing with gratitude for my well-being. "Thank God! Thank God you're okay!" Understanding the significance of the moment, I refrained from correcting her misconception, allowing her grip to tighten further. It became evident that these young women were likely Wil's sisters, their presence resonating with affection. Tenderly, I patted her back, offering a comforting touch amidst the emotional embrace. After a while, she released her hold on me, her tear-stained face radiating a mix of relief and fear. "Please ... please never do that again!" she pleaded, her voice trembling, as she leaned in to place a kiss on my cheek. "I don't know what I would do if I ever lost my big brother!"

A sigh escaped from the other girl. "Amelia, give him some space. You heard what the doctor said. He won't remember us."

Amelia, her voice trembling with a hint of desperation, released me from her embrace and stepped back, her tearful gaze fixed upon me. She sniffled and wiped her eyes, trying to regain composure. "Is it true?" she asked, her voice laced with vulnerability. "You don't remember any of us?"

The taller girl, aware of the doctor's assessment, approached Amelia and interjected, "And stop calling him *Wil*. You know the doctor said he thinks he's *Mark*," she stated firmly.

Apologizing sincerely, I sought to alleviate their distress. "I'm sorry," I uttered softly, my tone filled with empathy, "I don't want to upset you or cause any discomfort. It's true, I don't remember anyone."

Amelia's face contorted with dejection, and fresh tears streamed down her cheeks. Her voice quivered as she expressed her anguish. "You think you're someone else? A thirty year old married man with a kid? You think you're in a war, and in the army?" Her words carried a mix of disbelief and heartache, grappling with the stark reality of my memory loss.

I listened attentively to her frustration and confusion, understanding the weight of her emotions. Sensing the need for reassurance, I reached out to her, placing my hands on her shoulders in a comforting gesture. "You can call me Wil if you like," I offered gently, empathizing with her plight. "I'm sorry. I don't have a lot of answers for you. Yes, I'm married with a daughter named Katrina. I was fighting in the war, until I ended up here."

Amelia's frustration grew as she disputed my claims. "What war? There is *no* war!" she exclaimed, her voice tinged with exasperation. "You're certainly *not* thirty, *not* married, and you *don't* have any kids!"

"I know," I replied with a tinge of resignation. "That's what everyone keeps telling me."

She sniffled once again, searching for understanding. "You don't even know why you did it?" Amelia questioned, her voice filled with a mix of confusion and hope for answers.

Shrugging, I responded honestly, "I didn't do anything—certainly not to myself."

The older sister stepped in and embraced Amelia, offering support and stability. "It'll just take time, Wil," she reassured me, her voice filled with a mixture of hope and acceptance. "I'm Penny, your older sister by a year. This is Amelia, your youngest sister, also by a year." Penny paused for a moment, acknowledging the strangeness of introducing herself under these circumstances.

Nodding in acknowledgment, I let out a tired yawn and stretched my body. "They said I'm sixteen?" I inquired, seeking clarification amidst the uncertainty.

"Yep, sixteen," Penny replied. "Sixteen today, as a matter of fact. Happy Birthday!"

"And what day is it?"

"June the first," Penny replied.

"Happy Birthday, big brother!" Amelia sobbed. It had to be some odd coincidence that this boy and I had the same birthday. While Amelia continued to compose herself, Penny handing her a tissue, the weight of the situation settled upon us as we navigated the unknown together. I could sense their yearning for answers, and Penny's response prompted my contemplation.

"Do you have any idea why I would have ... you know ... done this?" I asked, hoping for any glimmer of understanding to shed light on the puzzling circumstances surrounding my memory loss and altered perception of reality.

"You weren't a happy person," Penny said with sadness etched on her face. "You've dealt with depression and anxiety for quite some time now. Your girlfriend, now ex-girlfriend, Rachel, left you recently."

Amelia, consumed by anger and protectiveness, couldn't hold back her emotions. "She's a stupid, cheating bitch!" she exclaimed, her voice filled with resentment. "She just left you! I hate her!"

Penny, still providing support, held on to Amelia's shoulders, attempting to diffuse the intensity of the moment. "Calm down, sis," she urged gently, understanding that anger wouldn't provide the answers we sought.

Amelia wiped away her tears, her sadness palpable. "So if you aren't Wil, if you aren't my brother, then where is he?" Her question struck me with its weight. I had grappled with the realization that I was alive but inhabiting another person's body, but the mystery of Wil's whereabouts intensified my confusion. How had this transformation occurred? I struggled to deny the reality before me, but the unfamiliar face staring back at me couldn't be ignored. Moreover, the absence of pain in my back indicated that I hadn't suffered a gunshot wound. It was enough to drive anyone to the brink of madness.

"I'm not sure, sweetheart," I responded softly, my voice tinged with a mixture of compassion and uncertainty. "I'm not sure of anything." Extending my hand towards Amelia, I sought connection, and she took hold, squeezing gently. "Can you tell me about Wil?"

Amelia nodded, her expression shifting to one of introspection. She glanced around, searching for a chair, and upon spotting a rolling chair, she settled into it. Penny remained close behind her, a constant source of support. "What do you want to know?" Amelia asked, her voice filled with a blend of curiosity and sadness.

"Anything. Everything," I replied earnestly. "Tell me what kind of guy he is." The desire to understand Wil and the life he had led drove me to seek any fragment of knowledge that could help me piece together the puzzle of my identity.

Amelia took a deep breath, her composure gradually returning as she wiped away the last traces of tears. "You're the best brother a sister could have," she began, her voice filled with a mixture of fondness and admiration. "You are always so protective of me, even though you can't fight to save your life, despite your size. But you have this incredible creativity. You love to read, write, draw, and especially play music. You are a talented singer too!" A genuine smile graced her face as she spoke about her brother, her admiration evident. So why had he attempted to take his own life? Was it really because of his ex-girlfriend?

"I sound like a cat that got run over when I sing," I joked, attempting to bring a lighthearted moment into the conversation.

"Oh no, you sing great!" she reassured me, her tone sincere. "Although, you haven't sung in quite some time. The doctors had you on various medications, but none of them seemed to help. Lately, your depression has been deepening, though I suspect that Rachel had a lot to do with it."

"My ex-girlfriend, right?" I confirmed, trying to grasp the details of my past relationships.

"Yes." Amelia nodded emphatically. "She was the only girlfriend you ever had. Rachel couldn't handle your depression, so she abandoned you. But, it's not your fault. You can't blame yourself. You're doing the best you can."

"I don't remember her, Amelia, so I *can't* blame myself. And if I did this to myself, the only person I can blame is *me*," I said, contemplating the weight of my actions. "But it sounds like he had a very loving family, considering ..." I gestured towards Amelia.

"Yes! *You* have a very loving family!" she affirmed, her eyes welling up again as she gently dabbed them with the tissue. "You just weren't happy. Something was missing in your life, I guess." The puzzle of my past continued to unravel, revealing fragments of a life marked by love, struggle, and an elusive search for happiness.

"Did he play any sports?" I asked.

Amelia looked at me, her grip on my hand tightening with a mixture of affection and concern. "Did *you* play any sports? Can we not talk about you as if you weren't him?" she gently requested.

"Amelia ..." Penny began, sensing the delicate nature of the conversation.

"No, no, it's okay, Penny," I interjected, understanding Amelia's perspective. "Of course, sweetheart, I'm sorry. Did *I* play any sports?"

Amelia shook her head, a small smile forming on her lips. "No," she replied. "You hate sports. You could barely throw a ball. It's strange because dad played a lot of sports. Mom played sports, too. Penny and I are cheerleaders, but you never wanted to participate at all. You were more inclined towards music, art, and those sorts of things."

I pondered this revelation, realizing that my interests and pursuits deviated significantly from the athletic realm. "Did I have a lot of friends at school?" I inquired, curious about the social aspect of Wil's life.

"Sadly, no," Amelia responded, her voice tinged with a touch of sadness. "You were usually a bit of a loner until you met Rachel."

Ah, Rachel, my previous romantic relationship. It seems she played a significant role in my life.

"Did I get along well with our parents?" I ventured further, seeking insights into my family dynamics.

Amelia nodded, her gaze filled with fond memories. "Yeah, mostly. About as well as any other teenage guy. They always encouraged you to go out and make friends, to embrace the joys of high school. But being you, of course, you resisted. Dad used to say that when he found out he was having a son, he was so excited to pass on his knowledge of sports. Unfortunately, that never happened." Amelia's grip on my hand tightened once more. "Oh, but don't think for a second that dad wasn't proud of you! He has always supported you and your creativity. You were always incredibly close to mom and me. And guess what? I'm your favorite sister!" Amelia exclaimed with a mischievous grin. I couldn't help but chuckle at her playful remark.

I glanced over at Crystal, who had been quiet but present throughout our conversation. A smile graced her face, but her eyes remained focused on the book in front of her.

"I sure would like to get out of here," I blurted out, feeling a sense of confinement in this unfamiliar situation.

Amelia's face instantly brightened with excitement. "We'll help you break out, Wil!" she exclaimed, her enthusiasm infectious. The room filled with a mixture of anticipation and amusement as we all glanced at Crystal, who had been observing us quietly.

Amelia quickly realized the need to clarify her statement, chuckling as she said, "Kidding!" But her subsequent silent message, mouthing "not kidding," conveyed a glimmer of possibility. It was endearing to witness her vibrant energy, her unwavering love and support, and her unexpected sense of humor.

Penny, on the other hand, adopted a more serious tone. "I don't know when they'll let you leave," she said thoughtfully. "Your belief that you're someone other than Wil might complicate matters." Her words struck a chord within me, reminding me of the complexities surrounding my current condition. The path to recovery seemed uncertain, and reconciling my new identity with the memories and relationships of Wil posed a challenge.

I sighed, my heart heavy with the pain I had unintentionally caused Amelia. "I'll convince you it's true," I said, my voice filled with a mix of determination and sadness. "I'm truly sorry, Amelia. I fear you might hate me if I find a way to prove that I'm not Wil."

Amelia's expression softened, her concern evident. "I could never hate you, big brother," she reassured me, her voice filled with genuine compassion. "But what you're saying … it's hard to believe. You look and sound like Wil, but your behavior has changed. You seem so mature now."

A deep frown formed on my face as I pondered her words. "I don't act like him because I'm not him, Amelia," I explained, my voice filled with a mix of frustration and sadness.

Amelia's distress resurfaced, and tears streamed down her face as she stood up from her chair and embraced me tightly. At first, I hesitated to reciprocate the hug, aware of the pain I was causing her. But eventually, I embraced her, unable to bear seeing her in such anguish.

Penny intervened, gently pulling Amelia away from me. "We should go," Penny suggested softly. "Our parents are here, and they'll want to see you again." I nodded in agreement, acknowledging Penny's words. As Penny led Amelia out of the room, I could hear Amelia's sobs reverberating through the hallway. The room fell into silence once again, leaving only Crystal and me.

Crystal's concerned gaze met mine as she asked, "Are you okay?"

I took a moment to gather my thoughts before responding. "I'm just trying to make sense of everything." I admitted, my voice tinged with a mix of confusion and longing. "I don't know who I am anymore."

As I lay there in the bed, I heard another soft knock on the door. I continued to lie in bed, my arms crossed over my chest as Sarah and Michael entered the room. I knew I had to approach the situation with a level of maturity and composure, considering the circumstances. Crystal glanced at me for permission before I responded, "Yes, of course. Come in."

Sarah took a seat in the chair that Amelia had occupied earlier, while Michael stood behind her. Crystal returned her attention to her book, giving us some privacy.

"How are you feeling, sweetie?" Sarah asked, reaching out and brushing a strand of hair off my forehead, a gesture of motherly affection.

I tried my best to maintain a calm demeanor as I answered her question. "I feel fine," I replied, my voice carrying a hint of fatigue. "Confused, of course, but fine."

"Do they hurt?" Sarah's hand trailed down to the bandage on my right forearm. I momentarily forgot about the injuries, but then recalled the pain medication I had been receiving through the IV drip.

"Oh, no, not really," I responded. "I believe they have me on some pain medication through the IV. I've been relatively comfortable in terms of pain since I woke up."

A sense of relief washed over Sarah's face as she expressed, "Oh, good! That's great, sweetie." It was clear that she cared deeply for me.

I mustered a small smile, trying to put her at ease. "Thank you for being here, both of you," I said sincerely. "I know this must be incredibly difficult for you, and I appreciate your support. I had the chance to catch up with Penny and Amelia earlier," I mentioned, attempting to engage in conversation. "They were wonderful company, especially Amelia. She did most of the talking."

Sarah's face lit up, a broad smile gracing her lips. "That's our Amelia for you! Oh, did any memories of them come back to you?"

Regrettably, I shook my head in response. "I'm sorry, I don't remember them. But I can tell they're genuinely kind and caring individuals."

Sarah responded with a swift, understanding smile. "I understand."

"I wanted to apologize for my behavior earlier," I began, my voice sincere. "I was really struggling and in a bad state, as you can imagine. But that's not an excuse for how I acted. I'm truly sorry. I understand that this situation must be a nightmare for both of you."

Sarah's smile softened, and she responded, "We understand, son. We know you've been going through a lot for a long time. Our main focus is getting you the help and support you need."

Michael chimed in, echoing Sarah's sentiments. "We're behind you, Wil, one hundred percent. We'll do whatever it takes to help you get better."

Feeling a sense of relief at their understanding, I nodded gratefully. However, Sarah's next words surprised me. "Don't worry," she said, sensing my uneasiness. "We won't pressure you or dismiss this *other life* experience you're going through. We may not fully understand how or why it has happened, but we had a conversation with Dr. Norris. She shared the life story you told her, with your permission."

I confirmed her statement, my voice calm yet filled with a mix of uncertainty and curiosity. "I'm still trying to make sense of it all myself."

Sarah nodded understandingly, her gaze filled with compassion. "Take your time, Wil. We'll be here to support you through this journey. We love you, and we'll do everything we can to help you find your way. Dr. Norris also mentioned that you provided such intricate details about this alternate life you believe you've lived. She was surprised that you consistently answered her questions about it."

I nodded in acknowledgment. "I understand, but I prefer not to talk about my other life right now. It seems to unsettle everyone, and I can't fully convince myself that it's not some elaborate trick or confusion. It's difficult to suddenly accept that I'm sixteen, never married, never had a child, and never experienced war. My question to both of you, as I asked Penny and Amelia, is: What if I'm right? What if, somehow, I switched bodies, as absurd as it sounds? What if your son is gone, and I'm here now?" Their reaction was a mix of silence and unease, clearly shaken by my inquiries. "Please, just indulge me this once."

Michael cleared his throat, struggling to find the right words. "Hypothetically, if what you're saying were true, and by some extraordinary miracle or horrifying nightmare, you died elsewhere and ended up in our son's body because he died too … I don't even know how we would begin to process that. It would be mind-boggling, deeply distressing. Frankly, it feels impossible to comprehend. My mind simply can't wrap around such a concept."

Sarah's voice trembled as she echoed his sentiment. "All we want is to have our son back."

Well shit, that sure wasn't happening.

At that moment, the longing to return to my true home, to be reunited with my wife and daughter, overwhelmed me. The prospect of finding a way back seemed impossible, and despair crept into my heart. "I can't promise anything," I said bluntly. "I'll work with Dr. Norris as much as possible, though, to see what can be done."

"That's all we ask, sweetie. They said you may never regain your memories at all, and that we should prepare ourselves for that," Sarah said, putting her hand on mine. "And that would be okay. If we have to start over, then we start over."

"And if I still insist I am Mark Fales?"

"We'll love you no matter what." Sarah stood up, gripping my hand. "Do you hear me, son? No. Matter. What. If you think you're Santa Claus, then we'll deal with it."

"They don't want us in here for too long. The doctors want you to get some rest," Michael informed me, rising from his chair. "We'll come back to see you soon."

"I'll be right here," I replied with a playful tone, looking over at Crystal. "That is, unless I can somehow slip past Crystal."

Crystal, engrossed in her book, suddenly perked up and glanced at me, a mischievous smile forming on her face. She playfully wagged her finger at me, indicating that she was onto my plan. Her gesture brought a genuine laugh from me, lightening the atmosphere in the room.

"We'll be back soon, son," Michael said as he walked past Crystal and exited the room.

Sarah leaned over me, planting a gentle kiss on my cheek. "I love you, sweetie." She paused at the door, facing me one last time, and blew me a kiss before departing.

I relaxed, placing my hands behind my head and exhaling slowly. "That went better than I anticipated, don't you think, Crystal?" I shifted my gaze towards her, but she remained focused on her book, only offering a serene smile in response.

*   *   *

My door slid open, rousing me from my sleep. The room was dimly lit, with only a small light illuminating the area where Crystal usually sat. However, it wasn't Crystal who stood there this time. Another girl had taken her place. She immediately sprang into action, intercepting the visitor and engaging in a hushed conversation with them. After a nod of approval, she gestured for the visitor to come in.

A young teenage girl entered the room, her long chestnut hair artfully gathered into a casual messy bun. She sported a comfortable ensemble, consisting of shorts paired with a tank top, and her purse casually slung over her shoulder. As she settled down beside me, her striking emerald green eyes finally met mine, and she softly greeted me, saying, "Hello, Wil." "Hello," I responded, feeling groggy and rubbing the sleep from my eyes.

Her gaze dropped to the floor. "How are you feeling?"

"I'm tired, but okay," I replied.

"That's good," she said, still speaking in a low tone. "How are they treating you?"

"Not to be impolite," I interjected, changing the subject, "but who are you?"

The girl appeared confused at first, then offended. "What?"

"I'm sorry," I quickly added, realizing my bluntness. "I mean, I don't recognize you. I don't know who you are."

"Really, Wil? Really?" she exclaimed, frustration evident in her voice. "I came here to check on you, to make sure you're okay, and you're going to play games with me? I understand you're upset with me for breaking up with you, for cheating on you, and I know you believe you did this to yourself because of me. But you don't have to treat me like this!"

The girl at the door rose to her feet. It was difficult to discern her features in the backlight. "Miss, he has amnesia," she interjected. "He doesn't remember anyone. Please, don't upset him, or I'll have to ask you to leave." She turned her attention to me. "Do you want her to leave?"

"No, it's alright," I replied, causing the girl at the door to sit back down.

"You seriously don't remember me? You don't remember anyone?" she asked, sounding amazed.

I shook my head. "Nope. But I'm guessing you're Rachel."

"Then how did you know that?" she inquired.

"You just mentioned breaking up with me. Amelia told me all about it earlier today," I explained.

"Of course she did," Rachel sneered. "She never liked me, or the idea of us being together."

"Well, it seems like you didn't like the idea of us either," I retorted. "So why does it matter to you what Amelia thinks?"

"It doesn't. I don't care what she thinks, I never did," Rachel replied, motioning towards the bandages on my forearms. "You did this because I broke up with you?"

I shrugged. "I don't know why this happened. I told you, I remember nothing at all."

Rachel leaned in closer, whispering, "Look, I just couldn't handle the constant doom and gloom. It became too much for me. I was starting to feel the same way, too. So when ... someone else ... offered me comfort and things you couldn't give me, I went with him."

"I understand how my depression could bring you down," I said, nodding. I was well aware of how depression could affect the people around you if they didn't know how to cope with it. "Are you trying to convince me or yourself? Look, I have nothing against you, even with the whole cheating thing. As I said, I don't even know you. I appreciate you coming to check on me, but I'm doing fine. Thank you for stopping by."

Rachel nodded, rising to her feet. "I'm really sorry, Wil. I am."

"Don't be. I'm alive."

"I'm glad, truly. I hope everything gets better for you."

"So, out of curiosity, who did you cheat on me with? Might as well tell me, not like I'll know who it is," I asked, attempting to inject a touch of humor into the conversation.

"It doesn't matter now. You'll tell Penny and Amelia, and they'll just make trouble for me," Rachel said, sounding defensive.

I shrugged. "I'm sure they'll eventually see you with this guy at school, right?"

Rachel shook her head. "No, they won't. He has a girlfriend, so we'll never be together. Like I said, he just offered me things you couldn't at the time."

"Before I tried to kill myself, did I know who the guy was?" I asked, trying to piece together the fragments of my past.

"You did, yes. He told you himself, but you didn't get the chance to tell your sisters or they would have paid me a visit by now."

I rubbed my chin, deep in thought. "Interesting. You don't sound like a very nice person—and I'm saying that as a stranger."

Rachel sighed, locking eyes with me. "You sure don't act like Wil at all. I do hope you get better, and that you won't try this again. Despite what I've done to you, I'm not a bad person."

"Whatever helps you sleep at night," I replied, my voice tinged with skepticism.

With that, Rachel turned swiftly and headed for the door. Before she walked out, she glanced back at me. "Happy Birthday, Wil," she said, her voice soft and tinged with emotion. Then, with a brief look down at the floor, she turned and was gone. The weight of her departure lingered in the air as I stood there, processing the encounter.

My Hospital Stay Ends

D r. Norris and I had countless conversations during my stay, delving into every aspect of my life. She made valiant efforts to trigger any memories of my current existence, but to no avail. Deep down, I didn't anticipate recollecting anything from this life, considering I wasn't here for any of it. Our discussions often revolved around my previous life, and she meticulously documented our conversations, even recording some of our sessions. The intricacies of my alternate existence fascinated her, and she confessed that conversing with me felt like engaging with a wise and mature adult rather than a young teenager.

At one point, I brought up the idea of finding a way back to my real life, although I held little hope for its feasibility. That's when Mia posed a poignant question: What exactly would I be returning to? I replied without hesitation, stating that I wished to reunite with my actual family. However, she reminded me of a harsh reality—one that pierced through my longing—I was deceased in the other world. Mia, in her wisdom, proposed that this could be seen as a gift, an opportunity to experience youth once more. She encouraged me to embrace my teenage years, to find my place, and to forge ahead with this life as a sixteen-year-old. It was a concept that took time to sink in, but as the days passed, I gradually accepted the reality that I had to move forward with the life I now inhabited. Despite my acceptance, the ache for Ella, Katrina, and fellow unit members remained ever-present. I longed to know of their well-being, if they were grappling with their own struggles in my absence. Yet, deep down, I understood that these were answers I would likely never obtain.

My "family" made frequent visits, bringing along a multitude of photographs in hopes of triggering my memories. However, their efforts proved fruitless. I referred to Sarah as "Mom," Michael as "Dad," and Amelia as "my lil sis." Penny, on the other hand, didn't fancy any nicknames, although she humorously suggested I address her as "Your Majesty." I did these things to provide them with some reassurance, to alleviate their concerns about my well-being. It didn't mean I had given up on convincing them of my true identity; rather, I simply didn't broach the subject until I could find a way to prove it convincingly.

Amelia's spirits had improved significantly since her initial reaction, and she radiated boundless energy. During her visits, which occurred frequently and sometimes without the others, she would talk incessantly, showering me with hugs and bringing along delicious treats. I learned from my "mother" that Amelia had always shared a strong bond with me.

As for Rachel, she didn't return for another visit, which I considered a fortunate turn of events. Both Amelia and Penny harbored deep resentment towards her, as Rachel had mentioned during my brief encounter. My parents had been informed by the hospital about her visit, and in turn, Amelia and Penny had learned of it. Their anger simmered for a considerable time, particularly Amelia's, who vented her frustrations at length. Gradually, the presence of the "watchers" diminished, although I cherished the time spent with Crystal. We even engaged in multiple rounds of card games, thoroughly enjoying each other's company.

The long-awaited day had finally arrived. After a month of staying at the hospital, it was time for me to leave and return to what was now considered my "home," wherever that may be. The entire family was present, ensuring my safe journey.

Although I was leaving the hospital, my appointments with Dr. Norris would continue. If I was going to fully embrace my newfound adolescence, I couldn't do it from the confines of the hospital. In the midst of my excitement, I hadn't taken the time to imagine where I would live or what my new school might look like, although it was still summer vacation. I hadn't even given thought to how I would decorate my room or make it my own. However, one thing did cross my mind—I would no longer have the privileges and responsibilities of an adult. I would have to navigate high school once again, starting as a sophomore. At least I could still drive, and the thought of my parents' reaction to me behind the wheel brought a smile to my face. After all, I had experience maneuvering an ambulance at high speeds through traffic.

The nurse removed the bandages from my forearms, revealing the angry scars. The stitches had been removed, but the remnants of the self-inflicted injuries remained. This "Wil" had truly intended to end his life. Unfortunately for this family, he had succeeded, and now I stood in his place. My mother had thoughtfully brought me a change of clothes—a pair of jeans, black shoes and socks, and a dark t-shirt. I had already taken a shower, realizing that I was now taller and more muscular than before. It amazed me that this guy had never participated in sports.

Nurse Cindy, who had been by my side throughout my stay, was there to bid me farewell. She wheeled in a wheelchair for me, inviting me to take a seat. "Hop in," she said, patting the back cushion.

"I'm perfectly capable of walking, Cindy. My legs are fine," I protested.

"Sorry, but it's hospital policy," she responded, shaking her head.

"Please, Wil, just follow her instructions," my mother urged firmly. "I want to get you home."

I really didn't enjoy being told what to do, but I reluctantly complied and took a seat. It was just a matter of minutes before I would be leaving this place. Cindy guided me out of the room, a room that had been my home for two to three weeks. Amelia stayed close by my side, followed by my mother and Penny. My father was on his way with the truck. As I didn't belong in this world, or what I called the "parallel universe," and President Simpson wasn't the president of the United States (there was some lady named President Sabrina Gavin instead, the third female president), I kept my eyes open for any other changes. Some things remained the same—they had soft drinks I liked, just different names, which was a relief. Amelia had introduced me to a soda called *Jabsi*. There also seemed to be slight technological advancements—For instance, the phones were more complex. Amelia mentioned that my phone was at home, and they weren't allowed to bring it to me. Figuring out the passcode was going to be a hassle. Unfortunately, there was nothing particularly thrilling that caught my attention as we reached the front of the hospital. I didn't know what kind of vehicle to look out for, but I stood up, ready to find out.

"Wait until your father pulls up," Nurse Cindy had said.

"We're outside the hospital now. I promise, I'm good. I'm getting antsy just sitting here."

Cindy pondered for a moment before nodding. "Take care of yourself, Wil," she said. I gave her a quick hug, surprising her, but she hugged me back before disappearing into the hospital. Amelia stayed close to me, seemingly concerned that I might stumble or something. A moment later, an unfamiliar black SUV pulled up. I could see my father in the driver's seat. Amelia insisted that I sit between her and Penny.

"I'd like to look out the window if that's okay with you," I said.

Amelia contemplated it for a moment. "Okay, big brother, but I'm going to sit next to you. If you don't feel good at all, you let me know right away."

"I promise, I will."

Amelia climbed in first, followed by Penny. I made my way to the other side of the truck and entered through the door. My mother sat in the front passenger seat after I was safely inside.

"Nice ride, dad," I remarked, taking in the interior of the truck.

"Thank you, son. It's fairly new."

My father steered the SUV away from the hospital, its architecture eerily reminiscent of the BWMC from my original world. The surroundings bore a striking resemblance to South Glen Burnie, though most of the storefronts displayed subtle differences. The roads, for the most part, remained familiar, but the absence of demolished buildings and the eerie quiet of a war-free environment was a profound relief.

My eyes were drawn to the unscathed buildings outside the window, beyond the pristine structures, the thriving storefronts, and the bustling streets were an affirmation that life here was untouched by the devastation of conflict. I found myself entranced by the thriving businesses, their open doors a symbol of prosperity and peace. It was a view that left me not only in awe but also humbled by the profound contrast to the chaos I had known.

"What town do we live in?" I asked, directing my question to anyone in the vehicle.

"Linthicum," Amelia replied.

"Ah, I used to live there," I said, nodding. "I know it well."

"You do?" she asked, sounding surprised.

"Well ... umm ..." I hesitated, not wanting to delve into the topic of my other life with them at that moment. "I don't know how I know, I just do."

"Maybe you're remembering stuff!" Amelia said excitedly.

"Maybe," I replied, though I knew deep down that I wasn't. Shortly after departing from the hospital, we drove past a series of strip malls and restaurants. Amid this scene, my attention was captivated by a specific establishment, causing me to nearly twist my neck in an attempt to catch a better glimpse. My sudden exclamation rang out, "Wait! Stop the car!" I exclaimed suddenly. My father, taken aback, applied the brakes, briefly stirring a touch of chaos on the road. "What? What is it?" my mom asked, looking around frantically.

"That place we just passed ... it had a sign that said 'World famous Milkshakes'! Do you think they actually have them? I mean, for real?" I asked with eager anticipation. Amelia and Penny burst into giggles, and I could feel my eyes widening with excitement.

"Jesus, Wil, don't do that to me," my father scolded me, his voice filled with relief. "You scared me."

"You want a milkshake, sweetheart?" my mom asked, looking back at me.

"I haven't had a milkshake in two years!" I exclaimed, excitement bubbling within me, as my dad turned into the shopping center to backtrack to the place I had spotted.

"You had a milkshake last week," Amelia pointed out.

Shit.

I had slipped up again. I had to be more careful not to mention my other life, especially around Amelia. I looked at her and shrugged, hoping to downplay the slip.

"What flavor do you want?" my dad asked.

"Chocolate."

"Girls?"

"I'll take chocolate!" Amelia chimed in immediately.

"Same," Penny added. Dad guided us through the drive-thru, placing an order for milkshakes to satiate our thirst—naturally, I requested a large. As I waited with bated anticipation, it conjured the same excitement one feels on Christmas morning. Following the exchange of payment and the handover in the drive-thru, he finally passed my eagerly awaited milkshake into my hands. "Oh my fucking god, I never thought I would have one of these again!" I exclaimed, unable to contain my joy as I immediately started savoring every sip. Amelia burst into laughter.

"William, language," my mom scolded, giving me a disapproving look. I relished every last drop, making audible sounds of delight throughout. Both girls giggled at how much I was enjoying it.

"If any of you can't finish your milkshakes, feel free to pass them my way!" I exclaimed, happily polishing off my own milkshake. I was so fond of the treat that when I reached "rock bottom," I even took off the lid and proceeded to lick the remaining bits from the inside of the cup.

"No chance! I love these!" Amelia giggled in response.

Penny couldn't help but burst into laughter, exclaiming, "Oh, Jesus, Wil! You go! Get it all!" The camaraderie and joy among us was infectious, making the moment even more delightful.

A little while later, we arrived in Linthicum, a charming older town in Maryland situated between Ferndale and Glen Burnie. Though not a sprawling city, it had its own unique appeal. As we drove through the main area of the town, I couldn't help but notice something missing.

"Hey, where's the Light Rail?" I inquired.

"The what?" Penny asked, puzzled.

"You know ... the Light Rail. The Metro?"

"Oh, sweetie, there's no Metro running through Linthicum," my mom replied, shaking her head. "Why would you ever think that?"

"Wow," I murmured, surprised. The absence of the Light Rail running through Linthicum, Ferndale, and into Glen Burnie was quite notable. It had been a topic of discussion and debate in the area, back in the day on my world. Nobody ever wanted it.

We continued down a road that was completely unfamiliar to me. It stretched for a long distance, with trees lining both sides. Eventually, we reached a gated entrance, and my dad pressed a button on his console to open it.

"We live in a gated community?" I asked, surprised by the entrance.

"Not exactly," my mom responded. "I realize we haven't really talked much about where we live."

A few moments after passing through the gate, an enormous house emerged from behind the trees.

"Are you kidding me? We live *here*?" I exclaimed, utterly amazed by the sheer size of the house. It seemed to stretch on forever. "Are we fuckin' rich?"

"Wil, please. Watch your language," my mother admonished firmly.

Damn, I had been swearing so freely. This adjustment wouldn't be easy.

"We're doing okay," my father replied modestly.

I was pretty certain that I had my own room in this grand house. As we came to a stop in front of the double doors, I couldn't contain my excitement. I quickly opened my door and stepped out, eager to explore everything.

"Wil, wait for me!" Amelia called out, sliding out of the car as fast as she could. My parents and Penny followed suit, but they didn't seem as rushed as us.

My father approached the double doors, and they opened automatically. "After you, Wil," he said, stepping aside to let me enter. I walked into the foyer, and my eyes were immediately drawn to the grand staircase, adorned with a magnificent chandelier hanging from the ceiling. The front entryway was filled with natural light from the surrounding windows. There were double doors on both sides and two hallways stretching ahead.

"Wow!" I exclaimed, unable to find any other words to describe the grandeur of the place.

Amelia and Penny burst into laughter, their voices echoing through the foyer. Even my mom couldn't help but smile, though my father didn't show much reaction.

"Oh, Wil, you're so funny!" Amelia said, still chuckling. "I'm thrilled that you're finally home!" She wrapped her arms around my neck, giving me a tight hug before releasing me. "Come on, let me show you around!" She eagerly took my hand and led me towards the open French doors on the right.

We entered a large living room with several couches and chairs, exuding a formal and pristine atmosphere. It seemed as if no one had ever sat in here. "Nobody really comes in here unless we have guests," Amelia explained, almost as if she could read my thoughts. "And there's no TV either." She briefly frowned but then quickly regained her smile.

"It's quite lovely," I commented, admiring the elegant surroundings.

"It's a stuffy room, you know, for stuffy people," Amelia added, offering her own perspective. She giggled, taking my hand and leading me to the next room. Each room she showed me was a marvel of space and luxury, stretching out before me in grandeur. My previous house could easily be engulfed within the expansiveness of each room. I may be prone to hyperbole, but the sheer magnitude was awe-inspiring. The rooms exuded a blend of exquisite craftsmanship and modern sophistication, adorned with state-of-the-art gadgets that pushed the boundaries of my familiarity. The kitchen, a vast expanse of culinary delight, boasted countless cabinets and an abundance of room to create gastronomic masterpieces. Adjacent to it, the informal dining room basked in the soft glow of natural light pouring in through the generous windows.

"This is where we usually sit to eat," she explained with pride.

As we kept exploring, we stumbled upon a fantastic workout room that practically screamed, "Fitness lovers, come in!" It was packed with a wide variety of weights and exercise stations, inviting us to test our physical limits.

And then, there was the indoor pool, a true haven for aquatic joy. It had a lazy river winding through the space and not one but two inviting hot tubs, each at the perfect temperature. It was like a little paradise under a roof. The room was lined with plenty of windows, offering breathtaking views in every direction. What made it even cooler was that you could adjust the windows' opacity, so you could decide whether you wanted to feel connected to the outside world or not.

Right next to the pool area, there was this fantastic game room that just screamed fun and friendly competition. It had a cool video arcade with both nostalgic classics and cutting-edge games that practically called out with their vibrant screens and joysticks.

You'd spot pool tables along one wall, and an air hockey table that buzzed with energy, just imagining the pucks zipping across its smooth surface, meeting skillful strikes from determined players. There were ping-pong tables too, ready for some thrilling rallies, their surfaces just waiting for lightning-fast exchanges.

But the best part was the movie theater, right in the middle of everything, a cozy haven for cinematic enjoyment. With comfy seats and top-notch audiovisual tech, it was the perfect place to lose yourself in the magic of storytelling on the silver screen.

"What the heck do our parents do?" I asked, feeling completely overwhelmed by everything I was witnessing.

"Dad created some device that became a huge success. I don't know all the details, but both mom and dad own the company called *Fenwick Industries*. It's pretty mind-blowing."

"Wait, there are only five of us in total living here?"

"Yep, just me, you, Penny, mom, and dad."

"I can't even wrap my head around it ..."

"Come on, Wil, let me show you our rooms." Amelia beckoned, her laughter filling the air as she intertwined her fingers with mine. With a skip in our step, we bypassed the elevator, opting instead for the graceful ascent up the stairs. As we arrived on the top floor, Amelia's gesture drew my attention to Penny's room, a haven of its own. Adjacent to it, we arrived at the grand entrance of her own abode. "This is my room!" she exclaimed, swinging open the door with a flourish. However, we stood at the threshold, not venturing inside. "If you ever need anything, just come and get me. My room is right next to yours!"

"Really?" I asked, a glimmer of excitement in my voice.

"Yep!" Amelia cheerfully shut her door and reclaimed my hand, pulling me along with an infectious excitement. As we traversed the hallway, she eagerly swung open the door at the end. I paused momentarily, hesitating just outside, but her reassuring gaze encouraged me forward. "Come on, Wil, it's okay," she assured me, her hand reaching out to mine once again.

With a gentle tug, she guided me into the room, unveiling a haven of serenity and comfort. The room embraced me with its grandeur, matching the opulence of the rest of the house. My gaze was immediately drawn to the French doors that beckoned me towards the balcony, offering a breathtaking view. Stepping farther inside, my eyes widened at the sight of the colossal Alaskan king-size bed, flanked by a convenient mini-fridge for late-night cravings. A desk commanded attention on the opposite wall, complemented by an astonishingly sleek and slim TV.

Adjacent to the bedroom stood two magnificent walk-in closets, spacious enough to comfortably house a small family. And then there was the bathroom, an epitome of indulgence, boasting an oversized jetted bathtub that promised blissful relaxation, a lavish shower with dual heads and sprayers for a luxurious experience, not one but two toilets, and twin sinks that spoke of effortless elegance.

Amelia walked over to the nightstand and handed me a phone that simply oozed elegance and sophistication. I couldn't help but admire the sleek, seamless design as I held it in my hand. Intrigued, I touched the screen, only to be greeted by a passcode prompt. I turned to Amelia, silently seeking her guidance, but she simply shrugged, leaving me to unlock the mysteries of the device on my own. "Don't look at me, big brother! We're super close, but you didn't share any passcodes, passwords, or anything like that."

I tossed the phone on the bed. "Not like I have anyone to call," I said with a shrug, feeling a tinge of loneliness. "I don't know anyone."

Amelia's expression turned somber as she nodded in agreement. "That's true," she said sadly. "But you could access your pictures, emails, and SocialStatus to see if any of it jogs any memories."

Curiosity piqued, I asked, "What's SocialStatus?"

"It's an app that allows you to connect with friends and family, see pictures, and stuff like that," Amelia explained.

"It sounds like something we used to have called Facebook," I replied.

Perplexed, she asked, "What's Facebook?"

"It's an app I used before. It sounds like the same concept to me," I clarified.

Amelia nodded absentmindedly. "Mom said that once I showed you your room, I should give you some alone time to get acquainted with your stuff."

I sighed, feeling overwhelmed. "This isn't my stuff, Amelia. I wouldn't want to touch anything."

She surprised me by embracing me in a hug. At first, I stiffened, unsure of how to react, but I eventually returned the gesture. After a few moments, she released me. A tear or two streamed down Amelia's face as she spoke. "Wil, this is your stuff. Don't be afraid to touch anything. You're home now. I'm going to make sure nobody ever hurts you again, I promise." She quickly wiped away the tears. "And don't worry, dad had a cleaning crew come in. There's no ... well ... you know ... it was all cleaned up."

I had to think about what she was saying before I realized. "I tried to kill myself in here?" I asked, my voice filled with disbelief and sorrow. Amelia nodded, her tears continuing to flow. The weight of the realization crashed down on me, and I struggled to comprehend the darkness Wil had faced within these walls. "How did you find me?" I inquired, needing to understand how she had discovered Wil in that desperate moment.

Amelia sniffled and took a moment to compose herself before responding. "I knew you were struggling after Rachel left you. I tried to keep a close eye on you, but you weren't answering your phone or the door when I knocked. So I let myself in, and I found you here, on the bed. In a panic, I called Penny. She and I held pressure with your sheets on both of your arms." She gestured towards the empty bed. "Oh, those sheets, pillows, blankets ... they're all gone now," she added before I had a chance to process it. "Dad replaced the entire bed ... even the carpet is brand-new."

Overwhelmed with gratitude and remorse, I looked at Amelia. "You ... you saved my life, Amelia. Both you and Penny. I don't know how to thank you, how I'll ever repay you for what you've done." Embracing her tightly, I felt her tears soaking into my shirt. I knew the pain that Wil had caused her, and I made a vow to her. "What *I* did ... that will never happen again," I whispered softly into her ear. "I promise you."

"Don't leave me again, big brother," Amelia pleaded between sobs. I held her even tighter, assuring her that I would stay by her side. We remained locked in that embrace for what felt like an eternity, until she finally released me. Wiping away her tears, she managed a smile through her sorrow. "I'm sorry, Wil. This has all been a lot for me. What happened, your memory loss ... it's been a lot. But I also know it's been even more for you. Just remember, I'm here for you," she reassured me.

As Amelia expressed her gratitude and held me to my promises, I placed my hand on her shoulder, offering a reassuring touch. "I can imagine, and I'm so sorry. Everything will be different from now on—a good kind of different," I assured her, hoping to bring some comfort.

Amelia's smile, though still tinged with traces of tears, conveyed a sense of hope. "I'm going to hold you to all those promises you just made, big brother," she declared playfully.

I chuckled softly. "You do that."

After composing herself, Amelia cleared her throat and spoke with a determined tone. "Well, I'll let you be for a bit. If you need anything, anything at all—if you need to talk, if you start to feel bad, depressed, sore, hungry—I'll be right next door! You come to see me *right away*, okay?"

I nodded, understanding the importance of her support. "I promise, Amelia."

"Okay, then ... I'll talk to you soon," she said, walking out of the room, leaving me in the solace of my own thoughts.

My Stuff

A s I explored the room, my curiosity led me to pick up the phone that was lying on the bed. I was eager to discover more about Wil's life, his memories, and the connections he might have had. Did he truly have no friends as Amelia had mentioned? It seemed strange considering the loving family he had, especially with Amelia being so protective of him. I couldn't help but feel a sense of awe at the grandeur of the house we lived in. It was clear that Wil's family had immense wealth and resources at their disposal. However, it also made me realize that Wil must have been going through something incredibly difficult to have resorted to such drastic measures.

I studied the phone intently, determined to crack the passcode. I tried a series of common combinations—1234, 1379, 9731—but to no avail. Disappointed, I tossed the phone back onto the sumptuous bed. My curiosity led me to the desk, where I rummaged through drawers in search of clues. I sifted through papers, drawings, and music-related items, but found no passwords. Just as I was about to give up, a stroke of luck struck. I lifted the keyboard and uncovered a jackpot—a collection of three passwords and two four-digit numbers. Eagerly, I entered the first password from the notes, successfully unlocking the phone. It felt like a triumph, an entryway to a world waiting to be explored.

Opening the photo gallery, I embarked on a visual journey through Wil's past. Selfies captured fleeting moments of self-reflection, offering glimpses into his inner world and the range of emotions he experienced.

Among the images, I discovered photos of Wil with Rachel at a carnival, enjoying some funnel cake, some pictures at a music festival of some type, showcasing the depth of their connection and the cherished moments they shared.

As I continued scrolling, a tapestry of familial love unfolded before me. Pictures depicted Wil alongside Amelia, Penny, and his parents, radiating warmth and happiness. The joy they experienced in each other's company was palpable. Birthdays held a special significance in Wil's life, evident from the snapshots that immortalized those celebratory moments. It appeared that Wil did manage to step out of the house occasionally, evident from the snapshots capturing moments with Amelia at what seemed to be a school concert, where they appeared to be enjoying themselves in a playful manner. I noticed photos of Wil playing the guitar, revealing his passion for music. As evident from one of the previous pictures, he was a member of the school band. I couldn't play any musical instruments myself.

Then, I came across a picture of cheerleaders, followed by one particular cheerleader who seemed to have caught Wil's attention — with her flowing, golden locks and enchanting azure eyes, she undoubtedly ranked as the most stunning girl I had ever laid eyes upon. It seemed that he had developed an interest in her, perhaps before his relationship with Rachel. I couldn't help but wonder what their story might have been and how it unfolded.

As I delved deeper into Wil's digital world, I couldn't help but feel a mix of curiosity, frustration, and even a hint of guilt. Discovering the limited number of friends on his SocialStatus account made me question why he seemed to be so isolated. However, the more I explored his interactions and messages, the clearer it became.

Rachel, the girl he had been dating, appeared to be a significant presence in his life. While she possessed physical beauty, her attitude and behavior left much to be desired. It seemed that she lacked empathy and understanding when it came to Wil's struggles with depression. The messages I read depicted her dismissive and insensitive remarks, urging him to simply "snap out of it" as if his mental health could be easily overcome. His status didn't seem to be updated too often. The latest update was a picture of him and Rachel together, and they were both smiling. If Wil was so unpopular, what drew her to him? The money his family had? As I went through the messages, I realized Rachel was not so attractive on the inside. I didn't like her—the way she talked to Wil, it looked like she tried to change him, wanting him to be something he wasn't.

The realization left a bitter taste in my mouth, and I couldn't help but feel disdain towards her. It seemed that she didn't truly appreciate him for who he was and had expectations that were unreasonable and unsupportive.

I stumbled upon an app on his phone that essentially functioned as a journal, akin to a personal diary. It was filled with countless pages, and a glimmer of anticipation welled up inside me as I contemplated delving into his innermost thoughts. As I began to scan through its contents, a wave of horror washed over me. Wil's self-esteem appeared to be virtually non-existent. In fact, from the initial entries alone, he expressed profound self-loathing and disdain for his own life. He grappled with the frustration of not being more outgoing and the sense of being different from everyone else.

Within the journal's pages, he described how people labeled him a *nerd*, and how their treatment made him feel utterly insignificant. He also chronicled numerous instances of being subjected to physical abuse, as if it were an everyday occurrence. It was painful to read; I had my own experiences with bullying in junior high school, and I understood the emotional toll it could take.

The journal painted a vivid picture of a deeply depressed individual who believed he had nobody in his life. However, amid the darkness, he frequently wrote about Amelia. He spoke of her kindness, love, affection, and the attention she showered upon him. There were also glimpses of positivity as he shared his profound love for music and the arts. He even expressed a desire to pursue acting, yet he struggled to summon the courage to audition or perform in front of his peers.

All of this was only within the first thirty pages of the journal.

Feeling a sense of frustration, I tossed the phone onto the bed, needing a break. I shifted my attention to the physical aspects of the room, hoping to find some solace or inspiration there.

Glancing at the clothes in the closets, I couldn't deny my disappointment. The style and choices didn't align with my personal preferences. It was all quite … *nerdy* looking things that I would not be caught dead in. Determined to create my own identity and carve out a new sense of self, I decided to seek out my parents' support and discuss my concerns about the clothes and my personal style.

One thing that caught my eye was an Andover High School yearbook from last year. I had attended the very same school in my world! Wil should've been a freshman. I immediately went to the index, to find he had a few pictures. As I perused the pages of the yearbook, I found myself drawn to the section featuring Wil's pictures. His freshman portrait didn't reveal anything out of the ordinary, just a typical school photo. However, it was the other two pictures that caught my attention.

In one picture, Wil was captured in a somewhat awkward pose, playing the guitar while sitting on a stool. It was evident that he was aware of the photo being taken, which might explain his self-conscious expression. Nevertheless, I couldn't help but admire his interest in music and his willingness to showcase his talent.

The second picture, which was bookmarked by a varsity music letter, the kind typically sewn onto jackets, depicted Wil as a member of the school band, playing one of the drums that he carried in front of him. I found this image particularly intriguing and cool. I found the music letter, an "A" for "Andover," to be interesting. I wondered why he had never sewn it to his school jacket—assuming he had one.

As I continued flipping through the yearbook, I noticed that there were only a few signatures on Wil's page. Amelia had left a heartfelt and lengthy message expressing her admiration for him as a brother. Penny, too, had written a message. Rachel's message, on the other hand, seemed to be more significant, and kind. Lastly, there was a signature from someone named Emily, whose connection to Wil remained unclear.

With a sigh, I carefully placed the yearbook back on top of Wil's dresser. *My* dresser.

Eager to explore the entertainment options in the sitting room, I strolled across the exquisite space and located the remote on the elegant end table. Settling onto the plush sofa, I embarked on a channel-surfing journey. Although the programs were unfamiliar to me, I stumbled upon a baseball game and caught a thrilling preview for the forthcoming hockey season, igniting my excitement. Lost in the captivating allure of the television, I was interrupted by a gentle knock at my door. Anticipating Amelia's prompt arrival, I marveled at her swift response.

"Please, come in," I invited, still seated on the sofa as I turned off the TV. Penny's head appeared around the doorframe, catching me off guard.

"Can I join you?" she asked.

"Of course, Penny. I thought you were Amelia for a moment," I admitted. Penny gracefully approached and took her place beside me on the luxurious sofa, her attire exuding casual elegance with shorts and a tastefully designed t-shirt. She reclined slightly, tilting her head back, momentarily evading direct eye contact.

"Don't worry, she'll be here soon," she reassured me, closing her eyes. "How's it been going? Adjusting to everything?" she inquired, her smile evident even without opening her eyes.

"It's been … okay, I suppose," I replied, unsure of how to fully express myself. Penny's smile grew as she took a deep breath and let out a sigh.

"You know … I know that you're *not* Wil," she stated abruptly. My heart skipped a beat, surprised by her revelation. I looked at her, awaiting further explanation.

"What do you mean?" I asked, my curiosity tinged with a touch of vulnerability.

She opened her eyes and turned her head towards me, her gaze held mine as she spoke, her words carrying a mixture of understanding and concern. "I know you still believe you're this other guy, *Mark*," she stated firmly. I remained silent, unable to find a suitable response. "It's okay, your secret is safe with me," she reassured me, her voice filled with compassion. "I don't want Amelia to be any more upset than she already is."

I nodded, grateful for her understanding. "She's a very sweet girl," I acknowledged.

Penny's tone shifted slightly, hinting at a touch of frustration. "She's also incredibly naïve. She wholeheartedly believes that you'll eventually regain your memories."

My gaze dropped to my hands, a pang of sadness creeping in. "I know she does," I admitted softly.

"I, on the other hand, don't believe you'll remember any of us," Penny said sharply, her words cutting through the air. "But here's the thing, I believe everything you've said."

Surprised, I looked back at Penny, searching for any sign of doubt. "You do?"

She nodded solemnly, her eyes filled with conviction. "I do. You don't act like Wil, you don't think the way he did. You're far more mature—*far more mature* than him, Amelia, and even myself. The things you say are different, as if you possess knowledge that he didn't. The only logical explanation is that you're not him." Her words echoed in my mind, resonating with a sense of truth. It was a relief to know that someone understood, even if it meant accepting the possibility of a different identity.

Taking a deep breath, I acknowledged, "You're absolutely right. I'm not Wil. I've come to terms with the fact that there's no way back to my previous life, and even if there were, I would essentially be dead. I wish I could bring your brother back to this body, but there's nothing of him here except occasional teenage urges, which is quite strange. I find myself thinking like a teenager from time to time."

Penny's voice carried a somber tone as she shared her revelation. "I believe he died the night you arrived. We held those sheets over his cuts for over twenty-five minutes before an Ambulance got here. When he got to the hospital, he was basically gone ... or at least, in a coma. Then he suddenly came back, and somehow, in that same moment, you seemed to have arrived."

A mix of frustration and confusion welled up within me. "Why didn't you mention any of this when I was in the hospital? I was losing my mind trying to explain everything to the doctors, your parents, and your sister."

Penny looked down, her voice tinged with resignation. "I'm only seventeen. I knew no one would believe my theories. My beliefs differ from my parents' religious views. I believe in something more expansive, grander than what the Bible states."

Understanding her predicament, I reflected for a moment, breaking eye contact before meeting Penny's gaze once again. "I understand your position. It must have been challenging for you. So, what do we do now?"

Penny shrugged. "I dunno. You live your life the way you want to, I suppose. What other choice is there? I mean, I know you must miss your family a lot, but being out of the war—that can't be so bad."

"I feel like I'm lying to everyone—that's my issue. If I say I'm Wil, then I'm lying. And I do miss my family—very much."

Penny's smile was understanding as she nodded in agreement. "That's something Wil wouldn't even consider, avoiding lies. I get it. Just be cautious, okay? Mom and Amelia have already gone through so much."

I nodded in acknowledgment. "You're right. Perhaps I just need to convince one person. Maybe I can start with your dad."

Penny burst into laughter, finding my suggestion amusing. It took her a moment to regain her composure. "Good luck with that! Dad isn't exactly open to the idea of reincarnation or a second life for someone."

Curiosity flickered in my eyes as I asked her, "If you believe me and believe that I'm not Wil, then why aren't you more upset about his permanent absence?"

Penny shrugged. "I loved Wil. I really did. He was such a tortured soul. No matter what any of us did to help him after Rachel left him … cheated on him, he seemed too far gone. I sure didn't think he would have taken his own life, or I would have stayed with him—day and night. I've cried my eyes out for him already. He's where he wanted to be—at peace."

"I hope so," I replied, a hint of longing in my voice. "I hope he has found peace, wherever he may be."

Penny's eyes softened, and she reached out to gently pat my arm. "As far as I'm concerned, you're my brother now. I'm here for you, *Wil,* if you need someone to talk to, vent, or even cry. I've got your back."

Gratitude filled my heart, and I couldn't help but express it. "Thank you, Penny. You're a genuinely kind person."

Penny chuckled, a mischievous glint in her eyes. "Don't say that too loudly. I've got a reputation to uphold, you know. Can't let people think I'm all soft and caring." She winked playfully. "So, how do you plan to convince our dad, the formidable figure that he is, that you're really Mark?"

A sudden realization dawned upon me, and excitement sparked in my eyes. "Oh! I've got an idea. You mentioned that Wil didn't play any sports, right?"

Penny leaned back on the sofa again, her gaze fixed on me. "That's right."

A grin spread across my face as I revealed my plan. "Well, I can. I can prove my athletic abilities and show him a side of Wil that he never knew existed."

* * *

I took a moment to change into a long-sleeved shirt, despite the sweltering heat, due to my self-consciousness about my scars. It struck me as odd that I would be concerned about such things, considering the scars I had on my body from war, previously. Penny located a football that her dad had somewhere, and she handed it to me. She gave me directions on how to approach our dad, who was standing in the backyard with his back to me, occupied with a garden hose.

"Hey, dad," I called out casually, tossing the football up and down in the air as I approached.

Michael turned around slowly, keeping the hose directed away from me. "Hey, son." He glanced at the football and nodded. "What have you got there?"

I shrugged, feigning nonchalance. "Oh, this? I thought I'd come out and see if you wanted to play a little catch."

Michael, or rather, my dad, let out a laugh. "You want to play catch … with *me*?"

"Yeah, why not? Haven't you always wanted me to be into sports?" I replied, trying to sound as if it were a natural desire.

He chuckled. "You *hate* sports."

I put on a comedic expression of confusion. "I don't remember *hating* sports." A small pang of truth ran through my words.

My dad turned to face me fully. "You don't remember anything."

"You're absolutely right," I replied with a grin. "So, what do you say?"

"You're serious about this, aren't you?" he asked, his grin widening.

I nodded affirmatively and tossed the football to him, underhanded, just a couple of feet away.

Well, what did he expect me to do? I didn't want to overwhelm him on the first throw!

He gently tossed the football back to me, underhanded, and I caught it with ease.

"Seriously, dad, scoot back some," I urged.

"Alright," he replied, sounding skeptical about my throwing ability.

He took two small steps back, but I was determined to prove him wrong. Frustrated, I walked back several yards.

"Son, you can't throw that far," he called out to me.

Ignoring his doubts, I continued to back up. "I'd hate for you to be running after the ball, dad!" I shouted back.

He stood back there, laughing at my persistence, but that laughter wouldn't last for long. While Wil's muscles hadn't fully developed yet, I knew that as a sixteen-year-old, I had the potential to sling the football much farther than a thirty-year old man just out of war. My father kept laughing, not realizing what was coming.

Without using all my strength, I heaved the ball toward him for the first time, launching it from about forty yards out. The pass soared through the air in a perfect spiral, arcing up and then descending right into his waiting arms. I felt a surge of satisfaction as I saw that I still had the skill.

My dad stared at me in astonishment, holding the ball as if it had materialized out of thin air. "What the heck was that? Did that really come from you?"

I couldn't help but laugh. "Are you gonna throw it back? Geez, I hate it when someone hogs the ball."

His eyes lit up with excitement as he reared back and threw the ball, putting all his strength into it. The ball made it to me, but I had to run a bit to catch it. I easily secured the catch, which only made him laugh even more. "Did that really just happen? You caught it!" I rolled out like a quarterback, passing him another perfect spiral into his waiting arms. He couldn't contain his amazement. "How are you doing this? You could barely throw a ball twenty feet, let alone a perfect spiral! Have you secretly been practicing?"

My smile faded as I approached my dad, who was still wearing a grin of astonishment. I could tell he was genuinely happy. "What would you like me to say, dad?" I asked earnestly. "That I practiced for three weeks while in the hospital?"

His beaming smile momentarily dimmed, and he paused, allowing a thoughtful silence to fill the air. "No, son, when would you have—"

"When would I possibly find the time?" I finished his inquiry for him. The once radiant smile on my father's face disappeared entirely, replaced by an expression of profound introspection. "It's almost like I've known how to do it for quite some time now," I added, emphasizing the peculiar nature of my newfound skill.

His gaze met mine, but his expression had turned somber. "I know where you're going with this, son."

"I just wanted to play catch with my dad," I replied simply.

He tossed the ball back to me, this time underhanded but with surprising speed. I didn't even flinch as I caught the ball effortlessly. "You hate sports. You can't play any sports. You can't catch, you can't throw—your eye-hand coordination is terrible," he stated firmly.

"It just looked really good to me. I love sports, and I can play a lot of them," I replied confidently.

"Is that so?" he questioned.

"Uh-huh." I nodded. "What sports does the high school offer?"

"Why, you're going to join football?" he asked, a hint of curiosity in his voice.

"Maybe, I don't know. It depends on what sports they have," I replied seriously. "Do they have ice hockey?"

My father nodded. "They do."

"Then can I get some hockey gear so I can try out for the team?" I asked eagerly.

My father appeared completely perplexed. "You have your own bank account with your own card—you can get whatever you want."

"Are you mad at me?" I inquired, my expression turning solemn.

He didn't answer immediately. "No, son, I'm not mad at you. I don't know what's going on, to be honest. Something isn't right."

I simply shrugged. "With that, we both can agree."

"I have this feeling that when you step out on the ice for the first time, you're going to know how to play hockey ... aren't you?" He eyed me curiously.

"We have to play catch again sometime soon, dad, okay? I really enjoyed it," I said, holding up the football. "I'm feeling tired, though. I think I'll go in for a while." I turned to head into the house.

"I love you, son," he called out from behind me.

I turned to face him once again. "I know you do, dad, and in time, I'm sure I will come to love all of you, too."

With those words, I turned back toward the house and began walking inside. As I glanced into one of the second-story windows, I saw Penny and Amelia watching me. I entered the house and made my way back to the stairway to reach my room. However, at the bottom of the stairs stood Amelia, her arms crossed in front of her. She was not smiling.

"What was that?" Amelia asked, her tone almost angry.

"What was what?" I replied innocently.

"You know what! I saw you throw the ball to dad and catch it, too. You made it look easy!"

"Yeah, so?" I nodded nonchalantly.

"You can't play sports, you suck at them!" Amelia exclaimed, as if it were news to me.

"Funny, dad said the same thing. I thought I did pretty good," I retorted, continuing up the stairs.

"But how?" Amelia demanded, following closely behind me. I stopped and turned to face her.

"Sweetie, ever since I woke up, I've been telling you that I like sports and enjoy playing them."

Amelia moved up the stairs to stand next to me, and we walked together down the hallway.

"Yes, but that doesn't mean you can just start playing."

"Sure it does, I just did. Now I need your help so I can play ice hockey."

"Ice hockey? You're going to play ice hockey?" Amelia exclaimed in disbelief. I continued down the hall toward my room, with Amelia keeping pace beside me.

"Yeah, why not? Don't you want me to pursue something I'm interested in?"

"You're not interested in hockey! You're interested in music and art! You … you don't even know how to play hockey!" she insisted. "You'll get hurt!"

"When do hockey tryouts start at school?" I asked, brushing off her concerns.

Amelia had grabbed on to one of my injured wrist, causing a surge of pain, making me yank away from her involuntarily. "Ow, Amelia, holy shit!" I exclaimed, wincing in discomfort.

Her hands flew to cover her mouth, her expression filled with shock and remorse. "Oh my god, Wil, I'm so, so sorry! I didn't mean to!" Her eyes welled up with tears once again, and I couldn't help but feel a pang of guilt for making her cry.

"Amelia, I'm okay … please don't cry," I reassured her, pulling her into a gentle hug. "I'm okay, I promise." I released the embrace, looking into her tear-streaked face. "Please, help me get some hockey gear? Dad said I have a bank account, and I need to know where to go to get the gear." She continued to stare at me, tears streaming down her cheeks. "Please, sis?" I asked sincerely, reaching out to wipe away her tears.

Composing herself, she nodded. "I didn't mean to hurt you. I just forgot," she said softly.

"I know you didn't mean to hurt me," I reassured her with a chuckle, wrapping my arm around her.

Amelia nodded, her voice softening. "Of course, I'll help you, big brother. Anything you need." Her concern for my well-being was evident. "But you have to be careful. Hockey can be pretty brutal."

I laughed in response, teasingly. "So is cheerleading!"

She giggled, acknowledging the truth in my words. Then, her expression turned serious. "I don't like this, Wil."

"It's okay, Amelia. I'll like it enough for both of us," I replied, trying to ease her worries.

Amelia assisted me in managing my bank account, and I was astounded by the amount of money in it. I promptly ordered the necessary hockey equipment after determining my new size. The items were expected to arrive within a day or two. I also made plans to visit the local ice rink to obtain my skates and have them sharpened.

Amelia pointed out which vehicles belonged to me, and I was surprised to learn that I had two: a sports car and an SUV. Opting for the SUV seemed out of character, even to Amelia. She couldn't recall why I had gotten it in the first place, as I rarely drove it.

I felt like a young teen again, actually trying out for hockey at the school, I wondered what else this new life had in store for me.

Keeping A Watchful Eye (PENNY)

———◇———

O ver time, I found myself closely observing *Wil*. He maintained a polite yet reserved demeanor in conversations with everyone. He often kept to himself, except when mom cooked a meal. He would actively engage, making it a point to savor every dish she prepared, leaving no trace of waste. He would eagerly consume each mouthful, appreciating the flavors and textures, showing his gratitude through his actions. It was as if he had endured a prolonged period of hunger, for his appetite seemed insatiable. Each bite he took carried a sense of urgency. The way he devoured the food hinted at a deeper hunger, not merely for sustenance, but perhaps for the comfort and warmth that a meal shared with loved ones could provide. Watching him eat like that tugged at my heartstrings; it was as if I wanted to shield him from any potential harm or deprivation, ensuring that he could savor every bite without any threat of loss or scarcity.

It pained me to witness the noticeable shift in my father's behavior towards Wil following their game of catch. It was evident that my father was deliberately keeping his distance, avoiding any meaningful interactions with him. The strained dynamic between them weighed heavily on my heart, and I could sense that Wil, too, was affected by this change. It was another blow to our already fragile familial bonds, deepening the ache within me. My father was seldom present from the start, constantly engrossed in his company affairs, managing everything and frequently working late into the night. It had become customary for us not to see him or have any meaningful interactions for days on end.

When I revealed to Wil that I wholeheartedly embraced the idea of him hailing from *somewhere else*, it wasn't just an empty sentiment. Unlike the rest of my family, my mind was open to the concept of reincarnation and the possibility that Wil was not truly my brother. It became increasingly clear to me that he possessed qualities and abilities that set him apart, such as his remarkable skill in playing sports and his maturity beyond his years, which even rivaled that of our parents. As the sole believer in his unique origin, Wil sought relief in confiding in me, understanding that I alone could comprehend the depth of his longing for the family he had lost and who had lost him. The weight of my worries for him grew heavier, fueled by the knowledge of his profound loss and the journey he was undertaking to find his place in our world.

During the nighttime hours, I would frequently bear witness to the fierce battles that raged within Wil's nightmares, remnants of the war he insisted he had experienced in a different lifetime. On occasion, I would stumble upon him seeking refuge from those haunting visions, finding comfort on the sofa in his private sitting room or even surrendering to sleep on the floor of one of his closets. These nocturnal scenes spoke volumes about the depth of his inner turmoil, the echoes of a past that seemed to linger relentlessly, even in the embrace of sleep. He never offered an explanation for his actions, and I never pressed him for one. Every time, those nightmares would engulf him, swallowing any peace of mind he might have.

Tonight was no exception. I could hear his struggles from my room, screaming at times, crying out for people I had never heard of before. Without hesitation, I swiftly left my bed, clad in my nightshirt and boxers, and made my way to the hallway. My room was to the right of his, while Amelia's was to the left. I knocked on his door, fully aware that he wouldn't hear me. I entered his room and swiftly made my way to the back room where his bed was located. As expected, he was tossing and turning, his forehead drenched in sweat.

Approaching his bed, I gently grasped his arms and shook him. "Wil!" I said firmly, my voice carrying urgency. "Wake up! You're having another nightmare!" It took a few shakes before he finally jolted upright, his eyes wide with fear. At first, he looked at me with a gaze of unfamiliarity.

"It's me, Penny." I said as comforting sounding as I could. Gradually, his expression transformed into one of relief, and he seemed to calm down, if only slightly. "I'm sorry, Wil. You were having another nightmare," I apologized softly.

"Penny," he whispered, his gaze scanning the darkness of his room.

"Yeah, it's me. It's okay, you're safe in *your* room," I reassured him. It took him a while to steady his breathing, and I placed my hand on his back, offering a gentle rub. Despite his sweat-soaked shirt, I didn't find it repulsive; I simply wanted to provide comfort.

"I'm sorry if I woke you," he finally said, meeting my eyes.

"It's completely fine," I replied. "Want to talk about it?" He shook his head, his gaze dropping to the blanket. "It might help you if you talk about it. At this point, I'm pretty much the only person you can confide in. I'm here for you, little brother," I encouraged.

He chuckled at the notion. "Little brother, huh?"

"Well, we have to maintain appearances, right?"

"Fair, fair."

"You were calling out names, telling people to take cover, that sort of thing," I mentioned.

He nodded. "I was dreaming about the war."

"What happened?"

"I don't know." He shrugged. "I've already forgotten most of the dream."

"I'm sure you witnessed some truly awful things," I sympathized.

"Many terrible things," he echoed.

"You should probably discuss all of this with Dr. Norris," I suggested, concern etching my voice. "You hold so much inside, and that can't be healthy."

"I don't have much of a choice."

"You do," I asserted with a smile. "You have me."

"And you've been amazing, Penny. I truly appreciate you," he expressed gratefully.

"Would you like me to make you something to eat, or get you a drink?" I offered, observing him draw the covers closer to himself.

"That's really kind of you, but no. You should probably get some sleep. I'm so sorry for waking you again," he replied, weariness and sorrow evident in his eyes.

"It's no trouble at all. It's summer. I can sleep all day if I wanted to."

"I'm good. I'll just try to get back to sleep."

"Okay, but remember, I'm here for you, day or night. You may *feel* alone, but you're not. Day or night, Wil, you can come get me. I promise you won't be disturbing me. It would make me happy to help you through all of this."

He leaned closer, wrapping his arms around me in a tight embrace, filling me with warmth and comfort. I reciprocated, holding him just as tightly, our bodies swaying gently in a tender moment. "You're the best, sis. Please get some sleep," he whispered.

I nodded, my heart filled with compassion and concern. As he settled back into bed, I felt a strong urge to take care of him. I approached his bedside, tucking the blankets snugly around him, a gesture he welcomed without resistance. With utmost tenderness, I placed a gentle kiss on his forehead, a silent reassurance of my unwavering support. Satisfied that he was settled, I reluctantly left his room, making my way back to my own, filled with a mix of emotions and hopes for a peaceful night for him.

Meeting Emily

I sat down at the kitchen table in the morning, after making myself a bowl of cereal to eat. I was about to dig in when my mom came in. She approached me with affection, kissing the top of my head and placing a gentle hand on my shoulder. Her concern for my well-being was evident as she offered to make me something else to eat.

I reassured her, "This is fine, mom, but thank you." I appreciated her thoughtfulness.

"Are you sure?" she asked.

I nodded, my mouth still partially filled with cereal, and mumbled, "I'm sure."

"Well, if you change your mind, let me know," she said, her voice filled with motherly love. I expected her to resume her daily routine, but instead, she took a seat in the chair beside me. I paused, observing her with curiosity as I continued to chew.

"I wanted to talk to you about something," my mom began, her tone gentle and comforting.

Curious, I finished chewing and swallowed before responding, "Sure, what's up? Did I do something wrong?"

She shook her head, a reassuring smile on her face. "No, honey, not at all. I just wanted to see how you're feeling and find out if you're up for some company today."

Raising an eyebrow, I asked, "Company? What kind of company?"

She nodded. "Well, the *company* isn't for you, per se, it's friends of your sisters. I didn't let them invite anyone over right away, since I figured that might overwhelm you."

Understanding her intentions, I reassured her, "Oh, of course! I'm fine, mom. Don't stop them from coming over on my account. There are plenty of places to hide if I feel the need to."

She expressed her concern about me feeling uncomfortable in my own home and wanted to make sure I was certain about it.

With a playful wave of my spoon, I replied, "I'm sure. I appreciate your concern, though."

A smile spread across my mom's face as she stood up. "Great! I'll let the girls know." She leaned down to kiss the top of my head once again before heading off.

*　　*　　*

As I explored the vast grounds of the estate, I marveled at the expanse of the property. The sprawling eight-hundred-plus acres seemed like a world of its own, with various landscapes and hidden corners waiting to be discovered. It was a perfect opportunity for me to acquaint myself with my new surroundings. I walked along tree-lined paths, taking in the beauty of nature surrounding me. The scent of blooming flowers filled the air, and the sound of birds chirping provided a soothing melody. I ventured through gardens, admiring meticulously manicured lawns and vibrant plant displays.

As I continued my exploration, I stumbled upon a serene lake nestled within the property. The shimmering water reflected the clear blue sky, and I couldn't resist sitting down on a nearby bench to soak in the tranquility. The peacefulness of the surroundings allowed my mind to wander and reflect on the changes I had experienced. Time seemed to slip away as I meandered through the estate, losing myself in its charm. The grandeur of the mansion, the vastness of the grounds, and the sense of serenity it offered created a sense of awe within me. Despite the lingering questions about my past, this new environment provided a much-needed respite. As I wandered, I couldn't help but wonder where Penny and Amelia might go to on such a vast property. I made a mental note to ask them about their favorite spots and if they had any hidden gems to share.

As the sun began to set, I returned from my exploration and entered the house through one of the back doors. The sound of laughter and cheerful female voices echoed from the lower level, indicating that the gathering was taking place in the game room. Intrigued, I followed the voices, drawn towards the heartwarming ambiance.

As I approached the doorway of the game room, a peculiar sensation washed over me—a sensation that defied description, akin to a comforting embrace. Despite my initial hesitation, an unexplainable force compelled me to step inside and join the gathering. Peering around the corner, I saw Amelia and Penny, accompanied by two unfamiliar girls, all of them turning their attention towards me.

I started to walk away, fighting the urge to go in, when Amelia called out to me. "Hey, big brother! Come say *hi!*"

Inhaling deeply, I gathered my resolve and exhaled slowly, allowing a newfound courage to guide my steps.

WTF is wrong with me?

"It's okay, Wil, they won't bite you." Penny chuckled. "Come in."

I offered a brief smile and gave a nod of acknowledgement. Despite not feeling particularly inclined to meet new people at the moment, circumstances had led me to this point.

Penny's touch on my arm sent a surge of anticipation through me as she guided me towards one of the girls across the room. As we approached, I couldn't help but be struck by the girl standing there. She was as tall as Penny, her long jet-black hair flowing down her back, framing a pair of mesmerizing blue eyes. Her outfit was effortlessly stylish, with a red crop top, short-shorts, and white socks that added a touch of playfulness. She exuded confidence and seemed to possess the allure of a magazine model.

"This is my best friend, Nikki. She's the cheer captain for our team." Penny's voice broke through my thoughts. I felt a tinge of shyness as I managed to greet Nikki with a polite, "Nice to meet you," extending my hand for a handshake.

To my surprise, Nikki's response was far from conventional. "Oh, come over here and give me a hug!" she exclaimed, pulling me into an embrace without a moment's hesitation.

"Oh … uh … you probably shouldn't do that," Amelia said with a protective instinct, but Nikki seemed unfazed, completely engulfed in the moment.

Caught off guard, I hesitated for a moment before returning the embrace, unsure of how to react. The warmth of her hug surrounded me, and a sense of familiarity washed over me. "You seriously don't remember me?" she asked, a mix of disappointment and hope in her voice. "I've spent the night here a million times."

My voice came out as a whisper, tinged with apology. "I'm sorry. I don't." The admission left me feeling unsettled, grappling with the void of forgotten moments that seemed to separate us. Yet, her smile persisted, her faith unshaken.

Our embrace lasted for what felt like both an eternity and a fleeting moment, a brief encounter that held a world of emotions. As Nikki leaned back to gaze into my eyes, a flicker of concern briefly shadowed her face before she mustered another warm smile. "It's okay," she reassured me, her enthusiasm undimmed. "We'll get your memory back!"

No, we won't.

Now it was Amelia's turn to take me by the arm, leading me towards the other girl, who had been hidden behind Nikki. "This is *my* best friend, Emily," she said, gesturing behind her.

As Nikki stepped aside, my gaze was immediately drawn to the girl. Emily, a vision of beauty that left me breathless. Her long, lustrous blond hair cascaded down her back in waves, dancing with the slightest movement. Each strand seemed to catch the light, turning her into a radiant beacon in the dimly lit space. Her eyes, a mesmerizing shade of blue, held an enchanting depth that drew me in. They sparkled with a hint of mischief, like two sapphires reflecting the secrets of the universe. I couldn't help but feel a magnetic pull towards those captivating orbs, as if they held the key to unlocking a world of untold wonders. She wore a sleek black dress that clung to her curves, accentuating her every graceful movement. The fabric hugged her form in all the right places, emphasizing her femininity and leaving me yearning to trace the contours of her silhouette. The dress spoke of sophistication and allure, an embodiment of understated elegance that only intensified her allure. Her legs were encased in black nylons, adding a touch of mystery and sophistication. They seemed to elongate her frame, accentuating the graceful lines of her figure. And as my gaze traveled farther down, I noticed the black heels that adorned her feet. They completed her ensemble with a touch of timeless class, leaving me captivated by the way they accentuated her poise and confidence.

In that moment, as our eyes met and our paths converged. The room around us faded into insignificance, and all that mattered was the undeniable connection that crackled between us. Her blond hair, her blue eyes, the black dress, nylons, and heels—they all merged into a symphony of beauty that made my heart race with anticipation.

In her presence, I found myself transfixed, unable to look away. Emily was more than just a striking appearance; she exuded an aura of grace that left an indelible impression on my soul.

Absently, I flung my hand out to shake her hand, and she, very daintily, shook mine.

"I'm … I'm sorry," I managed to stammer. "Hi, Emily, a pleasure."

Her eyes darted to the ground for a second, then back to me. "It's nice to see you again, Wil. You look so … different! I mean that in the best way possible." As if her looks weren't captivating to begin with, Emily had a British accent. Her voice was so soft and feminine, it was like an angel speaking.

"I'm going to guess you're British? Manchester area?" I asked, thinking I sounded stupid.

"Yes!" Emily exclaimed, her face lighting up with a big toothy smile. "I am from the UK originally, Bolton, close to Manchester! I've been here for a few years now. I'm surprised you could tell my accent is from the Manchester area." I couldn't help but feel a mix of confusion and awe. How did I know that? It was as if a small fragment of familiarity lingered in the depths of my mind, even though I knew it wasn't possible. I simply shrugged, unable to offer any explanation for this newfound knowledge. "No memory of me, either?" she asked.

Her question brought a tinge of sadness to my expression. I shook my head, my eyes filled with regret and uncertainty.

"It's okay," she said, her voice soft and comforting. "We'll make new memories together." Her words carried a sense of optimism and determination, as if she believed that our connection could transcend the boundaries of forgotten pasts.

"Why don't you hang out with us?" Amelia's question caught me off guard, and I could sense a hint of curiosity in her expression. Her gaze shifted between me, Emily, and back again, as if she was trying to piece something together.

A sense of overwhelm washed over me, though I couldn't quite pinpoint its source. "Uh … no, that's okay," I responded, my eyes briefly flickering from Amelia to Emily and back again. "I'm gonna go work out or something."

Amelia playfully persisted. "Aw, poo on that, Wil. Come have fun with us!"

I shook my head, appreciating her invitation but feeling a need to retreat. "I appreciate it, but maybe another time. Nice meeting you ladies," I said with a nod, gracefully inclining my head in a gesture that mirrored a respectful bow.

Penny seemed to understand my need for space, yet Nikki couldn't resist one last demand. "Okay, we'll let you go—but I want another hug!" Her arms opened wide, and I couldn't help but crack a smile at her infectious enthusiasm. I obliged, letting her embrace me, though my gaze instinctively drifted towards Emily, who observed the interaction with a focused intensity. Nikki's grip held on a little longer than expected, but eventually, she released me. "If you ever need anything, or need to talk, I'm here for you. I mean it! Don't ever feel like you don't have someone to turn to," Nikki reassured me, her words filled with sincerity.

I understood what she was trying to do, and I appreciated it. "You're very kind," I responded, grateful for her offer of support. My attention shifted to Emily, who stood beside Nikki, less inclined for physical contact and instead extending her hand.

"I'm glad you're feeling better, Wil," Emily said sheepishly as our hands gently shook.

"Thank you, Emily," I replied, feeling a sense of warmth in her presence.

With a quick turn on my heel, I made my way back up the stairs, the mix of emotions and encounters swirling in my mind. The need for solitude beckoned, a chance to process the whirlwind of introductions and the subtle yet powerful connections I had experienced.

* * *

After finishing my workout and taking a quick shower, I retreated to the comfort of my room for the remainder of the day. Flipping through the TV channels, I struggled to find any shows that interested me. However, sports remained a constant, offering some familiarity in this new chapter of my life.

While I appreciated the company of my sister's friends, particularly Nikki, who showed me an unexpected level of affection, my mind remained fixated on Emily. She occupied my thoughts throughout the evening, her beauty and magnetic presence leaving an indelible impression on me. It was a peculiar sensation, reminiscent of the connection I had with my wife, Ella. A surge of recognition washed over me as I pieced together the puzzle of Emily's familiar face. Memories flooded back as I recalled the pictures captured by Wil's phone—the vibrant cheerleaders, their infectious spirit embodied by one person in particular: Emily. It was evident why he would have been captivated by her, her allure drawing him in like a magnetic force. Perhaps his shyness had held him back from fully exploring the potential connection they could have shared.

Intrigued to learn more about her, I resolved to ask Amelia later. Perhaps she could provide some insights into this captivating woman who had captured my attention so profoundly.

I continued delving into Wil's journal, discovering that he had clinched victory in the county fair's art competition for portrait drawing. Scanning my surroundings, I noticed artwork adorning the walls, but no portraits in sight.

He also alluded to a girl in his writings, though her name remained unspoken. It was evident that he held deep admiration for this mysterious girl, praising her kindness and leaving me with the impression that she might be Emily. I grew increasingly certain that he had harbored a crush on her for an extended period, perhaps even years.

As I read further, he made reference to her British accent, further solidifying my belief that it was indeed her. I couldn't blame him; Emily's charm was undeniable.

A knock at my bedroom door interrupted my musings.

"Come in."

The door creaked open, and Amelia stuck her head in. "I just wanted to check in on you, if that's okay." She entered and closed the door behind her, offering a warm hug that I reciprocated. Taking a seat on the sofa, I motioned for her to join me.

Speak of the devil.

"Please, sit down," I said. Amelia took a seat next to me on the sofa, her presence bringing a sense of comfort and familiarity. As she settled in beside me, I couldn't help but appreciate the bond we had started to share as siblings.

"You're so formal, big brother." Her playful comment brought a smile to my face, melting away any remaining tension that lingered within me.

I chuckled softly, appreciating her ability to find humor in the situation. "I'm sorry, I don't mean to be," I replied, my voice laced with a hint of amusement.

"It's weird to hear you talk in complete sentences." She giggled.

With a playful grin, I quipped, "Are you sayin' I was an idiot or somethin'?" My words were lighthearted, reflecting the easy banter we had started to enjoy. Amelia's laughter swelled, her amusement filling the air around us.

"No, not at all!" she replied, still chuckling. "You just would normally answer questions with one or two words—maybe a grunt here and there." Her eyes sparkled with affectionate amusement, and I couldn't help but join in her laughter.

"Well, I mean … I can try that if you like," I offered, feigning a brief moment of seriousness before breaking into a grin.

Amelia shook her head, her laughter subsiding. "No, I like you this way. Is everything okay?" Her gaze softened, her concern evident as she studied my face. "You seemed like you might be a bit overwhelmed after meeting Emily and Nikki."

I took a moment to reflect, then met her gaze, offering a reassuring smile. "I'm okay," I assured her. "It was a lot to process, meeting them. I'm not sure why I felt the need to leave like that. I hope I didn't offend them."

She reached out, gently placing a hand on my arm, her touch a comforting gesture. "Nah, they're good. Honestly, they were both just glad to see you up and about, doing okay," she reassured me, her voice filled with genuine warmth.

"Nikki and I were close?" I asked.

Amelia shook her head and replied, "No, not really. The way she was with you startled me, and Penny. Don't get me wrong, Nikki was always kind to you, but never like that."

I nodded, trying to process the information. Curiosity got the better of me, and I asked, "So why do you think she was that way now?"

Amelia pondered for a moment before responding, "Honestly, I think it's because she was scared that we almost lost you—and she wants to be super supportive. Make sure you knew you had people to turn to."

"That's nice of her," I remarked, genuinely touched by Nikki's actions.

Amelia nodded in agreement. "It is. She's the most popular girl at school, so Penny says. It's easy to see why. She dates some guy who's away at college now, I don't even recall his name. She rarely ever gets to see him, which is really sad." I couldn't help but feel a sense of empathy for Nikki. Despite her popularity, it seemed like she faced her own challenges and sacrifices in her personal life.

"What about Emily?" I asked, my curiosity shifting towards her. "What's her deal? I mean, were we friendly?"

Amelia chuckled and replied, "Emily is one of the kindest people I've ever known, and she was always kind to you. Like Nikki, you rarely ever spoke to her."

I leaned back on the sofa, thinking about what Amelia had just said. "So I just ignored all these gals? Ignored everyone?" I questioned, a hint of disbelief in my voice.

Amelia nodded, confirming my assumption. "Pretty much. When Emily would talk to you, you would practically stutter your words."

I let out a sigh, realizing how much the original Wil had missed out on. "Well, she is really pretty."

Amelia raised an eyebrow and teased, "Really pretty?"

I corrected myself, "Okay, she's beautiful."

Amelia's laughter filled the room. "And don't think for a second, big brother, that I didn't notice the way you were looking at her."

I felt my cheeks heat up, slightly embarrassed. "What? I mean, like I said, she's beautiful, for sure."

Amelia continued to giggle, clearly amused by my reaction. "So is Nikki, but you didn't look at her like you did Emily."

I protested, trying to downplay the situation. "I didn't look at Emily in any weird way!"

Amelia grinned mischievously. "Oh, come on, Wil. I've seen that look before. You were definitely smitten. There's nothing wrong with it! All the guys ogle over her. There's just one teeny-tiny problem," Amelia said, her tone slightly exasperated.

"A problem? What problem?" I inquired, curiosity piqued.

Amelia let out a big sigh before explaining, "She has a boyfriend."

I raised an eyebrow, puzzled. "Why's that a problem?"

Amelia leaned forward, her gaze fixed on me. "Because I saw how you connected with her, right away!"

I shook my head, dismissing her claim. "Bullshit, Amelia. I didn't connect with anyone. In case you missed it, I left the room right after."

Amelia couldn't help but snicker, clearly amused by my defensive reaction. "Seeing how defensive you are right now assures me that I'm right."

I protested, adamant in my denial. "You're not."

"I am."

"Besides ... she has a boyfriend," I reminded her.

"Sadly, yes." Amelia sat up straight. "But there's more. Her boyfriend's name is *Greg*."

"So? Who gives a shit what his name is?"

"Greg is the guy who beat you up on a regular basis," Amelia said, wincing.

"*Greg*, huh?"

Amelia nodded.

I let out a quiet "Ah," as understanding dawned on me. Greg, the guy who had caused Wil so much pain and suffering.

"Well, that won't happen this year," I declared with determination. "Why would a nice girl like Emily go out with an asshole like that?"

Amelia shrugged, her face contorting with disgust. "He was nice at first, I guess. But he's always been a piece of shit, if you ask me. She's afraid of him now."

My expression darkened, anger simmering within me. "Afraid of him?"

Amelia nodded solemnly, her voice filled with concern. "Yeah, he's definitely hit her on a few occasions, if you ask me."

I clenched my fists, feeling a surge of protectiveness rise within me. "That's not cool, not cool at all. She needs to get away from him."

Amelia nodded in somber agreement, before her frown turned to a mischievous smirk. "Away from him ... and straight to you?" She teased.

I scowled, shaking my head. "I didn't say that. I just got here, Amelia. I'm not going out with anyone. Right now, I want to focus on rediscovering myself and adjusting to this *new* life."

Amelia's smirk softened into a knowing smile. "Fair enough. Just remember, you have people here who care about you and want to see you happy."

"I know, and I appreciate that very much."

"You certainly are a lot more outgoing than you used to be," Amelia stated, observing my newfound confidence. "Nobody at school is gonna know what to make of you now."

I shrugged, a faint, knowing smile on my lips. "I guess they'll have to get used to it."

Amelia leaned back, her eyes sparkling with amusement. "For the record, I think Emily was ogling over you too. After you left, she mentioned a few times how different you look, even how handsome you are."

I chuckled, dismissing her comment. "I just do my hair differently, wear different clothes. Hopefully, I'll catch up in weight soon, too. But Emily shouldn't be ogling over anyone other than her boyfriend."

Amelia sighed, a hint of concern in her voice. "I told you, she's afraid of him. There's no more *love* in that relationship, though she won't readily admit it."

"Like I said, she needs to break it off with him," I asserted firmly.

Amelia stood up, a heavy sigh escaping her lips. "Yeah, everyone in the world agrees with you," she said, standing up. "I gotta get back to the others now."

I followed suit and got up from the sofa. "They're still here?" I asked, curious.

Amelia nodded. "Yeah, they're both staying over tonight," she replied with a hint of excitement. "Shit, I was supposed to ask you about that earlier. Mom wanted you to be okay with it before—"

"I'm okay with it," I interjected, cutting her off. "I'm not a china doll or something broken, Amelia. I'm fine."

Amelia looked at me, her eyes filled with concern. "Wil, I want you to feel—"

I interrupted her once again, my tone resolute. "Amelia," I said firmly, meeting her gaze. "I said I'm fine. I'm not that insecure guy you knew before. I promise you, I'm stronger now, and I can handle having guests over. Besides, it'll be nice for you to spend more time with Emily and Nikki."

Amelia sighed, a mix of relief and apprehension evident on her face. "Alright, if you say so," she said, finally relenting. "Just remember, we're here for you, Wil. Don't hesitate to reach out if you need anything."

I smiled warmly at her, grateful for her concern and support. "I know, Amelia. And thank you. Now, go on, and enjoy the rest of the evening. I'll be fine on my own."

"Maybe you'll come down to hang with us at some point?" Amelia asked as she headed for the door.

"We'll see."

*   *   *

"You're back! Thank God!" Sally exclaimed, her face reflecting a blend of concern and relief. Cowboy, ever the steadfast companion, had joined me, his unwavering enthusiasm undiminished despite the peril that loomed around us. Confusion gripped me as I questioned how I had ended up back in Baltimore during the war, and the intensity of the firefight surged through my thoughts. "Where am I?" I demanded, my voice filled with a mix of urgency and bewilderment.

Cowboy, kneeling beside me, tried to reassure me. "You're in Baltimore, Doc," he said, giving my shoulder a reassuring pat. But before he could elaborate, duty called, and he vanished into the chaos, leaving me with my unanswered questions.

As the sounds of gunfire continued to punctuate the night, my attention shifted to Sally. "How ... how is he running? He was shot?"

The air crackled with danger as a bullet whizzed past, striking the top of Sally's helmet, sending it spiraling into the chaos.

Reacting instinctively, I reached out, my hand finding its way to her shirt, gripping it tightly. With a sense of urgency, I pulled her down, my voice strained with determination. "Stay down!" I shouted, the intensity of the firing escalating around us. Time seemed to slow as I sought cover, the weight of responsibility pressing upon me. The safety of those around me became my priority, and Sally's well-being was no exception. I dragged her with me. "Are you okay?" I asked her in earnest.

"Doc ... I ... I ... think I'm bleeding," she said weakly. The sight of blood on her head sent a surge of adrenaline coursing through my veins. I searched frantically for something to stem the bleeding, finding an old t-shirt that I pressed against the wound. "You hang in there!" I urged, my voice filled with concern.

When I looked down at her, it wasn't Sally lying before me; it was Emily.

"Emily!" I yelled, shooting straight up in bed, drenched in sweat, breathing heavily.

I took a moment to collect myself, my heart pounding in my chest as the remnants of the dream faded away. It was just a dream, I reassured myself, wiping the sweat from my brow. But it felt so vivid, so real. Looking around the dimly lit room, I realized I was back in my own room, my bed, far away from the chaos of the war zone.

Now, sitting upright in bed, my racing thoughts gradually subsided. I examined my own body for any signs of injury, finding none except for the two scars etched into my forearms.

"Fuck," I whispered, kicking off the covers and getting out of bed. Gently running a hand through my sweat-dampened hair, I allowed the weight of the dream to fade away. I decided I needed to walk around for a few minutes, maybe get something to eat. The comfort of sweatpants, a t-shirt, and white socks embraced me.

*　　*　　*

Entering the kitchen, I was greeted by a sight that brought a mix of nostalgia and delight. The shelves and cabinets were stocked with an array of food, including an abundance of junk food. Reaching for a tempting chocolate fudge treat, my ears perked up, capturing the sound of whispers echoing through the air. Intrigued, I instinctively closed the cabinet door silently, not wanting to disturb the clandestine conversation. Curiosity propelled me forward as I followed the source of the hushed voices.

I found myself standing outside the informal living room, hidden from view but close enough to catch a glimpse of the scene unfolding within. There, on the couch, sat Emily, her back to me. She was curled up, her bare legs drawn up against her, engrossed in a phone conversation. Her hair was neatly tied back in a ponytail, and she wore a long night shirt. My conscience tugged at me, reminding me that eavesdropping was an invasion of privacy. Yet, the desire to learn more, to understand this world and the people in it, tugged at my curiosity. I wrestled with conflicting thoughts, torn between respect and the yearning for knowledge. A mantra I had often shared with Katrina echoed in my mind: "Knowledge is power." With that thought in mind, I hesitated for a moment, debating whether to stay and listen or to respect Emily's privacy.

In the end, the pull of curiosity won over, and I quietly settled myself at a vantage point that allowed me to observe without being noticed. I justified my actions with the belief that this knowledge would provide insight into the lives and relationships of those around me, shedding light on the complexities of this unfamiliar world. In other words, I was being nosey. As I strained to listen, the conversation between Emily and a male became slightly clearer, though much of the male's words remained muffled. Emily's voice, on the other hand, held a mixture of frustration, defensiveness, and vulnerability.

"I dunno what you want me to say, Greg," Emily's voice rose slightly, still keeping her tone relatively hushed. "I told you I was spending the night at Amelia's."

The male's voice, Greg's voice, grew angrier, his words blending into an incomprehensible tirade. Emily's response was apologetic, her voice tinged with confusion. "I dunno why. I just blanked out, sorry."

There was a brief pause in their exchange, allowing me to catch my breath and brace myself for the continued conversation. Emily's voice regained some strength as she addressed one of Greg's concerns. "Yes, of course Wil is here. He lives here."

His voice grew even louder, his anger palpable even from my concealed position. I couldn't make out the specifics of his words, but the intensity was unmistakable. Emily, however, remained resolute, pushing back against his accusations.

"He got out of the hospital a day or so ago," she explained, her voice tinged with exasperation. "What are you, jealous of him? I talked to him for like two minutes, then he left. I haven't seen him since."

Greg's rage seemed to escalate, his voice turning into a series of aggressive outbursts. I could sense Emily's emotions bubbling to the surface as she fought back tears. Her voice quivered as she spoke, "Yeah, that's it ... I'm sleeping with him as we speak. Because I'm just a whore, right? Isn't that what you always say?"

The heaviness of the situation weighed upon me as I listened to Emily's raw vulnerability. It was clear that her relationship with Greg was toxic and abusive, leaving her emotionally battered and cornered. As she continued her conversation with him, his anger intensified, making it difficult for me to understand the exact words he was saying. However, the tension and frustration in his voice were unmistakable. Her voice wavered as she tried to explain the situation, defending my presence in my own house. I could sense the toxic dynamics of their relationship as his jealousy and insecurity seemed to fuel his anger. Her attempts to reason with him were met with further aggression.

Emily sniffled. "No, unfortunately, I don't feel safe anywhere I go. Thanks to you. Why can't you just be nice to me, for once? Why do you always have to get mad and yell at me? I deserve better!"

She sounded so sad, so alone.

"Yeah, that's right. You remind me all the time that I'm not good enough for anyone."

Feeling compelled to intervene, I moved closer to Emily, unintentionally making a sound that caught her attention. She turned toward me, startled by the noise. I quickly realized my mistake and stepped back, unsure of how to proceed.

Shit.

I snuck back as many steps as I could, before saying lowly, "Is someone there?"

"I have to go, Greg, I'll talk to you tomorrow!" Emily said in a hushed and hurried tone. I could hear him start yelling, but then I heard the beep when you're being disconnected. I turned the corner as she was wiping away her tears, and then she stood up.

"Wil!" she said, startled to see me.

"I'm sorry if I scared you, Emily," I said sympathetically.

"Oh … no, it's fine," she said, flashing a smile at me. I could see her more clearly now. She had on a pair of hot pink shorts and a long pink nightshirt. Emily didn't have any makeup on, but she looked every bit as beautiful as she had earlier, minus the red, puffy eyes from crying.

"Are you okay?" I asked.

Emily smiled again. "Yeah, of course," she replied, her British accent more prominent than before. "Why wouldn't I be?"

I heard Emily's phone vibrate, several times.

"Well, for starters, you're sitting here alone in the living room … in the dark."

"I … I just couldn't sleep."

I nodded. "I wouldn't be able to sleep if someone was yelling at me on the phone like that either."

Emily's smile faded and her eyes went wide. "You ... you heard that?"

Her phone started to vibrate several more times.

I gave her a sympathetic smile. "I'm really sorry, Emily. I didn't mean to." I looked down at the phone in her hand.

"It's okay," Emily said with a sigh, looking defeated. "I don't know what to say about it."

"Why do you put up with someone treating you like that?" I asked softly. Her phone vibrated some more. "Are you going to answer that?" I asked.

Emily backed up a few steps, then plopped down on the sofa with another sigh. "No. I know he's really angry with me right now. I dunno why I stay with him," she said meekly. "I'm not good enough for anyone else." Her phone continued to vibrate with Greg's angry messages, but with a sigh of resignation, she ended the call and turned off the device. Tears welled up in her eyes as she seemed to process the weight of the conversation and the toxicity of her relationship.

I came to the front of the sofa, crouching down like a catcher in baseball, "Emily, you are more than good enough for anyone."

"How would you know, Wil?" Emily asked while sniffling, "You don't even remember me."

"If you're Amelia's best friend, then I'm sure of it," I retorted.

This made Emily smile. She looked into my eyes, and her eyes had sort of a twinkle to them. "You don't act like the Wil I used to know. You would never speak more than a few words before. You certainly wouldn't have approached me."

"People grow up."

"They do, but this is a lot different than you just growing up. It's like you're a different person."

"I *am* a different person," I said honestly.

"For sure," she said, looking away, then back at me. Emily licked her lips before speaking again. "I'm so, so sorry for all that has happened to you. With Greg, then Rachel. You never deserved to be treated that way."

"It's not your fault."

"Greg's my boyfriend. He's treated you horrible since your first day of high school. I know you must've asked yourself why I would stay with a guy who is so mean?"

"That question has crossed my mind, yes."

Tears welled up in Emily's eyes as she shrugged, a heavy weight of sadness and resignation evident in her gesture. I could sense her inner turmoil, the battle between her desire for support and her instinct to shield me from harm. She got up hastily, passing by me as she made her way out of the room.

"Wait!" I called out, my voice unintentionally louder than intended. I immediately regretted it, seeing Emily flinch in response. "Sorry, I didn't mean to be that loud," I quickly apologized, following her out of the living room and standing in her path. In that moment, I mustered the courage to express my genuine concern and offer my support. "I'm here for you, Emily. If you need someone to talk to, or if you need someone to help you," I said earnestly, hoping that my words would convey the sincerity of my offer.

Emily's tears glistened in the dim light as she gave me a hug, a gesture that carried a mix of gratitude, sadness, and a hint of reluctance. Her embrace was warm and comforting, like a ray of sunshine on a chilly day. As she wrapped her arms around me, her body pressed gently against mine, creating a sense of closeness and security that enveloped me entirely. It felt as if our souls were embracing, not just our bodies. The connection was electric, a surge of energy passing between us that left me tingling. Every touch was filled with an indescribable warmth and familiarity, as if we had known each other across countless lifetimes. I felt an overwhelming sense of completeness and utter contentment that I could not explain. The embrace lingered a little longer than the one I had shared with Nikki, as if Emily held on to it as a brief respite from her troubles. Eventually, she let go, her voice filled with a bittersweet resolve.

"You're very sweet, Wil, but you can't help me. Nobody can," she said, her words laced with a deep sadness. "I don't want him to hurt you ever again. You've been through enough."

With those words, Emily swiftly passed by me, leaving me standing there with a sense of helplessness and determination. Her words echoed in my mind, but I couldn't accept her resignation. I knew deep down that I had to find a way to make a difference, to be there for her, even if it meant navigating the difficult and dangerous path that lay ahead.

I wanted to protect her and offer support, but I also recognized the complexity of the situation. I couldn't ignore the fact that I had a family waiting for me somewhere else …

… didn't I?

The Universe

———◁○———○———○▷———

Lying in the darkness, my mind was restless, replaying the conversation with Emily over and over again. The weight of her sadness and hopelessness weighed heavily on me, stirring memories that I had long tried to bury. I understood all too well what it felt like to be trapped in a situation where kindness was absent, where every day felt like a battle against an invisible force. The memories of my own past struggles resurfaced, and my heart ached for Emily, knowing the pain she must have endured.

In the midst of the darkness, a flicker of hope emerged. Perhaps, in this parallel universe, I could leverage the wisdom and experiences of my previous life to make a positive impact, to bring light into the lives of others who desperately needed it.

I had just fallen asleep, when the sound of a distant voice pulled me back to consciousness. The words were faint at first, but as I gradually emerged from the depths of slumber, they became clearer, seeping into my consciousness.

The sound of my name, uttered in such a soft and delicate tone, stirred something deep within me. I slowly turned my head, my eyes meeting the gaze of a figure standing at the foot of my bed. It was a woman, her presence emanating a gentle warmth that enveloped the room.

"Markus," she repeated, her voice like a soothing melody that washed over me. "I've been waiting for you."

I sat up, feeling a mixture of curiosity and awe. Her presence felt otherworldly, ethereal yet comforting. Startled, I jumped out of bed, my heart pounding in my chest. The presence of this mysterious young girl filled the room, her beauty captivating my senses. I couldn't help but be drawn to her gaze, mesmerized by the depths of her purple eyes. "Who are you?" I asked, my voice filled with wonder. Her presence felt familiar, as if she held the answers to questions I hadn't even formed.

I took a cautious step forward, my eyes never leaving hers. "Are you ... an angel?" I asked, my voice barely above a whisper. She smiled, a radiant glow illuminating her features. "I am an emissary of sorts, a guide to help you navigate this new path you've embarked upon." A faint smile curved on her lips, and she nodded ever so slightly. Her silence spoke volumes, as if words were unnecessary in her realm of existence. The glowing aura around her seemed to intensify, radiating a warmth and comfort that enveloped me.

Confusion clouded my thoughts, as I tried to grasp the meaning behind her words. "What do you mean? What path?"

The woman took a step closer, her eyes filled with compassion. "You have been given a second chance, Markus. A chance to rewrite your story, to discover new depths within yourself. But with this opportunity comes the responsibility to embrace the lessons and growth that await you."

Her words resonated deep within me, stirring a sense of hope and anticipation. "But why me? Why now?" I asked, my voice tinged with vulnerability.

"You have shown resilience, courage, and a capacity for compassion even in the face of darkness. The universe has chosen you to embark on this journey, to bring light where there were once only shadows."

I hesitated for a moment, feeling a mix of fear and excitement coursing through my veins. The path before me was unknown, but the prospect of transformation beckoned with irresistible allure.

"I'm ready," I whispered, my voice filled with determination.

She nodded, her eyes shimmering with a wisdom beyond comprehension. "Remember, Markus, you are not alone. There will be challenges, but there will also be allies along the way. Trust in yourself and the journey that awaits. Embrace the opportunity to become the person you were meant to be."

"What do I call you?"

"Feel free to address me as *Mary* for your comfort," she said, her voice carrying a soothing quality. "While I can't divulge all the details, I can share this: the universe, like humans, is fallible. When I transported you here, the intention was for you to assume the life of William Fenwick without retaining memories from your previous existence as Markus Fales. However, an unforeseen oversight occurred, allowing your past experiences to persist. Once this anomaly was realized, the universe chose to observe the unfolding of events, as humans often say, to see how the narrative would unfold."

"So, I was never meant to remember my past life as Markus Fales?" I asked, seeking further clarification.

Mary nodded, her gaze filled with a mixture of compassion and intrigue. "That's correct. You were intended to seamlessly assume the identity of William Fenwick, living out his life without the burden of previous experiences." Her gaze softened, understanding the weight of my emotions. "I can sense the depth of your longing for your family," she acknowledged gently. "It's only natural to miss them dearly. The bond you shared in your previous life lingers within you, and the pain of separation is real. Allow yourself to feel and acknowledge those emotions. They are a testament to the love and connections you hold deep within your soul."

"I miss them ... so much," I confessed, my voice trembling with heartfelt sorrow.

"Rest assured, I have a purpose for bringing you here, although I cannot disclose it to you at this moment," Mary assured me, her presence unwavering in the corner of my room. "Since your arrival, I have been working diligently to aid you in ways that align with that purpose, even if it remains hidden from your understanding."

"How do I know you're really part of the universe?" I asked suddenly, my voice filled with a mix of curiosity and skepticism.

Mary maintained her calm demeanor as she responded, "Would you like to see your family?"

The possibility of reuniting with my loved ones stirred a surge of hope within me. "You ... you can do that? I can see them? Are they okay?"

"You've been gone for short time now, but see for yourself," Mary replied, her voice steady and reassuring.

My heart raced with anticipation as I eagerly awaited the chance to glimpse those I held dear once more. The prospect of being reunited with my family filled me with a mixture of excitement and apprehension.

A moment later, I found myself transported to a different scene altogether. I observed Ella and Katrina, in unfamiliar surroundings, as they gathered around a table for a joyous family dinner. My heart swelled with happiness and relief at the sight of their well-being. Beside me stood Mary, a silent presence.

"Can they see me or hear me?" I asked, hoping for a connection.

"No, you can only see and hear them," Mary replied gently, her words dampening my hope.

Observing my family from a distance, I couldn't help but feel a mix of emotions. "They look okay," I murmured, turning to Mary for some form of reassurance.

"You're missed very much," she responded simply, her words piercing through my heart.

Overwhelmed with gratitude, I managed to say, "Thank you … for showing me this," my voice trembling with emotion.

But reality soon settled in as Mary's words sank in. "I'm sorry, I know what you're thinking, but you can never go back. The life you have now *is your life*," she explained, her tone filled with understanding.

Lost and conflicted, I felt a surge of uncertainty welling within me. "I … I don't know what to do," I confessed, my voice filled with both confusion and longing.

"To put in plainly: Live your life. You have parents, two sisters— make memories with them. Do what a normal person your age does," Mary advised gently, encouraging me to embrace the opportunities in my new reality.

Curiosity burned within me, and I couldn't help but ask, "You said you brought me over for a purpose. Does that mean you made sure I died that night in my world?"

Mary's response was swift and sincere. "No, I wasn't allowed to interfere. The events unfolded as they were meant to."

Seeking answers and guidance, I implored, "Why am I here, Mary? Please, can't you tell me something? Anything at all? I was so lost before you arrived, and now I feel even more so."

Her expression softened, conveying a sense of empathy. "I wish I could provide you with the answers you seek, but there are limits to what I can reveal. Just know that you have been given *nudges* along the way."

"Nudges?" I questioned, puzzled by her cryptic words.

A small smile played on Mary's lips as she explained, "Yes, gentle pushes in certain directions, subtle guidance to help you navigate your new life."

Taking in her words, I pondered the significance of her interventions. Suddenly, our surroundings shifted, and I found myself transported to a military base. There, I glimpsed Sally, visibly broken and seeking solace on a cot. The sight tugged at my heartstrings.

Mary affirmed, "Your unit is all alive. Sally took your death the hardest. She was deeply affected by the loss and has been removed from the front lines. With time, she will heal. She saw you as a father figure."

Observing Sally's sorrowful state, I felt a mix of emotions. "She looks so sad," I murmured, my concern evident.

Mary nodded, her voice filled with assurance. "In time, she will find her way to healing. She will be okay."

The realization sank in, accompanied by a sense of finality. "I can never go back," I whispered, my voice heavy with acceptance.

"You can never go back," Mary confirmed gently. "You must let go of your former identity and embrace the path before you. Follow your instincts, or as humans say, *follow your heart*." As Mary prepared to depart, I understood the weight of her words. Markus was no more, and I had to release my attachment to my past life.

As the bright light enveloped Mary, she disappeared, leaving me standing there, back in my bedroom, in disbelief. The weight of her departure settled upon me, and a flurry of emotions and questions flooded my mind.

"The fuck just happened?" I exclaimed, my voice filled with incredulity. "There is no way that just happened! I have to be sleeping still!"

Attempting to ground myself, I stepped out of the bed and paced the floor, hoping to find a logical explanation. Each step confirmed that I was indeed awake, dispelling any lingering doubts. Reality stared back at me, unyielding and undeniable. The encounter with Mary lingered in my thoughts, her cryptic messages and the glimpse into a different existence. It was a surreal experience, one that defied rational explanation. Yet, deep down, I knew it was real, even if it challenged the boundaries of my understanding.

With a mix of apprehension and curiosity, I contemplated the path that lay ahead. Mary had urged me to live my life, to embrace the present and forge new connections.

The room remained silent, the echoes of Mary's presence still reverberating within me. And as I stood there, ready to face the unknown, a sense of hope flickered, casting a glimmer of light onto the path that stretched before me.

TryOuts

The encounter with Mary left me unsettled yet strangely comforted. To assure myself that it wasn't just a dream, I stayed awake the entire night, confirming the reality of the experience. In the early morning, I observed Emily leaving, her tired appearance indicating a lack of sleep. I had informed Amelia about Emily's phone call with Greg, but she advised me to stay out of it, citing their turbulent relationship and reminding me of the past abuse I had endured from him. Too exhausted to argue, I silently vowed that Greg would never lay a hand on "*Wil*" ever again.

In the following weeks, I maintained a consistent workout routine, often exercising alone. Occasionally, Amelia and Penny would join me, as Amelia expressed concern about my solitary moments. Perhaps she feared that I might contemplate self-harm again, but I knew, of course, that I had never done that in the first place. Despite this, Amelia made an effort to be around me as much as possible. As for Emily, our interactions remained minimal, and she seemed to keep her distance, which suited me just fine.

I had made significant gains in terms of muscle size and strength, which delighted me. I made sure to skate as frequently as I could, building my confidence for the upcoming tryouts.

* * *

The highly anticipated day of high school Fall sports tryouts had arrived. Amelia and Penny had both dressed in athletic attire, sporting black yoga pants paired with tank tops, no-show socks, and tennis shoes. As for me, I had opted for shorts, a shirt, and tennis shoes. Taking the responsibility of driving, I had Penny seated in the back while Amelia guided me with directions from the passenger seat. Within a matter of minutes, we reached the school—a place I *thought* I had been intimately acquainted with.

Andover High School was proudly represented by the mascot, "The Archers." It was the name of the school I had graduated from in 2008, although it appeared both familiar and transformed. The building had expanded greatly, boasting an adjoining hockey rink. Pulling into the parking lot, I made a conscious effort not to reveal my overwhelming excitement. There was no need to disclose my personal connection to the school, especially to Amelia.

As we parked, I couldn't help but ask a question that popped into my mind. "What are our school colors?" I inquired, curious to see if things remained the same.

"Green and gold," they replied simultaneously, confirming that the school's identity had stayed consistent.

However, Amelia added a detail. "Well, more like forest green and gold/yellow." With a burst of school spirit, I began reciting the school song. Amelia's excitement was palpable. "You remember?" she exclaimed.

Smooth move, Mark, I thought to myself, realizing that I had slipped and referred to myself by my former name. Ever since Mary's visit, I had become accustomed to identifying as "Wil." I hadn't seen her since that eventful night.

Shaking my head, I admitted, "I don't know how I knew that."

Sensing the weight of the situation, Penny swiftly changed the subject, saving me from further contemplation. "C'mon, guys, let's get going," she said, redirecting our attention.

Come September, I would be a sophomore, Penny a junior, and Amelia a freshman. Penny had already secured a spot on the varsity cheerleading team, having been an assistant captain the previous year. As the assistant captain, she was involved in selecting the other assistant captain. This would be Amelia's first year in high school, so she had to try out for the team. I observed Penny and Amelia practicing some routines in our home gym, and they both seemed quite talented.

Cheerleading wasn't unfamiliar to me since my daughter had been a cheerleader before.

Stepping out of the truck, I retrieved my bag from the back. Despite its weight, my excitement overshadowed any discomfort.

A chance to play hockey again!

Mary's words echoed in my mind, their weight sinking in: I couldn't return to my original world. The realization hit me hard, but it also sparked a unique opportunity. I could now do all the things I either missed out on or was too timid to pursue when I was just sixteen in my previous life.

If I only knew then, what I know now.

With a newfound determination, I resolved to make the most of my current circumstances. This world was offering me a second chance, and I was determined to seize it with both hands, embracing the lessons I had learned and the wisdom I had gained over the years.

The three of us proceeded towards the gym area and entered through the propped-open door. To my embarrassment, my bag struggled to fit through the doorway, drawing the attention of several on looking girls.

"You sure know how to make an entrance." Penny chuckled, amused by the situation.

I rolled my eyes, determined to force the bag through the door. Eventually, I succeeded, but the effort nearly caused me to lose my balance. A brunette girl with a ponytail came to my rescue, steadying me to prevent a fall. Penny couldn't help but roll her eyes at my clumsiness. "Thank you!" I expressed my gratitude, offering a smile. "That would have been even more embarrassing."

"You okay?" the girl asked, gently touching my shoulder.

"I am, thanks to you," I replied, feeling a warmth in my cheeks.

Penny tugged at my jersey, directing my attention. "The ice hockey rink is down the hall, straight ahead," she informed me.

I smiled at her. "Thank you, sis."

Looking around, I couldn't help but marvel at the stark differences between this Andover and the one from my previous life. The first thing that struck me was the sheer size of the place; it was vast and lacked the familiar musty scent of old buildings. Every corner of this school seemed to exude a sense of newness, and even the Archers Logo had undergone a complete modern makeover.

The gym lobby, in particular, left me in awe. It dwarfed the one I remembered from my past, with trophy cases stretching along an entire wall. These gleaming showcases were filled with an impressive collection of championships, both from the past and the present. It was evident that the Archers had achieved far more success than we had during my time in my world.

As I continued to explore, I couldn't ignore the presence of a massive, eye-catching Archers Logo prominently displayed on one of the walls. It seemed like the perfect spot for students and visitors alike to take pictures with, symbolizing the school's pride and unity.

Penny and Amelia confidently made their way through the crowd of girls, with Amelia following slightly behind. They disappeared into the gym, leaving me to face the stares and whispers directed my way. The rumors about what had happened to me had likely spread throughout the school by now. I tried my best to ignore the attention as I walked down the long hallway towards the entrance of the ice arena, grateful for the solitude it offered.

Arriving at the arena, my attention was drawn to a conspicuous sign directing me to the men's changing room. Stepping inside, I claimed a vacant spot on the bench among the fellow aspiring hockey players. The intensity of their stares filled the locker room, creating an electric atmosphere. I felt a surge of relief, grateful for my choice to don long sleeves, shielding my scars from unwanted attention. Murmurs of curiosity rippled through the room, and as I glanced up, I discovered numerous pairs of eyes fixated on my presence, adding an air of intrigue to the moment.

Before I could respond, someone spoke up, breaking the uncomfortable silence. "Hey, why don't all you perfect assholes shut the fuck up, eh? He's sitting right there, he can hear you," the boy asserted.

He rose with determination, striding purposefully towards my position. "Move," he commanded the two individuals seated to my left. Without uttering a single word, the pair promptly collected their equipment and shifted to the opposite side of the locker room. The young man effortlessly settled down beside me, seamlessly claiming the space. Notably, the individual who had been seated adjacent to him prior to his arrival also relocated, taking a seat on the opposite side, forming an unexpected arrangement around me.

"How ya doin', Wil? You okay, man?" he inquired, extending a gesture towards the rest of the individuals in the locker room. "I'm sorry about the rest of them," he added, acknowledging the less-than-welcoming atmosphere.

I observed him for a moment, recognizing his familiarity with Wil. "I genuinely appreciate your support. Thank you," I responded sincerely. "I'm doing alright, thank you for asking."

"Good to hear. It shocked me when I heard," he said.

"I feel embarrassed to say this, but … I have no memories … at all. I don't remember my family. I don't know who you are," I said, waiting for his reaction.

As I revealed my lack of memories to him, he looked at another boy and then back at me, clearly taken aback. "Are you serious, dude?" he asked incredulously. I nodded, a sense of vulnerability washing over me.

"I swear. I don't remember my sisters or my parents. I don't know who you are."

He placed a comforting hand on my back. "Dude, I'm really, really sorry. That must be terrible. Where are my manners? I'm Henry, Henry Burke. This is my brother, Steve Burke."

"Wil … so they tell me. How do we know each other? Are we friends?" I asked, hoping for some connection to latch on to.

Henry chuckled. "Well, we are now. We were just acquaintances, never really spoke."

Curiosity piqued, I inquired, "What made you speak up now, Henry?"

"Dude, they were just over-the-top rude. I don't care who you are. Nobody needs to hear that shit," Henry replied with conviction.

I couldn't help but smile, genuinely grateful for his intervention. "Well, I appreciate you stepping in for me."

He shrugged casually. "Ah, no problem at all. I didn't take you for a sports guy, though. What made you try out for hockey?"

I shrugged as I focused on lacing up my skates. "I just think I would enjoy playing."

Steve, who had been silent until now, chimed in. "Have you ever played before?"

"Not really," I replied, feeling a twinge of guilt for lying. However, the truth about my past was too complex to explain, and I didn't want to risk losing my newfound friends.

"Don't worry, dude. You'll learn a lot here. If you don't make varsity, you could make JV," Henry assured me.

"I hope so," I said sincerely.

"Yeah, man, no worries. If you need any help at all, let me know," He offered, displaying his genuine willingness to support me.

After suiting up, I joined Henry and Steve as we made our way onto the ice, joining the group of eager participants. The coach, a distinguished older gentleman, stood alongside them, ready to assess our skills and potential. As we lined up for the drills, I stood behind Henry and Steve, feeling a mix of nervousness and excitement. Henry turned to me, patting me on the shoulder pad. "You nervous?" he asked with a friendly smile.

I shifted my head from side to side. "A little," I admitted.

"Don't be, dude. You're gonna do great," Henry reassured me, his confidence giving me a boost.

I chuckled, appreciating his support. "Considering I don't play sports, you sure have a lot of confidence in me."

He grinned. "Well, telling you that you'll probably suck won't help your chances any." We shared a laugh, and I genuinely liked his kind and encouraging nature. "The important thing is, don't give up, no matter what. If you fall flat on your face, get back up and try again. Never let them see you give up."

"Thanks, Henry. I'll keep that in mind," I replied, feeling motivated by his words.

Finally, it was Steve's turn, and he flawlessly maneuvered through the cones with the puck, showcasing his skill. "He's a freshman this year," Henry mentioned proudly. "He's good, though. He has a good chance to make varsity, regardless of his class."

"He's awesome!" I exclaimed, impressed by Steve's performance. As he finished, it was Henry's turn. My nerves intensified as I watched him effortlessly navigate the cones, executing the drill even faster than Steve had.

Now, it was my turn. I stepped up to the line, feeling the weight of anticipation. The assistant coach placed a puck on the ice in front of me and asked, "Ready?"

I nodded, my determination outweighing my nerves. "Yeah."

As the whistle blew, I sprang into action, effortlessly maneuvering the puck past each cone with impressive speed. It felt like second nature, and I didn't even need to think about my movements. Reaching the final cone, I deftly flicked the puck to the side with my stick, sending it soaring into the coach's waiting hand.

"What's your name?" the coach inquired.

"Wil Fenwick," I replied.

He nodded approvingly. "Nice job, son." I beamed with pride as he swiftly moved on to the next skater. Making my way back to the boards where Henry and Steve were stationed, they greeted me with wide-eyed excitement.

"The fuck? Dude, that was amazing!" Henry exclaimed.

"You guys were awesome too," I replied.

Henry chuckled, playfully tapping my shoulder with his glove. "You beat my time by a landslide! I didn't know you had it in you. How the fuck did you do that? You *never* played before? I always thought you were more into the artsy-fartsy stuff."

I realized then that there were many surprises awaiting me in the upcoming school year. We completed the remaining drills, with me winning the skating, shooting, and puck handling drills, while Henry triumphed in the passing drill. By the end, I was thoroughly exhausted. Henry assured me that I had a strong chance of making varsity, given my stellar performance in the drills. The team announcements would be made by 6:00 p.m. the following day, and we were instructed to wait for a phone call.

After changing in the locker room, I made my way towards the gym lobby, hoping to find Henry. Fortunately, he and Steve were waiting at the door, and Henry waved me over. "Hey, Wil, over here!"

I approached them, setting my bag down next to theirs with a grateful smile. "Hey, guys, I just wanted to thank you both for being so welcoming. It feels like I'm starting from scratch here, not knowing anyone."

Henry shrugged, giving me a reassuring pat on the back. "No problem at all, dude. You did amazing today. I was on varsity last year as a freshman, We went six wins, fourteen losses, but with you and Steve on the team, I think we have a real shot at improving our record."

I couldn't help but feel a twinge of uncertainty. "Well, I still have to make varsity first."

Henry shook his head with confidence. "Come on, man, you dominated almost every drill. Who in their right mind wouldn't pick you for the team?"

Taking a moment to gather my thoughts, I sighed and voiced my concerns. "I guess I worry that someone might hesitate because of my past ... you know, the whole suicide thing."

Both Henry and Steve immediately placed a supportive hand on my shoulders. "If anyone pulls something like that, they're just a bunch of douche canoes," Steve chimed in. "But I don't think that'll happen. Coach is a good guy."

Henry then had an idea. "Hey, let me get your phone number. We can hang out, shoot the shit, or even skate around sometime. Sound good to you?"

Despite being thirty years old, it felt great to make friends before diving into the high school experience. I gladly exchanged numbers with Henry and Steve, grateful for the opportunity. With my bag slung over my shoulder once again, I bid them farewell and headed out the door toward my SUV, excited to reflect on the day's events.

A few minutes later, I spotted Amelia and Penny emerging from the school doors, engaged in conversation with Emily and another girl who shared a resemblance to her. Amelia noticed me and nodded in my direction, prompting everyone to turn their gaze towards me. Emily's smile brightened as she caught sight of me. After a brief exchange, Penny and Amelia made their way towards me, their fatigue evident. Amelia's initial weariness faded as she approached, replaced by a smile.

"How did it go, big brother?" Amelia asked, closing the distance between us.

"It went alright. How about you?" I inquired.

"She did amazing!" Penny interjected, beaming. "We'll find out for sure tomorrow. The others already know I want her in, and I get a vote."

Amelia flashed a toothy grin. "Yay, me!"

I nonchalantly tossed my bag into the back of the truck as the girls climbed inside.

"By the way," I casually asked, "who was that you were talking to?"

Amelia fastened her seatbelt, her eyes bright with excitement. "Emily?"

"Well, yes, but I meant the other girl with her," I clarified.

"Oh!" Amelia exclaimed, a realization dawning on her. "That's Beth, her younger sister. She's a freshman."

I nodded, observing the resemblance. "She looks a lot like her."

"Not really. If you see them up close, they do look different. Beth also has less of an accent," Amelia explained.

"Interesting," I remarked as I maneuvered the SUV out of the parking lot, heading towards home. From the corner of my eye, I noticed a mischievous smile spreading across Amelia's face. "What's with the goofy grin?" I asked.

"Well, Wil, Beth happens to be available. She's not dating anyone," Amelia teased.

"And?" I responded with a shrug. "I've told you, I'm not actively seeking a romantic relationship."

"So ... are you going to wait and see what happens with Emily?" Amelia prodded.

I could hear Penny snickering from the back seat.

Turning my head briefly to look at Amelia, I frowned before refocusing on the road. "You just won't let that go, will you?"

"Do you like Emily?" Penny chimed in. "That sounds like a disaster waiting to happen."

"What the heck? No! I'm not interested in her! She has a boyfriend," I clarified.

"For now," Amelia interjected playfully.

"...and why would that be a disaster waiting to happen?" I questioned defensively, glancing at Penny. "Don't you like Emily?"

Penny chuckled and replied, "I adore her, but I'm thinking Greg wouldn't appreciate you hitting on his lady. He'd beat the holy hell out of you."

"I'm not hitting on anyone, and no one is going to beat anything out of me," I retorted.

"You sure are touchy about this." Amelia giggled, with Penny joining in.

"Look, you told me not to get involved with Emily and her problems. I agreed, and I'm sticking to that. So let's drop all this Emily talk," I asserted firmly.

Amelia cleared her throat. "You're right, Wil. I'm sorry."

"It's cool," I responded after a moment.

"So ... about Beth—" Amelia started to say.

"Zip it," I interrupted, not wanting the conversation to continue down that path.

Waiting

T hat night, sleep eluded me. I felt like a child eagerly awaiting Christmas morning, filled with excitement and anticipation. It was hard to believe that the possibility of making the varsity ice hockey team could stir up such emotions in me at my age—My real age. In my previous life, I actually ran Cross Country, Indoor and Outdoor Track. High school hockey wasn't even a part of my experience. I only played hockey during my senior year for a local league. Sometimes, I couldn't help but feel guilty about it, considering I had already spent twenty-three years playing the sport. But this was my reality now, a second chance that I was determined to seize. What else would I do with my time?

My thoughts often drifted to Ella and Katrina. I missed them immensely, and it pained me to think of the burden they had to bear, believing I had died that fateful night. I hoped and prayed that they were coping well, both mentally and emotionally, and that they weren't facing financial struggles. At least I had a substantial life insurance policy that would alleviate some of their burdens by paying off the house in full upon my death. That is, assuming they were even paying out life insurance during war. I wished there was a way to let them know that I was okay, but without any means of contact, I could only rely on hope.

Living each day in this new life was both a blessing and a mystery. I tried my best to embrace it, even though the circumstances baffled me. Why was I chosen to inhabit this boy's life? What purpose did it serve?

Did these kinds of events happen more frequently behind the scenes of life and death? Honestly, I couldn't wrap my head around it. As an agnostic, contemplating such matters often left me with a throbbing headache. Fortunately, I found solace in confiding in Penny. Despite being closer to Amelia, Penny provided a listening ear for me to vent about the loss of my family, my previous life, and the challenges of navigating this new existence as a different person, albeit with my older consciousness.

Both of my newfound sisters played crucial roles in my life. Penny accepted and embraced me for who I claimed to be, offering her support and understanding. Meanwhile, Amelia showered me with affection and watched over me like a protective little sister.

When I returned home from hockey tryouts, dad met me at the door. He inquired about how things went, and I assured him that it went well. I sensed that he was gradually grasping the reality of the situation, that I was not the boy he had known. However, I remained uncertain about how he would treat me if he fully believed my claims, considering I would close to him in age. As for mom, she wholeheartedly believed that I was her beloved "*Wil*," her son. I hadn't made any attempts to challenge her perception.

I watched as the sun began to paint the sky with hues of orange and pink, casting a warm glow over the room. It was a breathtaking sight, one that filled me with a sense of hope and anticipation. Today was the day I would find out if I made the team or not, and the hours until the evening announcement felt like an eternity. I knew deep down that even if I didn't make varsity, I would at least secure a spot on the junior varsity team. As long as I had the opportunity to play the sport I loved, I would be content. I couldn't help but wonder if Amelia was also anxiously contemplating her chances of making the varsity or junior varsity team. Despite Penny having a say in the selection process, there was still a chance she might not make the cut.

It struck me as surreal to be consumed with thoughts of making a team. In my previous life, my worries revolved around the war, taking care of my soldiers, life and death, real problems to deal with. But all those concerns had faded into the background, at least for now. Instead, I found myself immersed in a world of homework, social events, dances, proms, and sports—a life that seemed far removed from my previous reality.

Taking a deep breath, I left the comfort of my bed and made my way to the shower. After getting dressed in shorts, socks, and a t-shirt, I decided to leave my scars exposed. They were a part of who I was now, and hiding them felt unnecessary. With a sense of determination, I headed downstairs to the informal kitchen, where Penny and Amelia were already present. Amelia sat at the table, her leg bouncing with nervous energy. However, as soon as she caught sight of me, she leaped up from her chair and enveloped me in a tight embrace.

"Good morning, big brother!" she exclaimed, her voice filled with excitement and affection.

"Good morning, Amelia!" I greeted, returning her warm hug.

I made my way over to Penny and embraced her as well. "Good morning, Penny!" I said, grateful for her presence in my life.

Penny leaned in and planted a gentle kiss on my cheek, filling me with a sense of warmth and belonging. "Good morning, Wil! I'm making eggs for Amelia and me. Would you like some too?"

I nodded appreciatively. "Sure, if it's not too much trouble."

She shook her head, a genuine smile gracing her lips. "No trouble at all. I'm excited for both of you today!" Penny cracked open three eggs and began whisking them. "Three? Or do you want more?"

A smile formed on my face as I replied, "Three is perfect, thank you." The thought of sharing this morning meal with my newfound family brought me a sense of joy and gratitude. It also made me feel a sense of guilt—that my family, somewhere else, didn't have anything like this to enjoy. Now they had to do it without me.

"I'm so nervous," Amelia confessed, her leg bouncing uncontrollably as she took her seat.

"I am too, little sister," I acknowledged, empathizing with her anxiousness. "But I have a feeling you'll make it. I believe in you."

Amelia looked at me skeptically. "How can you tell? You've never seen me cheer before ... or at least, you don't remember."

A soft smile crossed my face as I reassured her, "I have faith in you, Amelia. Besides, Penny mentioned that both of you have been cheering for a long time."

Amelia's expression softened, and she seemed thoughtful. "You haven't mentioned music or art even once since you woke up," she pointed out.

I nodded, acknowledging her observation. "That's because I know very little about music, and I have no recollection of any artistic talents. I saw a lot of it on my wall, though. Interesting drawings, for sure."

Amelia protested, her voice filled with conviction, "But you do! If you could remember, you could play any instrument and sing beautifully!"

I chuckled, realizing the irony of the situation. "Unfortunately, I can't remember any of that."

Her tone turned wistful. "I still hold hope that one day you'll regain your memories."

I considered her words for a moment. "So, you'd prefer me pursuing music and art instead of playing hockey?"

Amelia appeared puzzled at first but quickly shook her head. "Oh no, no! I want you to do it all! I want you to find happiness in every aspect of your life. Even with what you're going through and losing your memory, you seem a thousand times happier than before. I just want to make sure it stays that way."

I couldn't help but be touched by her concern. "You're incredibly sweet, Amelia," I said sincerely, moving to sit beside her. "But you have nothing to worry about. I promised you, didn't I?"

A radiant smile adorned her face. "Good! Can you draw me something?" Amelia's request came out of nowhere, catching me off guard.

"What?" I asked, my confusion evident.

"Will you draw one of your pictures like you used to?" She persisted. "I know you've been saying you can't, but you haven't even tried."

"Right now?" I sought clarification.

"Yes, right now!" Amelia asserted, springing up from her seat and disappearing into the adjacent room. Moments later, she reappeared with a pencil and some paper, extending them toward me. With a pat on the paper and a hopeful smile, she settled back into her seat. "No pressure, just do your best."

I hesitated, contemplating a self-critique. "This might not turn out that great—"

Amelia jutted out her bottom lip, casting a melancholic gaze in my direction

"You little shit." I chuckled, playfully reprimanding her before picking up the pencil.

"Draw me!" Amelia exclaimed, her enthusiasm undeniable.

I embarked on the task of sketching her, stealing glances at her now and then to capture her unique features accurately. After a bit of time, I completed the drawing and held it up, shielding it so only I could see it. "Alright, I've finished," I announced.

"That was surprisingly quick. I swear to God, Wil, if you've drawn a stick figure …" Amelia's scowl deepened as she spoke, clearly skeptical. I turned the drawing toward her, and her reaction was nothing short of jaw-dropping. "What the fuck is that?" She exclaimed, her tone incredulous.

"It's you!" I retorted with pride.

"I look like a fucking hag from a horror movie!" Amelia snorted, her frustration apparent. Penny, who had been listening from the kitchen, couldn't hold back her laughter.

"No way! I poured my heart into it!" I insisted.

"It looks like you drew it with the pencil in your mouth," Amelia retorted, her frustration mounting.

"In my defense, I did warn you that I couldn't draw," I quipped, maintaining my sense of humor.

"Clearly, your memories haven't returned," Amelia remarked, crossing her arms in a mock stern manner.

Penny graciously served me a plate of delectable eggs, bacon, and toast, and I expressed my gratitude with a warm smile. She responded with a playful wink. "You're very welcome!" she chimed. "And for what it's worth, I think the picture looks just like her!" Penny's comment earned her a rather intimidating glare from Amelia.

Deciding to shift the topic away from our previous conversation, I decided to inquire about their dating lives. "So, let's change the subject," I suggested, hoping to ease any worries Amelia might have had. "Why haven't I heard about either of you dating anyone?"

Penny burst into laughter. "Well, I actually broke up with my jerk of a boyfriend, Fred, right as the school year ended. And, of course, he was on the football team."

Curious, I asked, "No prospects for now?"

Penny shook her head. "I'm not actively looking for anyone at the moment. I'll see what the new school year brings."

Turning to Amelia, I directed my attention to her. "And what about you? Who's the lucky guy dating my little sister?"

Amelia smiled and replied, "Nobody at the moment. I'm also waiting for the new school year. Besides, I didn't have time for a boyfriend this summer."

Penny interjected proudly, "But she had plenty of offers!"

Amelia playfully retorted, "So did you!" They both laughed together.

Realizing my own single status, I chimed in, "Well, I don't have a girlfriend either, so I guess we'll all have an interesting school year."

Amelia exclaimed, "This year will be the Fenwick Year!"

Curious about their plans while waiting for the team selection, I asked, "So, are you two having anyone over while you wait to see who made the team?"

Penny responded, "I have to head to the school to help select the team. Nikki, myself, and the coaches will be there."

Nodding absentmindedly, I turned my attention to Amelia. "What about you, Amelia?" I asked, trying to look nonchalant about it.

"Are you asking me if I'm inviting a certain somebody?" Amelia asked while grinning.

Caught off guard by Amelia's response, I tried to maintain my innocent façade. "I dunno who you would be talkin' about," I replied, feigning disinterest.

Amelia's grin widened as she saw through my act. "Right—so you didn't mean *Emily?*" she teased, emphasizing the name.

I nonchalantly shrugged, dismissing the notion. "We've discussed this before, remember? Emily is already in a relationship, so it's not worth dwelling on."

Amelia let out a weary sigh, expressing her intent. "I'm going to call her and invite her over. Hopefully she'll have a little bit of peace being away from that fucker. I'll check if Beth is available, too." She playfully coughed twice, accompanied by a wink, before making her way out of the room.

Curiosity piqued, I turned to Penny, seeking answers. "Why is Amelia so determined to set me up with someone?" I asked when Amelia had left the room.

Penny replied with a casual shrug, uncertain of the exact reasoning. "I think she believes it would make you happy and keep you from thinking negative thoughts."

A wry smile formed on my lips as I reflected on my unique situation. "We both know that I have no intention of harming myself. In fact, I consider this second chance at life a precious gift. I could have easily perished, but here I am."

Penny's response was filled with encouragement, her hair tossed over her shoulder. "If this second chance is a gift, why not embrace it fully? Let Amelia set you up with someone. It would make her happy, and who knows, it might bring you some happiness as well. It's a win-win situation."

I hesitated, feeling a sense of unease about the idea. "I must admit, Penny, it all feels rather strange to me. After all, I'm married."

She offered a compassionate perspective, acknowledging the reality of my past. "You *were* married. I don't want to sound mean, but you've moved on from that life. You're sixteen and unattached now. Take the opportunity to enjoy yourself."

I chuckled, playfully challenging Penny's response. "You should take your own advice first."

Her eyes narrowed with a mischievous glint. "What do you mean?" she asked, curiosity brimming in her gaze.

I seized the moment, teasingly suggesting a course of action. "Well, you don't have a boyfriend, do you? Why not follow your own advice and see what possibilities await you?"

Penny's face lit up with a mixture of amusement and anticipation. "Oh, believe me, I will. Once school starts, I'll be on the prowl." She playfully raised her eyebrows, eliciting laughter from me. "You know, the moment you open your mouth, nobody at school will know what hit them."

I nodded in agreement, acknowledging the truth in her words. "You're right. I should embrace this newfound persona and make the most of the surprises that await me—and everyone at school."

"After they look you over like a circus freak for the attempted suicide, your comments and playing hockey will really throw them off." Penny's words lingered in the air, and I considered their weight. The thought of being scrutinized for my past and then surprising everyone with my comments and involvement in hockey didn't seem all too bad.

"You're right," I acknowledged, realizing the potential of my unique circumstances. "They won't know who I am, and I won't know who they are. We'll all start on an even playing field."

Penny's smile hinted at a playful challenge. "Greg, he'll likely be your biggest hurdle."

I couldn't help but respond with a touch of sarcasm. "Oh, joy," I remarked, expressing my lack of enthusiasm.

Penny's demeanor remained unwavering as she continued, "I assume the reason you don't appear nervous or intimidated is that you can handle yourself in a fight?"

Slowly, I nodded, recalling my training. "Krav Maga, black belt, among other fighting styles. In this body, I am larger and stronger." Regret washed over me as soon as the words left my lips. "I didn't mean to upset you by referring to your brother's body like that."

Penny waved off my concerns, extending her hand to gently hold mine. "No offense taken. I loved Wil deeply, even if I didn't show it like Amelia did. But in all honesty, Wil made a conscious decision to be where he wanted to be. It wasn't a cry for help; he intended to die that night. The scars on his body, *your* body, tell that story. Your death, on the other hand, was violent and unexpected. You didn't plan to die, though I'm sure there were many times you could have. I believe that life wasn't finished with you yet. You were brought here to take over for my brother for a reason."

Her words struck a chord within me, resonating with Mary's previous statement about my purpose in this new life. I mulled over her words before responding. "You've given this a lot of thought, Penny. Your insights are remarkable. So, what do you think my purpose is in taking over for Wil?"

Penny shrugged, her expression thoughtful. "I'm not entirely sure, but the contrast between you and Wil is quite striking. You're outgoing, confident, considerate of others' feelings, and genuinely kind. Wil, on the other hand, had a more reserved and almost robotic demeanor. He wasn't necessarily selfish, but he didn't prioritize others as much."

"I'd love to have a more in-depth conversation with you about your thoughts and beliefs on religion," I remarked.

"I'm agnostic," she stated simply.

"Same here, although I do have some unconventional beliefs," I replied.

Penny laughed, her eyes sparkling. "Oh, I have some wild beliefs too! I'd love to share them with you sometime." Her smile widened as she squeezed my hand. "I can imagine you think about your family a lot."

A tinge of sadness colored my response. "I do. I always hope they're managing well without me."

"I'm sorry, Wil. I can't even begin to comprehend what that must feel like," Penny expressed sympathetically.

"It's okay. You all have been incredibly supportive and helpful, especially you. I feel comfortable talking openly with you," I acknowledged gratefully.

"Perhaps one day, you'll be able to have those open conversations with all of us," Penny mused.

"That would be wonderful, but for now, we'll continue with this ... charade," I replied, acknowledging the temporary circumstances we found ourselves in.

Penny winked at me just as Amelia burst into the room, brimming with excitement. "Emily will be over soon!" she exclaimed.

*   *   *

The evening approached, and I followed my usual routine, hitting the home gym for a workout session as planned. After a refreshing shower, I dressed in fresh attire—new shorts, a comfortable short-sleeved shirt, and socks. I wasn't precisely aware of Emily's arrival time, and I didn't shape my entire evening around it. My intention was not to intrude on their workout or their call from the cheer coach. Instead, I desired some solitude for my phone conversation with the hockey coach, regardless of the outcome. Seeking seclusion, I sought refuge in one of the spare rooms adorned with a few desks, situated conveniently close to my bedroom. This room seemed untouched and abandoned, making it my own personal hideaway whenever I craved some privacy. Settling into one of the plush, oversized chairs, I held my cell phone in hand, ready to answer my call.

To occupy my time, I delved further into Wil's journal. One particular entry resonated deeply with me; it chronicled an episode where he had been assaulted at school by his tormentor, Greg.

He beats me all the time, and nobody ever does anything to stop it, Wil had written. *My mind is growing numb to these beatings, and I've come to accept that this is just my life now.*

Reading those words kindled a fiery determination within me. It fueled an urge to confront this Greg on the very first day of school, to make him pay for the suffering he had inflicted on Wil. Unable to continue reading, I simply set my phone down on the desk, my emotions surging.

Just as I began to get comfortable, a sudden knock at the door jolted me from my thoughts.

Who the fuck even knows I use this room?

"Come in!" I called out, my voice slightly too loud. The door swung open, and Penny cautiously peeked in before entering the room. She closed the door behind her with a gentle touch. "How did you know I was in here?" I asked, genuinely astonished.

Penny smirked. "I saw you come in here a few times already." She looked around the room, almost as if she had never been here herself. "You hiding in here?" She chuckled. "You know you could hide in your own room, right?"

I laughed. "It's the first place everyone would look for me. What's up, sis?" I asked, holding up my phone. "Aren't you supposed to be at the school by now?"

"Shortly, yes." She replied, looking at me, "I'm sorry, I don't want to disturb you. I can go."

"Don't be silly!" I waved her thoughts away. "You're never bothering me."

"Amelia has been looking for you. She wanted you to hang out with her and Emily."

I raised my eyebrow. "I didn't want to intrude on their time together."

Penny laughed at this. "Are you avoiding Emily for a reason?"

"No, it just sounds like it could become drama with that *Greg* fella. That's shit I don't need."

"Yeah, that's probably true." Penny sighed. "Anyway, they're going to order some pizza. Would you like some?"

I was pretty hungry, but I wasn't sure I should eat with the girls.

"I think I'd rather not. I'm too nervous to eat anything, and I might not be good company, especially if I receive bad news," I replied.

Penny nodded understandingly. "I completely understand."

"I feel awful about it. I know Amelia really wants me to hang out with them, but I have enough on my plate right now."

"Hey!" Penny's voice held firmness. "You don't owe anyone an explanation. Focus on taking care of yourself and getting to where *you* need to be."

"Thank you, Penny. I really appreciate it."

"What are big sisters for?" she said with a smile and a wink, before walking out and closing the door behind her.

*   *   *

I scanned through SocialStatus while I waited, spending forty-five minutes immersed in its content. However, no call came during that time. It was still a bit early, and I began to wonder if I should have gone downstairs to be with the girls. Just as I was about to leave the room, my phone suddenly rang. I stood up quickly, recognizing it as an unknown caller.

Taking a deep breath, I answered, "Hello?"

"Hello, I'm looking for William Fenwick," Coach Babcock's voice greeted me over the phone.

"This is him," I replied, trying to sound nonchalant.

"Hey, Wil—this is Coach Babcock. I wanted to be the very first to congratulate you on making the varsity Andover ice hockey team. Congratulations, son."

"Really?" I exclaimed, excitement filling my voice. "Thank you, sir! Thank you so much!"

"I must admit, when I saw you at tryouts, I was genuinely surprised. I honestly thought it would go horribly, but you proved me wrong, son. I'm also going to make you one of the assistant captains. What number would you like?"

"Thank you, sir! I really appreciate that! Is number ninety-seven available, sir?" I asked eagerly.

"It is now. Congratulations again, Wil. You've earned it. We'll see you at practice starting Monday, 3:00 p.m. to 5:30 p.m., okay? Monday through Friday. Does that work for you?"

"It does! Thank you so much, sir!"

"Okay, Wil, see you soon."

"Bye, sir, and thank you again!" I expressed my gratitude before hanging up the phone, a sense of elation coursing through me.

Emily

I had spent a significant amount of time at Amelia's house since moving to America four years ago. It had become a second home to me, a place where I felt comfortable and welcomed. Whenever my sister Beth and I were there, Penny and Nikki would join us, and we would do everything together. From recreational cheerleading to eventually joining the high school cheerleading team, those moments were the best of times for me. During those years, I grew close to Mr. and Mrs. Fenwick as well. They treated me like family, and I appreciated their warmth and kindness. However, there was one family member I couldn't seem to connect with— Wil. He was always reserved and rarely joined our activities. The extent of our conversations usually amounted to a simple greeting or farewell. I always felt like he wanted to say more, but he never did, and I didn't press the issue.

All the joy and camaraderie came crashing down when I started dating Greg during my freshman year of high school. Greg was the epitome of popularity, the star of our football team, and I felt elated when he asked me to be his date for Homecoming. Initially, things were great between us, but it didn't take long for his true colors to emerge.

Greg became controlling, constantly accusing me of infidelity or flirting with other guys. Before I knew it, I had lost many, if not all, of my male and even some female friends. He dictated who I could talk to, how I dressed, and where I could go. His jealousy was especially directed towards my close friendship with Amelia, and he often forbade me from visiting her. Despite Greg's demands, I had chosen to spend time with Amelia tonight to find out if I made the varsity team again. It was an act of defiance, a small act of reclaiming my independence.

Beth had decided to wait for the cheerleading team news at Kara's house, another freshman cheerleader. That meant it was just Amelia and me, enjoying each other's company without any interruptions. It was a rare opportunity for us to have some girl time and catch up on everything happening in our lives. We were in their massive game room, filled with pinball machines, arcade games, consoles, pool tables, and large TVs. Amelia and I were engrossed in conversation, sharing laughs in that vibrant space. She had mentioned that Wil might be joining us, and that caught me by surprise. If Greg had known about Wil's presence, he would have undoubtedly tried to harm him at the first opportunity. I kept that information to myself during my last conversation with Wil, choosing not to bring up the painful memories of Greg's violent tendencies towards him. It was a dark chapter in our lives that I preferred to forget, and hoped Wil would never remember.

However, as I observed Wil, I couldn't help but notice how much he had transformed since his time in the hospital. He had undergone a remarkable change, both physically, mentally, and emotionally. In just a few weeks, he had opened up and spoken more to me than he had in the four years I had known him. It was refreshing to see him becoming more outgoing, confident, and compassionate. Not only had Wil grown as a person, but he had also physically transformed. He had gained muscle and become more physically imposing. The change was evident, and it intrigued me. I found myself drawn to this new version of Wil, appreciating the positive developments he had undergone during his recovery. Our brief conversation we had actually made me feel a lot better, especially when I hugged him. Yes, our hug had been on my mind a lot. In his embrace, I felt an overwhelming sense of security and acceptance, as if I had finally found my home. Time seemed to slow down, and the world around us faded away, leaving only the two of us locked in a timeless embrace. It was a hug that spoke volumes without words, a hug that left an indelible mark on my heart and soul. "Whatcha daydreaming about over there, bestie?" Amelia asked, playfully pulling me out of my thoughts.

"Huh?" I replied, a little startled. "Oh, um … nothing."

"You haven't been listening to a word I said!" Amelia exclaimed, poking me in the ribs and laughing.

"Just lost in my own thoughts, I guess," I said, trying to shake off my distraction.

"Don't worry, you have to know that you'll make varsity again," Amelia reassured me.

"There were so many talented girls trying out this year," I replied, voicing my concerns.

"Yeah, but you're amazing. I'm confident you'll make it," Amelia encouraged.

"Freshmen rarely make varsity, but I did last year. I have a feeling you'll make it too," I said, offering my support.

"What about Beth?" Amelia asked, referring to my sister. "Hopefully, she'll make it too. But she wanted to be there for her new friend, Kara. She was really nervous about tryouts," I explained.

"That's really nice of her," Amelia remarked, appreciating Beth's supportive nature of her friend.

There were a few moments of silence between us, and I glanced over at my phone, hoping for some distraction. It remained silent, offering no relief. Breaking the silence, I asked, "So, any potential guys catching your eye?"

Amelia shook her head. "We're not even in high school yet. My mom won't let me date until then."

"Well, I know that, silly. But have you noticed anyone interesting?"

"Not yet. What about you and Greg? Any improvement? Has he miraculously vanished yet? Died?" Amelia asked, a hint of frustration in her voice. The mere mention of Greg's name brought a wave of gloom over me.

"No," I replied, my voice barely audible as I looked down at my socks.

"Emily, you have to get rid of him," Amelia insisted, her tone filled with determination. "Take control of your life again. We're going to high school together, and it's going to be amazing."

"I can't just break up with him," I said, my voice tinged with fear. "He's threatened to hurt me and my family."

"Then you should call the police," Amelia suggested, her concern evident.

"Let's not talk about him, please," I pleaded, desperate to change the subject.

"But, Em—"

"Please?" I interrupted, looking into her eyes with a pleading expression. She frowned, reluctantly conceding.

"Fine," she said, her disappointment palpable.

"How has Wil been?" I asked, steering the conversation in a different direction.

"He's been okay," Amelia replied. "He works out every day, goes to hockey practice. He joins us for dinner but then retreats to his room most of the time. I try to drag him out whenever I can, and we have a great time together. You wouldn't even recognize him by talking to him. He's funny and witty now."

"Really?" I asked, surprised by the transformation. I couldn't imagine Wil being funny or witty. "He has seemed different lately. So why does he still keep to himself most of the time?"

Amelia shrugged. "You know how he was before. I think he's still trying to come to terms with everything that has happened, the fact that he has no memories. I keep reassuring him that his memories will come back eventually, but he insists that they won't. He doesn't even remember trying to kill himself and is literally baffled as to why he would even do that."

"Why does he think that way?" I inquired, curious about his perspective. "I mean—why does he think he won't remember?"

"I asked him the same thing," Amelia said, pausing for a moment. "He said, 'because I wasn't here before.'"

"What in the bloody hell does that even mean?" I exclaimed, perplexed by his statement.

Amelia hesitated, as if contemplating whether to share more. "It's not something I can discuss, Em. I'm really sorry. It's personal stuff that Wil mentioned when he first woke up."

"Personal stuff?" I turned to face Amelia directly, my curiosity piqued. "But if he had no memory, how can there be anything personal?"

"You'll have to ask him someday," Amelia replied. "It's not my place to talk about it."

"But—" I began to protest, wanting to know more.

"No, I can't," Amelia insisted, her voice firm.

"Okay, fine." I sighed in resignation. "I understand. It does sound intriguing, though. By the way, where is he right now?"

"I had hoped he would come hang out with us, but it looks like he's hiding somewhere," Amelia commented.

"Hiding?" I asked curiously. "Hiding from who?"

Amelia laughed and playfully teased, "Probably you."

I gasped, putting my hand over my mouth in surprise. "No way! He's hiding because I'm here?"

Amelia burst into laughter at my reaction. "I'm just kidding. Like I said, he's probably off by himself somewhere." We both shared a laugh, lightening the mood.

"Honestly, I think you may have a little crush on him," Amelia suddenly remarked, her tone mischievous.

"Amelia!" I exclaimed, caught off guard by her comment. "I do not!"

"Uh-huh, I see the way you check him out when he says, '*Hello, Emily,*' in that voice he has. You practically melt into the chair," Amelia teased, her laughter continuing as she imitated Wil's voice and demonstrated "melting into the chair."

"Oh my god, you've gone bonkers!" I laughed, shaking my head.

"It's okay, bestie. Your secret is safe with me," she reassured me.

"There is no secret," I said seriously, the laughter fading from my voice. "Do you know what Greg would do to me if he heard that? Do you know what he would do to Wil?"

"I know, I know. I was just kidding," Amelia quickly responded, her tone becoming serious.

I interjected, "Please don't joke like that. I would feel terrible if Greg ever attacked Wil again. He's already been through so much."

Amelia nodded in agreement. "Maybe you're right. Actually, I was thinking about the possibility of Wil and Beth getting together. That's why I wanted Beth to come over tonight. What do you think?"

Without thinking, I blurted out, "No! Don't do that!" Amelia's eyes widened, and a mischievous grin appeared on her face. "I mean ... I don't think they would be compatible."

She playfully hid her grin behind her hand and asked, "Really? You think they wouldn't connect?"

I hesitated, feeling flustered by the idea of Wil being with my sister. I knew I shouldn't entertain such thoughts, but they lingered in my mind. "I ..." I began, searching for the right words.

"Do you think Beth would be interested in him?" Amelia inquired.

I remained silent for a moment, contemplating her question. "I don't know," I finally replied, letting out a sigh. "Probably, yes. Why wouldn't she?"

Amelia seized on the possibility. "Yeah, she's single, Wil's single. I'm sure he's feeling lonely. They're both somewhat shy, and maybe being together would help bring them out of their shells. Perhaps we should give her a call?"

I made a face, visibly torn by conflicting emotions. Amelia seemed thoroughly amused throughout the conversation. "You need to stop," I pleaded, feeling my heart race in my chest. "I know what you're trying to do."

Amelia adopted a playful tone and asked, "What am I doing, bestie?"

"You're trying to make me jealous by suggesting Wil and Beth as a couple," I confessed, unable to hide my discomfort.

Amelia couldn't contain her giggle. "Are you feeling jealous? Why would you feel that way unless—"

"Don't say it, Amelia," I interrupted, not wanting to hear the words. "Just don't."

"Why don't you just admit that you like him?" Amelia persisted.

"I can't do that," I insisted, my voice firm. "I *have* a boyfriend."

"A real shitty one, yeah," Amelia commented, her tone sympathetic. "I'm your best friend, and I promise not to tell anyone."

I looked at Amelia with a mixture of apprehension and admiration. There was no denying that Wil was incredibly attractive, and his newfound kindness and maturity were undeniably appealing. However, I prided myself on being faithful and loyal to Greg, my current boyfriend. I couldn't simply entertain the idea of pursuing something with Wil while I was in a committed relationship. Besides, what would Wil think of me if I were to approach him, essentially cheating on Greg? "I do find Wil handsome, and I appreciate that he's more engaged in conversations with me now. He does seem mature," I admitted, "but I can't allow myself to develop romantic feelings for him. I'm committed to Greg, and I value loyalty. What would Wil think of me if I were to betray that?"

Amelia persisted, "I understand your loyalty, but things can change with one phone call. It wouldn't be cheating then."

"Amelia—" I started to respond, but before I could continue, her phone rang, interrupting our conversation.

"Holy shit!" Amelia exclaimed, her face lighting up. "This is it! It's Penny calling!"

"Answer it!" I urged her, sharing in her excitement.

As Amelia answered the call, I could hear Penny's voice announcing that both Amelia and I had made varsity. In our elation, Amelia tossed her phone aside, and we jumped up and down, embracing each other tightly. Amidst the celebration, I caught a glimpse of Wil peering through the doorway. He smiled at me before disappearing from sight.

First Day of School

As the weeks unfolded, my routine revolved around hockey practice at 3:00 p.m. from Monday to Friday. Alongside my teammates Henry and Steve, we formed a tight-knit group, spending ample time together both on and off the ice. I eagerly introduced them to my family, extending invitations for them to visit my home.

I formed strong connections with several of my hockey teammates, including Dean Campbell, our exceptional goaltender. His reflexes were akin to that of a cat, seemingly capable of snatching up almost every shot aimed at him. Another standout was Randy Jones, a left winger on the second line who displayed remarkable proficiency in delivering one-timers. In the locker room, his corny jokes never failed to elicit laughter from the team, but when he stepped onto the ice, he transformed into a formidable force to contend with.

As practice ended, I noticed a subtle connection seemed to blossom between Steve and Amelia, yet their unspoken feelings remained concealed, leaving me to ponder their unexpressed affections. Henry's ascension to the role of team captain was a remarkable achievement, and Steve, a freshman, was honored to be appointed as one of the assistant captains. Our team dynamic defied convention, with two sophomores and a freshman leading the charge. We embraced this unconventional arrangement, recognizing the strength that lay in our collective passion and dedication. Meanwhile, Emily's appointment as assistant captain for the varsity cheerleading team, alongside Penny, sparked an electric enthusiasm among them. Their shared dreams and accomplishments illuminated their path, though Amelia couldn't help but feel a tinge of disappointment that I hadn't joined in the jubilation downstairs.

Finally, the much-anticipated first day of school arrived, bringing with it a mix of excitement and trepidation. I meticulously dressed myself, adorning myself with black pants, socks, and shoes, complemented by a stylish black and gray polo shirt. Underneath, I wore a black long-sleeved shirt, while my hair, styled in a slightly longer and spikier fashion, reflected a newfound sense of self-expression.

Amelia commented on my altered appearance, "Wow, you look different!"

"Get used to it! Dress for success," I quipped playfully, emphasizing the importance of presenting oneself confidently to the world.

Together with Penny and Amelia, we embarked on our journey to school in my SUV, navigating the chaotic scene of cars and people flooding the parking lot. Seeking a spot close to the gym, we found respite amidst the bustling environment. Just as I was about to step out, Amelia's sudden grip on my arm halted my movements, causing Penny to remain inside the vehicle, sensing something was amiss.

"I want to talk to you before we go in there," Amelia said sharply. "I want you to be prepared."

I shrugged. "I'm ready for anything."

Amelia shook her head. "No, Wil. They can be mean as shit. At some point today, someone will be rude to you. It breaks my heart thinking about it."

I sat back in my seat but turned towards her. "I'm ready for it, I promise. You have nothing to worry about."

"You need to be careful of Greg, especially him! You're his favorite target. He knows you won't do anything. He knows what happened this past summer, and I have a feeling he'll come looking for you."

"Then he's in for a surprise this year." I grinned just thinking about it.

No sir, nobody was going to fuck with "Wil Fuckin' Fenwick" anymore.

Amelia grabbed my arm again. "Wil! He will start trouble with you! You need to take this seriously!"

"I'm prepared, Amelia. I'm prepared for all of it," I affirmed with determination. "I've undergone a transformation since last school year. I need to establish my new identity." Observing Amelia's frown, I let out a sigh. "I promise not to get in any fights unless provoked, alright?" Amelia nodded, her expression tinged with sadness. "Everything will be alright, you'll see."

"Yeah, well, I'm going to shadow you as much as I can," she said protectively.

I chuckled. "If it makes you feel more at ease." As I reached for the door handle, Penny followed suit. However, Amelia once again grabbed my arm and pulled it back, causing both of us to release the handle.

"Raaaawwwrrrrr!" Penny said in frustration.

I glanced over at Amelia, silently questioning her next move.

"Also, just a heads-up, mom called the school yesterday. I'm sure she told them everything that happened this summer," she said, letting go of me.

"Swell, I'm sure I'll see the guidance counselor a lot."

We stepped out of the SUV and made our way toward the gym. Strapped to my back was a backpack filled with school supplies, a tangible reminder of the academic world I was about to reenter. As I walked, I couldn't help but ponder how different this school experience might be compared to the one I had known in my previous life.

Among all the classes awaiting me, I anticipated that history might pose the greatest challenge. The unfamiliarity of the historical events and narratives in this world's timeline left me with a sense of unease.

As we entered the gym lobby, I followed Penny down the hall, aware that she was the only one familiar with the school's layout. My first class was located on the upper floor, almost above the cafeteria, so Penny guided me to my locker before attending to Amelia. Although Amelia protested about leaving me alone, Penny assured her that I could handle myself. I stored most of my belongings in the locker, only taking what I needed for my first class, which conveniently happened to be just a door down from my locker. The teacher was Miss Hemming, and it was an English class, serving as my homeroom.

I entered the classroom and scanned the room, noting that only a few students had arrived so far, which provided some relief. Choosing a seat in the first row closest to the door, three seats from the back, was a random decision without any specific reason. I simply preferred to establish a consistent spot in all of my classes if possible. Being a creature of habit, it gave me a sense of familiarity. As I settled into the seat, I placed my binder and pencils on the desk. The sensation of the desk was uncomfortable, as if I was being squeezed into it, requiring a shoehorn to get in or out. My increased size made the task more challenging. Soon, several students entered the classroom, their eyes fixated on me. Despite Amelia's warning, it was disheartening to witness the stares and whispered conversations, reminding me of the cruel nature of some kids.

A few moments later, the classroom door swung open, and in stepped the teacher. She was a striking figure, appearing to be in her mid-twenties, with an air of youthful energy about her. Her long, chestnut brown hair cascaded down her back, framing her face like a gentle curtain. Her captivating green eyes sparkled with a certain vitality, and they seemed to hold an intrinsic warmth within them.

Her choice of attire was both chic and stylish. She wore a black dress adorned with intricate patterns of red and white flowers, a design that added a vibrant touch to her overall appearance. The dress reached just above her knee, revealing a sense of confident femininity. Her choice of footwear was practical yet tasteful, with comfortable flats that allowed her to move gracefully around the classroom.

As she spotted me, she walked briskly toward my desk, her demeanor exuding a mix of confidence and approachability that instantly put me at ease.

"Hi, Wil, I'm Miss Hemming. By chance, do you remember me?" she said softly, kneeling beside me. "How are you feeling?"

I realized that questions like these would become a common occurrence. It seemed I would have to get used to them. "I don't remember you, but I'm doing great, Miss Hemming," I replied, trying to sound upbeat and kind. My response seemed to surprise her slightly.

"I'm told that you've lost your memory?" she asked cautiously. "I hope my question doesn't offend you."

"I'm not offended at all," I reassured her cheerfully. "That's correct, though. I have no memories of anyone or anything."

She nodded understandingly. "Well, if there's anything you need at all, please don't hesitate to ask, okay?"

"Okay, thank you. Was I in your class last year?" I inquired.

"Yes, you were in my homeroom, and you will be until you graduate," she confirmed.

"Oh!" I exclaimed. "I hope I was a good student for you." I chuckled.

Miss Hemming grinned. "You were always quiet and shy. I had no problem with you."

"Well, that's good to hear. You won't have any problem with me now either—although I'd like to think I'm not quiet, nor shy," I replied, emphasizing my newfound confidence.

"If you ever feel the need to leave the room, visit the Health Room, or talk to someone, please feel free to do so. Just let me know beforehand, okay?" Miss Hemming advised.

"Thank you. I'm sure I'll be fine, though. I appreciate your concern," I replied, expressing my gratitude.

"I'll be back in a few moments," She said with a smile, and left the classroom, I became aware of the curious gazes from my classmates, causing me to release a heavy sigh. It was evident that it was going to be a challenging and eventful day ahead. The classroom rapidly filled up, with only a few empty desks remaining, but nobody sat anywhere close to me.

As I sat there, already feeling bored, my attention was captured by the appearance of Emily in the doorway. She exuded sheer beauty. Her blonde hair was elegantly styled, partly secured with a small green bow, while the rest cascaded down her back. Clad in a black short-sleeved shirt that accentuated her features, she paired it with an enchanting emerald-green dress that fell just above her knees. Completing the ensemble was a green sash adorned with a black buckle, encircling her slender waist. Emily caught my gaze, but instead of feeling embarrassed, she responded with a warm smile.

To my surprise, she chose to occupy the seat in front of mine. "Hi, Will!" she greeted me with sweetness. "Do you mind if I sit here?" She nodded towards the seat in front of me.

"I don't mind at all, please," I replied, gesturing to the seat.

Her smile grew wider. "Thanks!" She settled down, placing her backpack on the floor. Retrieving a notepad and pencil from it, she neatly arranged them on her desk. She positioned herself sideways, crossing her legs elegantly, and her black nylons added a touch of sophistication. From her vantage point, she could observe the classroom and the prying gazes and hushed conversations directed our way. "Don't let them bother you, Wil," she whispered, leaning in close so that her words were meant for my ears only. Her hair emitted a delicate scent of fresh lilacs, enveloping me in its pleasant aroma.

"I appreciate your concern," I responded with confidence, "but I'm okay."

"They're just a bunch of nosy jerks," Emily whispered once more, her voice filled with assurance. "You don't owe anybody any explanations." She locked eyes with me, her thick lashes accentuating her gaze, before bashfully glancing downward, revealing a hint of green eyeshadow.

"Thank you."

Her smile illuminated her face, radiating warmth and genuine happiness. "It's wonderful to see you again! You look fantastic!" Emily's maturity seemed beyond her years. Her demeanor, speech, and even her gestures exuded a level of sophistication typically associated with someone in their mid-twenties. She possessed a poise and grace that surpassed many adults I knew, capturing attention with her refined presence.

I was about to ask her a question when a guy walked in the door. "Hey, babe!"

Emily's reaction was anything but expected. She seemed startled, swiftly turning around to face him. He was a tall guy, similar in height to me, with dark, curly hair and piercing brown eyes. His casual attire consisted of a t-shirt bearing an unfamiliar slogan and a pair of blue jeans. Above his right eye, there was a small scar, adding a touch of ruggedness to his appearance. I assumed this must be Emily's boyfriend, the infamous "Greg."

"Greg!" Emily exclaimed upon his arrival, as if she had heard my thoughts. She stood up and gently took his arm, seemingly guiding him towards the door.

"I hate when you talk in that stupid accent. You sound ignorant," Greg snapped angrily.

"I'm British. This isn't new," Emily retorted. "I try to tone it down for you."

I found Emily's accent quite charming, even though it wasn't particularly strong. I couldn't understand what his problem was, but it was clear he was an unpleasant individual. Just then, Greg's eyes landed on me, and a wide grin spread across his face. Emily attempted to drag him away, but he forcefully pushed her back into her seat. "We don't have to go in the hallway to talk, babe. After all, I wanted to say *hey* to my boy here." He gestured towards me while speaking. "How ya doin', pal?" he asked sarcastically. "Need some good tips on how to kill yourself, right?"

Emily stood up once again, surprise and anger contorting her face. "Greg! Stop! You're being so bloody rude!" Despite Emily's persistent tugging on his arm, Greg didn't break his gaze from me.

"You're Greg?" I asked, feigning boredom. "Here I thought you were some tough-looking guy ... but damn, if I didn't know any better, I'd say you were batting for the other team." Gasps and exclamations filled the classroom in response. His smile vanished quickly, and Emily looked genuinely startled by my remark, her eyes wide with fear.

"What did you just say, you no good piece of shit?" Greg retorted.

"Hey, dude, it's okay if you swing that way. No judgment here," I replied nonchalantly, holding his gaze without flinching. "I just thought you would be more ... you know ... *masculine.*"

Greg chuckled. "I guess a near-death experience made you either really brave or really stupid. Keep it up, and you might have another one." The classroom erupted in more gasps and exclamations.

I grinned and shook my head. "Wow, bro, you're actually terrible at shit-talking."

"Really?" he asked, moving closer to me. Suddenly, Greg grabbed my arm and attempted to pull down my left sleeve, hoping to reveal a small part of my scar. However, I swiftly retrieved my arm, preventing him from succeeding. "What kind of loser can't even kill himself, right?" Greg said coldly.

Emily's face contorted with anger. "STOP, GREG!" she shouted, desperately trying to intervene. As Greg continued to ignore Emily's pleas, the entire room remained captivated by the unfolding confrontation. Suddenly, I stood up from my chair, causing him to take a step back in surprise. The room fell into a hushed silence as I pulled up both of my sleeves, revealing the scars on my forearms. I showed them to Greg and then to the rest of the class.

"Is this what you all wanted to see?" I asked, my expression devoid of emotion. "What I did to myself this summer while you were all enjoying the break from school?" Some people looked away, while others gasped in response. "I'm not ashamed of what I did. In fact, I don't even remember what I did. I have no answers to any of your questions because I don't know them myself," I explained. "I don't know any of you. I remember nothing—*at all.*" I gestured towards Greg. "I don't even know who the fuck you are, dude. And frankly, I don't care. But if I have to resort to violence to earn some respect around here, then let's do it."

Greg seemed to be processing everything I had just revealed, and even Emily appeared taken aback by my words. "You've lost your fucking mind, Fenwick," Greg finally responded. "You're going to get your ass kicked on the first day of school! I think that's some sort of record for you!"

"So far, all I hear is a lot of talk," I retorted, briefly contemplating the idea of taking him down right then and there. However, I remembered my promise to Amelia, not to start a fight.

"STOP!" Emily's voice erupted with anger, her soft tone replaced by a fiery English accent. She clutched Greg's arm, desperately attempting to pull him away. "Just stop, Greg! Why must you constantly behave this way?"

He easily shook off her hold and grabbed her by her upper arm instead. He got his face close to hers and spoke in a menacing tone, "Don't you ever grab me again, you hear me, Emily?"

Emily appeared frightened, her shoulders slumping as she cowered down, anticipating further aggression from Greg. Determined to protect her, I instinctively moved forward to intervene, attempting to push him away from her.

"Of course you'll attack someone smaller than you," I interjected, hoping to divert his attention away from Emily. Greg let go of her arm and redirected his anger towards me, reaching for my collar. I swiftly evaded his grasp, my larger size giving me an advantage in the situation. Just as tensions continued to rise, the classroom door swung open, and Miss Hemming entered, her eyes widening at the scene unfolding before her.

"MR. MALLECK!" Miss Hemming yelled as she walked in the door. "Get out of my class!" Her stern intervention had interrupted the escalating situation, and she wasted no time in addressing Greg's disruptive behavior.

He turned to face her, clearly surprised by her assertiveness. "What?" Greg exclaimed, his frustration evident in his voice.

"I said, get out of my class! NOW!" Miss Hemming repeated, her expression unwavering. "I'm not putting up with your crap this year."

Greg let out a mocking chuckle and glanced back at me, pointing a finger in my direction. "This isn't over, Fenwick," he warned.

"I sure hope not. I'm not impressed," I replied, refusing to back down. He retreated, his eyes still filled with intense hatred. As he reached the front of the row, he forcefully pushed aside several desks and stormed out of the classroom. I turned my attention to Emily, who appeared terrified and trembling uncontrollably. I guided her to sit down and asked, genuinely concerned, "Are you okay?"

Emily's voice broke as she spoke, her fear evident. "Wil, he's going to hurt you! I've never seen him so angry with you before! You've never stood up for yourself like that!"

I smiled back at her. "I can handle myself, Emily," I reassured her with confidence. "But are you going to be okay?" She nodded silently but didn't say anything as she turned to face the front of the classroom. Feeling remorseful, I mumbled, "I'm really sorry. I didn't mean to start anything."

Emily turned back to me, her expression softening. "This isn't your fault, Wil. It never has been. I'm the one who should be sorry. He's *my* boyfriend." She turned back around, and Miss Hemming closed the door as the bell rang. Throughout the class, she remained quiet for the most part, sitting sideways with her legs crossed. Occasionally, I would catch her looking at me, and she even asked if I was okay at one point. I assured her that I was fine. Meanwhile, she doodled on her folder, lost in her own thoughts.

When the final bell rang, Emily hurriedly gathered her things. "I hope the rest of your day is better," she whispered to me.

"I'm sure it will be," I replied cheerfully. Emily offered me a sympathetic smile and then hurried off to her next class. I gathered my things and made my way to my next class. As I was leaving, Miss Hemming placed a comforting hand on my shoulder.

"If you need anything—"

"Thank you, Miss Hemming," I interrupted, expressing my gratitude before walking out of the classroom. I half expected Greg to be waiting for me in the hallway, ready to continue our confrontation, but he wasn't there. Instead, I was met with more whispers, pointing, and the usual negative attention that I had grown accustomed to dealing with already.

My next class wasn't as eventful as the first one, but Henry was there. We sat next to each other, and I shared with him what had happened with Greg.

"Fuck that guy," Henry said, his face contorting into a frown. "And the other four football stooges he hangs around with. If any shit goes down, you let me know. Steve and I *will* have your back."

"I really appreciate that, Henry. Thanks," I replied, feeling a sense of reassurance.

"Anytime, dude! Hockey guys stick together," Henry said with a nod, emphasizing the camaraderie among teammates. "And if he wants to escalate by bringing the entire football team, we're game! Our hockey team has always thought they were a bunch of pussies."

* * *

Most of the day was tolerable, with people approaching me and asking if I remembered them. Each time, I had to disappointingly admit that I didn't recall them, but they didn't seem too bothered by it.

At lunch, I sat with Henry and Steve. Several other hockey players joined us, including Dean and Randy, and they all made me feel very welcome. Henry even mentioned to them the incident I had with Greg, and they were just as supportive, ready to do whatever was necessary to protect one of their own.

"Don't let anyone give you any trouble," a hulking guy with a permanent sneer said. I recognized him as Damon Guthrie, the team's enforcer, who was never shy to drop the gloves to defend his teammates. I could see that this attitude carried over off the ice, too.

Finally, it was time for my last class of the day, history. The teacher, Mr. Stuart, welcomed me into the room as I scanned for a seat. That's when I spotted Emily sitting in the third row, second seat. All the surrounding seats were taken. I had hoped to sit near her, as she was one of the few people I recognized. Our eyes briefly met, but as soon as she realized it was me, she averted her gaze quickly back to her desk. Luckily, there was an open seat in the first row.

As the class began, I found myself genuinely intrigued by the subject of history. Since I had no memory of this world's past, it was all new to me. Throughout the class, I couldn't help but steal glances at Emily, hoping to catch her looking back at me. However, she seemed focused on the lesson, and I couldn't shake the feeling of disappointment, even though I knew she was already in a relationship. There was something about her that drew me in, something beyond her outer beauty.

When the final bell rang, signaling the end of the day, Emily swiftly gathered her belongings and hurried out of the classroom without even sparing a glance in my direction. I took my time collecting my folders and made my way out of the room. Before leaving, I briefly stopped by my locker to retrieve the items I would need for later that night.

Hockey practice went well under the guidance of Coach Babcock, who pushed us hard. I enjoyed the intensity; after all, no pain, no gain. Throughout the practice, I had conversations with Henry and Steve, mostly sharing my experiences from the day and how I was treated. Despite time flying by, I realized it had been a fulfilling two hours on the ice.

As I entered the gym lobby after practice, I noticed the varsity cheerleaders were also present. I casually tossed my hockey bag off my shoulder onto the floor. Emily was there, but she walked past me quickly, seemingly avoiding any interaction. However, Penny made her way over to me.

"How was your first day?" she asked with an amused expression. "I heard you met Greg."

I chuckled and replied, "Oh, I sure did. How did you find out?"

"Are you kidding? The whole school has been talking about it! Everyone said you stood up for yourself." Penny laughed. "You even suggested he might be *gay*?"

I joined in her laughter. "Hey, there's nothing wrong with that, but he's just a complete jerk. You should've seen the way he treated Emily."

"Yeah, Amelia has always mentioned that he can be really mean to her," Penny commented.

I couldn't help but feel a surge of anger. "So why does she stay with someone like that?" I asked, my frustration evident. "I guess I already know the answer."

"Fear, maybe? Who knows?" Penny replied.

I clenched my fists. "There's no way he and I won't end up fighting."

Penny grinned at me, and just as she did, Amelia approached us, her face displaying clear concern.

"What's wrong?" I asked, letting out a sigh, already anticipating her response.

"I heard about you and Greg!" she exclaimed, sounding upset.

I shrugged nonchalantly. "It was no big deal. Nothing physical happened."

"No big deal?" Amelia retorted sharply. "By standing up to him like that, you're forcing him to fight you!"

"He doesn't have to fight me. There's always a choice, Amelia. But personally, I hope he chooses violence," I responded firmly.

"Violence never solved anything," Amelia stated.

"Actually, violence, in the form of war, has resolved many issues throughout history," I countered.

"Wil, this is serious. He gave Emily a hard time after lunch today! He was really mean to her," Amelia emphasized.

"From what you've told me, that seems to be the norm for them. I know I sound repetitive, but she should break up with him. Why stay with someone like that? Emily could have any guy she wants," I said, frustration evident in my voice.

"It's more complicated than that! You don't understand," Amelia retorted.

"Okay," I said, narrowing my eyes at her, "then help me understand."

Amelia grabbed my wrist, causing me to wince. Realizing her grip was too tight, she loosened it but still pulled me towards the wall, away from the others in the lobby.

"Fuck's sake, Amelia, just let him be!" Penny said firmly, following us.

Amelia glanced around to ensure no one else was nearby and whispered, "She's afraid of him! She's afraid of what he might do to her if she ever broke up with him!"

"I would make sure he didn't hurt her," I stated confidently.

"Oh yeah? How would you do that, Mr. Macho?" Amelia exclaimed angrily, though I wasn't sure why. "Oh, that's right, you suddenly know how to fight."

"Well … yeah," I replied.

Amelia threw her hands up in frustration. "Even if that were true—"

"It is true," I interjected.

"Even if that were true," Amelia continued, "you couldn't be with her every minute of every day. He could wait for her outside her house, at school, or even after school. Then what?"

I paused, considering her words. The truth in her statement weighed on me.

"What would you have me do?" I said, my anger rising as I tried to keep my voice down. "Allow him to bully me? Or stand up for myself and make sure he knows he can't do it anymore?"

"Because I don't want to see you get hurt! I don't want Emily to get hurt!" Amelia exclaimed, her concern evident.

"But you're okay with watching me get bullied by him? Maybe that's what happened to me before," I retorted, my anger reaching its peak. "If the guy attacks me, I'm not just going to let him do it, nor should you expect that of me. I'll defend myself. I'll put him down." Taking a deep breath, I closed my eyes and counted to ten, trying to calm myself down. When I opened my eyes, I saw Amelia standing with her arms crossed in front of her. "Look, I promised you I wouldn't start anything. By that, I mean I won't initiate a physical fight. But I will stand up for myself. If someone decides to attack me first, I have every right to defend myself."

Amelia surprised me by leaning in close and hugging me tightly. At first, I didn't hug her back, as I was still simmering with anger. "I know you have to defend yourself. I just don't think I could handle seeing you get hurt by him again," she said, her voice filled with concern.

Sighing, I finally returned her hug. "I know, Amelia. I know. Everything will be okay." She let me go, and I could see a sad expression on Penny's face as she watched us. Just as I finished hugging Amelia, a short, blonde-haired girl approached us. She was almost the same size as Amelia, and I assumed it was Beth, Emily's younger sister.

"Is everything all right?" Beth inquired, her English accent bearing a hint of familiarity with Emily's, though somewhat more subdued. Her expression was one of genuine concern. "Yeah, Beth, just talking to Wil about what happened earlier," Amelia explained to her. "Wil, this is Emily's younger sister, Beth. Beth, Kara, and I are the only freshmen to make varsity cheerleading."

"Hello, Beth." I nodded to her. "Nice to meet you."

Beth smiled at me. "We've met before."

I offered her a sympathetic smile. "I don't remember, I'm sorry."

"It's okay. You look great!" Beth replied warmly.

I could feel a warmth spreading across my cheeks as I responded, "Thank you, you look lovely as well." It seemed that accepting compliments gracefully was not my strong suit.

Amelia turned to Beth with a small smile and asked, "Are you still single, Beth?"

Beth shrugged nonchalantly. "Yeah, why do you ask?"

Amelia seemed to hesitate, as if reconsidering her words. "Oh, no reason, just curious," she replied, trying to play it off casually. Penny couldn't contain her laughter, which only made me feel more self-conscious, my cheeks growing even hotter.

Breaking the lighthearted moment, Beth interjected, "Emily's waiting to talk to you. Do you have a minute?"

Amelia quickly responded, "Sure! I'll meet you two at the truck in a few minutes," addressing Penny and me.

"Yeah, no problem," I replied, with Penny simply nodding in agreement. I retrieved my hockey bag from the floor and slung it over my shoulder. Taking the lead, I walked out of the lobby, with Penny following closely behind.

When I got to the doors and looked back, I observed Amelia, Emily, and Beth engaged in conversation. It seemed that Emily had sent Beth over to fetch Amelia, possibly to avoid any interaction with me. Emily briefly looked my way but quickly shifted her focus back to Amelia, appearing concerned. Deciding not to interrupt, I pushed the door open, ensuring it didn't hit Penny as she followed behind.

Penny smiled at me and said, "Thanks, Wil," catching up to walk alongside me. "You know, I see the way you look at her."

I feigned innocence and asked, "Look at who?"

She playfully smacked me on the shoulder. "Don't play dumb with me. Who do you think I mean?"

Letting out a sigh, I acknowledged that she knew. "Emily?"

"Yeah, Emily."

"She's undeniably attractive," I responded matter-of-factly. "Beautiful even. But she's in a relationship, which makes her off-limits to me."

Penny wore that familiar know-it-all smile of hers but didn't push the matter further.

* * *

The next morning, I drove myself and my sisters to school and quickly arrived to Miss Hemming's class as early as possible. I casually tossed my belongings onto the desk, but of course, my pencil rolled off and fell onto the floor. It seemed like a sign of how the day was going to unfold. I leaned down to retrieve the pencil without bothering to stand up. As I sat back up, I noticed Emily shuffling towards her desk.

Her hair was down, partially covering the left side of her face. She was wearing jeans and a nice red and white striped top, with her varsity jacket left open. Emily kept her gaze down the entire time, avoiding any eye contact with me. She sat down, placed her backpack on the ground, and faced forward without uttering a word.

"Emily?" I whispered softly, concerned. "Are you okay?" She remained silent. "I'm sorry about yesterday," I continued. "Greg was getting under my skin." I heard her take a deep breath before slowly turning to face me. A dark ring was visible under her left eye. "Emily, what ... what happened?"

"I slipped and fell," she quickly replied. "Look, Wil, I'm sorry, but we can't be friends."

"You fell? Did Greg do this to you? Is this because of me?"

"No, Wil, I told you, I fell," Emily snapped, her voice filled with fear. She kept glancing towards the doorway and back at me. "We can't be friends, okay? I think you're a really nice guy, and I'm glad you're okay. I really am. I talked to Greg, and he promised he wouldn't touch you."

"Wait, what?" I said, confused. "If he hurt you—"

"No!" Emily interrupted sharply. Our conversation had caught the attention of some kids in the class, causing us to look up. She cleared her throat and whispered, "No, Wil. You can't do anything. Promise me you won't do anything."

"I'm not afraid—"

She cut me off again. "No! I don't want to hear it! He's my boyfriend. I'm going to ask Miss Hemming to move my desk when she comes in." She added softly, "I'm really sorry. It's not you, I swear." Miss Hemming entered the classroom just as Emily finished speaking. Emily promptly stood up and approached her. They exchanged whispers, occasionally glancing in my direction. After their brief conversation, Emily returned to her desk, grabbed her backpack, and walked over to another desk situated in the middle of the room. I couldn't help but feel bothered by this sudden change.

Lost in my thoughts, I failed to notice Miss Hemming approaching until she was right beside me. Startled, I looked up at her. "I'm sorry. I didn't mean to startle you," she said softly. "I want you to know that you don't need to worry about Greg. There won't be a repeat of last year. I'll make sure you feel safe, at least while you're at school."

"I don't remember last year, Miss Hemming," I replied, meeting her gaze. "But you're right, there won't be a repeat of it." She gave me a sympathetic smile, briefly placing her hand on my upper arm, before walking away.

I went through the remainder of the school day in a daze, only catching glimpses of Emily in my last class. She didn't utter a word to me or even glance in my direction for the rest of the day.

Hockey practice served as an outlet for me to release some of the pent-up frustration. Henry noticed something was off and asked if I was okay. I assured him that I was fine, not wanting to burden him with my inner turmoil. Truthfully, I didn't quite understand what was going on with myself either. Despite my reassurance, Henry and Steve checked in on me frequently, showing their concern, which I appreciated.

Freshened from a revitalizing shower and attired in my chosen ensemble, I embarked on my journey towards the gym lobby. Within its hallowed halls, an amalgamation of spirited camaraderie awaited—the football team, cheerleading squad, and hockey team unified in their presence. Navigating through the vibrant throng, I traversed the expanse, emerging into the open air and approaching my awaiting SUV. Mindfully arranging my equipment in the rear, I patiently bided my time, eagerly anticipating the arrival of my sisters. Their gradual emergence from the lobby, engaged in animated conversation with fellow cheerleaders, including Emily, seemingly stretched time itself. Finally, they drew nearer, their graceful strides carrying them towards our shared vehicle. Amelia's apprehensive countenance did not elude my observant gaze as she joined me in the car.

"Where were you? We looked everywhere for you," Amelia asked, her tone filled with worry.

I simply pointed down at my seat. "Well, you didn't look everywhere. I was right here."

"Are you okay?" Penny chimed in from the back seat, her concern evident.

"Yeah, I'm perfectly fine. Why wouldn't I be? I just didn't feel like engaging in small talk today."

"I talked to Emily," Amelia stated matter-of-factly.

"Yeah, I saw," I replied with a casual shrug, starting the truck and pulling out of the parking spot.

"Wait, what?" Penny exclaimed, sitting up so her face practically leaned into the front seat. "What happened?"

"Oh, for heaven's sake, nothing happened! She just doesn't want to be friends with me. I'm fine with that. It's not a big deal," I explained, my frustration seeping through. "So, let's not make it into one, alright?"

"Really? It sure sounds like a big deal," Penny said, her lips pursed as she settled back into her seat.

Amelia interjected, "She did it to protect you and herself. Greg was seriously pissed and was going to beat your ass—"

I raised my hand, cutting her off. "He's never going to beat my ass," I said angrily.

"He was going to fight you. You made him look like a giant pussy on the first day back at school. You really embarrassed him in front of everyone! Emily argued with him about it. I'm sure that's how she ended up with that bruise, despite what she says," Amelia explained.

"So he beats up Emily, and that's considered normal? All the more reason for me to knock his teeth down his throat," I retorted, my anger flaring.

"No, Wil," Amelia said firmly. "All you need to do now is avoid getting into it with Greg. For Emily's sake!" I let out a frustrated sigh.

"Alright," I reluctantly agreed. "No more promises from me, though. From now on, I'm going to handle things my own way."

Avoidance

—<o>—<>—

O ver the next two weeks at school, I couldn't help but notice Emily and Greg walking hand in hand through the hallways. However, her demeanor seemed different. She didn't smile when I saw her, and her style of clothing had changed. She opted for more casual and less stylish outfits, and she wore minimal makeup. But to me, she was just as beautiful without all the glamor. Whenever I saw her, she kept to herself and didn't interact much with others, not even the other cheerleaders. When Greg would talk to his friends, she would stand by his side silently. I caught her glancing at me a few times, but she quickly looked away. I couldn't understand why I cared so much about her actions or who she was with. It felt like there was an inexplicable connection between us, and we would often cross paths. No matter which way I went to my next class, it seemed like I always ran into Emily and Greg.

Amelia had confided in me that Emily was speaking to her less and less, and there were even rumors that she might quit the cheerleading team altogether. Amelia also mentioned that for the first two football games, Emily didn't wear her cheerleading uniform to school like the others, although she still cheered at the games. This caused tension between Emily and her coach, as they were required to wear their uniforms to school.

One day, as I exited my science class on my way to the restroom, I heard sobbing coming from the girls' bathroom. Intrigued and concerned, I paused outside the door to listen more closely. The crying persisted, and I felt an inexplicable pull, compelling me to investigate further. Tentatively, I spoke, "Hello, are you okay?" The crying ceased momentarily, as if the person inside tried to hide their distress. "Do you need any help?" I inquired.

"Please, just go away!" a familiar voice with a British accent shouted back.

"Emily? Is that you?" I asked, recognizing the voice.

Her crying resumed, and she pleaded, "Please, leave me alone!"

"I'm coming in, I hope you're decent," I said cautiously, entering the girls' bathroom for the first time. I quickly surveyed the area, making sure she wasn't in a vulnerable state. Emily sat on the floor, her knees pulled in close to her chest, rocking back and forth as tears streamed down her face.

"It's me, Wil," I said softly, kneeling beside her. "Are you hurt?"

"Go away, Wil. Please!" Emily looked up at me, her eyes filled with despair. "I don't want to talk to you!"

"Okay, I understand," I responded, respecting her wishes. "Just let me know if you're hurt, and I'll leave. I can get you the help you need."

"NO!" Emily shrieked, her anguish palpable. "I don't want your help! I don't want anyone's help! I just want to be left alone!" As I reached out my hands slowly, she jerked away, forcefully stating, "Don't touch me!"

"I only want to help you," I insisted gently.

"I don't want your help! I've already told you that!" Emily's voice quivered with a mix of pain and frustration.

"Okay, okay," I responded, feeling perplexed by the sudden hostility. "I'm sorry. I'll leave you be." As I exited the bathroom, Emily's sobs grew louder, tugging at my heartstrings. Every instinct urged me to go back and offer my support. However, she made it clear that she didn't want my help, and I couldn't force it upon her. The nearest room where I felt comfortable seeking assistance was Miss Hemming's classroom. Peering through the small window on her door, I saw her holding up a book, engaged with the class. I lightly knocked on the door, trying not to disrupt the lesson. Miss Hemming immediately turned her head towards me and swiftly approached, opening the door.

"Wil, is everything okay?" she asked, concern etched on her face.

"Uh, no. Not really," I replied.

"What's wrong?"

"It's not me, it's Emily." I proceeded to explain to Miss Hemming about the crying I heard, my encounter with Emily in the bathroom, and her rejection of my help.

"Class, open your textbooks to page 97 and read until 111. I'll be right back," Miss Hemming instructed before closing the door behind her.

"Which restroom?" she asked.

"The one next to your class."

Miss Hemming headed towards the bathroom while I decided to return to my own class. It seemed best if I wasn't directly involved in the situation. I put on a fake smile, nodding to Miss Hemming, and continued down the hall, concealing my concern.

*   *   *

Lunchtime arrived, although I had no appetite. Henry, Steve, Damon, Randy, and Dean were already seated at our usual table.

"Dude, where's your lunch?" Henry asked, noticing my empty hands.

"I'm not hungry," I replied, slumping down in my chair.

"You want some of mine? I got a turkey and cheese sandwich. I'll split it with you."

"No, that's okay, bro," I said, mustering a smile. "Very cool of you to offer, though."

"No problem. You don't look so good. You good?" Henry inquired, concern evident in his eyes.

"Are you saying I look like shit?"

"Dude, I'm saying you look like shit."

"Well, that's good because I feel like it."

"What's going on?" Henry set his food down, giving me his full attention.

"It's really hard to explain. I'm not really sure myself."

"Okay, well, try." He said, "You nervous about playing hockey? Is it a girl? Grades?"

"No, yes, no."

"Girls are always the problem," Steve mumbled between bites.

"They do nothing but cause a distraction, concentrate on playing hockey." Damon insisted.

"Okay, so which girl? You ask someone out and they shot you down?" Henry probed.

"No, no, nothing like that."

"Let's start simple. Who are we talking about here?" Henry pressed.

"Emily."

"Emily DuBrie?" Henry inquired.

"Yeah."

"Okay, what about her?"

I sighed, struggling to find the right words. "That's just it, I'm not sure. She has a boyfriend, if that's what you want to call him, but I find myself always thinking about her—even worrying about her."

"Dude, you and every other straight male in the Western Hemisphere." Henry chuckled. "She's one of the prettiest girls in the school."

"She is very pretty." Dean agreed, "There are a *lot* of cute cheerleaders this year."

"Yeah, but it's more than that. That's the part I can't explain." I said.

"Do you need my help with something? 'Cause if you do, just say the word, I'm there."

I smiled appreciatively. "You're a good friend, Henry. I appreciate you."

"As you should!" Henry replied, returning the smile.

I didn't notice her coming over, but when I glanced to the side, there was Emily, standing next to me at our lunch table, her expression clouded with unhappiness. "Emily!" I exclaimed, placing my hand over my heart. "You scared the shit out of me!" I felt a wave of fear, unsure if she had overheard our conversation.

"Well, look who's here." Damon remarked in his deep, resonant voice.

"I need to talk to you," she said firmly, ignoring the others, "Right now."

"Okay, sure," I replied, nodding. "What's up?"

"In private," she insisted.

"Oh!" I stammered. "Guys, I'll be back."

"Be cool to my bro," Henry said, giving Emily a meaningful look. "'Cause if you're here to *start* shit on Greg's behalf, we'll *finish* it."

Emily ignored him, focusing her gaze on me.

I quickly got up from the table. "I got this, bro, but thanks," I said to Henry, then turned to Emily. "Lead on."

Emily guided me out of the cafeteria and around the corner, heading towards the music wing of the school. Throughout the walk, Emily kept glancing around, presumably to ensure no one else was nearby. Once she felt we were in a secure location, she spun around to face me.

"I can't believe you sent Miss Hemming into the bathroom!" she snapped. "I told you I didn't want anyone's help!" Our eyes met, and I could sense the anger emanating from her.

"Yes, I know you did, but I had to make a judgment call. I wasn't sure if you were hurt or not," I explained.

"Thanks a lot, Wil!" Emily exclaimed, her voice filled with anger. "Thanks to you, I had to spend an hour and a half at the school counselor's office. Greg is furious with me!"

"I'm sorry, Emily. I really am," I said sincerely. "All you had to do was let me know you were physically okay, and I might have just walked away. I don't understand why your boyfriend would be against you talking to someone unless he has something to hide."

"Who do you think you are?" Emily's voice rose in frustration. "Before you tried to kill yourself, you wouldn't have done anything like that! You would have been too afraid that getting close to me would get you beaten up by Greg!"

I clenched my jaw for a moment, holding back my emotions. "Appreciate you bringing up the attempted suicide there. Thanks."

Emily began pacing back and forth, her anger seemingly overshadowed by fear. Despite her hostile appearance, there was an underlying sense of vulnerability. "You had better hope Greg doesn't take this out on me," she started. "I told you—"

"Enough!" I yelled, holding up my hand, which seemed to frighten her, as she cowered away from me. "I'm sick and tired of people telling *me* what to do, what *not* to do, how to act, how to think! Don't upset this person, don't upset that person! Oh no, Greg's coming for me! As if! I have my own problems, okay?" I held up my two wrists. "My *own fuckin'* problems! I've been nothing but kind to *you* from the very start, or at least from when I woke from slitting my fuckin' forearms open! Christ, I'm beginning to understand now why I did it! You told me you didn't want to be friends, *fine by me!* I haven't bothered you, I haven't talked to you, I have started nothing with that dumb-ass boyfriend of yours! If you weren't sitting in the bathroom crying, we would still *not* be speaking! We'd both be happy! Get over yourself! I didn't know it was you in the restroom, okay? You weren't crying in a British accent! When I found out it was you, I still wanted to help, and believe me, not everyone would have! I would've stopped to help anyone, 'cause that's what a decent person does! I know you hate me, I get it! Message received a while ago. I don't need a constant fuckin' reminder! I'm *not* your boyfriend, I'm *not* your ex-boyfriend—hell, I'm not even *your* friend! I'm not that pushover you knew before, and I will NOT be told what to do by *you*, or *anyone*!"

I was breathing heavily, the weight of my words hanging in the air. Emily stared at me with wide eyes, clearly shocked by the intensity of my rant. Before I could say anything else, she ran off, sobbing. Taking a deep breath, I tried to calm myself down. As the adrenaline subsided, regret washed over me for losing control like that. I didn't know what Emily was going through, and my outburst was unwarranted. Feeling a profound sense of guilt, I made my way back to the lunch table where Henry and Steve were packing up.

"I couldn't help but notice Emily running down the hall," Henry commented with a chuckle. "Guess things didn't go too well."

"It could've gone better," I admitted, a heavy sigh escaping my lips.

Living a Lie
(EMILY)

⊰◦─◇─◦⊱

I dashed down the corridor, my tears flowing ceaselessly. Wil's words struck me with an indescribable force. His anger towards me was palpable, and I couldn't blame him for feeling that way. It seemed as though he believed I harbored a deep-seated hatred for him, but the reality couldn't be further from the truth. In truth, I held great affection for him, but my commitment to Greg compelled me to suppress those feelings. I had believed that Wil reciprocated my emotions, but his outburst shattered my certainty. I was to blame for mistreating him initially, and witnessing him assert himself not once but twice was a revelation. It pained me to realize that I was the cause of his newfound strength. I never intended to inflict harm or distress upon him. I had purposefully distanced myself to shield him from Greg's wrath.

When Wil unexpectedly entered the restroom earlier, a part of me yearned for his comforting presence. Relief washed over me when he promptly informed Miss Hemming, who responded with remarkable understanding, cradling me as I wept uncontrollably. She convinced me of the necessity to confide in someone about the tumult in my life, and before I knew it, I was en route to the school counselor. After the session, I dutifully sent a text to Greg, adhering to the expectations of a "good girlfriend," divulging the events that had transpired. Naturally, he reacted with fury, as it seemed he was perpetually enraged with me, always finding reasons.

"*I saw you look at that guy*," '*You want guys to look at you with the way you dress*," "*Your accent makes you sound stupid*," "*You're a worthless bitch that nobody will ever want*," "*You wear that cheerleading uniform for attention.*"

I was a prisoner of my own existence, devoid of any control. Every facet of my life was under the oppressive rule of Greg. I had no say in what clothes to wear, where to venture, or even whom to associate with. Communication, even with my closest confidante Amelia, had been stifled. The suffocating isolation left me in a state of profound desolation. Deep within, I yearned to break free from Greg's clutches and flee the toxicity of our relationship. Who would willingly subject themselves to such mistreatment? However, it was far from a simple matter of walking away, despite what many may have believed. Fear gripped every fiber of my being. Each feeble attempt to liberate myself would be met with dire consequences. Greg relentlessly threatened to inflict harm upon me, my family, or both. I was ensnared, trapped in this agonizing existence for over a year. As the new school year dawned, I clung to the hope of a fresh beginning, a chance for transformation. I adorned myself, striving for beauty, primarily to appease Greg. In retrospect, I can't fathom what deluded thoughts possessed me. Yet, when Wil took a courageous stand against Greg, it became the turning point. It forcibly opened my eyes to the profoundly unhealthy and oppressive nature of our relationship.

As I drew closer to Wil at the lunch table, an inexplicable force seemed to guide my steps towards him. Surprisingly, anger was far from my mind; instead, a sense of genuine gladness washed over me at the sight of his friendship with Henry and Steve, two individuals radiating sincere kindness. His entire team was sitting there, watching me closely. It appeared that Wil had confided in them about our circumstances, evident from Henry's casual reference to me being on good terms with his "bro." Inexplicably, being in Wil's presence evoked a mixture of nervous anticipation and undeniable solace, despite the lack of logical explanation. As we walked together, a surge of exhilaration coursed through me, heightening the already rapid rhythm of my heartbeat. Yet, the words that escaped my lips during our conversation were not reflective of my true intentions. If only Wil could comprehend that my actions were motivated by a deep-seated desire to shield him, and that causing him further anguish was the last thing on my mind. He had already endured so much hardship. However, Wil held nothing back in firmly asserting his position, much like Greg often did. Although I should have grown accustomed to such confrontations by now, it stung all the more when they emanated from Wil.

Exhausted and emotionally depleted, I sought comfort outside the school, finding support against the sturdy embrace of the brick wall. The ceaseless display of my tear-streaked countenance had grown wearisome. The futility of adorning my face with makeup became apparent, for it invariably succumbed to smudges and smears, a reflection of my inner turmoil. With haste, I composed myself, determined not to be tardy for my impending class. Meanwhile, my phone persistently vibrated, a telltale sign of the identity behind the incessant notifications. The impending visit to Greg's abode loomed over me, an event inevitably shadowed by a singular expectation.

With the final bell signaling the end of the school day, I darted through the corridors, a relentless urge propelling me towards the gym lobby, desperate to steer clear of any encounter with Wil en-route to his hockey practice. As I stepped into the sanctum of the girls' locker room, a fleeting sense of respite enveloped me. Swiftly, I shed my ordinary attire, donning the vibrant practice attire of a cheerleader, and tightly bound my hair into an impeccably sleek ponytail. Approaching the practice room, a gathering of familiar faces awaited my arrival: Nikki, Amelia, and Penny. Their arms crossed, countenances etched with an unmistakable fury, casting an ominous ambiance.

"What's going on?" I asked, my voice low and cautious.

Nikki's eyes narrowed as she retorted, "Why don't you tell us?"

I shrugged and replied, "Nothing. Just practice."

Penny took a step closer to me, causing me to instinctively back away. "We understand you're dealing with issues with Greg, but why take it out on Wil?" she questioned, her tone filled with disappointment. "Of all people!"

Defensively, I said, "I'm not taking anything out on anyone. Please, things are already difficult for me."

Amelia's anger was evident as she added, "Wil told me about your argument with him during lunch today. Did you really feel the need to confront him like that? Are you trying to get him to hurt himself again?"

Lowering my head and gazing at my cheer shoes, I murmured, "I'm trying to protect him. I want him to stay *away* so Greg won't target him. I never want to see him hurt, by anyone, certainly not from himself."

Nikki scoffed, "Stay away? He hasn't bothered you at all! Get over yourself. He doesn't need your protection. You act as if he's stalking you or something, but he's not! If anything, you're the one stalking him!"

"He heard me crying in the bathroom and came in ..." I trailed off, attempting to explain.

"He was trying to help you, *stupid!*" Nikki's voice escalated to a yell. "He didn't even know it was you at first! It didn't matter to him who was in there; he went in with the intention of helping. He has his own problems, and he doesn't need you adding to them! Just leave him be!"

As they spoke their truths, the weight of their words bore down on me, sinking deep into my already shattered self-image. A single tear cascaded down my cheek, a symbol of my crumbling façade. "You're right," I murmured, my voice barely audible.

"And another thing ... wait, what?" Nikki's interruption broke the silence, but I stood firm in my admission.

"I said, you're right," I repeated, my gaze fixed downward, doing my best to hide my tears. "All of it. I've become a terrible person ... maybe I was never a good person to begin with, and that's why I'm where I am now. I deserve the miserable life I have. I'm sorry for failing as a friend to all of you."

Amelia, the first to recognize my vulnerability, abandoned her defensive stance and approached me with open arms. She enveloped me in a warm embrace, offering peace amidst the storm raging within me. "You don't deserve to be treated the way Greg is treating you," she whispered, her voice filled with empathy and compassion. Her words pierced through my anguish, igniting a torrent of tears that poured forth uncontrollably. In that moment of shared pain, Nikki and Penny joined the embrace, their support and understanding enveloping me.

Amidst my sobs, Amelia's voice reached my ears, her words resonating deeply within my wounded soul. "It's time for you to get your life back."

Crazy Week

$\Longrightarrow \!\!\!\! \longleftarrow \!\! \diamond \!\! \longrightarrow \!\!\!\! \Longleftarrow$

In the ensuing week and a half, I wholeheartedly immersed myself in the realm of hockey, finding solace in the company of my teammates, especially Henry and Steve. To my immense relief, my parents warmed up to them, fostering a sense of reassurance. They wholeheartedly encouraged our companionship, urging me to spend more time with these newfound friends, a proposition to which I eagerly acceded. With an open heart, I divulged the intricate details surrounding the enigmatic Emily, and Henry and Steve, in turn, voiced their vehement aversion to Greg's mistreatment of her. However, as time wore on, I reached a point where I no longer wished to dwell on the matter, firmly asserting that it was no longer my burden to bear. In response, Henry gently suggested that there were countless kind-hearted girls I could potentially encounter, even though neither he nor Steve had romantic partners themselves. Nevertheless, the horizon shimmered with the promise of exhilarating prospects.

As I delved further into Wil's journal, I stumbled upon a significant revelation—Wil had finally named Emily, the object of his affection. He had even penned a concise, imaginative narrative featuring himself and Emily, with her adoring him within the story's confines.

In addition to this, there was a disturbing list of bullies, and at the very top was Greg. One page in particular was haunting, with a repetitive mantra scrawled across it: *I hate him!* The intensity of those words echoed throughout the page.

What struck me most were the numerous entries detailing Wil's fantasies about being with Emily, and he meticulously noted each instance when she arrived at school bearing injuries to her face, arms, or legs. Each of these injuries fueled a deep-seated desire for revenge against Greg.

The impending Wednesday heralded my inaugural hockey game, a fiercely anticipated home match against the formidable Arundel. My elation knew no bounds. As a testament to my newfound dedication, the team generously bestowed upon me a collection of five jerseys, each representing a distinctive variation. The home jersey exuded a dominant green hue embellished with resplendent yellow trim, while the away jersey gleamed in pristine white accented by a harmonious blend of green and yellow. The third jersey sported a vibrant yellow canvas adorned with tasteful accents of green and white. Additionally, a yellow practice jersey and a resolute green jersey completed the ensemble. On game days, we dutifully embraced a formal dress code, meticulously donning dress pants, polished dress shoes, a crisply buttoned-down dress shirt, and a stylish tie.

I noticed that Emily had been absent from school for a few days, and when she finally returned, she continued to distance herself from me and avoided any interaction. It was disheartening to see her still walking hand in hand with Greg, and her bruised face was a painful sight. Amelia informed me that she had been frequently late for practice and hardly spoke to anyone. Beth had mentioned to Amelia that something terrible had occurred between Emily and Greg but didn't provide any further details. Concerned for her well-being, Coach Geller decided to have a talk with her after their last practice. Amelia, fearing that she might be removed from the team, approached the coach and shared her concerns about Emily potentially experiencing physical abuse. We all hoped that the coach would handle the situation in the best possible way and provide the support that she needed.

One morning, I entered Miss Hemming's class and assumed my usual spot. Just as the bell rang, Emily dashed into the room, narrowly slipping in before the door shut behind her. Her hair was neatly tied back in a ponytail, and a hint of makeup accentuated her features. She sported an oversized royal blue hoodie, distressed jeans, and a pair of well-worn chucks. No matter what she wore, Emily's beauty always shone through to me. As she hastened to her seat, her eyes briefly met mine before focusing on her own desk. Everything appeared typical, and I readied my notepad and pencil, poised for the English lesson ahead. Given my true age, English was a breeze, and securing an "A" in the class required minimal effort. I glanced over at Emily, observing her as she organized her materials and retrieved her distinctive pink pencil. She emitted a sigh, weariness evident on her face as she settled into her desk chair. "Okay, everyone," Miss Hemming started, moving to the front of the classroom. "Today, we will be working in pairs on a project. You will be writing together to create a short story, exploring the point of view of a boy and then from a girl's perspective." Collaborative work had never been my cup of tea, even during my previous school years. Whenever I found myself in a group, I would often take charge and handle the entire project on my own. It seemed that everyone wanted to be in my group solely because they knew I would do all the work. Today was no different, and I wasn't particularly thrilled about it. However, I decided to stick to my usual approach and extend the same offer to my assigned partner. "I took the liberty of selecting who you would be paired with, so when I call your names, sit somewhere together," Miss Hemming announced, holding a sheet of paper in her hand.

She began calling out names in pairs, assigning partners for the project. When she uttered my name, I prepared myself to be paired up with Kara Chellum, the diminutive cheerleader and Beth's closest friend. Kara occupied the seat closest to me, especially now that Emily had moved from our row. However, to my surprise, Miss Hemming spoke my name again, this time alongside Emily's. "Wil and Emily," Miss Hemming said, briefly glancing at me before continuing with the rest of the names on her list. I couldn't believe my ears. Was I really being paired with Emily? I turned to look at her, and the startled expression on her face confirmed it.

Well, shit.

I hesitated, unsure of whether I should approach Emily or wait for her to come to me. But before I could make a decision, Emily took the initiative and walked up to Miss Hemming, whispering something to her. The teacher paused in calling out names, a stern expression crossing her face. "I don't want to hear it, Emily," Miss Hemming responded, her tone indicating her lack of patience. "Go sit at your old desk. It's just for today."

"But Miss Hemming, you don't underst—"

"Go!" Miss Hemming commanded, directing Emily towards me. She glanced at me briefly, her expression filled with resignation, before gathering her belongings and making her way to the desk where she used to sit. It was an uncomfortable situation to be paired with someone who clearly despised me, especially when their protests were witnessed by the entire class. I was thoroughly embarrassed. Emily slouched in her seat, dropping her belongings heavily on her desk, deliberately avoiding facing me. We sat in an awkward silence for a few moments until I decided to break it by clearing my throat and whispering.

"I'll take care of the entire project, Emily. You don't have to do anything. I promise we'll both receive an 'A' for it."

"No, I'll do it all," she responded without turning towards me.

"Really, it's no problem for me to do it. I'll get it done quickly, and you can go back to your *own* desk. We don't have to speak to each other at all. I know you don't want to be near me, and that's fine. I didn't choose this pairing, so I would appreciate it if you just sat there silently, instead of going off on me again."

Emily swiftly turned in her seat to face me. I noticed a bruise on her face, near her left eye this time. Her eyes bored into mine, filled with anger and resentment. She opened her mouth to say something, but I raised my hand to stop her. "Seriously, Emily, don't. I can see you're already pissed off, and the absolute hatred you have for me, and I don't need it," I retorted in a whisper the best I could, my own anger showing on my face. "You said we didn't interact much before my attempted suicide, so let's just keep it that way. I don't need to be tortured by you. As I said last week, I have enough shit to deal with."

She appeared to ponder my words, and her expression softened, almost resembling the Emily I once knew. "I don't hate you, Wil," she whispered, looking down at the desk as I began writing on my pad of paper. "Not at all."

"You have a funny way of showing it." I offered a small smile.

"You don't understand—I'm *trying* to protect *you* ... and *me*," she whispered.

"I don't need your protection," I stated firmly, "or anyone else's."

Emily observed me in silence for a few moments as I hurriedly scribbled out a story, ensuring it would secure us both an "A." "You must know, I don't want to be mean to you, Wil," she said softly. "It's becau—"

"Then don't," I interrupted her, doing my best to keep a whisper, "I'd really appreciate it. Like I said before, I don't bother you, I don't talk to you—*just leave me alone.*"

"Please don't be like that."

I stopped writing and looked at her. She had a pained expression on her face, which left me dumbfounded. I slammed my pencil down on the desk, causing her to flinch. "Don't be like *what*? Since the moment you told me we couldn't be friends, I haven't said anything to you, except for the bathroom incident. Then you came to talk to *me* at lunch, to lecture *me* on what I could do, or could *not* do. I want you to tell me now: What do you want from me? What the actual *fuck* do you want from me?" I said, louder than I had wanted to, which caused a lot of our classmates to look towards us.

I expressed my frustration, noticing the tears welling up in Emily's eyes. Miss Hemming was watching us, and I could feel my anger growing, but I didn't want to contribute to Emily's problems. "I'm … I'm sorry, Emily. I am." I softened my tone, realizing the impact of my words. "I know things are rough for you. I promise, I don't want to add to your problems. When I met you, I thought you were awesome. You were really kind to me, and I enjoyed talking with you. I'm not here to make your life difficult. I just need to know what you want from me. What do you want me to do?"

A sob escaped Emily's lips as she hastily gathered her belongings and fled from the classroom. Miss Hemming appeared surprised but didn't pursue her. Instead, she approached me with concern.

"Wil, are you alright?" She asked in a hushed tone.

I shrugged and nodded. "I don't think I'm the one you should be checking on."

Miss Hemming took a seat at Emily's old desk, crossing her legs as Emily used to do. "I'm sorry for pairing you two. I thought it could do you both some good if you had to collaborate on something." she whispered.

"She hates me, so I don't think it would be a good idea, going forward." I also stated in a whisper.

"I don't think she hates you, Wil. I think that everything she does, her boyfriend is behind it."

I shrugged again. "I know it sounds mean, but there's nothing I can do about that. I have my own problems." Miss Hemming lightly touched my hand, offering me a sympathetic smile before getting up. "Miss Hemming?"

She stopped, turning back to me. "Yes?"

"Please give her whatever grade I get on this assignment? I think she has enough going on, and we both know she is more than capable of doing the work."

She smiled at me, leaning closer to whisper. "Despite you believing she hates you, you still protect her. Of course, I'll do that for you both."

* * *

The sun hung high in the sky, casting a warm, golden glow over the bustling school courtyard. Lunchtime was a cacophony of laughter, chatter, and the clinking of trays and cutlery as students queued up for their midday meals. I found my usual spot at our designated table, a sense of anticipation stirring within me. Henry, Steve, Damon, Dean, and Jared were there, and I enjoyed their conversation per usual.

However, as the minutes ticked away, it became apparent that Emily wasn't coming to lunch today. The cheerleading table across from ours remained vacant, the one Emily usually occupied. Her absence hung in the air like an unspoken question, and I couldn't help but steal glances at the doorway, hoping to catch a glimpse of her.

Eventually, my gaze settled on the clock, its hands moving steadily toward the end of the lunch period. The time dragged on, and I couldn't shake the feeling of unease that had settled in the pit of my stomach.

The lunch bell rang, signaling the end of the meal break, and I reluctantly gathered my belongings, the weight of disappointment heavy on my shoulders.

The afternoon classes passed by in a blur, each passing minute bringing me closer to the History lesson with Mr. Stuart, where I knew Emily would be present. The classroom buzzed with the energy of students, their voices filling the space as they took their seats.

As the minutes dwindled down to the start of the class, I kept a watchful eye on the doorway, anticipating Emily's arrival. When she finally entered, her entrance was as understated as her absence during lunch. Her eyes remained cast downward, her expression guarded, as if building an impenetrable wall between us.

Throughout the class, Emily continued to ignore me. Her silence was deafening, and it felt as though an invisible barrier had been erected between us. She made no effort to engage in conversation, avoiding any contact or acknowledgment of my presence.

With each passing moment, I couldn't help but wonder what had transpired between us to lead to this estrangement. The remainder of the day had indeed been uneventful, but the uncertainty of Emily's actions weighed heavily on my mind, leaving me with a lingering sense of unease as I navigated the challenges of high school life.

When the bell rang to signal the end of the school day, Emily hurried out, and was gone before I knew it.

Practice was a seemingly never-ending saga of relentless drills, sweaty teammates, and a nagging sense of fatigue that clung to my every move. As I concluded my hockey practice, I was practically running on fumes, my muscles throbbing with each step I took away from the ice.

The gym lobby buzzed with activity, a cacophony of voices and footsteps echoing off the polished floors. It was in this sea of post-practice chaos that Rachel, like an unexpected storm rolling in, made her approach. Her long, chestnut hair cascaded down her back in loose waves, a stark contrast to the cold, sterile surroundings of the lobby. The bright overhead lights played tricks with her appearance, casting alluring shadows that danced across her features.

Her eyes, hazel in color, seemed to carry an unspoken message—a message that had long eluded my understanding. They held a depth, a knowing, that hinted at secrets about us I could never quite decipher. Despite my reservations and discomfort in her presence, there was an undeniable allure about her that drew people in.

Rachel's attire was both casual and elegant, effortlessly combining comfort and style. She had a way of making even the simplest of outfits look sophisticated.

As she drew nearer, I couldn't help but sigh inwardly. Rachel had a talent for appearing just when I needed a moment's respite, even though our interactions often left me feeling conflicted and off balance. I knew deep down that her presence would once again offer some unexpected twist in the tale of my day.

Just what I need, more drama.

"Do you have a moment?" she asked.

I let out a heavy sigh, dropping my bag to the ground. "What do you want?"

"Nice to see you too, Wil," she said with a smirk.

"Rachel, I'm tired. Practice was rough, and it's been a terrible day. What do you want to talk about?"

"Do you still have no memories before your … *incident?*" she inquired.

I shook my head, reaching down to grab my water bottle and taking a long drink, wiping my mouth with the back of my hand, "No, not a single one. But you already knew that, since we spoke at the hospital."

"Really? You don't remember anything about you and me? *Still?*"

"Nothing at all. Just what I've been told," I replied.

"And what exactly were you told?"

"It's not important," I said, devoid of any emotion.

"It is to me. Amelia, Penny, and Nikki filled you in, right?"

"Yeah, they did," I confirmed.

She chuckled. "Of course they did. Have you ever considered that maybe you're only getting half of the story?"

I shrugged. "It doesn't really matter, does it?"

"Of course it matters! I don't want you to think I was some bitch to you. I even came to see you at the hospital," Rachel exclaimed.

"You did," I agreed. "Rachel, what is it that you want?"

"Why are you treating me this way? I'm just trying to have a conversation with you."

As we were talking, Emily emerged from the girls' locker room. She noticed me talking to Rachel and stared at us. However, her attention shifted when Greg approached her and placed his arm around her shoulders. He led her towards the door, and before she left, she cast one more glance in my direction.

"Wil? Hello!" Rachel said, growing impatient.

I looked back at Rachel, "Huh? Oh, sorry. I don't really have anything to say to you. Not about the past, the present, and certainly not the future."

"But you don't know what really happened." she insisted.

"You broke up with me, right? During my darkest time? Cheated on me? You mentioned that you couldn't handle it. Is any of that not true?" I questioned.

Rachel seemed to ponder this for a moment before responding, "I did break up with you, yes. I did cheat on you, but I admitted it. I dunno if it was your darkest hour or not. I doubt that. But yes, I did struggle with dealing with your depression."

"You *dunno* if it was my darkest hour?" I asked, focusing my gaze on her. "Rachel, I attempted to kill myself shortly after you left me. Both wrists ... up and down, not side to side. Apparently, I meant to do it. How is that NOT my darkest hour?"

"I had no idea you would do that to yourself!" she replied defensively.

"The point is, you broke up with me. Obviously, it's what you wanted. There's no point in this conversation because no matter what you want now, I don't care. I don't know you, I don't want to know you. I don't even care to know what you and I did together or went through. So you got your wish—now leave me alone," I firmly stated.

"Come on, Wil. I was young and dumb," Rachel pleaded.

"Just a few months ago, Rachel."

"I've grown from it, I really have!"

"I said: *Leave me alone.*"

"You heard him," Nikki's voice came from behind me, causing Rachel and me to both turn around. "Leave him alone, or I swear to God, I will rake your face across every trophy case in here."

Rachel stepped back, retorting, "Wow, Nikki. Shooting your shot with Wil now? I didn't think he was in your league."

"He's like a brother to me, you stupid bitch. That means anyone messing with my brother is messing with me," Nikki snapped.

"And us," Penny added, joining Nikki and Amelia by my side.

"None of this is necessary," I interjected. "Just go away, Rachel."

Rachel crossed her arms over her chest defiantly. "Fine," she said. "I gave you your chance. Don't come crying to me for a second chance later."

"No worries there," I stated firmly.

Rachel pivoted gracefully on her heel and pushed open the lobby door, her exit into the outside world marked by a swish of her departure. As she left, Nikki, Penny, and Amelia drew nearer to where I stood. "You okay, big brother?" Amelia asked.

"Yeah, fine," I said, flashing her a smile.

"It seems like you're not having the best week." She stated with a frown.

"I promise, I'm fine. Thank you all for coming to my *rescue*."

"It looks like you had it handled," Nikki said with a giggle. "I couldn't resist saying something to that bitch."

It *had* seemed like a crappy week, and it was only Tuesday.

Emily's Night from Hell

―――◦――◇――◦―――

Working closely with Wil wasn't something I desired, but my reasons were different from what Wil believed. The truth was, being near him made me feel alive and wonderful. It was a feeling I couldn't allow myself to indulge in because of Greg, my boyfriend. I didn't want to be with Greg anymore; I wanted to break free from him. However, I also didn't want to be near Wil because I was afraid Greg would target him again, just like he had done throughout the previous year. Even before I developed feelings for Wil, it pained me to see him being beaten up. I would try to defend him, but it only resulted in me getting hurt later. What Wil interpreted as hatred and anger on my face was actually frustration. I wanted everything that Wil had become, in a boyfriend. I admired everything about him—his smile, his way of speaking, his confidence, but most importantly, his kindness. So when he told me to leave him alone, it pierced me to the core. I attempted to explain that I was trying to protect him from Greg, but he wouldn't listen. The fact that he felt tortured by my presence was more than I could bear.

Overwhelmed by my emotions, I ran out of the classroom and found myself outside the building, behind the gym. I sat on the ground, crying for what felt like an eternity. Crying had become a constant in my life, and it wasn't fair. My life simply wasn't fair. Eventually, I pulled myself together, dusted off my clothes, and made a decision. Tonight would be the night I would end things with Greg. It was time to take control of my own life and break free from the toxic relationship that had held me back for so long.

* * *

It was late, well past the time I was supposed to be home. My phone vibrated on the nightstand, but I didn't make a move to answer it. I knew it was my parents, worried about my whereabouts. I couldn't go anywhere because Greg had driven me to his house. I glanced over at the darkened room where he was peacefully asleep, like nothing had happened. But something had happened, something that left me feeling violated and dirty. The memories flooded back, and I couldn't help but sniffle, trying to hold back my tears so as not to wake him. I carefully slid my naked and bruised body across the sheets and slipped off the bed, making sure not to make any noise. I had stood up to him, just as I had promised myself I would, but I paid a heavy price for it.

Gathering my torn and ruined clothes from the floor, I hurriedly put them on. My skirt and shirt bore the evidence of what had transpired. I had just managed to put on my shirt when Greg stirred. Heat washed over me, and my heart pounded in my chest. His eyes, once filled with love just a year ago, now opened with an expression of hatred and disgust as they settled on me.

"Where do you think you're going?" he demanded, swiftly getting out of bed.

"I have … I have to go home," I said softly. "My parents have been trying to reach me. It's past my curfew."

"I don't give a damn about your curfew or your damn parents!" he shouted, gripping my arm tightly. "Your parents don't tell me what to do!"

"Please, Greg, just let me go!" I pleaded, struggling to free myself from his grasp.

"You're mine, Emily, do you hear me? YOU belong to ME!" His grip shifted from my arm to the back of my hair, yanking it forcefully.

"PLEASE, GREG, YOU'RE HURTING ME!" I screamed, feeling the searing pain reverberating through my entire body. I hoped my cries would attract the attention of his parents, but it seemed they weren't home. Greg forcefully slammed my head against the door and finally released his grip.

I collapsed to the floor with a loud thud, disoriented and dazed. Before I could regain my composure, he spun me around, and his hands wrapped tightly around my throat. I fought desperately to break free, but his strength was overpowering. I thrashed and kicked with all my might, feeling the lack of air constricting my throat.

Panic set in as I choked and gasped, my struggle growing weaker. Darkness closed in, and Greg's enraged face became a blur. My arms fell limply at my sides, and my legs ceased their futile resistance. I had reached my limit, unable to fight any longer. This was how my life was going to end, in the grips of a monster.

Just when I believed my time had come and the vice-like grip on my neck was insufferable, he abruptly released his hold, allowing me to draw a desperate, ragged breath. Gasping for air, I lay on the ground, as he suddenly struck me in the face. My face was throbbing from the force of his punch. I tasted the metallic tang of blood in my mouth and desperately tried to breathe. The room spun around me, dizziness overwhelming me due to the lack of oxygen. Summoning every ounce of strength left in me, I managed to crawl to my hands and knees and pushed open the door. Greg seemed momentarily taken aback by my resiliency and began to give chase. I stumbled into the bathroom and locked the door behind me, just a second before he got there. Coughing violently, I feared I might vomit as I struggled to catch my breath.

Greg's relentless pounding on the door sent shivers down my spine. "BITCH, YOU'RE MINE! YOU'LL NEVER BE RID OF ME!" his voice bellowed through the bathroom. I clutched the sides of my head, sinking down against the wall, my sobs uncontrollable.

"Please, Greg," I managed to choke out, my voice barely audible, "I just want to go home." It was then that I realized I had left my purse and phone behind in his room. I pulled my legs close to my chest, rocking back and forth, consumed by a sense of hopelessness. Greg's vicious words reverberated in my mind, striking deep into my already wounded heart. He was right—I would never be free of him.

"NOBODY IS EVER GOING TO WANT YOU, YOU STUPID BITCH! I MADE YOU WHO YOU ARE! YOU'RE POPULAR BECAUSE OF ME! YOU'RE NOT GOOD ENOUGH FOR ANYBODY! YOU'RE JUST A STUPID BITCH! NOBODY WILL EVER WANT YOU! NOBODY CARES ABOUT YOU! NOBODY EVER WILL!"

I covered my ears, desperate to block out his vile insults. The tears continued to stream down my face, their salty sting mingling with the pain of my injuries. In that moment, I truly believed that I might not survive this night—and strangely, I was beginning to come to terms with it. At least in death, all the pain would finally cease, and my never-ending nightmare would reach its conclusion. With a heavy heart, I stood up, frantically rummaging through the drawers beneath the sink until I found what I had been searching for.

A razor.

My heart pounded in my chest as I held the razor in my hand. It felt like my only escape, a desperate solution born out of fear. I smashed it against the sink, blood trickling from my hand as I separated the blade from the handle. Trembling uncontrollably, I brought it closer to my wrist, paralyzed by a mix of terror and despair. This seemed like the only way, even though I was consumed by fear.

In a moment that felt like divine intervention, the sound of a car door slamming broke the silence. My instincts kicked in, and I rushed to the bathroom window, still clutching the razor. It was Greg's parents. The yelling had ceased momentarily.

"Listen, Emily." Greg's voice now held an unsettling calmness. "My parents are home. You better not say a word about what happened. Do you hear me? If you do, I swear to God, I'll kill you and your whole fucking family." Tears streamed down my face, my anguish overwhelming. I felt trapped, as if there were no way out. Even if I managed to leave tonight, I knew he would never let me truly escape. My hand shook violently, causing the razor blade to slip from my grasp and clatter into the sink. "Do you hear me, Emily?" Greg's voice grew louder, punctuated by a forceful bang on the door. "You better not tell anyone!"

I made my best attempt to compose myself as I heard the front door open. "I hear you, Greg," I responded, my voice quivering with sniffles. "I won't tell anyone. Just let me go home. Please, let me have my phone so I can call my mum."

"Who's in the bathroom?" Greg's mother's voice came from the other side of the door, slightly muffled.

"Emily," Greg answered flatly.

"Why are you leaning against the door like that? What ... what the hell happened to the *door*?" Her voice was filled with concern and shock. "Were you pounding on it?"

"We were just talking while she was in there, you know?" Greg tried to explain.

"Why are there fist marks on my door, Greg?" his mother demanded. "Emily, honey, are you okay in there?" Without hesitation, I unlocked the door and flung it open. I'm certain my eyes were swollen and bloodshot, my face bruised and bleeding. I pushed past Greg and made my way to his room, quickly locating my phone and purse. With a sense of urgency, I headed towards the front door.

"Emily, are you alright? Greg! What did you do to her? She's bleeding!" His mother's voice escalated, as she started to approach me. "Emily, honey, let me look at you!" I glanced back briefly and caught her shocked expression as she peered into the bathroom. I didn't answer her questions; I didn't stop or even slow down. My legs carried me out of the house as fast as they possibly could, practically running over Greg's father in my desperate escape.

I ran as fast as my battered body allowed me, weaving through side streets and alleys, constantly vigilant for any sign of Greg's pursuit. The darkness of the night and the hard rain added to my sense of urgency. I desperately needed to find a safe hiding place. My breathing was still labored, and each gasp for air reminded me of the brutality I had just escaped.

Finally, I stumbled upon a residential backyard and spotted a shed that provided a potential hiding spot. Its position behind the house shielded me from view, making it harder for anyone passing by to notice me. I quickly settled myself against the shed's wall, trying to calm my racing heart and regain control of my breathing. The silence was interrupted only by the distant sound of Greg's voice, calling out for me. "Emily! Please come back! I'm sorry, I really am! Let's talk about this!" His words carried through the night, becoming increasingly nearer. I held my breath, fearing that any sound I made would give away my hiding place. Tears streamed down my face, but I suppressed my sobs, desperate not to be discovered.

Feeling a mix of terror and determination, I mustered the courage to cautiously peer around the wall of the shed. I strained my ears, listening intently for any signs of danger. Greg's desperate pleas continued, growing closer with each passing moment.

"C'mon, babe!" His voice sounded dangerously near, and I realized I had underestimated his speed. My heart raced as I weighed my options.

With trembling limbs, I slowly crawled away from behind the shed, seeking cover behind a car parked in the driveway. From there, I moved from one driveway to another, using parked vehicles as temporary shields. When I deemed it safe, I sprinted to another house, praying that luck was on my side. The backyard gate was miraculously left open, offering me a pathway to potential safety. I hurried through the gate, silently grateful for the opportunity it presented.

Panic surged through me as I heard Greg's enraged voice drawing closer. His determination to find me was evident, and I knew I had to act quickly. Glancing down at my phone, I realized with a sinking feeling that he was tracking me through the SocialStatus locator app. He had forced me to keep it on, using it as a means to control and monitor my every move. With trembling hands, I desperately attempted to unlock my phone, but the pressure and anxiety caused me to fumble with my passcode. The first two attempts were unsuccessful, heightening my fear and urgency.

Shit! Shit!

Realizing that I had to keep moving to evade Greg, I mustered every ounce of strength I had left. However, my head injury left me dizzy and disoriented, making running a challenge. Despite stumbling along, I knew I had to overcome the chain-link fence obstructing my path to safety. I approached it cautiously, hearing Greg's footsteps drawing nearer.

Panic sliced through me, propelling me over the fence with a sob, and I crashed to the ground, dropping my phone in the process. Exhausted, frightened, and in excruciating pain, I desperately fought against the overwhelming urge to surrender. Leaving my phone behind crossed my mind, as it would lead Greg straight to me. But summoning my last reserves of courage, I reached for it, managing to unlock it this time. With trembling fingers, I disabled the locator feature on the SocialStatus app. Without hesitation, I forced myself to my feet and began running once more, pushing through the mounting fatigue.

"EMILY! You bitch! You're just making it worse for yourself!" Greg's voice pierced through the air, filled with anger and frustration. The knowledge that he could no longer track me fueled his outburst. Despite my exhaustion and waning strength, I pressed on, determined to put as much distance as possible between us.

Moving to a different street, I slowed my pace to a trot, strategically choosing side yards to avoid the need to scale any more fences and to minimize my visibility from the road. Breathing heavily and struggling to regain control, I sought refuge behind a parked car in a driveway, finding a brief respite with the sturdy stockade fence protecting my back. Tears streamed down my face as uncontrollable sobs wracked my body.

Greg's menacing shouts reverberated around me, but they seemed distant now, a faint echo of the torment I had endured. I attempted to regain my composure, brushing away my tears, but then the rain began to pour, compounding my distress. Aware that staying in one place wasn't safe, I got up and began briskly walking in a different direction. I hoped that by heading away from the direction of my house, Greg might be thrown off and I could find some temporary safety.

Clutching my phone tightly, I remained vigilant, constantly scanning my surroundings as I moved. Suddenly, a beam of light illuminated me as I passed through a side yard, causing me to let out a startled yelp. My instinct kicked in, and I started running, my flats splashing through the wet grass. When I glanced back, I saw no one pursuing me, but my heart continued to race with fear. I had never experienced such intense terror in my entire life. Greg's yells grew faint in the distance, and I began to feel a glimmer of hope that I had managed to escape his clutches. However, I couldn't afford to let my guard down. His determined shouts could still be heard in the rain-soaked air.

As I approached the Linthicum Library, I made my way to the parking lot at the back and found solace against the building, concealed from the view of the street. The partial overhang of the roof provided some respite from the rain. I remained alert, straining my ears for any signs of Greg's presence. The occasional barking of a dog echoed in the distance, but otherwise, I was alone.

Leaning against the building, I assessed my appearance. I was a disheveled mess, covered in dirt and completely drenched. Rainwater streamed down my face, mingling with my tears, and my nose was running. Mud coated my legs and feet from running through the grass, although the rain helped wash away some of the filth. I contemplated seeking refuge at Amelia's house, as it was nearby, but ultimately decided it was best to head home. However, as I was about to make my move, I froze at the sound of distant yelling. Uncertainty gripped me, and I realized it would be too risky to attempt the journey alone from where I was.

Unlocking my phone, I dialed my mum's number, praying for her swift answer. On the first ring, she picked up, her initial anger melting away at the sound of my distressed voice.

"Emily, where the hell—" she began, but I interrupted her, sobbing uncontrollably, pleading for her help.

"Mummy! Please, come get me!" I cried, my voice trembling.

Destined to Happen

It was finally Friday, and the past few days had been rather uneventful. However, one thing had been on my mind—I hadn't seen Emily at school since Tuesday. I tried not to let worry consume me, but I couldn't help but wonder about her well-being.

Practice that day was particularly challenging, but it ended on a high note with a friendly race between Henry, Steve, and myself. It was always a fun way to end the session, and this time, I managed to come out on top, with Henry finishing second. The friendly competition brought a brief moment of excitement and distraction.

After practice, I wasted no time in shedding my hockey gear, taking a refreshing shower, and getting dressed. I decided to throw on my yellow practice jersey, which I hadn't worn during today's session, over my t-shirt. I slowly walked into the gym lobby, my hockey bag thudding softly as I set it down on the ground. The scene that greeted me was perplexing. People were jostling and pushing to gain entry to the gym at the far end, which struck me as odd. There was no scheduled event today, so why the rush? What puzzled me even more was the cacophony of noise emanating from inside the gym. It was as if chaos had descended upon the usually tranquil space.

Avoiding the commotion, I made a beeline for the door closest to me, seeking refuge from the unfolding tumult. I had no intention of getting involved in whatever was transpiring. The closer I got, the louder the shouts became. A deep, booming voice reverberated through the air, mingling with the faint tones of a female voice. Though their words were indistinct at that moment, the intensity of their exchange was evident. Passing the bleachers, I caught sight of a crowd of onlookers gathered near the far wall, their attention fixed on a central point. Cell phones were held aloft, recording the spectacle for posterity.

Curiosity tugged at me, compelling me to join the throng and discover the source of the commotion. As my gaze settled on the focal point of the turmoil, my heart sank. Emily, disheveled and in distress, stood locked in a heated argument with Greg. Four imposing figures from the football team stood menacingly behind him, adding an intimidating presence to the confrontation. Emily's tear-streaked face and anguished cries painted a vivid picture of her emotional turmoil. She wore a white buttoned-down shirt, its neatness a stark contrast to the chaos unfolding around her, and a jean skirt that now seemed inconsequential amidst the tension. Her black flats grounded her in the midst of the tumult, but her ponytail, swaying with every emphatic gesture, mirrored the turbulence within her.

I came to a halt, rooted to the spot, transfixed by the unfolding drama. The urge to intervene warred with the fear of exacerbating the situation. The weight of the decision hung heavy in the air as I grappled with the consequences of my actions. For now, I chose to observe, hoping to glean some understanding of the conflict from the fragments of conversation that reached my ears. I listened intently, straining to decipher the words amidst the clamor, as I tried to make sense of the chaotic scene before me.

Greg's rage reverberated through the gym as he bellowed, "You just don't get to walk away from me, Emily!" His words echoed, filled with possessiveness and anger, cutting through the air.

Emily, her voice strained with determination, shot back, "It's over, Greg! My parents already called the police! You're going to jail!" Tears streamed down her face, her voice quivering with a mix of fear and defiance. She took slow steps backward, creating some distance between herself and Greg.

In an abrupt and shocking turn of events, Greg lunged forward, his fist connecting with Emily's left cheek with brutal force. The impact of the punch resounded throughout the gym, eliciting a collective gasp from the crowd. Emily let out a piercing scream as she crumpled to the ground, pain etched across her features. Voices from the onlookers rose in protest, urging Greg to stop his assault:

"Let her go, Greg!"

"Stop!"

Ignoring the pleas of the crowd, Greg leaned down, seizing Emily by her ponytail and forcefully yanking her back to her feet. Emily's cries intensified as she experienced the agony of his grip, her arms instinctively reaching back to protect her tender hair. "You're hurting me!" she sobbed, her plea echoing through the gym.

He tightened his grip on her ponytail, causing her to cry out once more, and declared, "Boys, if anyone tries to help her, you fuck them up! I don't care who it is." The weight of his words hung in the air, effectively intimidating the spectators into inaction.

"Please help me!" Desperation filled her voice as she implored someone, anyone, to come to her aid. Hearing this, Greg pushed her head into the wall, violently. As she started to fall, he grabbed at her shirt, ripping most of it, exposing her bra. Falling to the ground, she managed to put one arm over her chest, the other trying to fend Greg off.

Amidst the chaos, I found myself compelled to act. The cheerleaders were absent, and my hockey teammates were still in the locker room, oblivious to the unfolding turmoil. As I approached Emily, Greg, and the football players, it appeared that nobody noticed my presence until I was nearly beside them. The astonishment on their faces was palpable as I calmly continued toward Emily. Ignoring their stares, I focused solely on her, driven by a mixture of concern and a desire to protect her. Emily's terrified eyes met mine, pleading for help. Her face bore the marks of Greg's brutality, with a black eye, blood trickling from various wounds, and swelling evident. Dark bruising encircled her neck, a haunting reminder of the danger she was in. Without uttering a word, I kneeled beside her, acutely aware of Greg's proximity and the potential for violence. She reached out to me, her desperation tangible, and I gently took hold of her hand as I positioned myself between her and Greg.

"Wil! Wil, please help me!" Emily's voice trembled with fear, tears streaming down her battered face. "Please, help me!"

Her pleas resonated deep within me, and I wished desperately to offer comfort and reassurance. But in that moment, uncertainty clouded my thoughts. I wasn't certain if everything would be okay. Determined to shield her dignity, I swiftly removed my yellow practice jersey, draping it over her bruised form, covering the areas exposed by Greg's aggression. I quickly pulled Emily to her feet, eliciting a slight yelp of pain from her, but we were both aware of the imminent danger we faced. It took a moment to steady her trembling form, her breathing heavy and accompanied by heart-wrenching sobs.

As I turned around to confront Greg and his buddies, their stunned expressions met my eyes. Ignoring their astonishment, I gently guided Emily with my left hand, positioning her protectively behind me, away from the threat they posed. Her grasp tightened around my left hand, seeking support. Though I appreciated her gesture, I gently removed my hand, knowing that our focus should be on the impending confrontation.

Leaning in closer, I whispered to her, my voice filled with determination, "It'll be okay. I won't let them hurt you again." But even as I offered reassurance, the weight of uncertainty lingered in the air. Emily's strength waned, and she could no longer stand on her own. I carefully helped her to the ground, propping her against the wall, unsure if she would be able to remain conscious.

Greg's voice pierced the tense silence, causing me to shift my attention back to him. "Fenwick," he finally spoke, a smirk forming on his face. "I mean … I've got to hand it to you, you've got some balls. You've been asking for this since the day school started." His words dripped with arrogance, his intention clear: to intimidate me. However, his attempts to unnerve me only provided a moment to consider my next move. Five against one. "I guess you *really* forgot about all those other beatdowns I've given you," Greg taunted, his voice filled with misplaced confidence. His words served as a reminder of the torment the original Wil had endured before.

But this time, something within me had shifted. I refused to let the history of this world repeat itself. A surge of determination coursed through my veins as I met his gaze, my eyes reflecting an unyielding resolve. I prepared myself for what lay ahead. The echoes of my past merged with the present, fueling a fire within me. As I stood there, facing Greg and his buddies, a newfound strength took hold. Emily's safety became my priority, and I vowed to protect her at all costs. The weight of the impending confrontation settled upon my shoulders, but

I remained resolute. Greg had no idea I was not the *Wil* he had once known, and this time, things would be different.

"You're never going to forget the one I'm about to give you," I stated confidently, my voice filled with conviction. "Just remember—*you* asked for this."

Greg let out a laugh, attempting to mask his unease. "I'm sure," he replied, his voice laced with forced bravado. "You're gonna get your wish today, Fenwick. I'm gonna kill you."

I simply shrugged, refusing to be swayed by his empty threats. "I hope one of your buddies teaches you how to shit talk when you have all that time in the hospital because the things you say are really cringe. Seriously, like, right out of a bad movie," I retorted, narrowing my eyes at him. "We can settle this, you and I, but let her pass. She needs to get to a hospital, then we can fight it out."

Greg's laughter filled the air once more, but it held a sense of desperation. "Neither one of you bitches are going anywhere. My boys and I are going to kick the shit out of both of you."

Amidst the escalating tension, I couldn't help but chuckle. "You *and* your boys?" I questioned mockingly. "Are you afraid to face me one on one? It seems to me that all you're capable of is beating up on a defenseless girl." The crowd responded with collective murmurs and expressions of disbelief. They recognized the truth in my words, fueling their disapproval of Greg's actions.

"I'm not afraid of anyone, Fenwick," Greg retorted, his voice dripping with false bravado. "You're just not worth my time."

"But beating up Emily was?" I retorted firmly, my voice steady and resolute. "Let her pass. Be a man—for once. I'll fight all of you if that's what you want. Just let her go."

Greg's face twisted with a mix of anger and pride, his resolve hardening. "Oh, you're going to fight all of us, whether you like it or not," he declared, his words revealing a stubborn determination. The confrontation was now inevitable, and I braced myself for the battle that lay ahead.

I quickly turned to Emily, who was still on the ground but sitting upright while leaning on the wall. Her eyes were filled with fear and confusion. "If you get the chance to run, then you run. You hear me?" I urged, my voice filled with urgency. "No matter what's happening here, you go!" Emily seemed too scared and disoriented to respond, but I knew I had to emphasize the importance of her escape. "I mean it, Emily. Run if you get the chance." Though I was concerned for her safety, I couldn't afford to divert my attention for long. I turned my focus back to Greg, taking a few steps closer to him. The adrenaline coursed through my veins, fueling my determination.

"You wanna rumble?" I challenged, motioning with my hand for him to come at me. "C'mon!" Regardless of what might happen to me, my priority was ensuring Emily's escape. I was ready to face the consequences and protect her at all costs.

Greg wore a startled expression, finally realizing I had, indeed, intended to fight all of them. He exchanged a nod with his friends, and the largest guy among them surged forward, his fist poised to strike. Time seemed to slow down as my instincts kicked in. Drawing upon my military training, I swiftly reacted, aiming my foot directly at his groin. I felt a solid impact, but fortunately for him, there was no sickening "crack," indicating a severe injury. Nonetheless, it effectively incapacitated him, taking him out of the fight completely.

Without a moment to spare, I pivoted to confront the next attacker, who had attempted to circle behind me. My right elbow shot back and upward, connecting forcefully with his chin, causing him to stagger backward. Another adversary charged directly at my face, but I swiftly countered with a sharp elbow strike, utilizing the power of my right arm. As he stumbled, I seized the opportunity to neutralize another opponent coming from the side. Blocking his swing, I swiftly grasped his arm and deftly maneuvered my body, leveraging his own weight against him, sending him crashing to the ground.

The initial target of my elbow strike hadn't yet recovered, presenting me with an opportunity. I swiftly closed the distance and delivered a powerful uppercut, ensuring he would not pose a further threat. Amid the chaos, it became challenging to keep track of each assailant. Suddenly, a blow landed at the back of my head, momentarily dazing me. Reacting instinctively, I seized the collar of the assailant's shirt from behind and repeatedly drove my elbow into his face, each strike drawing him closer with a firm pull on his collar. The flurry of action unfolded, and I was focused on neutralizing the immediate threats, relying on my training and instincts to navigate the intense confrontation.

Two left.

I reacted swiftly, delivering a powerful roundhouse kick to one of the approaching adversaries, effectively halting his advance. As he stumbled, I swiftly followed up with a well-aimed right-hand punch, connecting solidly with his jaw. The impact seemed to have an immediate effect as he collapsed, rendered unconscious.

With one opponent left, the focus shifted entirely to Greg and me. I briefly glanced toward the distant doors, where my hockey team had just arrived, attracted by the disturbance. I quickly glanced behind me, where Emily remained, rooted to the spot, her fear palpable. It seemed she hadn't mustered the ability to run, even if she had wanted to. Instead, her eyes were locked on the intense confrontation, watching every move.

While concerned for her safety, I knew I had to stay focused on the immediate threat. In the midst of my momentary distraction, Greg seized the opportunity and swung at me. However, I turned back in time to block his strike, countering with a flurry of punches, my rage fueling each blow. One strike after another landed on Greg's face, causing him to stagger and eventually crumble to the ground, blood now trickling from various wounds on his face.

Hovering over him, my hands clenched tightly into fists, I addressed him with determination, my voice laced with anger and resolve, "You'll never terrorize her—ever again." The weight of my words hung heavy in the air as I stood victorious, ensuring his reign of intimidation would come to an end. But to my surprise and concern, Greg slowly rose to his feet, albeit unsteadily. He reached into his back pocket, retrieving something shiny that initially appeared to be a gun. My heart skipped a beat, but as the metallic sound of a switchblade being opened filled the air, my focus sharpened, preparing for whatever would come next.

Of course it was a fuckin' weapon.

"Wil, look out!" Emily's piercing scream jolted me out of my focused state, snapping my attention to the imminent danger.

Henry, Steve, Damon, Dean, and Jared, along with the rest of the hockey team rushed towards us, joining the chaotic scene just as Greg swung the blade at me. Instinctively, I intercepted his hand, countering with a swift knee strike to his wrist. The switchblade went flying out of his grasp, clattering to the ground. Consumed by an intense surge of anger and protectiveness, I unleashed a relentless barrage of punishing punches upon Greg's face, catching him off guard, with each strike fueled by the haunting memory of Emily's bruised and battered form and the agony she had suffered. The countless accounts in the original Wil's journal of Greg subjecting him to cruel beatings for his twisted amusement, it was all for them. As Greg staggered back, his eyes disoriented, I seized his right wrist and swiftly twisted it, sending him sprawling to the floor. Maintaining my grip, I leaned close to his face, my voice seething with determination.

"This ends now," I said through gritted teeth, ramming my knee forcefully into his already twisted elbow, the sickening sound of bones breaking filling the air.

I applied further pressure, intensifying his agony as he writhed and screamed on the gym floor. By this point, I was breathing heavily, my hands resting on my knees as I attempted to regain my composure. Gradually, Greg's agonized movements ceased as he succumbed to unconsciousness from the overwhelming pain. Part of me yearned to continue inflicting punishment upon him, to make him suffer as he had made Emily suffer. However, my rational self took hold, and I reluctantly stepped away from his broken body.

Finally, some teachers managed to break through the crowd and enter the gym, their belated arrival frustratingly ironic.

Where the fuck were they five minutes ago?

I glanced down at my right hand and elbow, feeling a sticky sensation. When I inspected them, I discovered blood coating my skin, unsure whether it belonged to my opponents or myself. Henry, Steve, and Damon looked at me in awe, prepared to defend me, though a bit late to the fray.

I turned my attention to Emily, who appeared slumped and visibly frightened. Her once radiant face was now a canvas of blood, the evidence of the brutality she had endured from Greg. "Emily?" I called out softly, my voice filled with concern as my anger subsided completely. Shifting my focus entirely to her well-being, I approached her gently.

Tears streamed down her face as she sobbed uncontrollably. It was evident that she couldn't walk on her own, so I carefully lifted her up, holding her close to me. Henry and Steve flanked me, providing a protective presence as we made our way through the crowd. People swiftly moved aside, opening a path for us as we headed towards the exit. Some kind individuals held the doors open, allowing us to pass into the gym lobby. The rest of the cheerleaders rushed in from the locker room.

Beth came running up, calling out Emily's name in a panicked voice. Emily appeared completely disoriented now, her arms wrapped around my neck, her eyes barely open. I gently set her down on the ground in the lobby, where Coach Geller, the cheer coach, immediately attended to her. "Someone call 9-1-1!" Coach Geller shouted, swiftly removing her jacket and placing it under Emily's head. I softly guided Emily's head onto the jacket, kneeling beside her.

"Oh my God, Em, what did he do to you?" Beth exclaimed, her voice filled with anguish and tears streaming down her face.

The events had left me dazed, trying to process everything that had just transpired. Her gaze shifted back and forth, as if searching for someone. When her eyes met mine, she reached out towards my hand, trembling uncontrollably. I gently held her hand, kneeling beside her.

"Please don't go!" she pleaded, her voice trembling with fear. "I'm so scared!"

Her hand shook violently in mine. "You're safe now, Emily," I reassured her, my voice filled with sincerity. "Nobody's going to hurt you."

"Please stay!" she implored, her grip tightening on my hand. I surveyed her injuries, realizing just how terrible she looked. I wish I had my Medic pack, the one I carried during the war, to treat Emily's wounds with. Cupping her hand with my other hand, I did my best to provide comfort and reassurance.

"I won't let *anyone* hurt you," I whispered softly, trying to convey a sense of strength and protection.

I felt a sudden grip on my sore elbow from behind, causing me to instinctively jump up, ready to defend myself. With a quick spin, I faced my "*attacker*," only to realize it was Mr. Benning, the assistant principal. He raised his hands to show he meant no harm, and I reluctantly lowered my fists, nodding in recognition. However, my guard was still up, the adrenaline from the fight coursing through my veins.

"Mr. Fenwick, you need to come to the office with me," Mr. Benning stated firmly, his voice carrying a sense of authority.

"Hold on!" Henry interjected angrily. "He just defended himself and Emily against five guys, and he's the one going to the office? What the fuck?"

"It's okay, Henry," I responded, attempting to calm the situation and control my breathing. I waved him off, silently urging him not to escalate things further.

"You have to come with me. Now," Mr. Benning repeated sternly from behind me, his tone brooking no argument.

I didn't want to leave Emily behind. All I wanted was to be there for her, to provide comfort and assure her safety. However, I knew I had no real choice in the matter. Several coaches, my sisters, and the other cheerleaders were now by her side, offering support. Reluctantly, I stood up and nodded at Mr. Benning, silently acknowledging his authority. I reluctantly let go of Emily's hand, witnessing panic wash over her face.

"Please, don't go!" she pleaded desperately.

"He has to go to the office," Beth explained to Emily, her voice choked with tears.

I turned to Henry, my voice filled with concern. "Bro, can you stay with her? Make sure she's safe?" I asked, entrusting him with Emily's well-being.

"Of course, I'll make sure. I promise," Henry replied, determination evident in his voice.

I nodded in gratitude, my eyes fixated on Emily as Mr. Benning led me away, gripping my arm firmly. I couldn't help but look back repeatedly, my heart aching as I saw her watching me, her hand still outstretched. Leaving her in that vulnerable state was one of the hardest things I had ever done, and the feeling of helplessness gnawed at me with each step towards the office.

At some point, I realized I was being restrained. "Let go of my arm," I said, maintaining my composure. "I'm walking to the office with you. There's no need for that."

Mr. Benning glanced at me, clearly taken aback by my assertiveness. He seemed about to respond when we were both interrupted by Miss Hemming approaching us hastily.

"Mr. Benning!" she exclaimed as she approached. "Perhaps you could let go of his arm? He's already been through so much, and he's not resisting you in any way. We don't even know what happened yet." We continued walking, and Mr. Benning reluctantly released his grip on my arm. Miss Hemming's eyes were drawn to the blood stains on my clothes. "Wil, what happened?" she asked urgently. She seemed genuinely concerned as she questioned me. "There's blood all over you."

I replied absentmindedly, "I'm not sure if it's mine."

Upon reaching the office, Miss Hemming excused herself, likely to gather more information. The distant sound of sirens reached my ears, adding to the tension in the air.

Great.

I didn't see anyone else involved in the fight at the office, just me. I may have been the only one in any shape to even be there. "Sit," Mr. Benning barked at me as we entered the principal's office. I obediently took a seat as Mr. Benning commanded, though I couldn't help feeling a surge of irritation at his authoritative tone. I resisted the urge to lash out verbally, recognizing that I was likely already in enough trouble. Sliding into the chair facing the imposing desk at the center of the room, I waited in silence.

After a while, Miss Hemming returned with Miss Potter, the sophomore guidance counselor, in tow. Time seemed to drag on as I sat there, the muffled whispers from outside the office door adding to the tension in the room. Eventually, the door swung open, and familiar faces filed into the office. The principal, whom I learned was Principal Wendle, my "mom," Mr. Benning, Miss Hemming, and Miss Potter all found seats, leaving Miss Hemming standing to my left. My "mom" immediately rushed to my side, her eyes falling on the blood-soaked arm.

"Why didn't someone tend to my son's wounds?" she exclaimed angrily. "Why is there blood all over his arm? You just left him like this?"

"The reason for that, Mrs—" Principal Wendle began, but my mom interrupted him.

"I don't care! That's *no* reason to ignore his wounds. He's bleeding!"

Principal Wendle nodded to Mr. Benning, who promptly left the room. "The school nurse will be here shortly."

My mom's voice brimmed with disbelief. "You expect me to believe my son just started a brawl, and he's the only one left standing? He can't even fight!"

"Mrs. Fenwick, we're not yet sure what happened, but I assure you, he is the only one in any condition to be here right now," Principal Wendle replied calmly.

"If my son hurt someone, it's because he had no other choice. He's not a violent person! He's never been in trouble—*ever!*" my mom protested vehemently.

Miss Potter interjected with a sympathetic tone, "Why don't you tell us what happened, Wil?"

I glanced around the room, noticing Miss Hemming engrossed in her phone. Shrugging, I began recounting the events. "It all happened pretty fast. I walked into the gym after hockey practice, and I heard a commotion. As I got closer, I saw Greg attacking Emily. He hit her several times … I couldn't just stand there and let him keep hitting her! I tried to avoid a fight, I swear. But they wouldn't let us pass."

Principal Wendle inquired, "Who wouldn't let you pass?"

"Greg and some other guys, the ones from the football team. That's all I know," I responded. "If you want to be sure, they're probably the ones sprawled out on the gym floor right now."

"This isn't funny, Mr. Fenwick," Principal Wendle snapped sternly.

"Oh, I don't find it funny at all!" I retorted, my anger bubbling to the surface. "Look at me! I'm covered in blood! That guy, Greg, beat the living shit out of Emily, and here you are questioning me? I don't think any of this is fuckin' funny! Last year, I was getting beaten up, and none of you seemed to do anything about it or care. But now, when I defend a girl who couldn't defend herself, you want to come after me? Let me make it clear—anyone attacking Emily again will get the same result."

"Don't you dare use that language in here!" Principal Wendle yelled, his voice filled with anger.

"Yeah, 'cause that's what's important right now—my language. Never mind that Emily was attacked by her—hopefully—ex-boyfriend. Have you seen her? Have you seen her face?" I interrupted, my voice filled with frustration.

"No, I haven't—"

"Then respectfully, shut up," I interjected, cutting off Principal Wendle before he could continue.

"How dare—" Mr. Wendle began to retort.

"There are several videos," Miss Hemming interjected, holding her phone out to the principal. "It's circulating on SocialStatus."

"May I see that?" Principal Wendle requested, taking the phone from Miss Hemming.

"It was self-defense, just like I told you. I was defending Emily and myself," I reiterated. "Does anyone know if she's okay?"

At that moment, the school nurse entered the office accompanied by Mr. Benning. She quickly retrieved a first aid kit and donned a pair of medical gloves. Without wasting any time, she began cleaning the blood off my arm and knuckles. "Does it hurt a lot?" she inquired. I simply shook my head.

"Is Emily okay?" I repeated urgently, my concern growing.

"We're not sure yet. There are several ambulances here to attend to the injured students," Miss Potter replied. "I'm not sure if she'll be taken to the hospital."

"She should go to the hospital," I insisted.

"That's a decision for her parents and the paramedics to make," Miss Potter explained.

"I need to know she's okay," I insisted, my worry mounting.

"We'll inform you as soon as we have any updates," Miss Potter assured me.

The ordeal in the office seemed to drag on endlessly. I had to explain the events multiple times, but luckily, the videos circulating on SocialStatus supported my claims. However, despite the evidence in my favor, the school administration was still considering a suspension for me, targeting Monday and Tuesday of the following week. My mother, on the other hand, was not willing to accept their decision. She vehemently objected, threatening a lawsuit and reminding them of the challenges I had faced throughout the previous year and summer. She made it clear that the school had allowed the bullying to persist unchecked for far too long, and now that I had taken action to defend myself and Emily, they wanted to punish me. She asserted her ability to hire numerous lawyers and involve the media if necessary.

In the end, my mother's fierce advocacy paid off. The school administration backed down, realizing the potential consequences of their actions. I didn't receive any form of punishment, not even detention. It was a small victory, but a significant one nonetheless. The police arrived at the office to inquire about the fight and the knife that Greg had used. I cooperated fully, answering all of their questions while my mother kept a watchful eye on their proceedings. She was truly remarkable, ready to defend me at the slightest hint of irritation in anyone's voice. I felt a sense of admiration for her strength. I did apologize to Mr. Wendle for my earlier outburst, and surprisingly, he was understanding, recognizing the emotional intensity of the situation. Once everyone was satisfied with the explanations provided, we left the office to make our way home.

My mother accompanied me to my truck, opting for a longer route to avoid the crowded gymnasium. I had hoped to catch a glimpse of Emily and check on her well-being, but Amelia informed me that she had already been taken away in an ambulance. She assured me that she would visit Emily as soon as possible to provide an update. My father was already waiting in the parking lot, and my mother explained that it was better for him to stay outside the office to avoid any potential confrontations. She would drive me, Amelia, and Penny home, while my father took charge of driving my truck.

In the car, Amelia attempted to engage in conversation with me, but my mother swiftly silenced her. I wasn't in the right mindset to discuss the incident, for sure. Despite my strong inclination to unleash my anger on Greg, I couldn't say I felt proud of my actions. However, I genuinely believed I had no other choice. I couldn't bear the thought of Emily enduring more harm than she already had.

Upon reaching home, I hastened towards my room, seeking solitude. Penny and Amelia caught up to me just as I reached the top of the staircase. Amelia, walking beside me, with Penny on the other side, called out my name.

I took a deep breath, feeling the weight of the situation, and turned to face her. "Yes, Amelia? I'm aware that I broke my promise to you. I'm sorry, okay? I couldn't stand by and let him hurt her—"

Before I could finish my sentence, Amelia interrupted me by wrapping her arms tightly around my neck, embracing me. In that moment, Penny joined in, enveloping both of us in her comforting embrace. We stayed like that for a while, finding support in each other's presence.

* * *

Amelia and Penny walked me all the way to my room, ensuring I was physically all right. As I entered my room, I collapsed onto the bed, not due to the physical toll of the fight, but because of the brutality Greg had inflicted upon Emily. The image of her terrified face and her desperate pleas for help lingered in my mind, haunting me. Despite the fact that two of the four boys, including Greg, ended up in the hospital, I couldn't shake off the feeling that I hadn't truly "won" anything. I struggled to understand the root of my distress. After a while, exhaustion overwhelmed me, and I drifted into a restless sleep.

*   *   *

A knock on my door jolted me awake. Uncertain if it was real or just a part of my dream, I heard the knock again, confirming its presence. "Come in," I mumbled groggily. No one entered, so I sluggishly climbed out of bed, clearly not ready to face anyone. The knock grew louder and more insistent. "Alright, alright, I'm coming!" I called out, making my way across the sitting room to the door and opening it.

Standing before me was Amelia. "Hi, Wil," she greeted softly. "Mom sent me to check on you. Sorry if I woke you."

I stepped aside, allowing Amelia to enter my room. She gave me a small smile as she walked in. I gestured towards the sofa, and she took a seat, placing her hands in her lap. Sporting her green yoga pants from cheer practice and a white t-shirt with bold green lettering that read "ANDOVER," she looked casual and comfortable. I noticed her no-show socks, even though she wasn't wearing any shoes. Leaving the door open, I made my way over to the couch and plopped down beside her. Amelia turned to face me more directly.

"How are your hands and elbow?" she asked thoughtfully.

I offered her a half-hearted smile. "They're fine, really. The knuckles are a bit bruised, and so is the elbow. The hit to the back of my head is a little sore, but overall, I'm doing okay. Probably better off than the other guys, I imagine. Thanks for asking," I replied.

Amelia gently took my right hand and examined it, then moved on to inspect my elbow. Once satisfied, her gaze fell upon the long scar on my right forearm, and she lightly touched it for a moment. "Does it hurt?" she inquired.

I shook my head. "Nope, not at all." I replied. Amelia let out a sigh. "What is it? Is Emily okay?" I asked, growing concerned.

"It's hard to say … She looked pretty rough." She nodded. "Her left jaw is swollen, her nose was bleeding quite a bit, and that black eye she had won't look any better after all this. They took her to the hospital by ambulance to make sure she's alright. Her mom texted me, saying the X-rays came back negative for any fractures, so that's good news. She should be home soon, according to her mom."

"Good," I replied absentmindedly.

"It's not the physical pain that concerns me," Amelia stated. "Emily always talked about what Greg would do to her if she ever tried to end things. I can only imagine how terrified she must be."

"It was a terrifying situation for everyone," I responded.

"No, Wil, you weren't scared," Amelia said softly, her eyes locked with mine. "You showed no fear at all."

"I was scared, Amelia," I insisted.

Amelia shook her head, her voice filled with conviction. "I watched the videos, Wil. There are so many on SocialStatus, and I watched them *all*."

I shrugged, not fully understanding her point. "So?"

Her tone turned earnest. "So, I saw something incredible. You walked over to protect Emily with this calmness about you. You faced off against five huge guys from the football team. It was the bravest, most heroic thing I've ever witnessed, and it came from *my* brother."

I tried to downplay my actions. "I just did what anyone else would have done."

Amelia looked at me thoughtfully. "That's the thing, Wil. Nobody else did. They may have shouted for Greg to stop, but not a single person put themselves on the line to help Emily. Only you did."

I wanted to defend the others. "The other four guys were blocking them from intervening—"

Amelia dismissed me with a wave of her hand, interrupting my words. "No way! There were so many people in that gym, they could have helped Emily if they wanted to. But they were scared, only thinking of themselves. What kind of men stand by and let someone like Greg beat on a defenseless girl like Emily?" Amelia's voice was tinged with bitterness. "And you, Wil, you kept your promise to me, even though you said you broke it. You tried to reason with Greg and the others, warning them multiple times."

I averted her gaze momentarily, but Amelia gently turned my head back towards her with her index finger. Her smile appeared, but it vanished just as quickly. "You're a hero, Wil," she said, her voice filled with both pride and sadness. "But the thing is, my brother was never a hero. He couldn't fight like that, he never had that kind of courage. He was never fearless and wouldn't have put himself in harm's way like you did. He would have just watched, like everyone else."

I looked at her, unsure of where this conversation was headed. "What are you trying to tell me, Amelia?"

Tears streamed down her face as she asked, her voice trembling with uncertainty, "You're ... you're not really *him*, are you? You weren't lying back in the hospital. You're *not* my brother. You're *not* Wil, are you?"

I didn't know how to respond to her anguish. I felt an instinctual urge to comfort her, to divert the conversation, but I couldn't bring myself to do either. "No," I replied softly, my eyes dropping to my lap.

Her tears continued to flow. "I talked to Penny. She told me everything she believes. She thinks *Wil* died when they were trying to revive him, and somehow you *appeared* right after, as if you brought him back."

I nodded, acknowledging what she had heard. "That's how it seems. I don't have all the answers either."

Amelia's sobs echoed through the room, and my instinct was to reach out and comfort her. However, she pushed me away, her anger evident in her voice. "No!" she exclaimed, her hands clenched into fists, striking my chest with weak punches. I stood there, absorbing the blows without resistance, understanding that her anger was a manifestation of her pain.

"Amelia," I began, but she suddenly collapsed into my arms, sobbing uncontrollably. Slowly, I wrapped my arms around her, gently patting her back. "I'm sorry, Amelia. I'm so, so sorry," I whispered, my voice barely audible. "I never intended for any of this to happen. I, too, long to be with my family, and I know I will never see them again. I miss them terribly. We can only hope that your brother has found the peace he so desperately sought, that he is in a better place now." I held Amelia tightly, providing a comforting presence as she poured out her grief.

Though it felt like an eternity, in reality, only a few minutes passed. She lifted her head and looked into my eyes, her own red and swollen from crying. Sniffles escaped her, and she tried to wipe away the tears. Her grip on my forearm tightened, her touch both firm and tender.

"I'm sorry I hit you," Amelia managed to say through her sniffles. "I know it's not your fault. None of it was your fault." Her gaze shifted to my scarred forearm, her fingers tracing the mark gently. "You didn't do this, Wil did. I'm so angry ... so angry at him for doing this to me, to our family ... to himself. Why didn't he come to me? Why did he believe there was no other way?" I sensed that speaking at that moment would offer little comfort, as her questions were more rhetorical than seeking answers. "It doesn't matter now," Amelia continued, wiping away more tears with her left hand. "None of it matters. He's gone forever."

"He was unwell, Amelia," I said softly, choosing my words carefully. "There was nothing you or anyone else could have done. Once he made up his mind, there was no stopping it." Amelia nodded, sniffling once again. Uncertain of whether it was the right time to ask, I cautiously posed the question, "So … where do we go from here?"

Amelia shrugged, her response simple yet profound. "You're my brother," she stated. "I will love you as if you were my brother. If you'll let me. Will you be my brother?"

A warm smile spread across my face as I looked at her. "I already am, Amelia."

"I'm heading back to the hospital to see Emily. Do you want to go with me?" she asked, her voice filled with a mix of hope and concern.

"I want to, but I don't think it's a good idea," I replied sadly, my voice tinged with regret. "We weren't friends when we last spoke, and I don't want to upset her."

Amelia nodded, understanding the complexity of the situation. "You're right. It might be best to give her some space for now. But know that when the time is right, we'll be there for her, together."

Emily's Injuries

<<o———o>>

Every part of my body ached, but my face was the worst. I had just returned home from the hospital, where they had kept me overnight for head and facial trauma. The pain was particularly intense in my left eye, the one Greg had struck just a few days before the gym incident. It had barely begun to heal when it was hurt again. The marks on my neck had become more conspicuous, displaying a range of angry shades. I had managed to conceal them from my parents by wearing turtlenecks every day, but they had seen the truth at the hospital. Now, in addition to my previous injuries, I had a sizable gash in my eyebrow, and my left eye was swollen, adding to the growing list of wounds. My nose throbbed, as did my mouth, which had been caked in blood on the left side. I felt tenderness in my cheek, and my chin displayed redness and bruising. There was also a painful knot on the back of my head from being forcefully slammed into a wall. The constant ringing in my ears made it difficult to think clearly, exacerbating my agony.

Looking at myself in the mirror proved to be a mistake, as the realization of how badly I looked overwhelmed me, causing me to break down in tears and intensifying my pain. Despite still being able to see out of both eyes, my vision would occasionally blur. No amount of makeup could hide the extent of my injuries. Likewise, no amount of therapy or love could erase the mental and emotional scars I carried. Even though I had escaped from Greg's clutches, I knew deep down that true freedom eluded me. I would forever have to be vigilant, constantly looking over my shoulder. The situation echoed the words he had always used to belittle me, making me believe that no one would ever want someone like me, burdened with so much damage and baggage. While I had hope that my physical injuries would eventually heal and my appearance would return to normal, it was the deep-rooted mental and emotional trauma that consumed my thoughts. The fear lingered within me, a constant presence, especially when it came to the possibility of Greg reappearing in our lives. Despite the reassurances from my dad that Greg had suffered significant injuries, I couldn't shake off the anxiety.

My dad informed me that Wil had unleashed a relentless assault on Greg, repeatedly striking him in the face until he lost consciousness. The damage was so severe that his face had become unrecognizable. Additionally, my dad mentioned that Greg's elbow had shattered, likely fractured in multiple places, rendering him incapable of pursuing anyone. I wasn't sure how my dad had acquired this information, and honestly, I didn't want to know the details. The mere thought of Greg's potential return sent shivers down my spine, and I clung to the hope that he would stay away, shattered elbow or not.

Despite the reassurances about Greg's condition, I couldn't shake off the lingering fear that he might still find a way to terrorize me. To ease my worries, I asked Beth to thoroughly check all the locks on the doors and windows in our house, ensuring that they were secure. My mum initially suggested that I lie on the sofa, but I insisted on being in my own bed, surrounded by familiar belongings. With great care, I changed into a loose-fitting nightshirt, boxers, and comfortable socks, wanting to create a sense of comfort and security for myself.

As I slowly made my way to my room, supported by my mum's steadying presence, she insisted on tucking me in. She stayed close by, doing her best to provide comfort and make me feel safe. To maintain a watchful eye on me while attending to other tasks around the house, she requested that I keep my bedroom door open. It was her way of assuring me that she would be nearby, ready to protect and support me whenever needed. Reflecting on the events that had unfolded, I remembered the pivotal moment when my mum had come to my rescue at the Linthicum library on Tuesday night.

Witnessing the state I was in, she wasted no time in contacting the police as soon as we arrived home. They arrived promptly and took a detailed report, assuring us that they would pay Greg a visit at his residence. We later learned that Greg had been arrested, though the specifics remained unclear. After the police left, I desperately tried to wash away the physical and emotional wounds inflicted by Greg. I took a long shower, hoping to cleanse myself of the blood, dirt, and the pain he had inflicted. But no amount of water could erase the trauma I had endured. To recover, I had taken Wednesday and Thursday off from school, allowing myself time to heal both physically and emotionally. I did not relay to my parents about my rape, I couldn't do it.

When I finally returned to school on Friday, it was already past lunchtime. I overheard some of my fellow cheerleaders mentioning that Greg hadn't been present for the past couple of days. This news brought a wave of relief, but it couldn't entirely dispel the lingering unease within me. Despite my anxieties, I intended to attend my last class, the one I shared with Wil. However, my plans took an unexpected turn when I was called to the guidance counselor's office.

Once that meeting concluded, I made my way to the gym for cheer practice. I had a doctor's note indicating that I couldn't participate for a couple of days due to my injuries, but even injured, we were expected to be at practice. It was there, in the gym, that I came face-to-face with Greg. I was taken aback by his presence since he was supposed to be in jail. Accompanied by his cronies, he wasted no time in approaching me, and that's when I mustered the courage to end our relationship once and for all. Little did I know that this confrontation would escalate into the horrifying attack that unfolded in front of everyone present.

I snapped myself out of the haunting memory, trying to find consolation in the fact that I was no longer confined to a hospital bed but in the comfort of my own. However, a lingering sense of insecurity remained, and I couldn't shake off the feeling of feeling unsafe.

My mum had left my phone on the nightstand beside me, but I wasn't ready to face the influx of messages, posts, and videos circulating on SocialStatus about the fight. Amelia had mentioned them during her visit to the hospital, expressing her frustration that people had chosen to film the incident rather than intervene and help me. Inquisitive about Wil's condition, I had asked Amelia, but she seemed unwilling to divulge any information for some reason.

Just then, my mum entered the room, holding a clear bag adorned with the hospital's logo. "Hello, sweetheart. How are you feeling? Do you need anything?" she asked, her concern evident.

"No change since the last time you were here," I replied, my voice laced with weariness.

My mum had a damp washcloth with her, as she set down the bag. "I'm going to attempt to clean you up a bit, sweetie. Get some of that caked blood off of you, especially around your nose, so you can breathe better."

"It's gonna hurt, mummy," I protested.

She nodded understandingly. "Your dad went to pick up your prescribed medications. He'll be back home soon."

"So, it's just the two of us at home?" I asked, my nerves getting the better of me.

Mum kneeled down beside my bed. "Beth is here with us too. Greg is still in the hospital, and he'll be returning to jail soon. He can't harm you anymore." Her words were meant to reassure me, but the underlying fear remained palpable.

"He will, mummy," I whispered, my voice filled with dread. "He'll find a way. His parents will bail him out."

"No, sweetheart, he won't," Mum asserted firmly. "The police are involved now. He used a knife in that fight with that boy." She started to gently clean some of my wounds, and as I thought, it hurt.

Tears cascaded down my face, exacerbating the pain in my already injured eye. "Mummy," I whimpered, on the verge of losing control. She enveloped me in her arms, being careful not to touch any of my wounds, and held me protectively.

"I know, sweetheart, I know," she reassured me in a soothing tone. But deep down, she didn't truly understand the full extent of the events leading up to our confrontation in the gym. I couldn't bring myself to tell her just yet, or anyone else for that matter.

Gradually regaining my composure, I delicately wiped the tears from my eyes. "What's in the bag?" I asked, diverting my attention to the item in her hand.

My mum stood up, clutching the bag. "These are just your clothes from the hospital. I'm going to wash them," she explained. Placing my flats on the floor next to my closet, she continued, "I'll take care of it." It was then that my gaze fell upon a yellow jersey nestled within the bag, catching my attention.

"Mum, wait!" I interjected suddenly, leaning over the bed but immediately feeling a wave of dizziness wash over me. I placed my hand on my head, trying to steady myself as a hint of nausea crept in. "Could you hand me that yellow jersey?"

"Sure, sweetie. But lean back into bed, you're moving too much," Mum cautioned, reaching into the bag and retrieving the jersey. Holding it up momentarily, she examined it before passing it to me. "I noticed you were wearing this when you went to the hospital. Where did you get it? Whose number is ninety-seven?"

"It's Wil's," I replied, taking the jersey from her. "He put it on me to cover my torn shirt when he came over to protect me."

"Wil?" Mum asked, a perplexed expression on her face. "Wil Fenwick?"

"Yes."

"William Fenwick is the one who saved you?"

I sniffled, tears welling up in my eyes once again. "Yes."

"And he plays ice hockey too?"

I nodded. "Yes! Wil Fenwick is the one who saved me from Greg and the others. He plays on the varsity hockey team."

"William Fenwick?" Mum repeated, her disbelief evident. "He beat the crap out of Greg and four other guys from the football team?"

"Yes."

"William Fenwick? Really? Amelia's brother? The one who was constantly bullied? I … I can't believe it."

"Damn, Mum, yes! How many times are you gonna ask?" I exclaimed, frustration mingling with the pain in my head. "You're making my head hurt. I was just as shocked. I knew he had changed a lot since his suicide attempt last summer, but it truly surprised me that he came to my defense. He's like a completely different person now. He beat them all effortlessly. It was unbelievable."

"Your dad said that he wasn't even sure it was Greg, his face was so torn up."

"How does daddy know? Did he see him?"

"Apparently, Greg was at the same hospital you were at."

I shivered, the thought of him being in such close proximity to me sending a chill down my spine. "Are you serious?"

Mum nodded solemnly. "Your dad found his room. He was ready to confront him, but Greg was still unconscious. His injuries made it look like he had been in a car wreck."

"Wil hit him so many times, so fast. When he turned to look at me, there was this determined and intimidating expression on his face—until he saw me. Then he looked genuinely concerned. He carried me out of the gym and into the lobby."

"You should call and thank him!" Mum suggested. "I can wash his jersey."

"No!" I exclaimed, sitting up abruptly before immediately regretting it as a sharp pain shot through my head. "I want to wash it myself before returning it to him. Right now, I just want to hold on to it, okay?"

"Sure, sweetheart, whatever you want to do. Just lie back down. You can't keep making sudden movements like that," Mum advised. "I'll wash your jean skirt and try to fix your blouse."

"Don't bother with either," I quickly interjected, gently lowering myself back onto the bed. "Please, just throw them away. I never want to see them again."

Mum nodded understandingly. "Okay, sweetie, I'll take care of it." She leaned down and kissed me on the head before leaving the room. I held up Wil's jersey, examining the front and back. A small stain of my own blood marked the upper left sleeve. I knew I should wash it immediately to ensure it came out, but all I wanted to do was hold it close to me. I brought the jersey to my face, inhaling its pleasant scent. Bundling it into a ball, I hugged it tightly against my chest. In the brief interactions I'd had with Wil since his recovery, they had been surprisingly nice. It made me ashamed to think of how mean I had been to him. I couldn't deny the attraction I felt, both in the past and even now. It was a conflicting realization, considering I had been in a relationship at the time. But that relationship seemed like a sick joke—my so-called "boyfriend" had subjected me to terrible things, causing me pain, terror, and worse. I couldn't bring myself to think about it at the moment. The tears flowed uncontrollably as I sobbed. A "boyfriend" who raped me. It was a truth I couldn't bear to share with anyone yet. I felt an overwhelming sense of hurt, embarrassment, and guilt. How could I ever trust someone again? When I was trapped in the bathroom at Greg's house, looking at that razor like it was truly my only way out, if that's how Wil had felt, when he did what he did to himself. I wondered this summer why he would do something like that to himself, and now I know the answer. He felt like he had no other choice, that there was no other way to escape the pain. We were both wrong, though. Somehow, he lived, and so did I — Almost like someone was watching out for us both. Clearly, we were meant for better things, and each new day was a gift, full of new hope and opportunity. Sounds great, for a girl who just got pummeled by her ex-boyfriend. Despite my brief positive feeling, I still felt terrible, ugly, and worthless. The weight of my emotions soon overwhelmed me, and I cried myself to sleep, clutching Wil's jersey tightly in my arms.

* * *

As I woke up, still clutching Wil's jersey, I noticed the daylight filtering through the blinds. I reached out to grab my phone from the nightstand, struggling a bit due to my weakened state. Unlocking it, I began scrolling through the numerous text messages I had received. Most of them were from people expressing concern and asking about what had happened. I searched specifically for any messages from Wil, but we hadn't exchanged numbers or connected on SocialStatus. Nikki had checked in on me, so I replied to her message, letting her know I was home. Penny had sent me a sweet message as well, which I responded to. Amelia had just messaged me a few minutes ago, expressing her desire to come over. Knowing my mum would be okay with it, I replied, giving her the green light to visit.

After going through all the messages, I placed my phone back on the nightstand and reclined, still holding on to Wil's jersey. Not long after, I heard a loud knock on our front screen door. My initial instinct was to hide, but I quickly realized it couldn't be Greg. He should still be at the hospital, and besides, my dad was likely home by now, and Greg wouldn't bother knocking. Nonetheless, I sat up in bed abruptly, which proved to be a mistake. Dizziness overcame me, and I instinctively held my head in my hands, feeling the intense pain. Before I knew it, my mum and Amelia were by my side, and I let out a small yelp. Amelia sat on my bed, enveloping me in her arms.

"It's just me," Amelia whispered softly.

"Sweetheart, how are you feeling? Is the pain returning?" my mother inquired with concern.

I slowly nodded, realizing that responding verbally would have been a better choice as the movement exacerbated my discomfort.

"I'll get your medication. It may make you quite drowsy, but rest is what you need," Mum assured before leaving the room.

"I'm sorry, Amelia," I murmured, feeling the weight of guilt.

"Shhh, don't apologize, Em. It's alright. Falling asleep would be beneficial for you. You need to rest," Amelia comforted, maintaining her embrace around me. "I can stay for as long as you need me."

"But you have school tomorrow," I whispered softly.

"Sweetie, it's the weekend," Amelia countered.

"Oh," I responded with a sense of realization.

Amelia released her hold on me, her gaze drawn to my neck. "Oh, Em." She sighed, a tinge of sadness in her voice. "I haven't been a good friend to you. I should have done more to protect you from him."

"There's nothing anyone could have done. It's not like you could have fought him off," I reassured, absolving her of any blame.

"No, but I could have involved your parents or the police," Amelia acknowledged, carrying a burden of responsibility. "I should have."

"It's not your fault. Please don't ever think that. I should have taken action myself before it escalated to this point. Now, your poor brother is involved. He's already been through so much without getting entangled in my problems. I'm truly grateful that he intervened," I explained, acknowledging the impact on Wil.

Just then, my mum returned with two pills and a bottle of water. "Here, sweetheart, take these. They should alleviate the pain," she said, handing me the medication. I obediently took the pills and placed them in my mouth, washing them down with a generous sip of water. I handed the bottle back to my mum, waiting for the drowsiness to take hold. "Good girl. Now lie back and rest," Mum said firmly, placing the water bottle on my nightstand.

"Okay, mummy," I replied, following her instructions.

"Amelia, would you like something to eat or drink?" my mum offered.

"Actually, some tea would be great. I'll make sure Em is okay," Amelia responded with a smile. "I promise."

My mum returned the smile. "I know you will. I'll get you some tea. I'll just be in the kitchen if either of you need anything."

Once my mum left the room, Amelia kicked off her shoes and moved to the other side of my bed. She propped up two pillows to lie next to me. We had always been incredibly close since I had moved here from England, like sisters.

"How's Wil?" I blurted out, my eyes turning towards her.

Amelia settled in and, once comfortable, looked over at me with a smile. "He seems to be alright, mostly. He had some bruising around his right elbow, and his knuckles are pretty badly bruised and cut up. Probably from taking care of those guys and Greg. He had a little pain in the back of his head from being hit there, but that seems to have subsided already. He hasn't said much about it, although he did ask about how you were doing."

I propped up one of my pillows slightly to have a better view of Amelia. "He did? He asked about me?"

Amelia nodded. "Of course he did! I told him I called you and you would be home soon. He was relieved to hear that."

"I want to call him, but I don't have his number."

"I'll have him call you when I get home, okay? Now might not be the best time."

"Not the best time?" I inquired.

"Yeah, I think he needs some time to process everything that just happened," Amelia explained, understanding the situation. I nodded, still not fully comprehending everything due to the drowsiness caused by the medication. "Can I ask you something, Em?" Amelia inquired.

"Of course," I replied, feeling the pain gradually fading away.

"This might sound like a stupid question, so don't get mad, but I just need to be absolutely certain: You're never going back with Greg, right?"

"No way!" I exclaimed, a hint of disgust in my voice. "Never! I would NEVER go back with him, ever, ever, EVER again!"

"Okay, okay, don't get upset. I just had to make sure. You know, sometimes girls go back to their abusive exes, so I wanted to be sure you wouldn't do that. I mean, you've been abused by him before and still got back together with him."

"I was scared, Amelia. Scared of what he would do to me if I left him," I said softly. "I'm terrified of him, even now. I know he will retaliate somehow ... and not just against me, but against Wil too."

"Well ... he'll have to do it with one arm, and from what I hear, his face looks like the Elephant Man at the moment." Amelia giggled. "Besides, if he tries anything, Wil will just beat the crap out of him again."

"I don't want Wil to have to do that ever again," I said. "He risked a lot by helping me like he did. Greg won't just let that go."

"Well, if he messes with Wil again, Greg has another arm that Wil can break," Amelia suggested.

"Amelia ... where did he learn to fight like that?" I wondered aloud.

She shrugged in response. "I don't know how he knows half the things he does, like playing ice hockey or why he's changed so much. Now he can't do anything related to music or art at all. I mean, I had him *try* to draw me ... and that mother fucker draws me like he was a five year old. My lips were flat, I had big ears, huge eyeballs, and like ... *three* strands of hair. Horrible! I looked like some crazy, haggard looking bitch right out of a horror movie."

I started to laugh, though it sent a sharp pang through my insides, "Ssssstttttooooppppp! Don't make me laugh! It hurts!"

"Just sayin', he *sucks* at art now." Amelia insisted.

"There's no way he just learned how to fight since he got out of the hospital," I pondered. Amelia shrugged again, remaining silent. I sighed. "He must hate me."

"No, not at all!" Amelia reassured me, placing her hand on my arm. "Why would you say that? He just took on five big guys to protect you. He was very protective of you when he carried you out of the gym. He would have stayed, but Mr. Benning took him to the office."

"Yeah, that upset me a lot. Did he get into trouble?" I asked.

"Nah, my mom showed up. I'm sure you know how that went." Amelia giggled.

I joined in the giggles. "I almost feel bad for the principal. I'm really glad he didn't get into any trouble. I would have felt even worse than I do now. I was really mean to him, Amelia. I even moved my seat away from him in Miss Hemming's class. I told him we couldn't be friends anymore."

"Yeah, I know all that, but he's not dumb. I told him it was because of Greg," Amelia stated. "I think he's just respecting your wishes."

"My wishes?" I questioned.

"Yeah, you wanted him to leave you alone."

"But you know that's not what I want, or ever wanted."

"I know," Amelia said, gently taking hold of my hand.

"If he had left me alone, I could be dead right now." I shivered, feeling a cold chill. Amelia noticed and reached down to pull the blankets up over me, tucking me in like a protective sister would. As she did, she noticed the yellow hockey jersey.

"Is this Wil's? The one he put on you?" she asked.

I sniffled, remembering when Wil had placed the jersey on me. "Yeah, that was the kindest thing anyone has ever done for me." I paused for a moment. "Until he protected me from Greg and the other guys, that is."

"I can take it back to him," Amelia offered.

"No!" I exclaimed more urgently than I had intended. "I mean ... I want to wash it and give it back to him personally."

"Sure, sure, I understand," she said, folding the jersey neatly. Amelia reached across my body to place it on my nightstand. I still longed to hold on to it, but I didn't want to explain why to Amelia.

"I have to tell you something," I said, looking at Amelia as she settled back into her comfortable spot.

"What's wrong?" she asked.

I took a deep breath. "You can never tell anyone, okay? You have to swear."

"Of course, bestie. What happened?" Amelia asked, concern evident in her voice.

I took another deep breath, and tears started to flow as I recounted to Amelia what had happened to me Tuesday night at Greg's place. I told her every horrifying detail: the rape, the brutal beating, how he almost strangled me, and how I had considered ending my life. Amelia held me close, and together we cried for what felt like hours.

"You have to tell your parents," she finally said when she drew back from our embrace. "You *have* to call the police."

"No!" I yelled, glancing towards my door to see if my mum was within earshot. "You promised you wouldn't tell anyone!"

"You can't let him get away with this, Em! He raped you!" Amelia insisted.

"I know, but I just can't right now, okay? I'm in a really bad place, I'm terrified. I don't want to add to it—not yet. Please, Amelia, please keep my secret!"

She sat silently for a moment before nodding. "I don't like it, but I won't tell anyone. I promise. But you do have to tell your parents at some point—or I will."

"I will … just please … I already have too much to deal with right now," I pleaded, looking at her. The room started to blur, and I suddenly felt overwhelming exhaustion.

"I think those pills are working," Amelia said, observing my drowsiness. "Your eyes are looking funny, like you're trying to focus on me."

"Uh-huh," was all I managed to utter.

Gently, Amelia removed the second pillow from under my head. "Get some rest, Em," she said softly. "And don't worry about anything— everything's going to be okay."

That was the last thing I remembered before drifting off to sleep once again.

*   *   *

I groggily awakened to the sound of my phone vibrating repeatedly, filling the dimly lit room. The only source of illumination came from the soft glow of the pink fairy lights adorning the border of my ceiling. Still feeling drowsy, I reached out for my phone to see who was so persistent in their attempts to reach me. As I held it in my hand, the device vibrated once again, signaling another incoming notification.

Fuck's sake.

As I turned my phone over and unlocked it, the screen displayed the name "Boyfriend" accompanied by two heart symbols. My heart sank, and fear gripped me in that moment. My gaze darted around the room, uncertain of what to do next. With trembling hands, I focused my attention back on the phone's screen. To my horror, I discovered eleven missed calls and thirty-three text messages from Greg. I couldn't fathom how he managed to send so many texts with just one functioning arm. The thought that he might have had someone assisting him made the situation even more terrifying. Frantically, I began reading through the messages. Each one was filled with threats directed at me, Wil, Beth, and even my parents. Greg warned of dire consequences if I dared to report the rape to the police. He vowed to harm me and my family if I blocked him. The content of each subsequent message grew increasingly horrifying.

But it was the final message that sent chills down my spine: *I'm outside your bedroom window right now, bitch!*

Panic surged through me as I scanned my surroundings, searching for any signs of an intruder. The feeling of vulnerability consumed me, and I didn't know what to do next. Despite the dizziness and pain in my head, I mustered the strength to stand up from the bed, albeit unsteadily. I clutched my head with one hand for support while gripping my phone tightly with the other. With a sense of urgency, I made my way to the window on the side of the house, hoping to catch a glimpse of any potential threat outside.

As I peered through the blinds, the darkness of the night made it challenging to discern anything clearly. I strained my eyes, scanning the area as best as I could, but there was no sign of anyone. Frustrated and fearful, I hurried to the window at the back of the house, above the AC unit. Yet again, there was nothing to be seen. The surroundings appeared calm and undisturbed. Feeling a surge of anxiety, I hastily closed the blinds, causing them to hit the top of the AC unit with a loud thud. My mind raced as I contemplated my next move. In an attempt to gather my thoughts and confront the situation, I began composing a text message in response to Greg.

Please, just leave me alone, Greg! You've done enough harm to me! Just go be with that other girl you cheated on me with, whoever she is!

My heart pounded in my chest as I anxiously awaited Greg's response, realizing the potential consequences of engaging with him. A sense of unease washed over me, questioning whether my decision to reply was a mistake that could further provoke his anger.

Time seemed to crawl by as minutes ticked away, and I started to believe that perhaps I had escaped his immediate retaliation. However, my hope was short-lived as my phone vibrated, jolting me back into a state of apprehension.

You're going to pay, you fucking bitch. You're going to pay! No college scouts will ever pick me now that my elbow is so fucked up!

Greg, please! I wrote with tears streaming down my face. *Just leave me alone! I've already paid enough! You're scaring me! I'm going to call the police!*

It took several minutes again, but he responded: *If you call the police, I will end you! You and Wil will both pay for this!*

LEAVE ME ALONE!!! I typed back, then removed and blocked his number. In that moment of vulnerability, I frantically took steps to sever any connection I had with Greg and his circle. I blocked his brother Reid's number, removing any avenue for their communication to reach me. With trembling fingers, I navigated through various social media platforms, removing Greg and his entire network from my contacts, blocking them to create a barrier of protection.

Gradually, my phone fell silent, void of his menacing presence. However, despite these efforts, fear still gripped me tightly, refusing to release its hold. Seeking comfort, I clutched on to Wil's jersey, the tangible reminder of his unwavering support and protection. Tears streamed down my face as I slid down against my closed bedroom door, overwhelmed by a mix of emotions. The weight of the situation pressed heavily on my shoulders, and I cried uncontrollably, my sobs echoing through the quiet room. Deep down, I knew that this wasn't the end, that the battle was far from over. The terrifying uncertainty of what lay ahead enveloped me, casting a shadow over any semblance of safety I had left.

Everything Happens for a Reason

◆

As the days passed since the incident at the gym, I found myself retreating from the outside world, seeking solace in solitude. I read more of Wil's journal, which just made me feel better about what I did to Greg. He deserved it — the only thing he understood was violence. This time, he was on the receiving end. I made a conscious decision to stay away from social media, avoiding the deluge of attention and discussions surrounding the fight. Instead, I immersed myself in moments of respite, spending time with my close friends Henry and Steve, trying to find some sense of normalcy.

On Sunday, Henry, Steve, and I opted for a casual outing to the mall, hoping to ease our minds with some food and distractions, attempting to alleviate the burden of recent events. Henry extended his apologies for not being present when everything had unfolded, carrying an unjustified sense of guilt. I reassured him that he couldn't have foreseen what would transpire, acknowledging his caring nature.

All my teammates were now seething with anger towards Greg, with no appropriate channel to vent their frustration. Damon, in particular, had issued threats to several football players who were involved in the altercation, sparking considerable tension between the two teams.

Amidst our time together, Amelia resumed her cheerful demeanor, treating me with the same warmth and affection she had before discovering the truth about our familial relationship. She updated me on Emily's condition, assuring me that she was recovering physically, but I still harbored concerns about her well-being.

Monday arrived too soon, and the thought of returning to school weighed heavily on my mind. I contemplated skipping, but Amelia convinced me otherwise, reminding me of the importance of not letting the situation define me.

As the first bell rang, signaling the start of the school, I noticed Emily's absence. People approached me throughout the day, offering congratulations and curious inquiries about the fight. Surprisingly, the overall response was positive, with no signs of negativity or animosity. Even one of the football players involved in the brawl approached me, expressing remorse and seeking forgiveness. I accepted his apology, sensing his genuine relief.

During lunch, our usual table saw an influx of my hockey teammates. Alongside Henry, Steve, Damon, Randy, Jared, and Dean, we were joined by Ben Harrow, a skilled center known for his potent left-hand shot, Charlie Powell, a formidable defenseman who delivered heavy hits along the boards in our zone, and Derrick, the smaller but lightning-fast defenseman.

The atmosphere grew tense as Jared had a heated exchange with Jake, one of the football players, earlier in the day. Damon was adamant that we should watch out for one another and confront Jake after practice. I emphasized the importance of maintaining composure and focusing on our game to avoid suspensions for unnecessary conflicts.

"We should also keep in mind that we don't want anyone getting injured," Dean pointed out, a hint of determination in his tone. "And while I like Miles, I'm not keen on giving him a shot at taking my position as the starting goaltender." Miles served as Dean's backup, always ready to step in if needed.

"Jake had a lot to say, thinking football is a tougher sport than hockey," Jared chimed in, his irritation evident.

Damon nodded knowingly. "That's the typical shit from football players. They don't understand what it's like to glide on ice with those tiny blades and take a hit from someone."

Charlie, our formidable defenseman, proposed, "You and I can pay him a little visit, Damon. We'll straighten things out quick."

I intervened firmly, "No, this is precisely what I said we should avoid. Getting suspended only hurts the team."

Charlie reluctantly conceded, "Alright, once hockey season is over, we'll handle it."

My last class passed by without Emily's presence, leaving me with a growing sense of concern. I hoped she was all right and wondered why she hadn't been at school. The remainder of my hockey teammates, eager to support me, congratulated me and insisted on watching the video of the fight multiple times. They assured me of their backing in case of any retaliation from Greg or his friends, but I doubted he would pose a threat to me for a while. I had witnessed the extent of his injuries firsthand, knowing that I had likely broken his elbow in a severe manner.

Practice offered a brief respite from the day's inquiries and attention. Coach Babcock, mindful of my injured elbow, decided not to push me too hard with the first game approaching. I appreciated the consideration and simply longed to go home, yearning for a moment of tranquility.

*   *   *

On Tuesday, the aftermath of the fight still dominated the school's conversations. Personally, I had mentally moved on, eager to put the whole incident with Greg behind me. Thankfully, he had been expelled for possessing a knife during the altercation, providing a sense of relief. I couldn't help but wonder if Emily had heard the news by now and how it might affect her.

As I sat at my desk in Miss Hemming's class, I tried to regain my focus on the lesson at hand. My notepad and pencil lay before me, the usual tools of my academic pursuits. However, just like many times before, my pencil had an annoying habit of rolling off the desk, mocking my attempts to stay attentive when class started.

With a frustrated sigh, I watched as the pencil made its escape, beyond my reach.

Maaannnnn, I don't feel like getting up.

"Fuckin' pencil," I muttered under my breath, preparing to retrieve it. However, before I could bend down, someone else's hand swiftly snatched the pencil away. Startled, I looked up and found Emily standing there, her face displaying a mixture of a smile and visible bruises. Her hair cascaded down, with the sides pulled back and adorned with a maroon-colored bow. She was dressed in a ribbed, long-sleeved turtleneck that matched the bow, complemented by dark blue jeans and knee-high black boots. Her eye shadow mirrored the shade of her top. I couldn't help but take in her appearance, realizing that it was the first time I had seen her dressed up since our estrangement.

Despite the remnants of her injuries, her nose and cheek appeared better, while her lower lip remained slightly swollen. Emily had even applied makeup to conceal most of the bruises, emphasizing her effort to present herself in a more put-together manner. She maintained her smile, doing her best to convey a sense of lightheartedness as she extended the pencil to me. I accepted it gratefully and returned to my seat, placing the pencil on my desk. However, to my frustration, the pencil seemed determined to continue its escape and rolled off once again. I couldn't help but roll my eyes in exasperation and let out a deep sigh, feeling a mix of annoyance and amusement at the pencil's persistence. Despite the small annoyance, I felt a glimmer of warmth in knowing that Emily was there, even in these trivial moments.

Fuck it. It can stay down there.

Emily giggled softly and ran her tongue over her lips, a gesture that made me aware of the lingering soreness she must have been experiencing. She looked at me with a sweet smile and asked, "Would it be alright if I joined you here for a little while?" Her voice sounded slightly strained, indicating the discomfort caused by her swollen lip.

"If that's what you want," I replied, trying to keep my tone neutral. I wanted to be supportive, but I also didn't want to push her if she wasn't ready for further interaction. Emily sat down, placing her book bag on the floor beside her. She leaned down to pick up my pencil once again, spinning around to face me and delicately returning it to my desk. I couldn't help but notice the bandage on her hand, indicating that she had sustained injuries beyond what was visible on her face. The sight made me feel even worse, knowing that she had suffered so much.

"You've been avoiding talking to me, Wil," Emily spoke softly, avoiding direct eye contact.

"I'm not avoiding you, Emily," I replied earnestly. "I just didn't want to add to your pain or make things more difficult for you. I wasn't sure if reaching out to you would have helped or made things worse."

Emily nodded, her smile fading as a hint of sadness crept into her expression. I could sense her inner turmoil. "I understand. I was really mean to you," she admitted, her nervousness evident as she licked her lips. Her eyes locked with mine, filled with a depth of emotion. "I just wanted to thank you ... so very much," she continued, her voice wavering as she fought back tears. "I wanted to tell you how much I appreciate you stepping in, defending me, and saving me."

I waved my hand dismissively, trying to downplay my actions. "You don't have to thank me for that."

"No, Wil, I do," Emily insisted, her voice laced with sincerity. "I was so awful to you. I befriended you, promised that we would create new memories together, and then abruptly pushed you away. It must have been incredibly confusing for you, especially since you had done nothing wrong. I treated you horribly, especially considering everything you had already been through. I would understand if you didn't want to be friends with me anymore, and I truly mean that."

"Emily—" I tried to interject, but she quickly cut me off.

"I did it, you realize, because of Greg's jealousy issues," Emily said, her voice filled with frustration. "But that's still no excuse. I didn't want him to hurt you. I didn't want him to hurt me."

I reached out to place a comforting hand on her arm, wanting to reassure her that I understood. "I understand why you made those choices. You don't need to explain yourself to me."

"No, I *do* need to explain," she insisted, her voice wavering with self-blame. "I was so stupid. You've been looking out for me, even when I was being an absolute jerk to you." Emily shook her head, glancing around the classroom and realizing that others were listening. She seemed to gather her resolve and straightened her posture in her seat. "I had friends, or so I thought," she continued, air quoting the word *friends*. "People I had trusted since I arrived in the States. Do you know how many of them helped me when I begged for it?" Her voice grew louder, as if she wanted everyone to hear. "I was *begging* for help, Wil."

I tried to find the right words to respond, but Emily pressed on before I could speak. "None," she stated, a mixture of pain and disbelief in her voice. "Not one of those '*friends*' lifted a finger to help me. They were content with just standing by, watching Greg beat the hell out of me, recording it all." Emily paused, her gaze locked with mine. "But you know who ultimately came to my defense," she said, her voice softening. Looking into her eyes, I could see the deep hurt that extended far beyond her physical injuries. It pained me to see her in this state. A tear rolled down her cheek, and she wiped it away with frustration. "The one person I treated so horribly. You came to my defense when I needed someone the most."

I swallowed hard, overwhelmed by her words and the weight of the situation. "I know why you acted the way you did," I said softly, my voice filled with compassion. "And when I said those things the other day, I was just upset. I didn't mean them."

Emily wiped away more tears, her vulnerability showing. "You should be upset, Wil. But I'm also upset with myself. I'm upset with my so-called '*friends.*' I need to reevaluate who truly is my friend and who I can rely on." She gently placed her hand on top of mine, her touch both fragile and sincere. "I don't deserve to be your friend. I deserve exactly what I got. I deserve to lose all the people I was close to and let them down. I'm not good enough for anyone."

I tightened my grip on her hand, my voice filled with determination. "Don't say that!" I said firmly. "You didn't deserve any of that. Nobody deserves to be treated that way. Greg ... *he* got what he deserved. You did nothing wrong. You're the victim here."

Emily sniffled and let out a chuckle. "You're too kind, Wil. I'll never forget what you did for me, as long as I live."

She reached down to a bag that had been beside her and handed it to me. I looked at it curiously. "What's this?"

"Your practice jersey," she replied, a smile gracing her face. "I washed it for you. It's clean."

I could smell her perfume lingering on the jersey even through the bag. "Thank you, Emily. You didn't have to do all this."

"No, Wil, thank you," she said sincerely. "I don't know how I'll ever repay the kindness you showed me."

"Don't be ridiculous," I replied, shaking my head. "You don't owe me anything."

Emily looked momentarily confused, her eyes searching for something. She let out a sigh and grabbed her backpack, getting up from her seat. "I hope one day you can forgive me for the way I've treated you. If you ever need anything, I'll always be here for you."

"There is nothing to forgive, Emily," I reassured her, my smile genuine. "I hope we can be friends again."

Emily's beautiful, toothy smile emerged, causing her to wince slightly from the pain in her lip. "Really? After everything I've said and done, you still want to be friends with me?"

"I do," I affirmed, my gaze unwavering. "Sit here again." I patted the back of her chair.

Her smile grew even wider, though the pain in her lip was evident as she quickly moved her hand to soothe it. "You're serious?"

"Yeah, I would really like that," I said earnestly.

"Alright," Emily promptly responded in a voice brimming with a potent blend of relief and elation, her words permeating the air. Settling back into her seat, she gently lowered her backpack to the floor, once again finding her place amidst the familiar surroundings. With a graceful inclination, she retrieved a notepad and her pink pencil, arranging them meticulously upon her desk.

As if choreographed by fate, Miss Hemming entered the classroom, her presence commanding attention. Catching sight of Emily, she gestured for her to approach. Concern briefly flickered across Emily's countenance as her gaze met mine, but she acquiesced to the request, stepping out of the classroom for a brief interlude. Before the melodic chime of the bell graced the airwaves, both Emily and Miss Hemming reentered the room, their unified return marking a sense of anticipation. Seating herself gracefully, Emily crossed her legs on the open side of the desk, her posture radiating an air of confidence. With a decisive click, Miss Hemming securely locked the back door from within.

While Miss Hemming taught, Emily reached into her backpack once more, fumbling for something. After a moment, she pulled out a bag of candy, opened it, and poured a handful onto my desk. She then turned to the side, and whispered, "Sour gummies," before popping one into her mouth.

"Thank you," I whispered back, excitement evident in my voice. "I love sour gummies!"

Emily grinned at me and enjoyed another candy. However, her smile faded, replaced by a look of concern. She set down her candy and seemed as though she wanted to say something but held back.

"Are you okay, Emmy?" I asked in a whisper, worried about her sudden change in demeanor. She simply nodded and returned to eating her candy, occasionally glancing at the front door, then back to Miss Hemming, and finally back to me.

As Miss Hemming continued with the lesson, Emily occupied herself by doodling on a piece of paper she had taken out, creating random designs. She would occasionally glance in my direction.

When class finally ended, Emily didn't rush to gather her belongings like she normally did. Instead, she took her time placing things back into her backpack, wincing a few times, which didn't go unnoticed by me. I gathered my own things and packed them into my backpack.

"Walk me to my next class?" Emily asked sweetly.

"Sure," I replied, walking out of the classroom alongside her. "You know … he can't hurt you here anymore, right?" I said, trying to reassure her.

Emily shrugged, adjusting her backpack on her shoulder as we walked. "You don't know him like I do," she said softly. "Look at my face, Wil. Those are just the visible injuries and bruises."

Hearing her words fueled my anger towards Greg, making me want to take matters into my own hands. "You're right, I don't know him like you do, but I'll do everything I can to make sure he doesn't get another chance."

"You can't be …" Emily began.

"Before you say I can't be everywhere, let me tell you this: if it comes down to it, I will make sure he suffers enough that he won't be able to harm anyone again."

"I don't want you to fight, Wil," she pleaded.

I shrugged, determined. "And I don't want to, but I will if I have to." Not wanting to dwell on the topic of Greg any longer, I decided to change the subject. "Which class do you have next?"

"Science," she replied.

"Mr. Fredrickson?"

"Yes! You have him too?"

I chuckled. "Yeah, but I have him for third period."

"That's so weird. I'm surprised we don't bump into each other when I'm leaving."

"Well, we did bump into each other quite a lot before," I said, recalling our encounters in the hallway.

"That's right, we did, didn't we?" Emily seemed more relaxed now, and it was a pleasant change. "Amelia told me about your first hockey game this Wednesday, at home. Are you nervous?" she asked.

I was glad that Emily and Amelia were talking again. "Um, not really. I'm sure the butterflies will start fluttering when I'm getting dressed, though."

"Aww, I know you're going to do great!" she reassured me.

"Thank you, I really hope so."

"You will. I wish we cheered for hockey instead of football."

"Really?" I raised an eyebrow, curious.

Emily nodded with a smile but didn't elaborate further. As we approached Mr. Fredrickson's class, she came to a stop. "This is me," Emily said, her voice filled with shyness, as she looked at me briefly before averting her gaze.

"Well, I guess I'll see you later today," I stated.

"I'm looking forward to it," she said, her eyes meeting mine once again. With a small wave, she disappeared into the classroom.

* * *

I arrived at my second period class, and as I walked in, Henry was already there, waving at me with his headphones on. I often wondered how he managed to pass his classes while always plugged in. I took my seat, dropping my backpack to the floor and unpacking my materials. That's when I noticed a pink pencil tucked away inside. Intrigued, I pulled it out and examined it.

"Dude, cute pencil you got there," Henry remarked when he noticed.

"It's not mine," I protested.

"Clearly." He chuckled. "Seriously, though, it's cool if you like pink. No need to be embarrassed."

I shot Henry a look, which only made him laugh even more. "I dunno what to do."

"About the pencil?" Henry asked, "Bro, who cares? It's just a pencil. A pink one."

I let out a sigh, my mind wandering to thoughts of Emily. It was almost unbelievable how much she had transformed, shifting from what had seemed like a strong aversion to me to becoming the sweetest person. It was evident that Greg had wielded complete control over her before, and it was heartening to witness her returning to the warm and friendly person I had first encountered. When my next class ended, I hurried to the science classroom, hoping to run into Emily so I could return her pencil. However, I didn't come across her. I must admit, I had been daydreaming about her more than I should have, and the pencil gave me a good excuse to see her.

* * *

During lunch, I occupied my usual spot with my teammates, Jared, Damon, and Dean. Henry, still ridden with guilt over the recent altercation, sat with a palpable unease. I made an effort to console him, steering the conversation towards our upcoming hockey game. Amidst our chatter, I noticed Damon repeatedly scanning the cafeteria, a gesture that sent a ripple of apprehension through me. I hoped he wasn't contemplating a physical confrontation with any of the football players right there in the lunchroom.

"Damon, who are you keeping an eye out for?" I inquired, monitoring his restless gaze. He ceased his surveillance and locked eyes with me, wearing an innocent expression. "You're not plotting something, are you?"

He let out a chuckle. "Do I make you nervous?" Damon teased. "You think I'm looking for a fight?"

I chuckled in response. "Well, the thought did cross my mind."

"I'm not all about fighting, you know. There's more to me than that," Damon defended.

"Oh, really? Like what?" I prodded.

Jared interjected with a mischievous grin, "He's into gardening, actually."

Damon shot Jared a disapproving glare. "Shut the fuck up, man! "

"You're kidding, right?" I burst into laughter.

Henry joined in, his laughter filling the air, asking, "Wait, did he just say that?"

Damon, now irritated, directed his furrowed gaze at Jared. "You fucker, why did you have to tell them that?"

Jared simply shrugged and laughed. "It's too funny not to share!"

"Are you serious?" I inquired, adopting a more earnest tone.

Damon's expression softened as he responded, "Yeah, I mean ... I enjoy it. Gardening relaxes me, helps me de-stress, you know?" Silence hung over the table for a moment before we all burst into laughter. "You guys are a bunch of assholes, you know that?" Damon added with a grin.

"That still doesn't explain why you were scanning the room like you were on a mission," I pointed out.

Damon began, "Oh, right, that. So there's this girl—"

"Didn't you tell us that girls were nothing but trouble and that we should focus on hockey?" Dean chimed in.

Damon chuckled. "Yeah, well ... *shut up.*"

Our laughter erupted once more. Clearing my throat, I continued, "Anyway, there's this girl, *and?*"

"Right. She's got long red hair and the greenest eyes," Damon elaborated.

"I swear, if he starts reciting poetry," Steve interjected.

Damon issued a playful threat, "You guys just wait until practice."

"Go on, Damon," I encouraged.

"Yeah, so anyway, she's really hot," Damon continued.

"What's her name?" Henry inquired.

"Stephanie. I'm not sure about her last name," Damon admitted, drawing chuckles from Henry and Steve.

"*Howell?*" I asked. "You just described *Stephanie Howell.*"

"Do you know her?" Damon inquired.

"Are you *not* paying attention during our locker room chats?" Steve retorted.

Damon shrugged, clearly needing a refresher.

"Wil went on a date with her," Steven confirmed.

Damon appeared puzzled. "I thought you were into Emily."

"I am, but it's a complicated story. She's a really nice girl, though, and I think you'd get along. Why don't you ask her to homecoming?" I suggested.

Damon hesitated, lacking confidence. "I'm not sure ..."

"You won't know unless you try," Henry encouraged, giving him a reassuring pat on the back.

"I suppose I'll have to give it some thought," Damon sighed.

As we continued our conversation, Henry suddenly nudged me in the ribs.

"Dude," he exclaimed.

"What? What happened?" I asked, startled, looking around.

"You sure seem nervous. Are you okay, brother?" he asked with a chuckle.

"Yeah, I'm okay. Just got a lot on my mind, I guess."

"Have you not noticed? Emily DuBrie has been looking over here a lot today."

"No?"

"Yep. Either you or one of us." Henry nodded. "I'm assuming it's you, since you were involved in the fight the other day."

"It sure aien't me." Damon chuckled, spooning some noodles in his mouth.

I looked to our right and indeed saw Emily and Amelia talking, occasionally glancing over at us. I wondered what they were discussing. "Yeah, I'm sure they're talking about the big fight, like everyone else," I mumbled. "Or maybe she knows I have her pencil."

"We both know that's *your* pencil." Henry laughed.

"Bruh."

"But since they're both smiling when they look over, I don't think it's anything bad. And Emily's sister keeps glancing over too. Personally, I think her sister is pretty hot," Henry commented.

"Whose sister? Emily's?" I asked, turning my attention back to him.

"Yeah."

"Her name's Beth. She's a freshman and a varsity cheerleader."

"Bro! You know her?" Henry asked sitting up more in his chair, excitement in his eyes.

"Not really. Amelia introduced me to her. She knows her well, though. Do you want me to ask about her?" I offered.

Henry smiled, contemplating the idea. "I don't know, man. She's really pretty. Too pretty for me. What are the chances she's looking over at me?" Henry was built like a tank, with perfect wavy brown hair and a strong jawline. Many girls had shown interest in him and even asked him out. I always wondered why he didn't pursue any of them. Perhaps he had his eye on Beth since the start of school. "I know nothing about her, but she's really pretty. She seems really nice from what I've heard."

"Let me see what I can find out for you, dude," I offered. Before Henry could respond, I continued, "I won't mention your name, cool?"

Henry pondered for a moment, then nodded and smiled. "You're a good friend, Wil."

I gave him a friendly slap on the back. "No worries, I got you, buddy."

I could see the seriousness in Henry's eyes as he looked towards Emily and Beth's table, then back at me. He spoke with a tone of remorse. "I can't even begin to tell you how sorry I am, brother, for not being there when you needed me."

"You had no way of knowing what was going on at the time, bro. No worries, it all worked out," I reassured him.

Henry shook his head. "I saw Emily's injuries when I passed her in the hall earlier today. If I had been there with you, it might not have ever come to that."

"Emily got those injuries before I stepped in," I explained.

"If Greg comes back to school—the moment he does, I'm jumping him," Henry declared, his determination evident. He was a powerhouse, both physically and in terms of his kind-hearted nature. Crossing him would be a grave mistake.

"I'm pretty sure he's expelled. Besides, you'd get suspended, and the team needs you," I pointed out, trying to dissuade him.

Henry nodded slowly, lost in his thoughts. "If he returns to school, I'm gonna break his other arm."

I let out a sigh, not wanting to dwell on Greg or the fight any longer. I took out Emily's pencil and examined it for a moment before deciding to return it to her. I stood up from the table, announcing my intention. "I'm gonna return this to Emily."

"Still pretending it's not yours?" Henry chuckled. "You know, admitting it is the first step towards healing, right?"

I rolled my eyes and let out another sigh. "I'll be right back."

As I approached Emily's table, a nervous feeling crept over me. It was surprising, considering I had my sisters and Nikki with me all the time, but this situation felt different. To everyone else, it would seem like I was just going to talk to them. Nikki was the first to notice me. Her expression turned from surprise to a warm smile, and she quickly got up from her chair to greet me with a hug. "Wil! What brings you over? Everything okay?" she asked.

In an enchanting tableau, Emily sat before me, her legs crossed and a radiant smile adorning her face. The unexpected sight of me seemed to ignite a spark of surprise within her. Our eyes met, creating an unbreakable connection, and I locked onto Emily's gaze with unwavering determination, making sure my words conveyed my sincere intentions. "Everything's fine, Nik. I just came over to return something to Emily."

Both of Emily's eyebrows shot up, and Nikki didn't return to her seat. Instead, she stood there with her hand on my back, creating an awkward silence. Emily and I continued to stare at each other until I realized I hadn't said anything substantial.

"Oh ... uh ..." I stammered, feeling the need to break the silence. I looked away and held up her pink pencil. "I think this is yours?"

Emily's eyes twinkled with delight as her gaze fell upon the very pink pencil, prompting a gentle, melodic giggle to escape her lips. "I've been wondering where it went," she confessed, her voice infused with a lighthearted playfulness. Extending my hand, I tenderly returned the pencil to its rightful owner, our eyes effortlessly finding one another once more. In that moment, an unspoken understanding seemed to pass between us. As our interaction unfolded, I couldn't help but notice the collective attention of the cheerleaders seated nearby, their watchful eyes fixated upon us, radiant grins etched across their faces. Emily, her voice now tinged with gratitude, finally spoke the words that lingered unspoken. "Thank you, Wil. I appreciate you coming over to give it back to me."

In an earnest attempt to quell my lingering embarrassment, I mustered the courage to respond, my voice betraying a hint of self-consciousness. "I ... honestly have no clue how it ended up in my backpack. It must have been a complete accident on my part. Sorry about that."

"It's no problem. I'm just glad you found it," she replied.

It felt odd to me that she was so appreciative over a simple pencil, but I kept my composure. There was another bout of awkward silence, and I only looked away when I addressed the rest of their table. "Well, I'm gonna head back," I said, gesturing towards my own table. I could feel Nikki patting my back with a gentle rub, and an oversized grin on her face.

"Thanks again, Wil," Emily's words cascaded from her lips with an enchanting sweetness that melted away any reservations in that moment. In response, I offered a nod of gratitude, the sincere gesture a silent acknowledgment of our shared connection. Eager to regain my composure, I briskly retraced my steps, heading back towards the familiar presence of Henry, Steve, and the others. Echoes of lighthearted giggles and whispered conversations gently enveloped me, a symphony of playful mirth accompanying my journey. The telltale warmth of a blush gradually tinged my cheeks, a subtle testament to the emotions swirling within me, yet I pressed forward, determined to navigate this spirited atmosphere with grace and poise.

With a casual glance, Henry directed his attention towards me, his voice laced with playful curiosity. "So, did you finally part ways with your little pink companion?" he inquired, an amused twinkle in his eyes. Responding with a nod, I affirmed the notion. However, his observant gaze honed in on my flushed complexion, unable to mask the evident hue of embarrassment. "Dude, you're like ten different shades of red right now," he quipped, his tone tinged with good-natured jest.

"Yeah? Thanks for noticing," I replied, feeling a mixture of embarrassment and affection for Emily. As Henry playfully slapped my back, my gaze shifted towards Emily's table. They were all glancing over, their mocking laughter filling the air. I observed Emily swatting at them, attempting to silence their ridicule while stealing glances in my direction. Where had my confidence disappeared to? Why was I feeling so unsettled? My heart raced in my chest, urging me to escape from this situation. "I think I'm gonna head out," I stated, my voice tinged with unease.

"Are you okay, bro? I was just joking around," Henry replied, his sympathy evident in his expression.

I chuckled, attempting to brush off my discomfort. "I know, it's all good."

"I'll come with you," Henry offered, nudging Steve.

As our lunchtime drew to a close, the three of us disposed of our trash and exited the cafeteria. From the corner of my eye, I noticed Amelia practically skipping over to me, a wide grin adorning her face as she bumped her hip against mine.

"What's up?" I inquired, puzzled by her excitement.

"Nothing at all," Amelia replied, her grin unyielding as she swiftly walked away from the cafeteria.

"We'll catch up with you later, bro," Henry said, bidding farewell.

"Yeah, see you at practice," Steve added.

I noticed Steve and Amelia exchanging flirty glances, an odd interaction that left me intrigued. As Henry and Steve disappeared down the hallway, I caught up with Amelia, determined to satisfy my curiosity.

"Hey, is Beth seeing anyone?" I asked, eager to know more.

Amelia gave me a perplexed look. "Beth?"

"Yeah."

"Why do you want to know that?" she asked, her smile fading. "I thought you liked ... well ... you know."

"It's not for me, sis."

"Ohhhhh!" Amelia exclaimed, her smile returning. "Who's it for?"

"I promised I wouldn't mention any names."

"But I'm your favorite sister!" Amelia protested.

"Sister or not, a promise is a promise, right?"

Amelia sighed. "Yeah, I guess. Beth isn't seeing anyone, but if your friend wants to go to Homecoming with her, he better ask soon. A lot of guys have been hounding her about it."

"I'll let him know, thanks. How's Emily?"

"I think you made her day when you came over to our table."

"What about it?"

Amelia's smile grew wider. "Oh, come on! How did that pencil magically end up in your bag?"

"Are you insinuating that I took it on purpose?" I asked, a frown forming on my face.

"No, I'm suggesting that *she* put it in *your* backpack."

"Why would she do that? It seemed important to her."

"Why do you think, *stupid?*" We stared at each other for a moment. "Oh my god, you are so dense! Do you really think she gave a shit about the pencil? It was so you would have to come see her to give it back."

"Nuh-uh. I could have simply waited until last class to give it back to her."

"But you didn't, did you?" Amelia challenged, raising an eyebrow. Her words echoed in my mind, and suddenly, it all made sense. A rush of realization washed over me, mingled with a hint of excitement. The possibility that Emily had orchestrated the pencil incident as a way to connect with me ignited a spark of hope. I suppose always thinking like an adult wasn't a good thing, I needed to think more like a teen.

"Anyway ..." I said with a sigh.

"Did she return your practice jersey?" Amelia asked.

I nodded. "Yeah, it smells really nice," I said with a slight grin.

Amelia returned my grin and started laughing. "She sprayed her perfume on it, didn't she?" The grin on her face grew even bigger now. "Did you know she was hugging it when she slept? It brought her a lot of comfort."

That revelation caught me off guard.

"I'm sorry, I probably shouldn't have said that," Amelia said, her tone apologetic.

"It's good to know," I replied, still processing what she had shared. Before I knew it, Amelia hugged me and then skipped off down the hall.

*   *   *

I went to my locker to exchange the folders from the beginning of the day with the ones for the end of the day. After I finished, I made my way down the hall towards my next class. As I walked, I noticed Emily coming down the opposite side of the hall, engaged in conversation with a few other cheerleaders. My heart fluttered, and butterflies swarmed in my stomach at the sight of her.

What in the hell is going on with me?

As Emily's eyes landed upon me, an infectious joy swept across her countenance, illuminating her features with a radiant smile. "Hi, Wil!" she greeted me with the sweetest, most delightful British accent, accompanied by a wave. Her eyes held a confidence that never wavered as she walked past. The girls with her watched, their faces filled with knowing grins.

"Hi, Emily!" I greeted her, my voice touched with shyness as I looked away. The cheerleaders passing by couldn't resist imitating her British accent and saying, "Hiiii, Willll."

Effortlessly, Emily attempted to suppress the laughter of her friends, playfully urging them to "Sttttooooopppppp," evoking another round of infectious giggles. Amidst the cheerful commotion, she stole a momentary glance in my direction, that familiar, radiant smile gracing her lips. Witnessing her engaging effortlessly with her friends and teammates filled me with a sense of contentment, grateful to witness her genuine interactions once again.

*   *   *

As the final period commenced, Emily entered the classroom with perfect timing, taking her seat in the familiar spot within the third row. Throughout the class, her gaze intermittently wandered in my direction, a subtle acknowledgment that didn't go unnoticed. I, too, found my attention gravitating towards her, observing her with a mixture of curiosity and concern. Engrossed in her own world, she indulged in the rhythmic strokes of her pink pencil, effortlessly doodling on her notepad. Yet, every so often, she would turn her head, locking eyes with me, her left eye seemingly darker when viewed from a distance. The realization of the pain she had endured weighed heavily on my heart, an ache that underscored the profound impact of the abuse she had faced.

As the bell signaled the end of class, a sense of urgency washed over Emily, prompting her to swiftly gather her belongings while keeping a watchful eye fixed on me. With purposeful strides, she hastened her departure from the classroom, her determination palpable. I, on the other hand, maintained a more measured pace, mentally preparing myself for the upcoming hockey practice.

Anticipating that today's session would be relatively light, considering our scheduled game for tomorrow, I focused on channeling my energy accordingly. Stepping out into the hallway, a delightful sight greeted my gaze—Emily, leaning effortlessly against the lockers, patiently awaiting my arrival. In that moment, a surge of exhilaration coursed through me, a familiar thrill that evoked a sense of youthful enthusiasm. With Emily's presence, I couldn't help but feel like an ordinary high school student, captivated by the timeless allure of young attraction. It made me think of the first time I had met my Ella, the butterflies I would get every time I saw her.

"Are you guys practicing today?" she asked, clutching a bunch of folders in her arms. "Do you practice the day before a game?"

"Are you stalking me?" I teased, smirking.

"Oh!" Emily seemed taken aback by my sarcastic comment. "I'm sorry, I was just—"

I laughed, interrupting her. "I'm just kidding, Emmy! I'm glad you're here."

"Really?" she asked, her gaze fixed on me.

"Yeah, I genuinely enjoy your company," I replied, scratching my head and shifting my backpack to the other shoulder. "Truly! We have practice, but it'll be light, I'm sure."

A smile spread across Emily's face. "Oh, good!" She seemed eager as she looked at me. "Walk me to the gym lobby?"

"Sure," I readily agreed, and we embarked on our shared journey. During our walk, I couldn't help but notice the subtle closeness between us, as if an invisible thread drew us together. Her arm occasionally brushed against mine, each gentle contact sending a flutter of anticipation through my being.

"Are you feeling okay?" she asked. "Amelia told me you hurt your knuckles and elbow in the fight." Before I could respond, Emily reached for my hand, examining it. Her touch was warm and soft, sending shivers through me. "I'm sorry, did I scare you?" she asked, noticing my hand twitch.

"It just startled me," I responded, my voice steady as I endeavored to regain composure. With a keen attentiveness, Emily examined the deep hues of purple adorning my knuckles, her expression morphing into a concerned frown.

Sensing her worry, I hastened to reassure her, a hint of deception lacing my words. "I'm alright, truly," I insisted, masking the discomfort that lingered beneath the surface. It pained me to fabricate the truth, but I wished to spare her unnecessary distress. Utilizing her other hand, Emily delicately traced her thumb across my bruised knuckles, a tender gesture that evoked a surge of conflicting emotions within me.

In a soft, heartfelt tone, Emily spoke, her words resonating with remorse and empathy. "I'm really sorry this happened to you because of me," she confessed, her voice carrying a gentle weight.

"It's not your fault," I insisted. "Please stop blaming yourself."

Suddenly, a vivid flashback from my old life on the battlefield hit me like a lightning bolt. In the flashback, I could see Sally and Cowboy by my side as I leaned over a fallen comrade who had succumbed to a gunshot wound. The memory flashed before my eyes and vanished just as quickly. When I turned to Emily, her wide eyes and startled expression indicated that something unusual had just occurred. She released my hand and stared at me in bewilderment.

"Hey, are you okay?" I asked, genuine concern etched across my face. "You look like you've seen a ghost."

"I ... I don't know what just happened," Emily replied, her confusion palpable. "I saw ... *something*."

"Something?" I inquired.

She nodded, "It was like a vision or a daydream. I saw people in military uniforms, standing around someone who had just passed away. It happened so quickly, and then it was gone."

I couldn't believe what I was hearing. Had Emily experienced the same vision that had just flashed through my mind? It didn't make sense; she had never been part of my former life. I wanted to ask her more questions, like if she had seen any names on the tape of the soldier's uniform or other details, but I hesitated. I wasn't prepared to handle this, and she might have her own set of questions for me.

"Wow, that was so weird," Emily remarked, brushing off the strange experience. "Anyway, what were you saying?"

I pushed aside the unsettling vision and decided not to alarm Emily. "Uh … Oh … I was saying you shouldn't blame yourself for what happened," I replied.

She sighed, her uncertainty evident. "I'm not sure I can do that, Wil."

"You're gonna have to," I asserted firmly. "It wasn't your fault, and I'm perfectly fine."

Her gaze locked on to mine, her eyes searching my face for understanding and forgiveness. The weight of her words hung heavily in the air as she mustered the courage to speak her truth. "Wil, I'm truly, deeply sorry for all the trouble I've caused you," she began, her voice laced with remorse. The memory of her past unkindness lingered, haunting her with a deep sense of regret. With sincerity pouring from her heart, she confessed, "I never intended to be so mean. I genuinely believed I was doing the right thing back then, feeling like I was protecting you, but now I realize how foolish and misguided I was."

The consequences of her relationship with Greg, she admitted, had inflicted pain upon countless individuals, driving a wedge between her and those she cared about. Shoulders slumping, she took responsibility for her actions, acknowledging that she alone bore the blame for allowing the toxicity to persist for as long as it did. A somber air hung around us as she stepped in front of me, positioning herself as a barrier on my path. With a heavy sigh, she expressed the bitter truth. "I did stand up for myself, and the result is exactly what I thought it would be," she lamented, gesturing to her bruised face with a profound sadness in her eyes. "At least I'm free of him, but he'll try to get back at me."

"I don't blame you for any of it. I wish you'd believe me when I say that," I assured her.

"I guess I don't know how you can be so kind to me after everything that's happened," Emily confessed, her voice expressing genuine confusion. With a subtle shift, she returned to my side, resuming our shared stride as we continued our leisurely stroll.

In that moment, I yearned to reveal the truth, to confess that my kindness stemmed from a growing affection towards her—an affection

I couldn't explain. However, the fear of vulnerability held me back, prompting a simple shrug as my response. Time seemed to slip away unnoticed, and before we knew it, we found ourselves standing in the familiar embrace of the bustling gym lobby. Reluctantly, we bid each other farewell, our gazes lingering as Emily gradually disappeared into the gymnasium. Even as she vanished from sight, her eyes continued to seek mine, a silent reminder of the connection that lingered between us.

* * *

The vision I had experienced with Emily weighed heavily on my mind throughout practice, making it exceptionally challenging to focus on the task at hand. Fortunately, it was a low-intensity practice, and Coach Babcock remained cautious about my elbow. Despite my assurance that there was no pain, he insisted on playing it safe. As the practice drew to a close, I noticed Amelia and Penny eagerly awaiting my arrival near the door of the gym lobby. A noticeable air of anxiety and concern enveloped Amelia, evident in her demeanor. Closing the distance between us, I gently lowered my hockey bag to the ground, positioning my trusty stick atop it.

"What's wrong?" I asked with concern.

Amelia stopped fidgeting and looked at me with a serious expression. "Emily has been receiving threatening texts from Greg. She's terrified."

I couldn't help but make a lighthearted comment. "One-handed threats? Because he's definitely not using both hands."

Amelia scolded me, urging me to take the situation seriously. "Wil, this is serious. He's been threatening to hurt her and her family. He even mentioned getting back at you."

I nonchalantly shrugged it off. "Idle threats. He couldn't do anything to me even when he had two good arms, a knife, and four friends. It'll be a lot harder for him now."

Amelia's worry deepened. "He only needs one arm to harm Emily, and what if he has a gun?"

The mention of a gun caught me off guard. I hadn't considered that possibility, and I realized I should have. After all, it was a gun that had ended my previous life. "You're right," I acknowledged, a touch of concern in my voice. "I see your point." Amelia seemed relieved that I understood the gravity of the situation. "Why not have Emily stay at our house for the night? Maybe it'll help calm her nerves. We have a high iron fence surrounding our property and security alarms everywhere."

Amelia's face lit up with enthusiasm as she eagerly voiced her approval. "That's a great idea!" Her excitement overflowed, propelling her to rush towards me with a tight embrace that enveloped us both. "We can take her to school tomorrow and everything! I'll send a text to mom first and ask. I'm sure she won't care, then I'll text Emily. The hardest part will be convincing her mom. You're the best! I'll text mom right away and then reach out to Emily. We'll figure this out."

Overnight (EMILY)

I couldn't fathom the method behind Greg's ability to text me from different phone numbers, or if he had enlisted his friends to do it. Regardless of how it was happening, the messages instilled immense fear within me. Some were explicit threats directed at me and my family, while others were even more disturbing. To address the severity of the situation, I decided to show all the texts to my parents. We took screen captures of each one, ensuring we had a record of the evidence. My mother took charge and contacted the police, who arrived to document the incident. Although they promised to investigate and trace the numbers, the absence of concrete evidence linking them to Greg limited their immediate course of action. My father, on the other hand, took matters into his own hands. He repeatedly checked our property, making sure we were safe. I caught glimpses of him discreetly concealing his gun, a clear indication that he understood the gravity of the situation and was prepared to protect us.

When Amelia called and offered a haven for both me and Beth at her house for the night, an overwhelming sense of relief washed over me. Given the circumstances, I anticipated a challenging task of persuading my father, but to my surprise, he agreed *without* hesitation. His swift approval reassured me that he genuinely regarded Greg's threats as a serious matter.

With a glimmer of comfort in my heart, I quickly changed into black tights, paired with black socks, and donned a pink t-shirt beneath a vibrant hot pink hoodie. I gathered my hair into a ponytail, a practical choice for the night ahead, and readied myself to leave.

Wil will be there.

The very thought of him compelled me to apply some makeup, opting for a subtle touch. I brushed on some pink eyeshadow and mascara, trying to enhance my features. Despite the lingering bruise around my eye and the slight one beside my lip, I aimed to look my best. I re-tied my hair up in a ponytail, making sure it was as neat as possible. Grabbing my overnight bag and slipping into my varsity jacket, I made sure everything was in order. Once Beth and I were prepared, my mum drove us to Amelia's house. It was already nighttime, and the atmosphere added a layer of solemnity to the situation.

As we approached the Fenwicks' main gate, the imposing sight of the tall iron fence with its pointed spikes at the top greeted us. It encompassed the entire property, spanning over their vast multi-acre land. Mr. Fenwick's protective nature was evident in the fortress-like design. Mum rolled down her window and pressed the intercom button, signaling for the gate to be opened.

"Remember, girls, call me if you need anything, anything at all," Mum reminded us, her gaze fixed on me.

"We will, Mum, but I'm sure we'll be safe here. It's practically a fortress," I reassured her.

"Mind your manners," she added.

Beth sighed from the back seat. "We've been here a million times, Mum."

"Right. Emily, remember to take your pain medication as needed," she reminded me.

"My face serves as a constant reminder," I replied with a wry smile.

A buzzing sound resonated, and the massive gate began to open before us. As we entered, it swiftly closed behind us, securing the premises. The drive from the gate to the house only took a couple of minutes. To the right, there were dense trees, while the left offered an open view of the grand mansion. Even after all these years, I still found myself in awe of its size. I had never experienced anything like it before. The fascination lingered within me, contrasting with Amelia's nonchalant attitude. It seemed she had never known any other life.

"We're here," Mum announced cheerfully, snapping me out of my thoughts.

I turned to her and leaned over to hug her. "I love you, mummy. I'll text you from time to time."

She chuckled. "I'm walking you both in, dear."

"Really, mum, we'll be—"

"I want to talk to Mrs. Fenwick," she insisted.

I nodded and stepped out of the car, followed by mum and Beth. With my overnight bag and school backpack slung over my shoulder, I began climbing the stairs just as Amelia swung open one of the double doors, a wide smile on her face.

"Bestie! Beth! I'm so glad you're here!" Amelia exclaimed excitedly. Her genuine enthusiasm always melted my heart. She rushed towards me in her socks, nearly knocking me over with her hug.

"Let me take those for you," she insisted, grabbing my backpack. "Beth, do you need any help?"

"I'm good, Amelia, but thank you," Beth replied, her voice sounding shy.

"Thank you for inviting us," I said, beaming at her.

Amelia turned to my mum, addressing her politely. "Mrs. DuBrie, thank you so much for letting them stay over. I promise, they'll be super safe here."

"Hello, Amelia," Mum greeted her cheerfully. "We appreciate you looking out for them. Is your mom at home? I'd like to talk to her for a minute."

"Sure, sure—come in!" Amelia invited, leading the way.

We followed her through the entrance, stepping into the welcoming confines of the foyer. She clicked a button on the wall, which shut the doors behind us. With an aura of graceful authority, she advanced and extended her offer to assist with our coats. Before any words of dissent could escape my lips, she deftly swooped in, skillfully freeing me from the weight of my bag and slipping my jacket from my shoulders. In a display of seamless efficiency, she transitioned, smoothly retrieving Beth's coat with equal care and attentiveness.

"Mom!" Amelia's voice resounded loudly. Startled by her sudden burst of volume, I couldn't help but jump slightly, caught off guard by the sudden loudness that permeated the space. "Mrs. DuBrie is here!"

As we waited, Amelia vanished for a moment to hang up our coats, then returned a moment later.

Within the span of a heartbeat, the distinct sound of Mrs. Fenwick's heels reverberated through the vicinity, their rhythmic click steadily growing louder as she drew nearer. Anticipation filled the air as her presence materialized, stepping into the foyer, a poised figure embodying grace and sophistication. "Charlotte!" Mrs. Fenwick exclaimed upon seeing my mum, moving towards her with open arms for a hug.

"Sarah, so good to see you," Mum replied, embracing her. They held each other for a moment before mum spoke again, "It's been too long. We should really get together more often."

"I agree. You just let me know when you're available," Mrs. Fenwick replied.

"I will definitely do that," Mum said happily. "I just wanted to talk to you for a sec about my girls before I go." Amelia and I stood silently, observing our mum's conversation.

"Sure," Mrs. Fenwick agreed.

"If anything happens, anything at all, you'll be sure to call me?" Mum asked with concern.

"Of course, Charlotte, but believe me—*nothing* will happen. Why don't we go into the dining room and talk, so these girls can go do whatever it is they do."

"That sounds nice," Mum agreed. She turned her attention towards me and Beth, enfolding us in another warm embrace and tenderly planting kisses atop our heads. Her parting words resonated with a familiar, loving admonishment, "Be good girls."

"Mum," I protested with a sigh.

"Come on, guys!" Amelia exclaimed, grabbing my arm. "Let them talk about boring stuff." She swiftly led us up the elegant, winding staircase and down the hall to her room. Pushing the door open, we hurried inside.

Amelia's room was ridiculously large—it surpassed the size of my living room and kitchen combined. It was divided into two main sections. The front half featured a large TV, a sofa, chairs, and even a kitchenette. The back part served as her actual bedroom, complete with a spacious king-size bed, a bathroom boasting a large tub with jets, a walk-in shower with misters, and two walk-in closets. We entered her bedroom, where all three of us could comfortably sleep in her bed without touching each other. I placed my bag on the floor, and Amelia placed my backpack nearby. Beth, on the other hand, promptly flopped onto Amelia's bed.

"I forgot how wonderful your bed is!" Beth exclaimed, snuggling into it, which prompted laughter from Amelia and me. "I'm just gonna live here from now on."

"Fine by me!" Amelia replied. "It's not like I have to share my room with you two. We have plenty of bedrooms."

"If only," I said glumly. Suddenly, my phone started vibrating in the pocket of my hoodie. Without thinking, I took it out and checked the messages.

It was Greg.

Not a day will go by where you won't be afraid of when I might turn up, bitch!

I immediately tossed my phone onto the bed and let out a sob. Amelia was instantly by my side, wrapping her arms around me. "Greg? He can't hurt you here," she whispered softly in my ear. I saw Beth grab my phone and block that particular number.

"We have to get your number changed, Em," Beth suggested.

I nodded, tears streaming down my face. "That's a good idea."

"Why don't we just keep your phone off for tonight?" Amelia suggested, looking at Beth. "Beth can text your mom to let her know, and she can contact you through her."

Again, I nodded and sniffled. "Okay." I moved out of Amelia's embrace. "I'm really, really scared."

"I know you are, and I'm sorry. But you're safe here, I promise. Not only would we know if he sets foot on the property, but my dad would fill him with holes."

"Yeah, I know," I replied, but my voice lacked conviction.

"My dad has many guns, and Wil is in the house, too. Nobody is coming here unless they plan to leave in a hearse."

I was overwhelmed with fear, causing me to momentarily forget about Wil's presence. Despite knowing that Amelia's parents were just down the hallway, it didn't provide much comfort. I recalled that Wil's room used to be adjacent to Amelia's, but I wasn't sure if he had relocated since then.

"Take your pain medication, Em," Beth gently reminded me, concern evident in her voice.

Letting out a sigh, I understood that the pills would likely make me drowsy, which could be beneficial in this situation. I reached into my purse, retrieved two pills, and swallowed them without water. "There, happy now?"

"Well, you'll be happy soon when you drift off to dreamland," Beth replied with a hint of playfulness. Silence enveloped the room for a few moments, with only the sound of a ticking clock breaking the stillness.

"Is Wil's room still next to yours?" I asked, my voice trembling.

Amelia nodded in confirmation, saying, "Yep, right next door. He can come over in a heartbeat if needed." While the knowledge that Wil was nearby did provide some reassurance, I still yearned for the security of seeing him in person. In truth, I simply wanted to set eyes on him. Almost as if she could sense my thoughts, Amelia added with a playful tone, "I'm going to get him real quick, so you can get the warm fuzzies and all, for more than one reason." Her infectious grin brought a smile to my face, and I couldn't help but giggle. "I'll be right back!" With that, she swiftly exited the room. "You're going to be alright, Em," Beth whispered, sitting up in bed. She patted the space next to her, signaling for me to join her. I slipped off my shoes and settled into the bed beside her. She placed her hand on my trembling arm. "You're shaking."

"We can't stay here every night," I whispered, acknowledging the reality of our situation. While part of me wanted nothing more than to remain in this safe haven, my growing interest in getting to know Wil better overshadowed my immediate concerns about Greg. The kindness and compassion he had shown earlier had made a profound impact on me, and I craved more of that connection. It was a strange sensation I would get anytime I was around him.

"Well, we're here now," Beth stated matter-of-factly. "Let's just breathe a sigh of relief. Tomorrow, we'll take care of changing your number, and hopefully, that will be the end of it."

I nodded in agreement just as Amelia entered the room, followed closely by Wil. He looked incredibly handsome, with his neatly cropped brown hair and his fitted navy blue t-shirt that accentuated his well-toned physique. He wore pajama pants featuring a logo of a hockey team, and his white socks completed the casual ensemble.

As soon as my eyes met his, I couldn't help but hop off the bed, overcome with a mix of emotions. A sympathetic smile graced his face as he observed my state. With every fiber of my being resisting the urge to rush into his arms, I restrained myself. Surprisingly, Wil approached me and enveloped me in a warm, comforting hug—a hug that felt like being embraced by a big, soft teddy bear. In that moment, all the hurt and fear melted away. His voice, soft and soothing, reached my ear, sending shivers down my spine. The scent of his fresh cologne, with its masculine allure, filled my senses, causing my heart to race.

"I won't let anything happen to you, Emmy. I promise," he whispered, his words carrying a genuine sincerity that touched my soul. If only he knew how much I craved that sense of safety and protection. "I'll be next door if you need anything." Reluctantly, he released me from his embrace, and a cold emptiness replaced the warmth he had brought. In that fleeting moment, I yearned for him to continue holding me, to provide that comfort throughout the night. Had any other male hugged me like that right now, I would have lost my shit. The very thought of someone touching me, a male, made me ill. But not Wil—It was the exact opposite effect when it came to him.

"Thank you, Wil. You're very sweet," I said, my voice betraying my infatuation with him. '

He shifted his gaze to the wounds on my face, his expression turning into a frown. Despite my attempts to cover them up with makeup, I knew they were still visible. Tentatively, he raised his arm, as if contemplating touching my face, but decided against it. His eyes then traveled down to my neck and widened in realization when he noticed the marks left by Greg.

"I'm really sorry I didn't get there sooner," he murmured, his voice barely audible.

"You arrived just in time," I said in a whisper, wanting to reassure him.

Turning his attention to Amelia, Wil asked, "Do you want me to hang out for a while, or are you all okay?"

"I think we're okay, big brother," Amelia replied. "We're probably just going to get ready for bed and talk about girly stuff." An awkward silence filled the room as Beth and Amelia observed Wil and me. Sensing the tension, Amelia finally spoke up. "Ahem. Why don't you two get ready for bed? I'll walk Wil out."

Reluctantly, I accepted the reality that Wil had to leave, though I didn't want him to. "Thank you again, Wil," I said, expressing my gratitude.

Wil smiled, and followed Amelia out of the room. Just as quickly as he had arrived, he was gone. She returned to the room moments later, wearing a mischievous grin on her face.

"What's that look for?" I asked innocently, though I suspected it had something to do with the hug Wil had given me. Amelia burst into laughter, joined by Beth, who appeared equally amused. Confused, I pressed, "Oh, bloody hell, what are you two on about?"

"Honestly, I thought we were gonna have to get a crowbar out to pry you and Wil apart," Amelia teased, giggling at me.

"It was just a simple hug," I defended.

"You had the biggest smile on your face!" she countered.

"I did not," I protested.

"You really did, sis," Beth chimed in. "Like ... I've never seen you smile like that before."

"Pure rubbish," I dismissed their observations.

"He had the same smile," Amelia said, sitting next to me on the bed. "If that makes you feel any better about it."

"He was smiling?" I asked, surprised.

Amelia and Beth both nodded and started to giggle again.

I shrugged, attempting to exude an air of nonchalance and composure, as if unfazed by the situation at hand. "It was just a hug to make me feel better. Wil's a nice guy. It doesn't mean he likes me or anything."

"Oh, bestie ... you're either playing dumb with us or you're really naive," Amelia remarked.

"Someone like him wouldn't be interested in someone like me," I mumbled, glancing down at my hands. "He wouldn't be interested in someone with all the damage I have."

"There is *no way* he doesn't like you, Em. He took on part of the football team to protect you," Beth reminded me.

"Because Wil's a good guy! He would have done that for anyone."

"I doubt that," Amelia countered, shaking her head in mild disbelief. As the bedtime routine commenced, she chose to slip into a comfortable nightshirt, a choice mirrored by Beth. However, I opted to remain in my black yoga pants and donned a cozy pink t-shirt, removing only my socks for added comfort. Initially, Amelia had positioned me in the middle of the bed, a thoughtful gesture aimed at providing reassurance. However, I mustered the courage to express my preference, requesting to occupy the far-right side of the bed, with Amelia willingly taking the middle position, accommodating my desire for a greater sense of security.

*   *   *

Despite my tiredness, sleep eluded me. My mind was still racing with thoughts of the recent events and the lingering fear of Greg's presence. Every creak of the house seemed magnified, causing my heart to race. I reached for the pain pills on the bedside table, hoping they would help calm my nerves and lull me into sleep. As I lay there, trying to find a sense of calm, I couldn't shake off the feeling that something wasn't right. The noises, although seemingly innocent, had taken on a sinister tone in my mind. With a mix of curiosity and apprehension, I decided to investigate the source of the sound.

Silently, I slipped out of bed, careful not to disturb Amelia and Beth. Tiptoeing towards the door, I pressed my ear against it, listening intently. The silence was unnerving until I heard the noise again, confirming my suspicions. Determined to confront the source of the sound, I opened the door quietly, my heart pounding in my chest.

In the dimly lit room, I noticed the closed doors leading to the balcony and Amelia's bedroom. As I approached the couch, I saw a figure lying there, covered by a blanket. Relief washed over me when I recognized the scent of Wil's cologne. He had been there all along, protecting me even in his sleep. Approaching him, I couldn't help but smile at the sight. Carefully, I covered him up with the blanket, ensuring he stayed warm. It felt like an intimate moment, knowing that he was here for me, offering his presence and protection. The tenderness I felt for him swelled within my heart.

Unable to resist, I gently ran my fingers through his soft hair, savoring the tranquility of the moment. He stirred slightly but remained peacefully asleep. I could have stayed there indefinitely, watching over him, but I knew I needed to rest. Before leaving, I couldn't resist the urge to show my affection. Placing my hand gently on his cheek, I leaned down and softly kissed his forehead, expressing my gratitude for him. With a sense of peace settling over me, I made my way back to bed, knowing that my protector was close by.

I lay there, thoughts of Wil filling my mind, and I drifted off to sleep, feeling safe, knowing that he was watching over me.

The First Hockey Game

Having spent the night on Amelia's sofa, a less-than-ideal sleeping arrangement, I made the conscious choice to remain close to Emily, should she require my support. As the new day unfolded, I harbored a silent hope that, if the need arose for me to enter the room, everyone would be appropriately attired. Deep within, I harbored a flicker of confidence that Greg would not dare set foot in our home, particularly considering his present state. Reflecting upon the previous night, I found myself reminiscing on the spontaneous hug shared with Emily, a moment so fleeting that its significance only dawned on me afterward. In that singular embrace, an indescribable sense of warmth and connection enveloped us, and I cherished every passing second, reluctant to release her from my grasp.

On the day of my highly anticipated hockey game, a surprising nervousness coursed through my veins as I prepared for the imminent competition. With meticulous attention to detail, I dressed in a refined ensemble: black dress pants, complemented by matching socks and shiny black shoes. A crisp white button-down dress shirt with long sleeves adorned my frame, while my black tie, featuring shades of gray and a subtle pattern, added a touch of sophistication. Perplexed by the intensity of my jitters, I sought to understand their origin, but time betrayed me as I realized I was running behind schedule.

Sacrificing breakfast in the name of punctuality, I hastened to the garage, eagerly making my way towards my trusty truck. To my delight, the girls, including the radiant presence of Emily and Beth, had already congregated near the truck.

"Sorry I'm late," I blurted out, feeling a bit flustered.

"Wooooo, look at you, big brother!" Amelia exclaimed as I approached them.

"Looking pretty sharp, Wil," Penny chimed in with a smile as I unlocked the truck doors, and they all hopped in.

"I can't tell if you're serious or not," I replied, slightly perplexed.

"I'm serious!" Amelia insisted with enthusiasm.

"You look very handsome, Wil," Emily said softly, her cheeks turning a faint shade of pink. "The girls will all be ogling you today."

I playfully rolled my eyes at her comment. "Oh, great," I replied sarcastically.

I only wanted one girl to admire me, and that girl was Emily. Starting the SUV, I drove to school while the girls settled into their seats. Throughout the ride, silence filled the air, except for the occasional giggle and the sound of tapping on phone screens. It was evident that they were engrossed in their own conversation. I caught a glimpse of Emily's reaction when she gasped and playfully hit Amelia's arm.

Once we arrived at school, I hurriedly made my way to my first class. However, I heard footsteps behind me and turned to see Emily trying to catch up.

"Walk with me to class?" she asked, surprising me since I had expected her to walk with Amelia.

"Yeah, sure," I replied, a hint of excitement in my voice. We walked in silence, the weight of unspoken thoughts lingering between us. I couldn't help but wonder about Emily's intentions—was she genuinely interested in me, grateful for my support, or seeking comfort and safety in my presence? The uncertainty made it difficult to find the right words to say.

Upon reaching the classroom, I noticed that only a few people had arrived. As I took my seat, my mind continued to wander, contemplating the possibilities of a relationship with Emily. The mere thought brought a smile to my face. Lost in my thoughts, I was interrupted by Emily tapping my desk. I looked up at her and noticed how she had styled her hair in a ponytail for the day, complemented by a simple pink v-neck t-shirt tucked into a denim mini-skirt. Despite the makeup she wore, I couldn't help but notice the faint traces of the bruises Greg had inflicted on her. However, her radiant smile managed to overshadow any signs of previous harm. The marks on her neck from last night surprised me, but I was relieved to see that they were gradually fading.

"Thank you so much for watching over me last night," Emily expressed her gratitude. "I know you were in Amelia's sitting room."

I looked at her, surprised. "How did you know? I left pretty early in the morning."

"I heard some noises last night, so I went to see what they were," Emily explained.

"That probably wasn't a good idea, investigating noises on your own," I remarked, concerned for her safety.

"You're probably right." She nodded in agreement.

"Did I make the noises?" I asked, curious. "Was I snoring?"

Emily giggled, shaking her head. "No, it sounded like you were trying to get comfortable. I don't think that sofa was designed with sleeping in mind."

"I'm sorry I woke you," I apologized, feeling a pang of guilt.

"Oh, no! I couldn't sleep!" she reassured me. "After I saw you out there, it made me feel really safe, so I was finally able to get some rest."

I felt my face blush as I absorbed her words. "I'm glad I could help in some way."

An awkward silence settled between us, and I found myself looking away. However, I could sense Emily's gaze fixed on me. "You really do look very handsome today," Emily complimented, her words slightly stumbling. "Not that you don't look handsome all the time, of course. I quite like this look on you."

"Thank you!" I responded, my own cheeks turning warm with a blush. "You look beautiful, as always."

A delightful expression appeared on Emily's face, her eyes widening with joy. "You really think so?"

"I do!" I replied, though my thoughts ran deeper than my words allowed me to express.

"You're very sweet," Emily replied, her cheeks tinted with a blush. "I'm sure all the bruising isn't helping, especially the ones on my neck."

"They're not from the fight in the gym," I stated knowingly.

Sadly, Emily nodded. "From a night or two before. I tried my best to hide them with turtlenecks all week."

"I don't really know what to say, except that I'm so very sorry, Emmy. I can't say it enough," I expressed sincerely. She offered me a quick smile, settling into her seat and placing her backpack on the floor. Shifting to the side of the desk, she positioned herself to face me more directly, crossing her beautiful bare legs. One of her flats slipped off, prompting her to quickly put her foot back into it and cross her legs again.

"I don't feel like working today." She sighed, making no move to retrieve anything from her backpack.

"No?" I asked curiously. "Why not? Lack of sleep?"

Emily frowned momentarily before responding, "I just haven't felt right … I mean … since the whole fight in the gym thing … I …" She struggled to find the right words, visibly frustrated.

"You don't need to explain anything to me, Emily, if you don't want to," I reassured her.

"I have trouble putting into words things that are troubling me."

"Anything you want to talk about?" I inquired, concerned for her well-being.

She briefly diverted her eyes to the floor before meeting my gaze again. "I'm scared—all the time."

"I know, but he really can't get to you now. You're protected at school by the teachers, and by me in this class, during lunch, and the last class," I reassured her.

"He attacked me in the school," she reminded me. "I wasn't protected."

"I know, but it's over now," I responded, hoping to provide some comfort. "He's in no condition to hurt anyone."

Emily nodded. "There is so much more to the story than anyone knows. It's just too much for me right now. If I took off all my makeup to show you what my face looks like after Greg got to me, you'd see why I'm so scared. My face was so swollen, and my lip is just now starting to look normal."

"I'm sorry, Emily," I reiterated, my sympathy evident. "Is there anything I can do to make you feel better or safer?"

"No, you've already done enough, but thank you. It's my problem that I have to deal with." Emily's frown transformed into a smile as she abruptly changed the subject. "You know, you've changed so much since the … since the summer. It's like you're an entirely different person."

"You don't say," I replied, chuckling lightly.

Just as Emily was poised to speak, the classroom door swung open, granting entrance to a young man, who immediately caught sight of Emily. With an air of both anticipation and apprehension, he ambled towards her, his hands casually tucked into the pockets of his jeans. In that fleeting moment, Emily's gaze briefly flitted in my direction, a silent exchange passing between us before she pivoted to fully face the newcomer.

"Hey, Emily!" the guy said enthusiastically.

"Hi, Sean," she replied in her usual sweet voice. "How are you?"

"I ... I'm ... well, how are you?" he stammered.

"I'm doing okay." There was an awkward silence that permeated the room, making me feel uncomfortable as well.

"How's your face?" he asked, immediately regretting his choice of words. "I'm sorry, that didn't sound right."

"It's okay. My face will heal."

"I mean, it looks great!" he quickly added. Emily simply nodded without saying anything. "So ... you know Homecoming is in a little under two weeks ... and ... uh ... and I was wondering ..." I leaned forward in my chair, eager to hear what he would say next. "Yeah ... I was wondering ... if you would like to go with me?" His hand emerged from his pocket to nervously rub the back of his neck. He started sweating, and I found myself feeling just as nervous, realizing I should have asked her myself. I couldn't see Emily's face since she was facing him, but she seemed to ponder his question for a moment or two before responding.

"You're so sweet to ask!" she began. "The fact is, I don't think I'm going to Homecoming this year ... you know, with all that has happened. I'm not sure I'm ready for that yet."

"Oh!" he finally managed to say, shaking a bit more now. "That's cool, I totally understand." He turned to face the door as if to leave but then turned back to her. "Maybe ... maybe we could go out on a casual date? You know ... something smaller? Coffee?" he persisted, undeterred by her initial response.

"I really appreciate you asking. I do. I'm just not ready to start going out again."

He nodded at her. "Okay, maybe some other time?" he asked, his voice filled with hope.

"Sure. Maybe some other time," Emily replied, leaving the possibility open, which made him smile, albeit looking a bit disheartened. With a quick wave, he turned and made his way towards the door. Emily remained facing the front of the room as more students arrived, but soon she spun around to face me again, crossing her legs as she usually did. It seemed like she was seeking some sort of reaction from me regarding the encounter. I struggled to find the right words to say.

"You should get used to that. I'm sure it'll happen a lot," I finally managed to say.

Emily frowned. "I hope not."

"He seemed like a decent guy, and he's not bad looking. Are you not interested, or is it because of the breakup?" I asked, trying to understand her perspective.

"He's on the football team, and he was in the gym when Greg attacked me. I don't recall him coming to my rescue. He was content with watching," she explained, disappointed. I offered her a sympathetic smile. "It's okay, really. It's certainly not your fault. You're the reason I'm sitting here today," she said, clearing her throat. "Are you excited about your game today?"

"I am! Although now I'm feeling a bit nervous. I'm not sure why," I admitted.

"You see, I knew you would be!" Emily giggled. "It's completely natural. After all, it's your first hockey game!"

Not my first, for sure.

"I wish I could see you play, but I have cheer practice," Emily said, a hint of disappointment in her voice. "I hope to catch one of your games at some point."

"That would be awesome!" I replied, perhaps a little too enthusiastically. As the class bell rang, Emily reached into her bag and retrieved her usual items. She sat sideways with her legs crossed and even pulled out more sour candies, placing them on my desk throughout the class.

When the bell finally signaled the end of the class, I gathered my belongings and headed out into the hallway. Emily followed closely behind me. "Walk with me to class?" she asked, her smile making it impossible for me to refuse. I nodded happily, and we started walking in comfortable silence, occasionally brushing arms. It made me feel giddy, like a high school boy with a crush—well, I suppose I was one all over again. We strolled through the hallway towards her class, Emily's ponytail swinging from side to side as she chattered about stunts and cheers. Her eyes sparkled with enthusiasm at her memories, and I couldn't help but smile in response. We arrived at her science classroom and she turned around and gave me a quick hug before slipping inside, the door closing behind her with a soft click.

Throughout the day, I caught sight of Emily in the crowded hallways as she laughed and talked with her cheer friends. In between their conversations, when our eyes met, she'd send me a bright smile that lit up her entire face, while her friends would giggle and jokingly nudge each other. I wasn't sure what was so funny, but whatever it was had them all full of joy.

The rest of the school day passed with relative ease, albeit punctuated by the numerous compliments I received on my outfit. During lunch, I spotted Emily engaged in conversation with my sisters, and of course, Henry couldn't resist poking fun at me when he caught me stealing glances in her direction. Yet, these minor distractions paled in comparison to the exhilaration I felt when I walked into my last class and found Emily already there.

As I settled into my seat, my heart quickened its pace. I couldn't help but steal a few glances in her direction. Her eyes met mine, and a warm smile graced her lips, growing wider when I reciprocated with a smile of my own.

*   *   *

When the school day came to an end, I hurriedly left the classroom, eager to focus on the upcoming game. Suddenly, I felt a gentle tug on my arm and heard Emily's voice calling out to me.

"Hey, Wil, are you okay?" she asked, her voice filled with concern.

"Emily!" I exclaimed, startled by her sudden presence. "You scared me!"

She giggled apologetically. "I'm sorry, I didn't mean to. You just rushed out of class so quickly."

"I'm just still a little nervous, I guess," I admitted.

"Don't be. You're going to do great!" she reassured me. I slowed my pace, realizing she was struggling to keep up. "You'll have to tell me all about it tomorrow morning."

"I will!" I replied, grateful for her support. There was a brief pause in our conversation, and I could sense that Emily had something she wanted to say.

"Well ... good luck today, Wil. I'll be rooting for you!" she said as we continued walking towards the gym. Upon reaching the entrance, she squeezed my hand briefly, smiled, and then disappeared into the gym without saying another word. My thoughts began to shift, focusing more on Emily rather than the game, despite my intentions.

* * *

I headed to the ice arena and stepped into the locker room. Swiftly, I donned my hockey gear and settled onto the bench in front of my locker. Henry and Steve, my teammates in the midst of their own preparations, flanked me as we got ready for the game. "You look nervous, Wil," Henry commented, observing my leg bouncing rapidly up and down.

"Just a little," I replied.

Henry chuckled. "A little? At this rate, you're going to dig a hole in the mat."

I sheepishly smiled at his remark. "It's not so much about the game."

Henry finished tying his skate and placed his hand on my shoulder pad. "What's on your mind, brother?" he asked, concern evident in his voice.

Taking a deep breath, I replied, "I dunno ... my head is somewhere else. I need to concentrate on the game."

Steve, finishing up with his gear, chimed in with a chuckle, "Sounds like a girl. Is this about Emily?"

I glanced at Steve and then back at Henry. "Yeah! How did you know?"

"I know that feeling, buddy," Steve said thoughtfully. "I've been there. It's always at the worst moments, too ... like right before a game."

"I told you guys, girls are nothing but trouble." Damon said, "Hockey is life."

"I'm conflicted. I know Emily just got out of a relationship, but a big part of me wants to ask her to Homecoming. I'm just not sure if it's appropriate or not to do so," I explained, not paying Damon much mind, "She turned down a guy named Sean today, saying it was too soon for her. So, I'm assuming I would get the same answer."

"I wouldn't assume anything," Henry advised. "You won't know until you ask her, and if you never ask, you'll never know."

"And if you don't ask her, you'll kick yourself if she ends up going with someone else," Steve added.

"Besides, Sean's a douchebag, of course she would turn him down." Damon said with a chuckle.

I let out a sigh. "I dunno, man. I have to get through this game first, and then I'll worry about that," I said, putting on my game jersey. Our team wore predominantly green jerseys with yellow trim. The sound of people settling into their seats echoed through the arena. It seemed like there weren't many spectators.

"I wouldn't expect a lot of spectators," Henry remarked, as if reading my thoughts. "We've never had a winning record."

Playing in front of a crowd didn't make me nervous. I always had butterflies until the linesman dropped the puck, signaling the start of the game.

"It's go time, gentlemen," Henry declared as we all stood up, ready to walk out onto the ice.

The *crowd* was buzzing with excitement, and it was quite impressive considering it was a high school ice hockey game. The arena was filled with spectators, and even the presence of an announcer added to the sense of grandeur. The lights dimmed, except for a couple of spotlights moving around on the ice, creating a captivating atmosphere.

"Please welcome to the ice ... the visiting Arundel High School," the announcer proclaimed in a somewhat monotonous tone. The opposing team skated around in the darkness, illuminated by the spotlights. "And now, please welcome to the ice ... yourrrrrrr Andoverrrrrrrrr Archerrrrrsssssss!" The announcer's voice was brimming with enthusiasm. I burst onto the ice as the third player from our team. Skating alongside Henry and Steve, we circled the net, building up anticipation. Although I had played as a left defense in the past, I was now assigned to the left wing. The unfamiliar but catchy music filled the arena, adding to the energy. Soon, the regular lights illuminated the rink, revealing the sizeable crowd that had turned up to support us, despite our team's underwhelming record from previous years.

Scanning the audience, I spotted my parents, who had kept their promise to be there. My father wore an ANDOVER shirt and a ball cap, looking thrilled and eager. I had no idea where he got the merchandise, but it brought a smile to my face. My mom seemed a bit uneasy and concerned, while my sisters were absent, occupied with their cheer practice. I skated towards the boards near our bench but didn't hop over just yet.

"First line: me, Wil, Steve. Jared and Mike on 'D,'" Henry declared, laying out the lineup.

I nodded and made my way to the designated spot on the left wing. Steve, being left-handed, took the right wing, and Henry played as the center. Jared manned the right defense, while Mike covered the left. Our goalie for the night was Dean.

With the team set and the game about to begin, I felt a surge of adrenaline. It was time to focus on the game and give it my all. The cheers from the crowd faded into the background as the anticipation built up, and I prepared to take my first shift on the ice.

Arundel's colors resembled ours, but they sported green and white jerseys for the game. As the referee blew the whistle, signaling the start of the game, we prepared for the face-off. Thankfully, I wasn't the one taking it—I always found face-offs a bit challenging.

Henry emerged victorious from the face-off, and I swiftly sent the puck back to Jared, our right defenseman. Jared began his rush up the right wing and swiftly passed to Henry, who crossed into Arundel's offensive zone. I entered the zone from the left wing, with Mike positioned in the center. The opposing defense closed in on Henry swiftly, so he made a quick dump pass to the corner.

The puck ricocheted around the boards to my side of the rink, and I collected it as it came around the net. Just as I released the puck, the defender hit me from behind, but I managed to put the puck in play right in front of the goalie. Steve fired a shot at the net, but the goalie made a graceful save. Any remnants of butterflies had vanished by now—I was completely focused and in the zone. Arundel struggled just to touch the puck; they were clearly slower and less experienced.

The puck made its way back to Henry, who passed it back to our left defenseman, Mike. With precision, Mike unleashed a powerful one-timer at the goalie, who barely managed to make the save. The rebound came straight to me, and I executed a quick juke on the goalie before unleashing a wrist shot. The puck slid beneath the goalie's pads and found the back of the net!

I raised my arms in triumph as my teammates converged for high fives. The sound of the siren echoed throughout the arena, and the red light above the net illuminated, resembling a police car's lights.

We skated back to the bench, making way for the second line. I glanced at the crowd, searching for my parents, who were both standing and cheering. My dad looked incredibly proud, and I found myself feeling even happier for him than for myself. A bit to their left, I spotted my sisters in a space behind my parents' seats, enthusiastically cheering for me. And there, right next to them, was Emily, cheering as well. Our eyes met, and it felt like a special moment amidst the excitement of the game. I took a swig of water from the bottle on the bench, noticing her beaming smile directed at me. It seemed like she was waving to me.

The second line returned to the bench, but Coach Babcock wanted the first line back on the ice, so we quickly headed back into the game.

Stay focused, Fenwick.

The face-off was in our defensive zone, near the boards and almost shoving me into them. I squared off against an opponent slightly bigger than me, but I never let size intimidate me during a game—I knew I could hold my own. Arundel won the face-off, sending the puck back to their right defenseman. Trusting my instincts, I skated aggressively up the center, just as the opposing player passed towards their left defenseman. I intercepted the pass and immediately accelerated towards their net as fast as I could.

A defender was trailing me through the center. Employing a move called a "spin-a-ronie," I slammed on the brakes, causing the defender to trip over his own feet. I found myself alone with the goaltender, faked right, and swiftly switched to my backhand, sending the puck soaring over his right shoulder and into the net!

The goal light flashed, and the blaring siren echoed through the arena once again. I back-skated towards the far boards, arms outstretched in triumph. Goal number two! My teammates surrounded me, exchanging high fives as we celebrated our success on the way back to the bench. As I reached the bench, I glanced up into the crowd, spotting my sisters and Emily cheering for our team.

Damon had left a physical mark on a few players who had dared to target me, asserting his dominance as he forcefully checked them into the boards. On the second line, Randy showcased his prowess with a blistering slapshot, while Dean, our goaltender, made the art of saving shots appear effortless, snatching up everything that came his way. Occasionally, Randy would step in for me on the first line, and I would take his place on the second line. However, for the majority of the time, I found myself on the first line alongside Henry and Steve. When the final buzzer sounded, we had completely dominated Arundel throughout the game, preventing them from scoring a single goal. I ended the game with a hat trick of three goals and two assists, while Henry contributed with a goal and three assists, and Steve with a goal and an assist. The final score was eight to zero in our favor. We shook hands with the Arundel team, and I commended them on their efforts, acknowledging that they had played a great game.

Slowly, we made our way off the ice and towards the locker room. Emily remained in the stands, clapping enthusiastically, her eyes fixed on me until I disappeared from view.

The air in the locker room was thick with celebration. Players pounded each other on their backs, and coach Babcock walked towards me with a wide grin on his face. He placed my first goal puck and the game puck into my hands before embracing me in a huge bear hug.

After showering and getting dressed, I walked out of the ice arena and into the gym lobby. There, my parents, Amelia, and Penny awaited my arrival. Amelia's excitement was palpable as she hugged me tightly. "You were incredible! I wouldn't have believed it if I hadn't seen it myself!"

A radiant glow of pride illuminated my father's face, his wide grin stretching from ear to ear. "I couldn't be prouder of you, son. You played like a seasoned professional out there," he praised, his words laced with genuine admiration.

Following Amelia's hug, my mother embraced me next, her eyes holding a hint of wistfulness. While she pressed a tender kiss upon my cheek, her silence spoke volumes, conveying emotions that words could not capture. After a fleeting moment, she gently stepped back, leaving an unspoken sentiment hanging in the air.

Penny embraced me and gave me a kiss on the cheek too. "I'm also super proud of you, Wil!"

"Thank you, everyone. I really appreciate it," I replied with a grateful smile, still clutching my hockey bag. "But where's Emily? I saw her in the stands," I asked suddenly, realizing she wasn't present.

Amelia's grin grew even wider, and she clasped her hands together. "I knew it! I *knew* you liked her!"

Raising an eyebrow at her playful assumption, I clarified, "I never said that. I just noticed her in the stands and wondered where she was."

Penny chimed in, revealing the reason for Emily's absence. "She received a text. The police put a car outside her house to keep an eye on things, so her parents made her go home."

Unexpected

<hr/>

On the following day, positioned in the hallway just outside my first-period class, I exuded a relaxed demeanor in my casual ensemble. Suddenly, the distinct sound of a throat clearing reached my ears, prompting an instinctive swivel of my body to face the source. There, before me, stood an enchanting redhead, her vibrant locks cascading around her, folders clutched close to her chest. It was a moment of pure serendipity, as this encounter marked the first time our paths had crossed, igniting a sense of intrigue within me.

"Hi, Will!" she greeted me with a pleasant tone.

"Hello …" I responded, hoping she would provide her name.

"Stephanie," she said, her expression slightly disappointed.

"Hello, Stephanie!" I replied with a smile and nod. "I apologize, I have trouble with my memory."

"Hi!" she repeated nervously. "It's totally fine! I forgot about your memory issue." There was a long, uncomfortable pause, before she spoke again. "I was wondering, if you don't already have a date, would you like to go to Homecoming with me?"

Oh, shit …. now what?

My mind raced, as I hadn't considered the possibility of going with someone else if Emily wasn't interested. My focus had been solely on asking her to the dance. "That's really kind of you to ask, Stephanie," I said, maintaining eye contact. "But I don't think I'll be going this year.

It's been a tough year for me." She continued to look at me, waiting for more. "I'm truly sorry," I added.

Finally, she seemed to snap out of her daze. "Oh! That's okay, Wil. I understand," she said, her face displaying uncertainty. "Can I give you my number? You know, just in case you change your mind? Or want to go out on a date?"

"Sure," I replied.

What harm could it do?

Stephanie's sad expression transformed into excitement. "Okay!" She reached into her folder, tore out a piece of paper, and quickly wrote down her number. She handed me the torn sheet a moment later. "Call or text me!" Stephanie said with enthusiasm. "Maybe we could go out sometime this weekend?"

"Uh, maybe," I mumbled, struggling to come up with a response.

"Okay, great! Call me anytime!" Stephanie exclaimed, turning away and practically skipping down the hallway.

I glanced at the paper with Stephanie's name and number on it, noticing the heart symbol she had drawn. I punched the number into my phone contacts, and quickly stuffed the paper into the top of my locker and closed it. Just as the locker door shut, I was startled by Emily's presence behind it, causing me to jump back in surprise.

"Holy shit, Emily!" I exclaimed, clutching my chest. "You scared the shit out of me!"

Emily smiled, finding amusement in my reaction. "I'm sorry, Wil. I didn't mean to scare you, although it seems like I manage to do that a lot."

We walked into the classroom together, with me gesturing for Emily to take her seat before I did. She settled into her chair, allowing her backpack to drop to the floor. She, too, was dressed casually today, with her hair tied back in a ponytail. She wore ripped jeans, a plain light-blue t-shirt, low-cut socks, and Chucks for shoes. As I sat down and placed my folders on the desk, I noticed that Emily's gaze was fixed on me.

"You were so great in your game last night! I couldn't believe the things you were capable of out there!" she exclaimed, her voice brimming with genuine astonishment.

"Thank you! It felt amazing! It's hard to believe how well it all came together!" I shared, the thrill of the victory still coursing through my veins.

"You were absolutely amazing! I would never have guessed in a thousand years that you could skate, let alone play like that!" Her face lit up with excitement. "You continue to surprise me, Mr. Fenwick."

"Well, I hope that's a good thing," I said, slightly unsure of her reaction.

She gave me with a warm smile and replied, "It is! I apologize for having to leave before the game ended. My parents called me home, and the police had more questions for me. They even stationed a car outside my house for the night."

I reassured her, saying, "That's alright; I'm just grateful you made it. Is everything alright with the police?"

Emily appeared somewhat preoccupied but nodded, saying, "Yeah, they were mainly interested in knowing more about what had transpired between Greg and me. They mentioned they couldn't keep a police car parked outside my house every night, but they did so last night."

Concern etched my features as I asked, "Are you holding up okay?" Emily seemed composed on the surface, but my experience as a Medic had taught me that appearances could be deceiving.

Emily just nodded, blushed and looked away shyly. There was a moment of silence, a hint of awkwardness in the air. "Stephanie's a nice girl," she suddenly remarked, turning her gaze back to me.

"Who?" I asked, not immediately grasping whom she was referring to.

"Stephanie. The girl who asked you to Homecoming, and on a date."

"Oh," I responded, caught off guard. "You, uh, saw that, huh?"

Emily nodded, biting her lower lip slightly. "You would like her. She's really smart, and very kind ... and as you can tell, very pretty. She's on the pom-pom squad."

"I don't even know her," I said, feeling unsure about how to navigate this conversation.

"You aren't going to Homecoming?" she asked, her gaze locked with mine.

"Uh, well ... you see ..." I began, feeling her intense gaze on me. "I *do* want to go to Homecoming, I just didn't want to go with *her*. You know ... not really knowing her and all."

"Ohhhhhhhh, I see," Emily said with a smile that almost resembled a grin. "But ... how are you going to get to know anyone by that theory?

I mean, you don't remember anyone. Maybe you should go on that date with her."

"I …" I started but couldn't come up with a satisfactory explanation that I was willing to share. "Heh, I don't know. It just didn't feel right, you know?"

"So you do plan to go? To Homecoming, that is."

"I'd like to, sure," I replied, feeling the weight of the awkwardness between us. The bell rang, signaling the start of class, and the other students began entering the classroom.

As the day unfolded, Emily's presence seemed accompanied by a quiet demeanor, her words held in reserve. Nevertheless, I remained steadfast in my commitment to accompany her to science class, a comforting routine that continued to foster our connection. The absence of our shared last period class stirred a sense of concern within me, prompting worries about her well-being. Uncertainty cast a shadow over my thoughts, leaving me to wonder if everything was indeed all right.

* * *

Hockey practice concluded prematurely, courtesy of Coach Babcock's scheduled appointment, affording us the luxury of an unexpected thirty-five-minute early release. My body still bore the remnants of soreness from the previous day's game. Hastily, I indulged in a refreshing shower before attiring myself. Stepping out of the locker room, I found Henry and Steve, faithful companions, catching up with me in the vibrant expanse of the gym lobby.

"Hey, brother!" Henry's enthusiastic greeting reverberated through the air, accompanied by our customary "brotherly" handshake, a series of intricate gestures symbolizing our close bond, which seamlessly transitioned into a heartfelt, manly embrace. Steve, mirroring our camaraderie, swiftly joined in, completing the trio with a firm, supportive hug.

"Did you ask Emily out yet?" Henry asked once the formalities were over.

"No." I sighed. "But some girl named Stephanie asked me on a date … and for Homecoming."

"Stephanie Howell? The redhead, right? Dude, she's gorgeous. What did you say?" Henry inquired.

"Yeah, that's her. I said *no* to homecoming and *maybe* to the date. The thing is, Emily was right there and heard everything."

"So what? You're not dating Emily. Are you going with Stephanie then, or are you going to ask Emily out?" Henry pressed.

"*No* to Stephanie," I replied.

"Bro, why not?" Henry asked sympathetically. "She's really good looking, and really nice!"

"Looks aren't everything, although she does seem nice. I really want to go with Emily, but she said she wasn't going to Homecoming."

"I told you, ask her anyway! She's waiting for someone she wants to go with, I'm sure!" Henry encouraged. "Just like you are. I know I'm right."

"What if she genuinely doesn't want to go because she feels it's too soon after Greg?" I thought aloud, realizing I was overthinking like a teenager. What was wrong with me? I was supposed to be braver than this, right? I was in World War III, I ran through a hail of bullets to get to a wounded comrade, time and time again—and here I was, afraid of what Emily might think about my asking her to homecoming.

"Then you'll look pretty foolish, get embarrassed, and have no way to backtrack," Steve chimed in with a big grin.

"Dude," Henry scolded Steve, frowning. "Not helping."

"Well, what about you two, huh? Have either of you asked anyone to Homecoming?" I redirected the conversation.

"Funny you should mention that …" Henry began with a chuckle, his eyes shifting towards Steve.

"I asked your sister, Amelia, earlier today. She said *yes*," Steve blurted out nervously.

"Subtle," Henry muttered with a sigh.

"Are you kidding me right now? Bro! Why didn't you mention it to me? You didn't even tell me you were interested in her!" I exclaimed, feeling surprised and a bit betrayed.

"Well, I kind of did," Steve replied, his voice trailing off. I stood there for a moment, staring at him. "No?" Steve asked, seeking confirmation.

"No," I repeated.

"Sorry about that, bro," Steve apologized, looking genuinely remorseful.

"It's cool, man," I assured him with a laugh. "I'm happy for you. Amelia's great! Just remember, hands off. Seriously," I added, narrowing my eyes playfully. We all shared a laugh, and I knew Steve would be respectful towards my sister … or at least, I had hoped he would.

Henry interjected, "Did you have a chance to talk to Amelia about Beth?"

I nodded, replying, "Yeah, I did. Amelia told me that Beth isn't as outgoing as Emily, but she's really kind and sweet. She's a freshman, varsity cheerleader, and a flyer. So far, she's not dating anyone, but you better act fast."

"What the fuck is a *flyer*?" Henry asked, sounding puzzled.

"It's the cheerleader who gets tossed into the air during stunts. Same role as Emily," I explained.

"Oh, got it," Henry responded. "Well, I guess I should take my own advice and ask her out this week." Both Henry and Steve picked up their hockey bags. "Hey, brother, we gotta run. Catch ya tomorrow?"

"Yeah, man, see you guys," I replied.

Moments later, solitude enveloped me within the expansive confines of the gym lobby, my trusty hockey bag nestled by my side. Inquisitively, my gaze swept across the area, searching for a telltale sign of the cheerleaders' practice location. Uncertain of the precise room, I deduced that they were not occupying the main gym. Stepping forward with purpose, I navigated through the gym, making my way towards the recesses where various sports teams honed their skills. With the football team gracing the field, I surmised that the cheerleaders were unlikely to be found there. Tuning my ears to the ambient soundscape, a symphony of female voices harmoniously counting in unison carried faintly through the air, leading me closer to my desired destination, "5, 6, 7, 8 … and 1, 2, 3, 4, 5 …"

It was the cheerleaders. I was getting closer. The door to their practice area was propped open, allowing me to hear Coach Tabitha Geller, the varsity cheerleading coach, giving instructions to the team.

Her voice echoed through the room, urging the cheerleaders to improve their dance routine. "Let's get it right this time, ladies. It's a dance, it's not fucking hard," she yelled. Curiosity getting the better of me, I peeked into the room from the hallway just as the coach pressed "Play," and the music started playing.

Immediately, I spotted Emily in the stunt group on my left, Amelia in the group on my right, and Penny in the center group. The cheerleaders moved in perfect synchronization, their bodies flowing to the music. It was an impressive sight to behold. Suddenly, Emily seemed to spot me, our eyes met, and a smile illuminated her face. Though she quickly returned her gaze to the front, the smile remained, as if it was meant just for me. As the song progressed, there was a captivating moment when all the cheerleaders placed their hands on their hips, swaying from side to side. They spread their legs wide, assuming a firm stance while their arms moved up and down, side to side. The sight was undeniably captivating and alluring.

Once the routine came to an end, Coach Geller threatened them with the consequence of running the stairs if they didn't improve. The cheerleaders took a well-deserved break to grab some drinks. It was then that Amelia noticed my presence and gently nudged Emily, signaling towards the door. Emily's eyes followed Amelia's gesture, and upon spotting me again, she bit her lower lip, radiating excitement.

I raised my hand in a wave, and she reciprocated with a small wave of her own. The anticipation in her expression revealed her genuine enthusiasm at seeing me there. My emotions were in turmoil as I stood there. I felt a growing sense of loneliness, and I realized that being alone wasn't something I desired. I knew I had to make a decision, to figure out what I truly wanted.

Emily's Regret

—◇—

As I entered our home, the sight of the police car parked outside only added to my frustration. Ignoring my mom's attempt to talk to me, I stormed into my room and forcefully shut the door behind me. I couldn't believe I had foolishly encouraged Wil to go out with Stephanie. What was I thinking? Stephanie was undeniably beautiful, and it was only natural for Wil to be attracted to her. I dreaded the thought of him asking her to Homecoming instead of me. All I wanted was to be Wil's date, or I'd rather not go with anyone at all. My infatuation with him was consuming me, and I couldn't shake the desperate desire to be close to him. Frustrated, I kicked off my cheer shoes and flopped onto my bed, burying my face in the covers. Within moments, there was a knock at my door.

"Go away," I mumbled, my voice muffled by the fabric.

The door opened anyway, and I heard it close shortly after. Someone sat on my bed next to me. "Want to talk about it?" Beth asked gently.

"No," I replied with a mixture of frustration and vulnerability.

"Yes, you do," Beth insisted.

I spun around, sitting up to face Beth directly. "Stephanie Howell! I actually told Wil to go out with Stephanie Howell! Am I bloody stupid?"

Beth chuckled, acknowledging the absurdity of my decision. "Yeah, that wasn't your best idea."

I shot her a look of exasperation. "He's going to like her and ask her to Homecoming! She doesn't have all the baggage I have!"

"He might," Beth conceded, "unless you ask him first."

"I can't do that," I protested, looking away. "Have you seen him up close? He's gorgeous! He's kind and sweet. I'm just not good enough for him."

Confusion filled Beth's expression as she tried to understand my self-deprecating perspective. "Em, why would you ever say that? You're amazing! Everyone likes you! You're funny, smart, and beautiful! You're the prettiest girl in the school!"

"No, Beth, Greg made me popular when I was with him. I'm okay with not being popular if it means I don't have to be with him. And Nikki is the prettiest girl in the school," I replied, my voice tainted with jealousy.

Beth sat beside me on the bed and embraced me in a comforting hug. "Greg is a nobody. Especially now. You have all those qualities I mentioned, even without him. I see how your face lights up, how you laugh when you're around Wil. It's as if he came into your life at the darkest moment, like he was sent from God. Embrace it, for goodness' sake! And I'm willing to bet that if you ask Wil, he thinks you're the prettiest girl in school." I remained silent, taking in Beth's words and finding comfort in her support. "Wil talks to you a lot, Em. He walks you to class, he walks you to practice. There's no way that guy doesn't like you! Remember when he came over to our lunch table just to return that silly pink pencil to you?" Beth exclaimed.

I sniffled, my emotions overwhelming me. "Yeah, a pencil I sneaked into his bag."

"Exactly! If you don't make a move, you might miss out on something wonderful," Beth asserted firmly. "And then you'll only have yourself to blame." Frustration and sadness engulfed me, causing me to throw myself back onto the bed with a growl. "Why not call Amelia and have her drop a hint to Wil about you wanting to go with him?" she suggested.

I sat up again, considering her suggestion. "I've already mentioned it to her at least once, maybe more."

"Well, mention it again! We can always resort to the *nuclear option*," Beth declared.

I raised an eyebrow, curious. "What the bloody hell is the *nuclear option*?"

Beth chuckled mischievously. "I could simply tell him that you want to go to Homecoming with him and to ask you. It may sound absurd, but it could work."

I protested, finding the idea slightly ridiculous. "That's ... unconventional, to say the least." I giggled. "Let's call it Plan B."

Beth laughed and hugged me once more. "Hey, didn't you mention seeing him during our practice and noticing him smiling at you? Even waving to you?" I nodded, a glimmer of hope emerging as she held me in her embrace. "Now why would he come looking for the cheerleading room if he wasn't interested in you?" Beth questioned, her tone filled with disbelief.

I leaned back, pulling away from her hug. "I don't know, maybe he got lost?"

Beth raised an eyebrow, not convinced. "Have you ever seen him get lost or heard him mention it? It's Andover, it's not that big of a school."

"Maybe," I mumbled uncertainly. "Maybe he came looking for you."

"Oh, Em." Beth sighed, embracing me once more. We sat in silence, finding companionship in each other's presence. It had been a challenging few days, and I had only confided in Amelia about what Greg had done to me. Beth released me from her hug and looked into my eyes. "Have you received any more texts from Greg?" she asked, seemingly reading my thoughts.

"A few, from different numbers. I blocked them all," I replied, my voice filled with determination.

"We still need to change your number," Beth stated firmly. I nodded, my mind preoccupied. Just then, my phone vibrated on the nightstand, catching both Beth's and my attention. It vibrated again, indicating an incoming call. "It's a call," Beth whispered, as if it held some special significance.

"No shit," I muttered, taking a deep breath before reaching for my phone, which was face down. Relief washed over me as I saw that it was Amelia calling. I quickly answered, trying to sound composed. "Hi, Amelia!"

"Hey, bad news. Wil is going on a date with Stephanie Howell tonight," Amelia revealed, her voice filled with disappointment.

"What?" I exclaimed, my worst fear materializing. Greg's hurtful words echoed in my mind, fueling my insecurities. Maybe Wil didn't like me after all.

"What's going on?" Beth whispered, curiosity evident in her voice.

"Hang on, Amelia. I'm gonna put you on speaker. Beth's right here," I said, flipping the speakerphone on so Beth could hear the conversation. "This is terrible!" I exclaimed, my voice filled with sadness. "I should've done something earlier. Why didn't you stop him?"

Amelia's annoyed tone came through the phone. "First of all, my mom is the one who told me he went out with Stephanie. I wasn't even here when he left. Second, he's going on this date because you keep telling *everyone* that you're *not* going to Homecoming. He assumes you don't want to go with him either. He thinks it's because of your recent breakup with Greg. And let's not forget that you actually *encouraged* him to go out with Stephanie. What the fuck, Em?"

"I know, I know … I don't know what got into me. I feel so bloody stupid," I admitted, my voice trembling with regret. Amelia sighed, and a heavy silence filled the room.

"Yeah, you're stupid," Amelia agreed bluntly. "I mean, who tells a guy they like to go out with someone else? That's what I would fucking do if I liked a guy. Tell him to go out with someone else!"

"Stephanie and her stupid red hair!" I exclaimed, my frustration boiling over. "Wait, what am I saying? I love her hair! And she's on the bloody pom squad too! Wil will probably love that! She's gorgeous! What if Wil doesn't even like me that way? What if—"

"Oh, shut the hell up," Amelia interrupted sternly. "He likes you, I *KNOW* he likes you, so stop that shit. Calm down. We can fix this."

"But they're already going on the date. It's not like he's going to hate her. She's super sweet, smart, and funny. Oh, did I mention how fucking gorgeous she is?" I babbled, my thoughts spiraling out of control.

"You might have mentioned that once or twice," Beth chimed in, confirming my previous comments.

There was a brief silence as we contemplated the situation. "Okay, I will think of something. Leave it to me," Amelia finally said, determination evident in her voice. "I got you, bestie!"

The Unexpected Date

I parked my truck in front of the house Stephanie had given me the address to. It was a pleasant cul-de-sac in a nice neighborhood. Taking a deep breath, I gathered my courage and walked up to the door. As I approached, I could hear a small, yappy dog barking from inside, clearly not thrilled with my presence.

What am I doing here?

Stephanie had exuded kindness, intelligence, and undeniable attractiveness, but a lingering sense of unease gnawed at me. Nonetheless, loneliness had begun to seep in, and I yearned for companionship. This wasn't the same as the camaraderie I shared with my hockey buddies; rather, I felt the desire to embark on a date. I didn't want to add any undue pressure to Emily, especially given all she had recently endured with her breakup from Greg. And with Stephanie readily available, the idea seemed appealing.

I hesitated before knocking, but before I could, Stephanie appeared at the door with a big smile. The little dog now barked at her feet. "Princess, stop!" She reprimanded the dog, looking down. "It's just Wil. Hi, Wil!" She stepped out of the house and closed the door behind her, despite Princess's protests.

This was the first time I had a chance to really take in Stephanie's appearance. She was even more beautiful than I remembered, with her long red hair and captivating green eyes. When she smiled, adorable dimples appeared on her face. She wore a green dress that hung slightly above her knee, along with black nylons and heels.

"Hey, uh, Stephanie," I greeted her, originally extending my hand for a handshake, which suddenly seemed like a foolish idea. She ignored my hand and hugged me tightly. Her perfume smelled lovely, and her embrace was warm. "You look really nice."

"Thank you, cutie," Stephanie replied, lingering a bit longer in the hug than I expected. She readjusted her purse strap and looked up at me. "Are you all ready to go?"

"Uh, don't your parents want to meet me or something?" I asked nervously.

"Nope," she responded, linking her arm with mine. "Well, they're not home anyway. Otherwise, I'm sure they would. I'm glad they're not here. They'd have so many questions."

We walked towards my truck, and Stephanie's hand moved slowly up and down my bicep.

"I'm sorry for the last-minute call. Is there somewhere specific you'd like to go, or should I decide?" I inquired, trying to make conversation.

"Your choice, cutie," Stephanie cooed. "And I'm really glad you called me!"

I opened the SUV door for her, assisting her inside before closing it behind her. Within moments, I settled into my seat, and we started driving down the road. "We can grab a coffee or a bite to eat?" I suggested.

Stephanie giggled. "Let's go for coffee. It's less pressure for both of us."

I nodded in agreement. "Okay, cool."

I steered us towards a local coffee shop called Franklin's Coffee, even though I wasn't particularly fond of coffee myself. I was certain they would have soda as well.

Once we arrived, I held the door open for Stephanie as we entered. We walked up to the counter, and I glanced at the menu.

"What would you like?" I asked Stephanie.

"Just a regular coffee with cream and sugar," she replied.

I acknowledged her choice and approached the counter. A friendly server greeted us, his nametag read "Paul".

"What can I get for you two?" Paul asked, radiating pleasantness.

"I'll have a regular coffee with cream and sugar, and a soda without ice," I ordered.

Paul nodded. "Cream and sugar are available on the tables or the side counter. For your soda choice, will that be a Jabsi? And will that be all?"

"Yes, sir," I confirmed. It struck me as peculiar that despite the identical taste of the sodas from my universe, they bore different names. Jabsi reigned as the predominant soda, renowned worldwide. Yet, the origins of the name remained shrouded in mystery to me.

A moment later, Paul informed me of the total.

"Wait, do you have chocolate shakes?" I asked with genuine excitement, scanning the menu board in search of the delightful treat.

"We do, sir. So a chocolate shake as well?" Paul replied.

"Yes, please!" Stephanie glanced at me with a small grin, curious about my sudden enthusiastic outburst.

Paul calculated the new total, all the while smiling.

Handing him some money, I smiled and said, "Keep the change."

"Thank you, sir," He acknowledged with a smile. A few moments later, he handed me the coffee and then the soda. I carefully passed the hot coffee to Stephanie.

"Careful, it's hot," I cautioned.

"Thank you, Wil," she responded sweetly.

Moments later, Paul presented me with the chocolate shake, and I looked at it as if I had just won the lottery.

Guiding Stephanie to a secluded table at the back of the shop, unoccupied by other patrons, I courteously pulled out her chair. She appeared pleasantly surprised by the gesture but gracefully accepted it, settling into her seat. The cozy and inviting ambiance of the place set the perfect stage for an enjoyable conversation. "Wow, I'm getting the entire gentlemen treatment tonight," Stephanie remarked with a big smile. Returning her smile, I settled into my seat as she busied herself with the packets of sugar and creamer, adding two of each. Meanwhile, I made quick work of my chocolate shake, savoring every delightful sip. I couldn't resist the urge to enjoy it to the last drop, and my enthusiasm was quite evident when I hit the bottom.

Looking up at Stephanie, I noticed her large grin. "Do you need some alone time with your shake?" she teased playfully.

"Oh!" I replied, slightly embarrassed. "Sorry about that. I don't have these very often, and, well ..." I stumbled, realizing I might have sounded ridiculous.

Thankfully, Stephanie seemed more amused than anything. "I'm just playing, cutie. I think it's adorable."

Feeling my cheeks warm, I skillfully changed the subject, wanting to move away from my shake-induced embarrassment. "So, you know I lost my memory for real, right?" I began, eager to share my story with her.

Stephanie nodded as she stirred her coffee. "I heard all about it. I'm pretty sure the entire school knows," she replied. "I'm really, really sorry, Wil. You know, for what happened to you."

"It's okay. It was self-inflicted ... though I don't know why. I mean, I was told why, or at least why they think I did it."

"That must feel really strange, waking up not knowing why you tried to ... well, you know," Stephanie said, taking a small sip of her coffee. "Oh wow, that is hot."

"Believe me, everything's been strange since I woke up."

"I can't even imagine," she sympathized, twisting a strand of her hair with her finger.

"Did we know each other before?" I asked curiously.

"Not really," she replied. "Just in passing. You weren't a very talkative person."

"I see," I said. "Out of curiosity, what made you ask me out then?"

Stephanie set her coffee down and pondered her answer. "If I'm being honest, you've gotten a lot cuter and a lot more buff since last year. Your personality has changed completely."

I chuckled. "Thanks? For noticing, I mean."

"Oh, all the girls noticed, believe me." Stephanie laughed.

"I literally just changed clothes and my hair a little."

"Let's not forget about being more buff," she added with another laugh. "Your personality changed more than anything. We have math class together. I'm not sure if you noticed me there."

"We do?" I asked, surprised that I hadn't known this earlier.

"We do," she confirmed. "I sit on the other side of the room, last row, second from the back."

"I didn't know that."

"Well ... now you do." She giggled.

"Can I ask you an odd question about me?" I raised an eyebrow.

"Sure, if I can answer it," Stephanie replied, intrigued.

"How many times did I get beaten up last year? Who did it, and who came to my defense, if anyone?" Stephanie was taking a sip of her coffee and practically choked on it when I asked my question. She coughed a few times, and I leaned over to pat her on the back. "You okay?" I asked.

Stephanie nodded, regaining her composure. "Well … that is a strange question, for sure. I mean, I sure didn't keep count. Greg was the person who bullied you the most. As for who stood up for you? I wasn't physically present at very many of those altercations, but when I was, Emily would try to stand up for you. She would normally come in the next day with a black eye."

"So everyone just stood by while I got the crap kicked out of me?" I asked, feeling a mix of frustration and disappointment.

"Everyone's afraid of Greg, and several members of the football team," Stephanie replied.

"I see."

"I'm sorry, Wil," she added sincerely. "I really wish there was something I could have done to help you. I'm not very big, nor am I much of a fighter."

"Nah, there was nothing you could have done." We sat in awkward silence for a few moments. "So, tell me about you!" I said, trying to change the subject and bring some positivity to the conversation. "What do you like to do?"

Stephanie smiled and began listing her interests. "Let's see—I like to dance. I love reading books, especially romance. I enjoy watching movies, the classics and romantic comedies are my favorites. I like going for walks, especially in the spring, preferably with the right guy. I'm on the Pom squad, which I love, because I get to dance." As she was talking, my phone kept vibrating. "Are you going to get that?" She asked, noticing the persistent notifications.

I shrugged. "I'm out with you right now. It can wait."

"It could be important," she suggested.

I sighed and turned my phone over on the table. "It's one of my sisters," I explained.

Stephanie nodded. "See? It's probably important."

"Somehow, I doubt it," I said with a sigh. Reluctantly, I answered the call, trying not to sound annoyed. "Hello, Amelia. I'm assuming someone died, since you keep calling?"

"*Hi, big brother, where are you right now?*" Amelia asked.

"I'm at Franklin's Coffee," I replied to Amelia's question. "On a date. But you knew that already."

"I knew you were on a date, I just didn't know where," Amelia clarified.

"What difference does it make?" I asked, growing increasingly annoyed. "Plan on joining us?"

"Uh, no ... but you need to come home, right now," Amelia insisted.

"What? Why?" I questioned, feeling frustrated by the sudden interruption.

"You just need to. I can't explain right now," she responded firmly.

"Amelia, I'm on a date. Why do I need to come home right now?" I pressed.

"It's super important. Trust me on this. Do you trust me?" Amelia asked.

"Of course, I trust you, Amelia—" I started to say.

"Then take your date home and get here," she interrupted.

I let out a sigh. "Okay. I hope this is important because I sure am irritated now."

"It is," she assured me.

"Be there soon," I said before ending the call. I looked over at Stephanie, who was still smiling at me.

"You have to go?" she asked, sounding understanding.

"Yeah, I'm so, so sorry. I don't know what's so goddamn important," I replied, frustrated by the situation.

"It's okay, I understand," Stephanie said sweetly. "Rain check?"

"Yes, of course," I replied, genuinely meaning it. I helped Stephanie out of her chair and assisted her with her coat. She didn't seem upset or disappointed that I was cutting the date short. We walked together to my SUV with her holding on to my arm for support.

I drove her home safely and walked her to the door. I wasn't sure what she was expecting at that moment, but I knew I didn't want to overstep any boundaries. I don't kiss anyone on the first date.

"I had a nice time, albeit short," Stephanie finally said, looking up at me.

"I did, too. I'm sorry again," I apologized sincerely.

"Go take care of your family," Stephanie whispered, kissing me on the cheek. "We have plenty of time." With that, she hurried into the house, waved, and closed the door.

* * *

It didn't take me long to arrive home, a mix of annoyance and relief swirling within me. I couldn't quite grasp what was happening with my emotions. As I stomped into the house from the garage, I found Amelia waiting for me in the foyer, her arms crossed as if I had just ruined *her* date.

"Okay, Amelia, what's the urgent matter?" I demanded, shedding my jacket and hanging it in the front closet.

"You were out with the wrong girl," Amelia stated, maintaining her crossed-arm stance as I turned to face her.

"What's that?"

"I mean exactly what I said. You were with the *wrong* girl," she reiterated.

"Are you kidding me? You called me home, claiming there was an '*emergency*,' and now you tell me I'm with the *wrong* girl?"

"That's right."

"Okay, Amelia, what's going on here? This is really underhanded of you, and it's not like you at all."

"Really? If there's one thing I prioritize in life, it's looking out for my bestie and my big brother. Who do you truly want to be with, Wil?"

My eyebrow raised in curiosity. "You already know I want to ask Emily out, but she just got out of a difficult relationship."

"I've hinted at it before, but now I'll be blunt: ASK EMILY TO HOMECOMING!"

I brought my jaw forward, trying to keep my frustration in check. "Amelia, I've seen her reject numerous guys, claiming she won't go to Homecoming because—"

"Because she wants YOU to ask her, STUPID!" Amelia interrupted, her voice filled with exasperation. "I swear, you can be clueless when it comes to women!"

"Teenagers," I corrected, a wry smile forming on my lips despite my annoyance.

"Whatever!" Amelia exclaimed, throwing her hands in the air. "I just saved you from making a huge mistake! We both know you wouldn't have gone to Homecoming with Stephanie, only with Emily."

"It was just a date. I don't even know why I went. I guess I'm just lonely."

"Yeah?" Amelia shifted her weight from one foot to the other. "Well, Emily knows about that date."

"That's impossible! I didn't even know about the date until tonight! Unless—"

"Unless I told her."

"Why would you do that?"

"I already told you. You were making a mistake," Amelia said firmly. "And honestly, it served as a wake-up call for Emily too. The fact that she encouraged you to go out with Stephanie was ridiculous. Tonight, she has been really upset with herself for doing that. She thinks she's ruined everything."

"She thinks she messed up everything … with *me*?"

"No, with fuckin' Santa Claus! Yes, with you!" Amelia said. "Tomorrow, you're going to prove her WRONG by asking her to Homecoming! Holy shit, so can the two of you stop doing stupid shit and just go to Homecoming with each other?"

"Well, I—"

"Wil! I don't want to hear another word, except that you'll ask her to Homecoming! By the time I reach lunch tomorrow, I expect to hear from Emily that YOU have asked HER to Homecoming!" Amelia's voice rang with determination. "Or I will go fourteenth century on your ass!"

The Choice

"**M**arkus," a voice called out, piercing through the depths of my dream. I recognized that angelic voice immediately, perhaps because Mary intended for me to.

I reluctantly peeled my eyes open, initially shielding them from Mary's radiant light. As my vision adjusted, I could see her clearly once more.

"You again!" I exclaimed, sitting up in bed with a jolt. "I have so many questions!"

"I'm not here to answer questions," Mary replied, her eyes and lips remaining still while her voice resonated clearly in my mind. "I'm here to inform you that there is a way for you to return home."

"There is? How? I want to go home!" Excitement coursed through me.

"I can create a portal for you to return home right now, if you wish. However, things will not remain the same for you, and there will be consequences in this life if you choose to leave," Mary explained.

"What will change? What are the consequences?" I inquired, my curiosity piqued.

"You would not return as *Markus Fales*, the thirty-year-old Combat Medic. Instead, you would be *William Fenwick*, the sixteen-year-old boy," Mary revealed.

"That's unbelievable! I'd be only a few years older than Katrina! I wouldn't even look like myself," I exclaimed, taken aback by the revelation.

"That is correct. Even when you find your beloved, Ella, she is unlikely to believe that you are who you claim to be. Even if she did, nothing would ever be the same for any of you, including your daughter," Mary confirmed.

"That's disheartening," I muttered, struggling to accept these new details.

"I have been in contact with someone from your world. I can bring her here for a brief time if you wish to speak with her," Mary offered.

"Ella?" I asked, my excitement returning.

Mary's arm rose with a deliberate and authoritative motion. As her hand ascended, the air before her began to quiver and ripple, reminiscent of the surface of a pond disturbed by a gentle breeze. This disturbance converged into a mesmerizing circular shape, hovering mere inches from her outstretched fingertips.

Within this otherworldly circle, the very fabric of reality appeared to warp and contort, crafting a vivid and enigmatic gateway to an alternate universe—my own. The portal emitted a soft, ethereal glow, casting an otherworldly radiance upon Mary's determined countenance.

Mary's command over this portal was unequivocal, a testament to her formidable mastery over the mystical rift that bridged worlds. With her arm extended, she wielded the gateway to the unknown, a living embodiment of the extraordinary forces under her control.

From this portal, a figure emerged—a young woman who took graceful steps through, crossing over into my new world, or rather, my bedroom. With her arrival, the portal dissolved into nothingness, leaving Mary and Sally in its wake.

"Sally?" I uttered in a hushed tone, scarcely able to believe what I had just witnessed. "Is that really you?"

She nodded, her gaze flitting over to Mary, then back to me. "Who are you?" Sally inquired, directing her question to me, then turned back to Mary, "You mentioned taking me to see Mark."

"And I have," Mary affirmed. "He stands before you."

Sally turned her attention toward me as I climbed out of bed. "This *can't* be him … this is a teenage boy," she remarked, her scrutiny focused on my altered appearance.

"Sally, it's me, Mark. Mark Fales," I replied with enthusiasm, overjoyed to see her. I reached out and embraced her tightly. At first, she didn't reciprocate, leaving me hanging in the hug, but after a moment, she finally embraced me in return.

"This is impossible," Sally murmured, her disbelief evident.

"We used to call you S-O-S," I reminded her, evoking memories of our shared experiences. "You gave me half a chocolate bar for my fiftieth birthday." I chuckled. "Well, you gave me half, and you polished off the other half."

"I don't ... I don't understand," Sally stammered, her eyes wide with astonishment.

"It's just as I explained. When Markus was killed in your world, he was transported here to live a new life while retaining all his memories from there," Mary reiterated.

"I have so many questions, Sally!" I exclaimed with enthusiasm. "How's Ella? Have you seen her? And Katrina? Are they doing well? Is the war still raging?"

"Oh my ... it's really *you*, isn't it?" Sally's realization dawned on her. "Doc!"

"Yes, it's me! Please, tell me about my family," I practically pleaded.

"Oh! Um ... they're all alive. I saw them not too long ago. They pulled me off the front lines after ... well, after you were shot," Sally replied.

"I can go back!" I exclaimed with excitement. "But I would have to return like this!"

Sally shook her head. "Mark ... things are still dire. The war persists, and despite our efforts, it shows no signs of ending soon."

"The war ... it's still ongoing?" I inquired, disbelief in my voice.

She nodded solemnly. "They're even recruiting senior citizens now for combat duty. After I get myself together, I'll have to return to the front lines again. Is there a war here too?"

"No! World War III never happened here! We're living in a time of peace!" I exclaimed.

"Then don't come back, Mark. Your family ... they've done their best to move forward. If you returned like this, I fear you would do more harm than good. I'd love to see you again, but I wouldn't wish our lives on my worst enemy," Sally said with a heavy heart.

"But ... I miss them!"

"And you'd never see them. You'd just return to war and possibly face death all over again," Sally reasoned.

"Well … maybe you could stay with us here! It's safe, there's no war!" I suggested eagerly.

"No, she must return," Mary asserted.

"But why? She's here now, just let her stay!" I implored Mary.

"She must return," Mary insisted.

"I have to go back, Mark. If this is your life now, I'd stay here and embrace it. This is a beautiful room with nice things. Enjoy it, you deserve it," Sally said, offering a warm smile, then chuckling, "I'll bet you've even had a chocolate milkshake here."

I turned to Mary, pressing further, "What are the consequences here, if I go back home?"

"The most apparent consequence would be that when you step into the portal I create for Sally to return, Wil Fenwick would disappear from this world. Your parents, your sisters, they would never see you again, never know what happened to you, and their hearts would break," Mary explained.

"That … that sounds devastating," I murmured. "What else?"

"Yes," Mary replied, her gaze finally meeting mine for the first time. "Because you wouldn't be here to prevent it, a terrible fate would befall someone you care about."

"What? What fate? What happens?" I urgently inquired. I couldn't let anything harm someone I cared about due to my actions. Somehow, I knew she meant Emily. "You mean Emily, don't you?"

"I cannot say," Mary responded, still locking eyes with me.

"Oh, for fuck's sake! Why always riddles? Why can't you just tell me?" I exclaimed, growing frustrated.

Mary gestured gracefully with her hands, and the portal reappeared. "If you wish to return home, step into the portal with Sally. Be aware, this is a *one-time opportunity* — I can never bring you back here, and this is your *sole* chance to go home."

Sally began to move towards the portal but paused to gaze at me. "It was wonderful to see you again, Mark. I'm overjoyed that you are alive and living in a world without war. Please stay here; it seems like they *need* you. Ella is looking after Katrina."

"I … have to stay …" I whispered, my voice filled with anguish. "I can't go with you, Sally."

"It's for the best," she said, offering me one final embrace. "You've always been like a father to me, and now I won't have to cry myself to sleep, night after night, worrying about you. You're safe here. You've done enough, and you deserve to have this life."

"Please, convey my love to my wife and Katrina!" I implored Sally.

"I promise I will," She replied with a reassuring smile, and she vanished into the portal just as it sealed shut.

I stood in silence for a moment, grappling with the weight of my decision, with what I had just surrendered.

"You heartless, merciless bitch!" I yelled at Mary, tears welling up in my eyes. "I can't believe you forced me into that choice!"

"I had to demonstrate to you that even with the option to leave, you would be unable to. Your destiny is bound to this place, and there is no way around it. Embrace it. You are needed here," Mary explained calmly.

In another flash of blinding white light, Mary disappeared, leaving me alone in my room with my swirling thoughts.

The Big Question

<<o—◇—o>>

With hardly a wink of sleep, I wearily extracted myself from the clutches of my bed, Mary's astonishing display still fresh in my thoughts. The sight of Sally, her presence reassuringly alive and temporarily removed from the harrowing front lines of war, had offered me some comfort. Yet, the disheartening news of the ongoing conflict gnawed at my sense of hope.

Amidst the tumultuous swirl of emotions, a small but comforting refuge was the knowledge that my family remained unharmed, under Ella's diligent care. As I contemplated the daunting task of shelving these troubling thoughts and soldiering on with the day, I couldn't help but acknowledge the new reality that had been thrust upon me.

The weight of my responsibilities and the reality of my existence loomed heavily, and I grappled with the challenge of compartmentalizing it all and adopting a semblance of normalcy. There was no choice but to carry on with the day's demands, for this was the life fate had thrust upon me, a life that I had to accept, willingly or not. The first order of business to deal with was that I had my hockey game today, which meant I had to dress up. I decided to change things up a bit and added a gray vest to my outfit. But my nerves weren't because of the game this time; it was because I planned to ask Emily to Homecoming. I had no specific plan in mind for when or how to ask her, but I knew it had to be today. A few girls had already asked me to Homecoming, but I politely declined all of them. They were understanding about it, and I felt a pang of guilt for turning them down. However, my heart was set on going with Emily or not going at all. There was just something about her that drew me in. She was undeniably beautiful, the most stunning girl in the school, judging by the number of guys vying for her attention. But it was more than that. Her kindness was genuine, she was intelligent, and she had a great sense of humor.

*　*　*

Stephanie caught up with me in the hallway, asking if everything was okay at home. I assured her that everything was fine now and that it had been taken care of. She was dressed in jeans, wearing a tight-fitting light blue top, and had her hair pulled back in a ponytail. "Do you think we could go out again?" Stephanie asked me, looking hopeful. "I had a really nice time."

"I'm not sure, Stephanie," I replied, feeling overwhelmed by the internal conflict I was grappling with. "There's a lot happening in my life right now, and I'm trying to sort through it."

Disappointment etched across Stephanie's face as she clutched her folders tightly. "Is there someone else you'd rather be with?" she asked, her voice tinged with uncertainty.

I took a deep breath, exhaling slowly before attempting to explain. "Stephanie," I began, searching for the right words.

To my surprise, a small smile curved on Stephanie's lips. She held herself with grace and understanding. "It's okay, Wil," she reassured me. "I've always been attuned to the nuances of romance, thanks to my love for novels. I have a feeling I know who it is, and if it's true, she's a really lucky girl."

Her perceptiveness struck me, and I struggled to find a response. "I … I don't even know what to say," I stammered, feeling a mix of guilt and confusion.

Stephanie's warmth continued to shine through as she gently spoke, "You don't have to say anything, cutie. If things don't work out and I haven't found my *knight* yet, perhaps our paths will cross again."

Leaning in, Stephanie planted a tender kiss on my cheek, expressing her appreciation. "Thanks for the coffee," she said with genuine affection. "You're truly a sweet guy and a gentleman."

With those words, Stephanie turned and walked away, blending into the bustling hallway filled with students. I couldn't help but feel a pang of regret and self-criticism. Amelia had been right all along—I was fumbling my way through understanding relationships in high school, feeling like a complete fool. Still, these high school issues I was currently worried about, paled in comparison to the war I chose to leave behind. Mary's words echoed in my mind, that I was needed here, or I would miss an event that could hurt Emily. I had no idea what the event was, or even to what degree of hurt she had meant.

I took my seat in Miss Hemming's class, slouching and feeling my nerves take hold. The pencil in my hand became my fidgeting companion as I anxiously awaited the opportunity to ask Emily to Homecoming. As my classmates trickled into the room, I scanned the crowd, but Emily was nowhere to be seen. The idea of asking her in front of everyone suddenly felt overwhelming, and a wave of shyness washed over me. I didn't want to risk being rejected and embarrassed in front of my peers. It was a typical teenage concern, but it seemed to have taken hold of me. It was strange how I could be so outgoing as an adult, yet falter in these moments of vulnerability.

The sound of Emily's voice drifted in from the hallway, and I strained to listen. I caught a glimpse of her, saying, "I'm really sorry" to someone. Shortly after, she entered the classroom accompanied by a guy I didn't recognize. She was radiating beauty in her cheerleader outfit. Her hair flowed freely, but she had adorned it with a bow in green, yellow, and white, matching the colors of the school's team. The dark green uniform with its yellow trim and hints of white suited her perfectly. A cheerleading turtleneck in green and gold, accentuated with white trim, added a touch of elegance. The cheer skirt complemented the rest of her uniform. Her bruises, if any remained, were skillfully concealed by makeup or had faded significantly. Nevertheless, she exuded a breathtaking beauty that captivated my attention.

"You shouldn't miss Homecoming because of that jerk," the guy said as Emily took her seat.

Emily quickly sat down, placing her backpack on the floor. "I'm really sorry," she replied. "Please just respect my decision."

"I can make you forget all about Greg," he insisted. "I promise we'll have a good time."

"I already gave you my answer. I don't know why you keep pressuring me. No means no."

He seemed taken aback. "You don't have to be mean about it. Do you know how hard it was for me to even ask you?"

Emily took a deep breath. "I'm sorry, I'm not trying to be mean. I understand it's nerve-wracking for you, but I've been kind with my responses. When I said I wasn't going, that was my way of declining. Then you asked me again, and I was kind with my second response, which was also *no*. Now, this is the third time, and I feel like you're pressuring me into going with you. My answer isn't going to change. *No, thank you.*" The guy crossed his arms and stood there, staring at her. "You're making me nervous now," Emily pleaded. "Please, just go."

The guy went to touch Emily, but she yanked away quickly, looking scared. He backed away, quickly, and finally, he threw his hands up in frustration and stormed off, muttering, "Whatever."

I felt a surge of nervousness as Emily turned towards me, sitting sideways in her desk and crossing her legs. "Hi, Wil!" she greeted cheerfully, seemingly undeterred by the scene that had just unfolded in front of the entire class.

"Are you okay?" I asked, concerned.

She nodded. "I feel bad when I have to turn people down, I really do. I know they're really nervous, and nobody wants to be embarrassed … but when they persist, it starts to make *me* nervous. It reminds me of things Greg would do."

"I'm really sorry," was all I could offer in response.

Changing the subject, she asked with a smile, "What did you think of our practice yesterday?"

"It was great! You're a flyer!" I replied. Emily beamed, showing her toothy grin.

"That's right, I am! So, you know about cheerleading?"

"I know a little something about it," I said.

"That's impressive! Most people think we just stand on the sidelines for football and basketball, looking bored."

"No, no. I know about your competitions. They can be brutal. Cheerleading is as much a sport as any other."

"Wow! Acknowledging cheerleading as a sport too! I had no idea you were such a fan," Emily said excitedly. "Are you going to the football game tonight? You could watch us perform!"

I frowned. "I wish I could, but I have a game this evening."

"Ohhh, that's right. Duh. You're all dressed up today ... more so than usual. Very handsome, I might add!" She lowered her gaze a moment before looking back at me, "I've heard a lot of girls asked you to Homecoming."

I gave her a weak smile, not wanting to delve into the topic at the moment. "Yeah, well—"

"And you went on a date with Stephanie last night, too?" she interrupted.

"Uh, yeah ... about that—" I began.

"I'm sorry, Wil. I didn't mean to embarrass you," she said softly, sensing my discomfort. "It's none of my business."

"Not embarrassed," I replied coolly, forcing a laugh. "It was a rather short date."

"Short?" she questioned.

"Yeah. Amelia called during the date and told me to come home for some emergency."

Emily giggled. "An emergency, huh?"

I nodded. "It's a long story." I had a feeling that Emily might have known more about that "emergency" than I did. But my main concern at the moment was how and when I would be able to ask Emily to Homecoming, without feeling embarrassed. I had to wait for a time when there were fewer people around, just in case ... I mean, if she said *no*, then we'd have to sit next to each other for the rest of class, which would be super awkward. I had witnessed how stressed out she was when that guy just asked her out. All I knew was, Amelia had better be right about this. I didn't even want to think about it right now, honestly.

Emily and I engaged in casual conversation about the upcoming football game and my hockey game as we waited for class to start. She had brought some new candy, which she happily shared with me. Her arm rested on my desk for most of the class, causing our hands to brush against each other several times. Occasionally, I would catch her watching me while I took notes, and she didn't look away when our eyes met.

After the class ended, we walked together into the hallway, heading towards Emily's science class. Our hips occasionally brushed against each other as we walked, sending a tingle down my spine. I couldn't help but wonder if she was doing it intentionally. My mind was filled with countless scenarios on how I was going to make this work. Amelia had already told me that Emily wanted to go with me, so what was the problem?

"Earth to Wil ..." Emily's voice brought me back to reality. "Are you okay? You seem worried. Is it because of your game?"

We paused outside her classroom, and I knew it was now or never. "Uhhhh ..." I struggled to find the right words, my nerves getting the best of me. I must have appeared a mess in front of her.

Emily placed her hand on my forearm, lightly gripping it, which was unusual for her, "This isn't about your game. You're never this nervous. What is it, Wil? Did I do something wrong? Was it your date last night?"

"No! Emily, no," I hurriedly assured her. "I think you're great!"

"Really?" Her eyes searched mine, searching for the truth.

"I do! Ummm ... errr ... soooo ..." I stammered, taking a deep breath and trying to compose myself. "I wanted to know if you would like to go to Homecoming with me. You're the only girl I want to go with. I know you said you didn't want to go, but—"

"Yes!" Emily exclaimed, cutting me off with the brightest smile I had ever seen. "Yes! I'd love to go to Homecoming with you!" She bounced up and down a little, biting her lower lip in excitement before hugging me tightly.

"What? Really?" I asked, surprised and relieved, returning her embrace and taking in a deep breath.

Emily giggled. "Yes, really! I've been hoping you would ask. I just didn't want to hurt the other guys' feelings. Didn't Amelia mention it to you?"

"She did, but I guess I'm just an idiot. I thought she was assuming ..." I raised my hands in frustration. "Like I said, I'm an idiot."

"You're not an idiot," she said softly. "I'm really looking forward to going with you! What about Stephanie, though?"

"What about her? She's a nice girl, but she's not you," I replied, exhaling and feeling a wave of relief wash over me.

Emily looked at me with a mixture of surprise and tenderness. "But you don't even know me," she insisted. "How can you be so sure you wouldn't enjoy Homecoming more with Stephanie?"

I was taken aback by her question. "Are you trying to get me to go with Stephanie?" I asked, trying to understand her intentions. I knew she had self confidence issues, most girls who are abused by their boyfriends go through a lot of self-doubt and feelings of worthlessness.

"No!" Emily quickly clarified, "That's not what I'm saying at all." She sighed and continued, "Sometimes, I feel so stupid. I want to go with you. I just wanted to know why you picked me. I was so *mean* to you."

I didn't have a specific answer for her question. I had always felt a strong connection to Emily, even though we hadn't known each other for long. The truth was, I felt the same way when I was near her, as I had around Ella. "When I first saw you, I was captivated by your beauty," I confessed. "Your eyes, the bluest of blue, held a certain allure that I couldn't resist. Every time you looked at me, I couldn't help but stare. I was mesmerized. I thought you were the most beautiful girl in the entire school. And when you spoke, your voice sounded like that of an angel—soft, sweet, and with a hint of your British accent. You showed me kindness, especially on our first day together. I know you think you were mean to me, but we've already discussed that. I understand why. The truth is, I've wanted to ask you to Homecoming for a long time. I only went out with Stephanie because I thought you didn't want to date anyone after everything with Greg. I felt lonely."

Emily watched me intently as I poured my heart out to her. "I've never heard anything like that before," she murmured, her eyes filled with warmth. "That's the sweetest thing I've ever heard! I didn't expect that at all. And you really didn't want to go to Homecoming unless it was with me?" She pouted playfully. "Wil, that is so cute! I'm sorry for sending the wrong signals. I would go out with you, anywhere, anytime."

I smiled at her response, feeling a surge of happiness. "Why did you only want to go with me?" I asked, genuinely curious.

Emily blushed, caught off guard by my question. Her cheeks turned a rosy shade as she cleared her throat. "I've mentioned it before, but you've changed so much. You were always handsome, but now you're incredibly attractive. Your confidence in the way you carry yourself, the way you speak, and your kindness towards others has captivated me. You've become more mature, intelligent, and wise. Everything about you intrigues me, but what impresses me the most is when you stand up for me, even if it puts you in danger."

Her words filled me with warmth and gratitude. "Thank you for saying that. It means a lot."

"You see?" Emily continued, a smile dancing on her lips. "That's what I mean. Not many guys would respond like you just did. Most would just say, 'Thanks, that's nice.'" I shrugged, not quite knowing how to respond to such praise. "Can I see your phone for a moment?" Emily asked, extending her hand towards me.

"Uh … sure." I reached into my pocket, retrieving my phone and handing it to her.

Taking my phone, she giggled a moment, then handed it back. "You have to punch in your code."

"Oh, right!" I punched in my four-digit code and handed it back to her.

She swiftly typed on the screen, her smile never fading. I could hear the faint vibration of a phone coming from her purse as she pressed the enter button. "I added my number to your phone," she said sweetly, handing it back to me. "I hope you won't play the *playing it cool* game and wait a few days to call or text me."

"I'm not like that," I assured her. "And please don't think I'm a loser if I reach out to you today."

Emily laughed, her eyes sparkling with joy. "You're funny, Wil! I would never think that. In fact, I would love it." She glanced at the clock on the wall. "You should hurry to class before you're late. Talk to you soon?"

"Yes, absolutely!" I replied eagerly.

"Bye, Wil." Emily waved goodbye before disappearing into her classroom.

I spun on my heel, a surge of excitement coursing through me.

She said yes!

I hadn't taken more than two steps towards the classroom when Rachel appeared in front of me.

"Hi, Wil," she greeted me. "You look nice today."

"Oh, hey, Rachel," I replied, my tone neutral. "Thank you."

"I've been looking all over for you," she said, her voice slightly hesitant.

I wasn't sure what to expect from this encounter. "What's up?" I asked, keeping my response brief.

"I'll get straight to the point," Rachel said, shifting her weight to her other leg. "I know we have a history together, which you apparently don't remember, but I believe we can work through things. I'd like us to go to Homecoming together … as a couple."

I was taken aback, trying to process her request. My ex-girlfriend, whom I had no recollection of, and whom my sisters didn't like, just asked me to Homecoming? "Homecoming?" I repeated, seeking clarification.

"Yeah, you know … the football game, dancing, dresses, suits … Homecoming," she explained.

"It's nice of you to ask, but I'm already going to Homecoming with someone," I said, surprising Rachel.

"What? WHO are you going with?" she demanded, her tone filled with anger.

"Emily DuBrie," I stated bluntly.

"Emily?" Rachel exclaimed, her upset evident as she glanced briefly behind me before locking eyes with me. She stormed off without another word.

I turned towards Emily's classroom and saw her standing there, arms crossed over her chest, wearing a pleasant smile. I shrugged at her, reciprocating the smile, before quickly making my way to class.

*　　*　　*

The remainder of the day proved arduous as my mind became consumed with thoughts of the upcoming Homecoming with Emily, posing a considerable challenge to maintain focus on my classes. Although tempted to reach out to her immediately, I restrained myself, mindful of not interrupting her during school hours.

At lunchtime, I joined my hockey team mates at our customary table. As anticipated, Henry promptly inquired about Emily's response, leaving no room for delay.

"She said *yes*?" Henry eagerly inquired.

"She did," I replied, trying to maintain a semblance of coolness, but my smile couldn't be contained.

"That's great, brother!" Henry exclaimed, and the rest of the group chimed in with congratulations. "Now I just have to ask out Beth, maybe after our game."

"Will there be enough time?" I questioned, slightly concerned.

"Yeah, man, our games start before the football game, so we should be good," Henry reassured me.

"Well, I hope you're right," I replied.

"Makes two of us, brother."

From our vantage point at the table, I caught sight of Amelia, Beth, Penny, Nikki, and Emily occupying their customary place among the cheerleaders. A radiant smile adorned Emily's face as she waved in my direction. Amelia, exuding her usual enthusiasm, erupted into applause and jubilantly exclaimed, "Congratulations, big brother! It's about time!"

"Incredible, man! That was unbelievable," Henry commented with a chuckle. "You've got the whole cafeteria's attention now."

"Us, Henry. They're watching *us*," I corrected him, feeling a mix of embarrassment and excitement. I briefly contemplated sliding under the table to hide, but I remained in my seat. Emily playfully swatted at Amelia's hand, looking mortified as their table erupted into laughter. It seemed like they were teasing her good-naturedly.

As lunch drew to a close, Emily departed alongside the other cheerleaders, leaving me to navigate the remainder of the day with a persistent yearning for her presence, regardless of the topic at hand.

* * *

Finally, the last class of the day arrived, and I settled into my seat, eagerly anticipating Emily's arrival. A few moments later, she entered the room, giving me a radiant smile. "Hello, handsome!" she warmly greeted me.

"Hi, Emily!" I couldn't help but wear a silly grin, feeling like a complete goofball, all giddy inside.

As Mr. Stuart began the class, I found myself completely disinterested in his lecture. My attention was solely on Emily, and it seemed like she was keeping an eye on me too, though she had to turn her head to do so. At one point, I saw Emily pass a folded-up piece of paper to the girl sitting on her right. She leaned in and whispered something to her, gesturing subtly towards me. The girl nodded and reached over to hand me the note. I glanced back at Emily, and she was smiling at me before quickly redirecting her attention back to the teacher. With my folder held at an angle to hide my actions from Mr. Stuart, I carefully opened it and discovered a note inside. It was written in the most girly handwriting imaginable. The note read: *I am so excited to go to Homecoming with you! I was scared you would never ask me.*

I couldn't help but smile, and when Emily looked over to gauge my reaction, she smiled back. *I'm excited too. You could have asked me!* I wrote in response. Folding the note back up, I leaned over and tapped the girl on the shoulder, the one who had passed me the note. She smiled at me and took the note, tapping Emily on the shoulder and smoothly handing it to her. She quickly checked if the teacher was watching, but the coast was clear. She opened the note, read what I had written, and immediately scribbled something in response. Folding it back up, she handed it to the girl, who promptly passed it back to me.

"What's your name?" I whispered to the girl.

"Kim," she replied, her voice accompanied by a slight, shy smile.

"Thank you for doing this for us," I expressed my gratitude.

"It's no problem at all," Kim reassured me with a friendly tone.

I carefully read the note, still hiding it within my folder: *I'm more of a traditional type of gal. You know, the boy has to ask the girl. Can we walk together after class?*

I like "traditional" and I agree. Sure, we can walk together. I like that, I wrote back, a smile spreading across my face.

Passing the note back to Kim, she then handed it to Emily. Emily glanced over at me, nodding before tucking the note into one of her folders. When class ended, Emily met me in the hallway.

"I haven't passed notes in forever." Emily giggled. "I forgot how fun it was. It's like there's a danger aspect to it."

"I may have passed notes ... once?" I said, trying to be a bit guarded in my response. It was true that I had only passed notes once before, back in high school.

"Really? It can be kinda scary ... you know, if you get caught, and the teacher makes you read it out loud in front of the entire class."

I chuckled. "Sounds like you're speaking from experience."

Emily laughed too, making a funny face. "Oh, I am!"

"It's nice to see you laugh and smile," I remarked.

A slight blush graced Emily's face, lending her an endearing charm. "Well, you're the reason it's happening. Without you, I can only imagine I'd be in a dreadful state right now," she confessed as we began making our way towards the gym.

After a brief moment of contemplation, I finally gathered the courage to voice my thoughts. "You're not accompanying me to Homecoming solely because of what I did, right?" I inquired.

"No!" she quickly responded. "Not at all. I'm going with you because I quite like you, Wil."

"I'm glad. I like you too." We strolled together in harmony, relishing a few serene moments of silence. As we continued our path toward the gym, I mustered the courage to break the quietude. "I have a question for you," I finally ventured.

"Sure, shoot," Emily replied, curious to hear my question.

"Would you go out with me on a date … a casual date, so we can talk, spend some time together? Homecoming seems so far away."

I felt a rush of anticipation as Emily's smile widened, indicating her positive response to my proposal. "I'd absolutely love to!" she exclaimed, her enthusiasm evident in her voice.

Encouraged by her answer, I proceeded to ask, "Are you busy on Saturday?"

Emily's eyes lit up with excitement as she replied, "I am, but only because I'll be going out with you." My heart skipped a beat, and a wave of joy washed over me. It was settled—we had plans for a casual date on Saturday, and I couldn't contain my excitement for the time we would spend together.

* * *

I stumbled upon Emily's contact entry on my phone, where she had saved her number as "Emily DuBrie :)", accompanied by a cheerful smiley face and a heart. Before my game, I summoned the courage to compose a text message and send it her way. The anticipation during the wait for her response felt like an eternity, but when her message eventually appeared, it proved to be worth every second. *I'm so happy you reached out! Best of luck with your game today. I'll be thinking about you the entire time!* Her words enveloped me in a comforting embrace, filled with warmth and unwavering support.

During the thirty-five-minute trip to Annapolis, Emily and I indulged in a spirited exchange of text messages, immersing ourselves in lively conversation. Our discussions revolved around our eagerly anticipated upcoming date, and after careful deliberation, we agreed on a rendezvous time of 2:30 p.m. The realization dawned upon me that I would have the opportunity to meet her parents, an experience that had long been distant in my memory.

Curiosity piqued, Emily sought clarification on the dress code for our outing. I promptly responded with "casual," emphasizing the paramount importance of her comfort. In turn, she shared her intention to wear a dress or skirt, igniting vivid images in my mind of her breathtaking beauty on that day.

The game itself was intense and highly competitive. Annapolis boasted a formidable lineup, but we emerged victorious with a score of seven to two. I played a crucial role, scoring four goals and providing three assists, while Henry and Steve also contributed with a goal each.

Back in Andover, the varsity football team was playing at home, coinciding with Henry's plan to ask Beth out. Initially distraught, he found cheer in the fact that the football game was still ongoing as our bus approached. He would have the opportunity to ask her afterward. I tried to boost his confidence with a pep talk, but his nerves were evident. We were aware that Beth had other potential suitors, and none of us knew if she had accepted any of them.

After getting off the bus, and dropping our gear off at the ice arena, we were greeted by the resounding cheers of the crowd and the spirited chants of the cheerleaders. While spectators typically had to pay for admission, athletes were granted free entry. Moreover, as the game was nearing its end, with the third quarter already underway, the officials were more lenient.

Nestled within the heart of Andover High School's vibrant campus, the Football Stadium stood as a proud testament to the school's sporting legacy. It was capable of accommodating up to 5,000 spirited fans, this stadium is a true symbol of athletic enthusiasm and community unity.

A meticulously maintained eight-lane, all-weather urethane track surrounds the expanse of the field, providing a sleek contrast to the lush, sprawling real grass that forms the stage for thrilling competitions. Along one side of the field, a fence encloses the domain, embracing a colossal ticket booth area that hums with anticipation on game days. Two entrances, strategically placed, beckon fans into the exhilarating world of high school football, while on the opposing side, a generous concession area thrives, flanked by a sturdy building housing four locker rooms catering to football, lacrosse, soccer, and baseball players. By the entrance gates, twelve Maryland-shaped monuments stood, commemorating the 3A Maryland State Championships. Four for football, five for lacrosse, and three for soccer. They proudly displayed the years of victory with meticulously etched inscriptions, bearing the names of the players, coaches, and staff who contributed to the successes. Dominating each flank of the field, two grand stands rise majestically, providing seating for the spirited spectators. The home side, marked by a towering multi-story sports booth, offers an elevated vantage point for the announcer, videographer, and media personnel to capture every electrifying moment.

Positioned with commanding presence at the end zone near the bustling concession stands, an immense scoreboard commands attention. With its colossal frame, it features an instant replay video screen that relives the most breathtaking plays, while adjacent sections proudly display scores and an out-of-town scoreboard, keeping the crowd engaged throughout the event.

Crisp white lines stretch across the verdant field, punctuated by yard markers every ten yards, in perfect alignment with the hallowed traditions of football. However, it is the heart of the field that truly captivates—emblazoned with the resplendent ANDOVER ARCHERS Logo, it radiates the indomitable spirit of the school.

In harmonious synergy with the fervent student body, the spirited cheerleaders take their place in front of the exuberant student section, positioned just to the right when facing the stands. Their lively performances and infectious energy infuse the atmosphere with a palpable sense of unity and pride, making Andover High School Football Stadium an iconic stage where dreams are chased, victories celebrated, and memories etched into the annals of time.

As we neared the bleachers, the scoreboard displayed the score: Andover 28, Annapolis 17. I positioned myself near the fence, to the right of the bleachers, to get a close view of the track where the cheerleaders were performing. Among them, Emily stood out as the flyer in the closest stunt group to me. Her right foot was lifted by the side base and the main base, with assistance from the back spot. Meanwhile, she extended her left leg upward, holding it with her right hand. Her left arm stretched out horizontally, with only her index and middle fingers extended—a challenging pose known as the Bow and Arrow.

With a mischievous wink, she maintained the finger position while turning to point at the crowd, mimicking a gun motion. Moments later, they called for dismount, and she was caught safely by the group. Excitement filled the air as the cheerleaders jumped up and down, grabbing their pom-poms and cheering for the football team. Standing beside me at the fence was Henry, with Steve standing next to him. The cheer coach instructed the girls to take a break and get a drink of water, prompting them to walk over to the fence where their matching backpacks were neatly lined up.

Emily spotted me, and a wide grin lit up her face. She quickly made her way over to where I stood. "Wil, you're here!" She exclaimed, her accent adding a charm to her words. She wrapped her arms around my neck, catching me off guard, but I gladly embraced her. Her warmth and softness were comforting, and her intoxicating perfume filled my senses. After a moment, she pulled back slightly. "How was your game? Did you win?"

Still feeling the impact of her hug, I smiled. "Yes, we won. seven to two."

"Did you score?" she asked, her smile growing wider.

"I scored when you said you would go to Homecoming with me," I joked.

She laughed. "Aww … you're so adorable." Her smirk appeared as her eyes focused on me, and she tilted her head. "I meant in the hockey game."

I nodded. "Four goals, three assists, seven points."

"He's a beast!" Henry chimed in, chuckling, as he briefly put his arm around me for a playful shake.

"I just have an amazing team. They make me look good," I added modestly.

"That's very humble of you," Emily remarked.

"He's a great guy," Henry interjected. "Easily the best player we have."

"It certainly sounds like it," Emily replied.

"No, no," I protested, feeling slightly embarrassed. "We simply have a very talented team."

The other cheerleaders began heading back to the benches, ready to cheer. Emily glanced at them and then turned her attention back to me. "I have to go now," she said with a pouty face, pushing out her lower lip. "Can you meet me after the game?"

"Of course, I will," I assured her.

"Great!" She beamed. "See you soon!"

Emily started to walk back to her team, but before she could get too far, I called out to her. "Emily! Wait!" I yelled, a sense of urgency in my voice.

She turned back with a concerned expression and quickly returned to me. "What's wrong?" she asked.

"Did Beth find a date for Homecoming?"

"You're going with me, mister," she said, playfully nudging my arm.

"I know, but I have a friend who wants to ask her, and I want to save him from any embarrassment," I explained.

Emily glanced at Henry with a mischievous smile before returning her gaze to me. "Nope, she hasn't accepted any offers yet. Whoever your *friend* is, he should hurry, though," she said, winking at me and briefly gripping my hand before jogging back to her team.

I turned to Henry, who looked utterly mortified. "There you go, brother," I said, chuckling. "Ask her after the game."

"Bro ... she totally knows it's me," Henry replied, his nerves evident in his voice.

"So what?" I shrugged. "It's not like Beth won't find out by the end of the game anyway."

"I suppose that's true. Still, I'm really nervous."

"I don't think you have any reason to be."

"Dude, you were nervous as hell to ask Emily, and your sister practically told you she would go with you."

"True dat." I grinned, patting him on the back for reassurance.

Our football team ended up winning the game, 31-20. Henry paced anxiously for most of the game, while I tried my best to keep him calm as we watched Emily perform her incredible stunts. Her backflips, back tucks, cartwheels, and flips were all mesmerizing. Every time she reached the top of her stunt, her eyes would briefly meet mine. She made my heart race, and I felt the pleasant butterflies in my stomach. Watching her perform was thrilling, but being near her was even better. It was hard to put into words—she was just so easy to talk to, and I admired everything about her.

With the game now over, all the cheerleaders gathered near where we stood. Emily swiftly grabbed her bag and made her way towards the opening in the fence, standing right in front of me.

"It's cold!" Emily exclaimed, a smile on her face as she rubbed her upper arms.

"I'll carry that for you," I offered, gesturing to her backpack.

"That's very kind of you, Wil. Thank you," she replied, handing me her backpack.

I took off my school jacket, a forest green one with gold sleeves, though it didn't have a varsity letter yet. Moving behind Emily, I helped her put it on.

"No, you'll get cold!" she protested.

"I like the cold," I retorted.

Emily nodded and slid her arms into the jacket's sleeves. "Thank you, you're so sweet."

With her backpack casually draped over my shoulder, we embarked on our journey towards the school, followed by the others. As we strolled side by side, a newfound closeness enveloped us. as our arms would occasionally brush against one another.

"Are you warm?" I asked, gazing into her eyes.

"I'm getting there," she replied, holding my gaze and smiling.

In an instant, the sound of someone clearing their throat echoed behind me. "Beth, can I have a word with you?" Henry's voice cut through the air. Both Emily and I turned our attention towards him. It seemed that the long-awaited moment had arrived—Henry was finally going to talk to Beth. "In private?" Henry added, emphasizing the need for a secluded conversation.

Beth responded with a shy smile and a nod. "Sure," she agreed. I couldn't help but feel a surge of hope for Henry as they departed, venturing off as a pair, their conversation set apart from the rest of our group. Amelia and Steve continued their lively discussion as they walked, while Penny trailed closely behind Amelia, engaged in a spirited conversation with Nikki.

"It appears that everyone is finding their own connections," Emily astutely remarked. Her concern for my comfort prompted her to delicately graze her left hand against mine.

A sudden curiosity welled up within me, and I couldn't help but ask, "Are you nervous?"

A hint of self-awareness colored her response. "Is it really that obvious?" she replied, a touch of playful vulnerability in her tone.

"Well, I've actually noticed that your accent becomes more pronounced, almost slipping through, when you're feeling something other than happy, whether it's nervousness or being upset. And I have to confess, I absolutely love your accent," I openly admitted.

Emily responded with a delightful giggle. "You caught on to that, huh?" she playfully remarked, giving me a wink. "Yeah, when I'm feeling upset or nervous, it tends to come out a bit more. I'm so glad you appreciate it. Greg, on the other hand, despised it! He used to claim it made me sound ignorant. So, whenever I was around him, I would deliberately speak with my American accent."

"LOVE it!" I quickly corrected her, emphasizing my enthusiasm. "Speak with whatever accent you want, Emily!" I said as we walked, and my hand once again brushed up against hers. The others were behind us, but were engaged in their own conversations.

With an air of excitement, Emily exclaimed, "Oh, I can even do an American Southern accent! I enjoy practicing different accents just for fun."

"Alright, let's hear it," I said, letting out a playful chuckle.

Emily cleared her throat a few times, building up anticipation, and then proceeded to deliver her rendition in an exaggerated American Southern accent, dramatically declaring, "Ah'm tahrd, ah caint wawk the dawg." It was the most over-the-top accent I had ever heard, and I couldn't hold back my amusement. I erupted into boisterous, uncontrollable laughter, and Emily joined in, our laughter filling the air. It took us a while to regain our composure, our laughter turning into the kind that starts to hurt after a while.

"Oh my goodness, you are absolutely precious!" I exclaimed, unable to contain my delight. "Do it again!"

Emily's grin widened, and she cleared her throat once more, preparing for another amusing display. "Mama, ah caint find mah draws!" she exclaimed, fully embracing the comedic Southern accent. The hilarity overwhelmed me once again, causing me to burst into laughter, joined by Emily. Our uproarious outbursts attracted the attention of the others, who turned to look at us. Tears streamed down my face as I struggled to regain control amidst the uncontrollable laughter that made it difficult to breathe. After what felt like an eternity, I finally managed to compose myself.

"Emily, that was absolutely incredible!" I exclaimed, still wiping away the tears from my eyes. "I can't believe that came from you!"

She teased, "I can try speaking in that accent all the time if you want."

"No, no. Your natural English accent is truly beautiful," I assured her. "But, oh my god, I haven't laughed like that in such a long time."

Emily giggled once more, and we walked together in silence for a brief moment. Sensing her mood, I asked, "Are your nerves settled now? You have no reason to be nervous around me."

"I'm sure I'll still feel a little nervous for a while. Aren't you?" she responded.

"A little. I get those good kind of butterflies whenever we're together. Is that too cheesy?" I wondered aloud.

"No, it's not cheesy at all! It's incredibly sweet," Emily reassured me as we arrived at the school's entrance. She turned to face me as I lowered my arm to my side. The rest of our friends had already entered the school building, leaving us alone in that moment. "I've only had one real boyfriend in my entire life, and he wasn't very kind to me. He's nothing like you, so all of this," she continued, gesturing with her hands, "is new to me."

"What's new to you?" I inquired, genuinely curious.

"All the little things like putting your coat on me, carrying my bag, treating me with such care and respect. It means a lot. And the way you asked me to Homecoming, and then on a date, was incredibly cute. The way you talk to me, the way you look at me … it's all so overwhelming, but in the best possible way. I just want to make sure I don't mess it up," Emily confessed, her voice filled with genuine appreciation.

"You can't mess it up, Emily. I really like you," I responded sincerely. "I genuinely enjoy every moment spent with you, which is why I'm thrilled that we're going out tomorrow evening."

Emily's face lit up with excitement, her smile widening. "I love that you're not trying to play it cool. It's something new and refreshing. I can't quite put my finger on it, but I really like it. I have this incredible feeling about us, about you." Extending my arm towards her, she gladly accepted it, her smile never fading, as we walked into the school together, embracing the promising path ahead.

It's Always Something

<img referring to decorative divider>

L
ater that night, I lay in bed, my mind occupied with thoughts of the upcoming date with Emily. As I began to envision the details of our date, my thoughts involuntarily drifted back to a different time and a different life—a life where my wife, Ella, held a special place in my heart.

In that previous existence, before the shadows of war had descended upon us, our paths had crossed through mutual friends. Ella was a member of the Navy, while I pursued my career as a Systems Engineer. The memories of those initial encounters with her were etched vividly in my mind, a tableau of excitement and anticipation.

I vividly recalled the sensation of exhilaration and the fluttering butterflies in my stomach that accompanied our first meeting. The mere thought of her had been enough to set my heart racing, and those moments had felt almost surreal in their intensity.

The memory was a cherished one, etched deeply into my heart. It was a crisp autumn evening, with the leaves adorned in hues of red and gold, gently swaying in the cool breeze. I had been nervous, almost jittery, as I awaited her arrival. Ella and I were introduced, virtually, by mutual friends.. This was our first official date.

She walked through the café's entrance, her smile was radiant. Her presence had a way of brightening even the dullest of days. She was a vision of grace and elegance, her striking features framed by her long, flowing brown hair. Her captivating blue eyes were like tranquil pools of sapphire, reflecting the world with a depth and clarity that drew people in.

On that special day, she wore a resplendent emerald green dress that complemented her complexion and highlighted her natural beauty. The dress was a testament to her impeccable taste, hugging her slender figure with an air of sophistication and charm. Its rich, deep hue seemed to mimic the lush shades of a forest on a sunlit day, adding a touch of enchantment to her presence.

As she moved, her dress swayed gently, the fabric whispering secrets of elegance and refinement. The color brought out the subtle undertones in her eyes, making them appear even more enchanting, like two precious gems set against a backdrop of lush greenery.

That night, we had shared a simple meal, but the conversation flowed effortlessly, as if we had been talking this way for years. Her laughter was like music, filling the air with joy and warmth. We discussed our dreams, our past adventures, and the little quirks that made us who we were.

As the evening wore on, we decided to take a leisurely stroll through the nearby park. The moon hung low in the sky, casting a gentle glow over the world around us. The park was quiet, and the only sounds were the rustling of leaves and our hushed voices.

We found a secluded bench beneath an ancient oak tree, and there, we shared some of our most intimate thoughts. It was a perfect evening.

And then, as we sat there, bathed in the soft moonlight, Ella reached for my hand. It was a simple gesture, but it spoke volumes. In that touch, I felt a connection, a bond that would grow stronger with each passing day.

That night, as we said our goodbyes, I couldn't help but feel that I had just embarked on the most incredible journey of my life. Little did I know that our first date would be the beginning of a love story that would span years and fill our lives with countless moments of happiness and warmth.

Reflecting upon that evening, my thoughts inevitably turned to my daughter, and a wave of longing and nostalgia washed over me. The absence of her presence in my life weighed heavily on my heart, and as I prepared to go out with Emily, it felt as though I was committing an act of betrayal against them.

Mary had firmly closed the door to any possibility of reconciliation, leaving me with a profound sense of longing for my wife and daughter. I yearned to know what they were doing at that very moment, to share with them that I was okay and embarking on a new chapter of my life elsewhere.

The persistent ache in my heart remained, and I wished for some magical conduit to bridge the chasm that separated us. A way to convey my love and reassure them that, despite the physical distance, my love for them was as strong as ever.

Nonetheless, I recognized the need to set these thoughts aside. My date with Emily was on the horizon, and I didn't want the weight of my past and the absence of Emily and Katrina to overshadow our time together. Emily had faced her own formidable challenges, and I had come to appreciate her perceptiveness in detecting when something weighed on my mind, despite our relatively brief acquaintance. So, with a determined effort, I pushed these thoughts aside, ready to embrace the present and the potential for a brighter future.

Feeling Badly (EMILY)

═══◁○═◇═○▷═══

Sleep eluded me that night; the anticipation of my first date with Wil had my heart and mind racing with excitement. I found myself in a wardrobe dilemma, uncertain about what to wear, but determined that it had to be super cute. It was a pleasant surprise that Wil had asked me to homecoming, let alone invited me on a date, considering how unkind I had been to him. I couldn't help but replay in my mind the hurtful words I had hurled at him and marveled at his capacity for forgiveness.

A part of me was trembling with fear at the prospect of going out with someone, but an irresistible magnetism drew me to Wil, an indescribable pull I couldn't resist even if I tried. Honestly, I felt like he was leagues ahead of me, not necessarily in terms of looks, but in every other aspect. Despite the struggles he had faced during the past summer, he seemed to have everything together, and I held onto the hope that I could follow suit. If there was hope for him, even after enduring his darkest moments, then surely there was a glimmer of hope for me as well.

The truth was, the shadow of that terrible night still loomed large in my thoughts, and I couldn't shake the feeling of being irreparably broken. No matter how many showers I took or how many clothes I discarded, I never felt truly clean. Yet, whenever I was with Wil, the weight of worthlessness seemed to lessen. He had a unique way of making me forget the haunting memories, and I felt an unfamiliar sense of safety in his presence. No one else had ever made me feel that way, not even my own father.

Whenever I found myself near Wil, I made a conscious effort to push aside the negative self-perceptions that constantly plagued me. I was determined not to be a Debbie Downer and jeopardize what we had. After all, Wil was battling his own inner demons, and I didn't want to burden him with my problems.

To soothe my restless mind, I replayed the sweet words Wil had spoken to me, like how endearing it was when he had been shy about asking me to homecoming. A significant part of me yearned to reach out and hold his hand, yet I grappled with the readiness for such physical contact. I had initiated that hug when he asked me out, but the idea of further intimacy felt daunting.

Eventually, I decided to rise from my restless state, opting to lay out my outfit for the upcoming date with Wil. My closet became a treasure trove of possibilities as I spent hours searching for the perfect attire—a balance between not too extravagant and not too casual. Once I had settled on an outfit, there was nothing left to do but await the arrival of morning.

I climbed back into bed, slipping under the covers and hoping to clear my mind for restful slumber. I desperately wished for a night free of nightmares, one where I could dream of Wil and our upcoming date, unburdened by the haunting memories that plagued my sleep.

The First Date

Saturday evening had finally arrived, and I was determined to be punctual for picking up Emily. Remembering that she mentioned wearing a skirt or a dress, I decided to dress up a bit. I opted for a dark purple dress shirt paired with a black tie that had touches of purple. Completing the outfit were black shoes, socks, and dress pants. With a sense of urgency, I hurried down the stairs and glanced at my watch—it read 6:10 p.m. Emily lived just a few streets away, so I still had around twenty minutes. Taking a moment to check my appearance in the mirror of the informal living room, I made sure everything was in place.

I made the decision to read the conclusion of Wil's journal, although a part of me wished I hadn't. It chronicled his time with Rachel, detailing his initial elation at having a girlfriend and even delving into intimate moments of their relationship. I couldn't help but appreciate his impressive command of the English language. However, the narrative took a dark turn as it progressed.

Wil wrote about how things began to deteriorate with Rachel, how she attempted to change him and cloaked herself in secrecy. He noted the sudden addition of a passcode to her phone, which had previously been accessible. Numerous arguments followed, with Rachel repeatedly urging him to "be a man." I quickly skimmed through the pages and discovered the heart-wrenching revelation of her infidelity. When she came to discuss it with him, she confessed to her betrayal and ended their relationship that very night.

The subsequent journal entry, dated May 24th, shook me to my core: *May 24th – I died tonight.* I felt sick to my stomach. It was the night Amelia had found Wil in his room after he had attempted to take his own life. He spent a week in the hospital, and it was on June the first, both of our birthdays, that I had arrived. Reading through all of this had been a heavy burden, especially just before my first date with Emily. I put my phone aside, and began to pace the floor.

In an effort to divert my thoughts from what I had just perused, I reminded myself that Amelia had already left with Steve, and Penny was at Nikki's place, presumably preparing for their evening plans. Just last night, I received a text from Henry, excitedly sharing the news that Beth had agreed to accompany him to Homecoming. While he apologized for the late message, he couldn't contain his joy. They had spent the majority of the night exchanging text messages, and now they were preparing for their first date later in the evening. Glancing at my watch again, now showing 6:19 p.m.—I made a quick decision. I couldn't bear staying cooped up any longer. Briskly, I made my way to the garage and hopped into my SUV. I always preferred being early, as I disliked lateness. Time was precious to me, and I never wanted to waste it.

The drive to Emily's house was a mere four minutes, hardly any time at all. As I pulled up, my gaze fell upon her family's single-story residence, which possessed a cozy and modest appearance. The driveway accommodated two cars, with two more parked along the street. Opposite their home, there was a park, prompting me to choose parking along the fence there.

Despite the successful time I had spent with Emily just last night, a wave of anxiety washed over me as I stepped out of my SUV, nervously adjusting my tie. It felt peculiar to experience such nerves, especially considering the pleasant memories we had created together. However, the anticipation of meeting her parents kept my apprehension intact. The situation felt unfamiliar, particularly since I was technically older than all of them. Nevertheless, I couldn't shake off the teenage thoughts and urges that accompanied this scenario. With trepidation, I slowly made my way up the walkway, my hand trembling as I gently knocked on the screen door. To my surprise, the noise it produced reverberated much louder than expected, with certain parts detached from the metal frame. The unexpected clamor left me completely unsettled.

Oh, Jesus Christ.

The sound was impossible to ignore. It was as if even the most distant souls would have been alerted by the reverberation. With a nervous anticipation, I stood there, anxiously awaiting a response. Soon enough, the inner door swung open, revealing a middle-aged woman with cascading blond locks. Her beauty was undeniable, mirroring her daughters in an uncanny manner, and her vibrant blue eyes caught my attention. Clad in a professional ensemble, she donned a black skirt paired with a crisp white button-down shirt, emanating an air of sophistication.

"Hello, Wil!" she greeted me warmly, her pleasant smile accompanying the opening of the outer door, which had proved to be obnoxiously loud, worse than when I had knocked. "I almost didn't recognize you! You look so—"

"Different?" I interjected, finishing her sentence. "I've been told I've undergone some changes, ma'am," I responded politely.

"You look very handsome," she complimented, her gaze assessing my appearance. "We've actually met before, but I don't think you remember."

"Thank you, ma'am. When did we meet?" I inquired.

"Several times over the past few years when we dropped off Emily and Beth to spend time with Amelia," she recalled.

"Ah," I acknowledged. "That was before my *accident.*"

She nodded, a hint of understanding in her eyes. "I dropped her off the other night at your house, but I suppose you were preoccupied with something else." An uncomfortable silence fell upon us. "Well, come in, come in, have a seat." She gestured toward the interior. I stepped inside, finding myself in a modest foyer. "Let me take your jacket."

I handed my jacket to Mrs. DuBrie, and she carefully hung it on the back of a door, presumably a closet. There was a second door, though I wasn't sure where it led to. She then motioned for me to take a seat, and I began to lower myself onto a chair. However, before I could fully settle, a man of similar stature to me approached. Dressed in a sharp black tie, crisp white button-down shirt, and sleek black dress pants, he had a commanding presence.

"Oh, this is Emily's father, Roger ... you remember Wil, don't you, sweetheart?" Mrs. DuBrie addressed him.

"Nice to see you again, Wil," Mr. DuBrie greeted me, extending his hand.

I shook his hand firmly, maintaining eye contact. "Nice to meet you, sir," I responded respectfully.

Mrs. DuBrie motioned for me to sit down once more, and this time I complied. However, both Mr. and Mrs. DuBrie remained standing. "Emily will be out in a moment," Mrs. DuBrie informed us. "You know girls, always taking forever to get ready."

"Only because I have two sisters." I chuckled, and Mrs. DuBrie joined in for a brief moment. However, their expressions soon turned serious.

"Wil," Mr. DuBrie began, clearing his throat and loosening his tie, "before Emily joins us, Charlotte and I wanted to talk to you."

"Sure!" I replied, anticipating a typical "protective dad" conversation. One I would have given, myself, had someone come to date Katrina. It was sad to think about the possibility of my daughter dating, or even being married – and I would never know. I would never get to be there for any of it.

Mr. DuBrie took a deep breath, gathering his thoughts. "We wanted to thank you for what you did for Emily—for standing up for her and protecting her. You put yourself at risk by doing that."

"We saw the videos online," Mrs. DuBrie added. "Covering our baby with your shirt, then fighting off five of them to ensure nobody else would harm her—we saw it all." She brought her hand up to cover her mouth, her eyes welling up with tears.

Mr. DuBrie put his arm around his wife to offer comfort as she became emotional. "The thing is, we don't know what would have happened if you hadn't stepped in, though we have a pretty good idea. So thank you, son, for what you did. It's something we'll never forget. Ever," he expressed sincerely.

I stood up, feeling a sense of humility. "You don't have to thank me, sir. Emily is an amazing girl. She didn't deserve to be treated that way. Nobody deserves to be treated that way," I said firmly, emphasizing the importance of standing up against injustice.

Mrs. DuBrie wiped away her tears, and Mr. DuBrie extended his hand once more. I shook it, but to my surprise, he pulled me into a brief "bro hug," patting me on the back. "We'll never forget it," he added.

From the periphery of my vision, I noticed Emily standing in the hallway, her presence unbeknownst to me until that moment. My breath caught as I beheld her exquisite beauty. She was adorned in a stunning royal blue dress that descended just above her knee, tastefully cinched at the waist by a black belt. Her legs were enveloped in sleek black stockings, and she completed the ensemble with elegant black closed heels. "Emily!" I couldn't contain my excitement, my exclamation bursting forth as a testament to my elation. Immediately, she skipped over to me, embracing me tightly. It was a warm and heartfelt hug, and I felt a pang of emptiness once she let go.

In a gentle whisper, Emily expressed her contentment. "I'm glad you're here."

A smile graced my lips as I couldn't help but offer a sincere compliment. "You look absolutely beautiful."

With tenderness, Emily extended her hand towards my tie, carefully adjusting the knot. "You're incredibly sweet," she responded, her words filled with warmth and appreciation.

Mr. DuBrie gave a mock cough, capturing our attention. "So, I still have to play the *dad* here," he said playfully. "What time do you plan to have her home, so we don't worry?"

"Is eight-thirty okay?" I suggested.

"It's Saturday, make it ten," Mr. DuBrie responded, giving his approval.

"You two go out and have a wonderful time!" Mrs. DuBrie said with a warm smile.

"Thank you, ma'am, thank you, sir. I'll make sure she's safe, don't worry," I assured them.

"Oh, I know you will, son." Mr. DuBrie chuckled.

Emily guided me towards the door, pausing momentarily to retrieve a jacket from the closet, as I grabbed mine off the door. With a graceful motion, I slid her jacket onto her. As she opened the noisy screen door, she offered a brief wave to her attentive parents, who observed us with keen interest. Side by side, we strolled along the walkway. I reached into my pocket and retrieved my keys, pressing the button to unlock the doors. Opening the passenger door for Emily, she appeared pleasantly surprised, followed by a radiant smile as she hopped inside.

"Such a gentleman," she sweetly remarked. Returning her smile, I closed her door before taking my place behind the wheel.

As I settled into the driver's seat, I couldn't help but notice a trace of nervousness in Emily's expression. Our eyes met, and she responded with another smile. "I'm excited," she confessed, revealing her innermost feelings.

"You're feeling a bit nervous." I chuckled, starting the SUV's engine. Glancing over at Emily's house, I noticed her parents still observing us from the doorway.

"My accent again?" she guessed, sensing my amusement.

"Yes. But I told you, there's no reason to be nervous with me," I reassured her, aiming to ease her concerns.

"You can't tell me you're not nervous at all," Emily countered playfully.

"I'll admit, I was a bit nervous to meet your parents," I confessed, honesty coloring my words. "And yes, there's a hint of nervousness about our first date as well. I want it to be absolutely perfect."

"I'm sure everything will go perfectly," Emily replied, her enthusiasm radiating. "To be honest, I'm pleasantly surprised my parents allowed me to go out. They've become quite protective, especially after everything that's happened."

Curiosity piqued, I asked, "So, why did they give their approval for our outing?"

Emily's face lit up as she explained, "Well, my parents are good friends with yours, they have been since we arrived here. And Beth, my sister, showed them all the videos online of the ... *incident* in the gym. Seeing how you stood up for me and protected me, they felt reassured and agreed to let me go with you."

A genuine smile spread across my face. "I'm really glad they did."

Breaking the brief moment of silence, Emily's cheery voice filled the air, "Where are we going?" she inquired, her curiosity palpable.

"To a small place called Reagan's. It's pretty casual. I didn't want to go somewhere that was *stuffy*. I want you to be comfortable with me—always," I explained.

"Oh, that sounds lovely! I've heard about it, but I've never actually been there," Emily responded with a hint of intrigue. "You'd think I would have visited, considering it's so close to home."

"I think you'll like it," I said, my own nervousness creeping in. "Did I mention that you look really beautiful?"

"Aw, thank you, Wil. You look incredibly handsome as well." Emily blushed, returning the compliment.

The restaurant was just a short drive away, so we arrived promptly. Stepping out of the SUV, I extended my right arm to Emily, and she delicately placed her right hand on my bicep. As we entered the restaurant, I led Emily towards a table situated at the back, near a window adorned with twinkling white fairly lights. The warm and inviting ambiance created by the lights embraced us, filling the air with a cozy aura. Positioning myself behind Emily, I assisted her in removing her coat, and her radiant smile persisted throughout the process. Gesturing for her to sit on one side of the booth, I settled in on the other.

"I absolutely adore the cozy atmosphere here," Emily remarked, as if she could read my thoughts, "I have fairy lights in my room, too, except they're pink."

"Yeah, it's definitely one of my favorite aspects too," I replied, sharing in her sentiment.

Her curiosity piqued, she inquired, "So you've been here before?"

I nodded, answering, "Yeah, with Amelia and Penny, although we usually sit near the other wall."

Emily grinned mischievously. "So you haven't brought any other dates here?"

I chuckled and shook my head. "Nope. I've only had the one other date since I left the hospital."

"Really?" she exclaimed, intrigued. I met her gaze with a smile.

"Yep."

Emily's smile grew wider. "I'm pretty sure Amelia won't be interrupting us on our date. At least, I hope not." She giggled. "I'm really sorry it got disrupted."

I laughed lightly. "Well, it did bring me home early, but it didn't ruin anything. Are you feeling less nervous now?" I inquired, genuinely interested.

"You know ... I am," she replied, placing her hands on the table. I noticed a pretty silver ring adorning her right index finger. "You put me at ease. It's so easy to talk to you."

"I'm glad you feel that way," I responded genuinely.

I reached out, aiming for a gentle touch of her hand, but she swiftly withdrew it.

"I apologize; I have a habit of touching people's hand to make them feel at ease," I admitted sincerely, feeling a tinge of regret for my forwardness. "I didn't think, it caused the opposite effect." In truth, I often found myself reaching out to touch the hand of the soldiers I was tending to in my world, hoping to offer them some comfort in their time of need. It was a well-intentioned but unwise habit, one I resolved to break—no more such gestures to anyone. Emily returned her hand to the table and reassured me, saying, "No need to worry. It's not about you; it's about me, I promise." She sighed softly, adding, "I just have a lot of personal issues to deal with. It's not like we haven't touched before, I've hugged you on several occasions."

I had seen this type of behavior before, normally in females that had previously felt ... violated. I was hoping that was not the case, but my training told me otherwise.

"No, my fault. I shouldn't have done that. We're just getting to know each other." I insisted. Clearing my throat, I proposed a suggestion, breaking the silence. "How about we take this opportunity to get to know each other better tonight? I'm open to answering any questions you have. If there's anything you'd rather not discuss, we can skip it. Sound good?"

Emily's response was immediate and filled with enthusiasm. "Yes! This will be so much fun!"

"Ladies first," I encouraged, signaling for her to begin.

After a brief moment of thought, she posed a simple question. "What is your full name?"

"William Michael Fenwick," I replied carefully, ensuring the accuracy of my answer. I would have had a lot of explaining to do if I told her my *real* name.

Curiosity driving her next question, she inquired, "Are you named after someone?"

"Yes, my middle name is my father's first name. What about you? What's your full name?" I inquired.

"Emily Renee DuBrie," she proudly responded.

Recalling our previous conversation, I asked, "You mentioned being from Bolton, right?"

"Bolton, UK! Yes! I'm impressed you remembered! It's just north of Manchester, although I don't really have the Manchester accent," she explained.

"It's your turn!" I declared, observing her eyes wandering up to the ceiling as she tapped her lips in contemplation. Eventually, she formulated her question.

"What do you hope to gain from our relationship? Is Homecoming just a one-time event for you, or are you open to dating others? Maybe I'm getting ahead of myself," she asked directly.

Her straightforwardness momentarily caught me off guard, but I quickly composed myself and responded honestly, "I don't date around. You're the only person I want to be with. If Homecoming was meant to be a one-time thing, then we wouldn't be out together right now. I'm seeking a stable, long-term relationship."

Emily's pleased expression made it evident that she appreciated my response. "Good answer! That's exactly what I want too. Now it's your turn!"

Contemplating my next question, I asked, "When did you come to the United States?"

"We moved here when I was twelve. Interestingly enough, we actually met before then when we were in the same class. However, you didn't really talk to me back then. I became friends with Amelia shortly after, and eventually, Penny too," Emily explained, reminiscing on our shared past.

"Noticing the accents in your family, I've observed that your mom doesn't have an accent, while Beth and your dad have a slight one," I observed.

Emily nodded, affirming my observation. "Yes, with Beth, her accent can vary. Sometimes it's subtle, and other times it becomes more pronounced ... I guess it just depends on her mood. My mum's not English; she's actually American. And when my dad gets angry, his accent comes out in full force."

"Alright, it's your turn," I prompted eagerly, anxious to hear her question.

Emily's eyes sparkled with excitement as she giggled. "Yay! Um ... What is your ideal date night?"

Smiling at her infectious enthusiasm, I replied, "That's an easy one: any date that involves being with you."

Emily blushed at my response and praised, "Oh, you're quite witty. I love it!" Just then, our server approached our table.

"Hey, guys, I'm Lauren. Welcome to Reagan's! What can I get you two?" she greeted us with a friendly smile.

Glancing at Emily, I asked, "What would you like?"

"Can I have a Jabsi and maybe some nachos?" Emily requested.

"Sure!" Lauren replied cheerfully. "And for you?"

"I'll have the same, no ice in my soda, please," I responded. "Oh! Can I have a chocolate shake, too?"

"Certainly! I'll have those for you in no time," Lauren assured us before hurrying off. As we waited for our order, my focus returned to Emily, who was watching me intently.

"I'm sorry, where were we?" I inquired, trying to recall our previous conversation.

Emily giggled, reminding me, "We were asking each other questions. I have one!" she exclaimed.

"Alright," I responded eagerly, prepared.

With a serious tone, Emily shifted her gaze down to the table and asked, "Serious question, and I want you to be honest, no matter how bad it might make you look, okay? Can you do that?"

"Yes, absolutely," I assured her, understanding the importance of honesty in our conversation.

Taking a deep breath, Emily appeared slightly nervous as she moistened her lips. Her unwavering gaze encouraged me to respond sincerely. "In an argument, is winning what is most important to you? If so, why?" she asked, her voice filled with curiosity and anticipation.

A smile formed on my lips, and I replied, "So deep." Her eyes remained fixed on mine as she patiently awaited my answer. "Arguments aren't about *winning* or *losing*; they're about *listening* and *learning*," I began, adopting a more mature perspective. "An argument often arises from a misunderstanding or when one person feels that their concerns or issues are not being properly addressed. In such situations, it's important to remain calm yet assertive, relying on evidence rather than mere opinions. It's crucial to avoid sarcasm or belittling the other person's concerns or fears. However, it's also essential to choose our battles wisely, as constant arguing can be draining. While I can't claim to execute this perfectly in every argument, I always strive to do my best. And as a general rule, I believe it's important to avoid going to bed angry with each other, if possible." My own statement made me think of Ella, and how we vowed never to go to bed angry with each other. A promise we held true to our entire marriage.

A smile bloomed on Emily's lips as she chuckled. "Well, I certainly wasn't expecting such a profound response. You seem much more mature for your age than ... well, anyone I know," she commented, acknowledging my perspective. I responded with a knowing smile, appreciating her compliment. "I really like that answer, Wil. I'm curious about where you got such an ideology, considering you've only remembered from this past summer until now," Emily remarked, her curiosity shining through.

I shrugged, drawing a parallel between another aspect of my life. "How did I learn to play hockey since the summer?"

"That's a great question!" Emily replied, perking up. "How did you manage that?"

Once again, I shrugged, acknowledging the inexplicable events that had unfolded in my life. "A lot of strange things have happened to me since I woke up in the hospital."

"Amelia mentioned something similar," Emily added.

Raising an eyebrow, I responded, "She did, huh?"

"Oh! Don't be mad at her. She refused to tell me anything—I swear," Emily quickly reassured me.

I nodded, acknowledging her words. "Maybe one day, we'll have a conversation about it." I didn't want to delve into that topic tonight, but I left the possibility open for future discussions.

"It's none of my business," Emily said, her smile remaining intact.

"One day," I promised, assuring her that there would be an opportunity to share more in the future.

Lauren returned with our nachos, Jabsi sodas, and my chocolate shake. As soon as the shake was placed in front of me, I couldn't resist diving in like a caveman, which immediately caught Emily's attention. "Do they not feed you at home?" she teased playfully, her giggle sounding like music to my ears.

I let out a mock sigh, pretending to be dramatically deprived of food. "Nothing. They feed me nothing," I replied with a hint of humor. Emily's laughter was contagious, and her face lit up with delight. "I'm just kidding—I really like chocolate milkshakes."

"I can see that!" she said, thoroughly entertained by my enthusiasm for the treat. The joy in her eyes made me realize how lucky I was to share these lighthearted moments with her.

"Whose turn is it?" I inquired.

Emily's face lit up with a grin, though there was a hint of nervousness in her demeanor. "I seem to have lost track," she admitted. "But I do have a question for you, and it might be a bit personal. If it's too much, just say so."

"Go ahead, don't worry about it," I responded with confidence, trying to ease her discomfort.

"Do you think your breakup with Rachel played a role in ... well, you know," Emily asked cautiously, "I realize it's an intimate topic for a first date—"

"I honestly don't know," I admitted. "Supposedly, that's what led me down that path, but I can't recall any of it. I've been reading through a diary I found, though. It's clear he was in a dark place."

"A diary, really?" Emily inquired, her curiosity piqued.

I nodded, displaying my phone. "Yes, it's all documented here. There are hundreds of pages, but I haven't mustered the courage to read it all yet."

"Aren't you curious about it?" she asked.

I shrugged, conflicted. "I'm not sure I want to know. It's emotionally challenging to read through."

Emily nodded empathetically. "I'm so sorry, Wil."

"It's alright, just promise me you won't mention it to my sisters, okay?" I requested. "I think the contents could really hurt them. It seems he had given up on himself years ago."

"*He?*" Emily questioned, seeking clarification. "You mean, *you?*"

"Exactly," I confirmed with a faint smile. "Me."

"Did you mention anything really bad in your journal?" Emily inquired. "He talked about suicide, a lot. I feel like if Amelia and Penny knew, they could have helped him long before he did what he did." I said.

"Once again, the distinction between *he* and *you* arises," Emily observed. "You speak of it as if it were someone else."

"Well, considering I can't recall anything before my accident, it's challenging for me to take ownership of those actions," I clarified.

"I suppose that makes sense," Emily conceded, seemingly accepting my explanation. "Did *he* ... I mean, *you* ... *whoever* it was, did they ever explain why they wanted to go down that path?"

I hesitated, reluctant to reveal that she had been a source of inspiration in the journal, even part of several stories he had written, or that Greg played a significant role in it all. "It just seemed like everything was falling apart, and I was in a very dark place."

"But you don't feel that way now, do you? You seem perfectly fine," Emily observed.

"Sometimes, it's those who appear strong on the outside that need the most support, the ones who are silently struggling," I replied seriously.

"Is that what's happening with you right now?" She asked, her concern evident.

I shook my head, offering reassurance. "No, I'm genuinely happy and feeling great."

"Are you saying that because society has conditioned men not to show weakness?" Emily inquired.

"I can't recall being conditioned since this summer," I replied with a smile, "but I'm telling you the truth. When you agreed to go to homecoming with me, it meant a lot."

"Oh my god, Wil, you're so sweet!" Emily blushed. "And to be clear, I don't ever want you to feel you can't showing your feelings around me, sadness, or otherwise. I don't see that as being weak, I see it as being human. It would be terrible for a man to have no outlet for his feelings. I know this is our first date, but I want you to promise me right now, that you won't hold in your feelings. You can always talk to me about anything."

I thought about it for a moment, before nodding, "I'll do my best."

There was a moment of awkward silence, during which I considered sharing my own dark past from the other world—my battles with depression, the loss of loved ones, and even my own death. However, it felt too soon for that conversation.

"So, what about you? If you don't mind me asking, you've likely faced some difficult moments, given everything," I inquired.

Now Emily appeared noticeably uncomfortable, shifting in her seat as she contemplated my question. "There are some things I'm not ready to talk about," she admitted.

"I understand," I began to say, but she interrupted me.

"But I've been in the darkness for a long time, especially with Greg. So many terrible thoughts have crossed my mind," Emily confessed. "I've often wondered if this misery was my life now. I'd sit there in a daze, feeling helpless and worthless. He would always tell me that nobody else would want me, that he was the only one willing to put up with me."

"That's absolutely not true," I countered with a smile, trying to lighten the mood. "I'm living proof of that. Many guys asked you to homecoming, too." "Just because of how I look." Emily pointed out, "Greg had control over every aspect of my life, as you know. I couldn't even talk to you, let alone show kindness to you. I wore what he told me, interacted only with people he approved of, which was a small circle. He humiliated me in front of everyone, cut me off from my family and friends, and stripped away any self-esteem I had. Even now, as happy as I am with you, I can't shake the feeling that I'm not worth your time because of the damage he caused."

"You are absolutely worth my time, Emily. Everyone carries some scars from life, even at your young age," I reassured her.

Emily smiled, "*Our age*. Did you suddenly become older than me?" She teased, letting out a laugh.

I chuckled, realizing my slip. "I suppose I'm just an old soul," I quipped.

"You've matured so much compared to how you used to be. I know I mentioned it before, but it's really striking," Emily remarked.

"Is that a bad thing?" I inquired.

"Not at all! I really like it!" Emily replied with enthusiasm.

We continued asking each other questions for the next two hours, fully engrossed in our conversation. Emily listened attentively, laughing and smiling throughout. It was delightful to see her happy and carefree. When we decided it was time to leave, I took care of the bill and left a generous tip for our server. Emily had offered to split the cost, but I declined her offer. As we sat in the SUV in the parking lot, Emily had a wide smile on her face.

"If that smile on your face is any indication of how tonight went, I'd say you had a good time," I remarked, noting her joyful expression.

"I had such a fantastic time!" Emily replied enthusiastically. "Thank you so much! It was so much fun!"

"Thank you. You're a lot of fun to be with," I replied sincerely. We sat in comfortable silence for a moment before she cleared her throat. I noticed her tendency to bite her lower lip when she was nervous or shy.

"It's 9:45 p.m.," she said softly. "I have to get back … but I don't want this night to end."

"I feel the same way, Emmy," I confessed.

"I've never felt this comfortable with someone before," she said, her accent shining through. "I still feel nervous, but in a good way. Do you know what I mean?"

I nodded, understanding her sentiment. "I do. It's like the nerves before a game."

"Yes, exactly!" she exclaimed, her excitement evident. "Only better!" She gave me a shy look. "I hope this isn't all going to your head."

I laughed, appreciating her playful remark. "I may have trouble getting out of the truck later, yes."

She put on a mock surprised expression and playfully slapped my arm. "Sttttooopppppp."

"I'm just kidding," I said through laughter. "Seriously, I'm really enjoying being with you." I sighed and checked the time again. "I suppose I should get you home before we end up being late. I want to make sure to get you home in plenty of time, so your parents are happy."

I started the truck and headed back to Emily's house. We drove in silence for most of the way. Occasionally, I noticed her stealing glances at me from my peripheral vision. My hand rested on the shifter, while her hand shifted between her lap, her thigh, and eventually settled next to the shifter. It didn't take long for us to reach her house. It was still early, only 9:54 p.m. We sat in my truck, not making eye contact right away. Finally, Emily looked at me and smiled.

"Well, here we are."

"Here we are," I echoed.

"Thank you again for tonight," she said, turning more towards me. "Maybe we can talk or text later, after you get home?"

"Sure, I'd like that a lot," I replied enthusiastically.

"Well, I should probably get inside," she said, breaking the silence.

"I'm going to walk you to your door, make sure you get inside safely."

Emily's smile returned. "Oh, I'd like that! Mum and dad would, too."

I got out of the truck and glanced around, noticing there was no police car in sight. There was an odd smell in the air as I walked to Emily's side, opening the door and gently taking her hand to help her out. "This is going to take some time getting used to," She said, a hint of excitement in her voice, as I closed the door behind her.

"Well, get used to it," I said with a warm smile. We walked across the street and up her walkway, our arms brushing against each other often. As we approached her house, I could see her parents peeking out the windows, curiosity evident on their faces. Once we reached the door, I turned to face Emily. "Where are the police?" I inquired.

"They've stopped coming; they claim they don't have the manpower to stay out here all of the time," Emily replied.

I nodded, and looked as her house, "Your parents seem to be looking out the windows," I remarked.

Emily rolled her eyes playfully. "That figures. They're probably wondering why you walked me to the door." She giggled. "This is uncharted territory for them ... and for me!"

I shifted my weight from one foot to the other, feeling a nervous lump in my throat. "So, um ..." I started, trying to clear my throat. "Gosh, sorry about that," I said, sounding a bit nervous.

Emily laughed, finding my nervousness endearing. "You seem so nervous, Wil."

"Yeah, well, a little," I admitted.

"Is everything okay?" she whispered, concern in her voice.

I nodded, gathering my courage. "I, uh ... wanted to know if you would ... you know ... go on another date with me?"

"Awww, Wil, you don't have to be nervous with me," she reassured me. "Of course, I'll go on another date with you."

"Really? You will?" I asked, a mix of relief and excitement flooding through me.

"Yes, of course! Why would you think I wouldn't want to go out with you again? I told you I had a wonderful time, and we're already going to Homecoming together."

"I didn't want to assume anything," I replied honestly.

"I quite like you, Wil," Emily said, looking up at me with an intense gaze.

"I like you too, Emily," I said, my heart swelling with affection. "When would you like to go out again?"

She pondered for a moment, considering her options. "What about tomorrow? If you're not already busy?"

"Tomorrow? Really? Sure!" I exclaimed, trying my best to contain my eagerness but failing miserably. "What time?"

Emily pondered her words for a moment and let out a giggle. "I can be ready whenever you want me," she playfully remarked. "Whenever you want me to be ready," she added, blushing slightly.

"How about ten?" I suggested, a delightful plan forming in my mind for our next outing. "In the morning, that is."

"Sure. What do you have in mind?" she asked, her eyes fixed on me.

"I think I'll keep it a surprise," I replied with a grin, enjoying the anticipation building between us.

"Ohhh, surprises are the best! I can't wait," she exclaimed, her excitement contagious.

"I feel the same way," I admitted sheepishly, glancing at the time on my phone. "It's 9:56 p.m. You should head inside."

Emily made a disappointed face. "Oh poo, they already know I'm home. Can you call or text me when you get home? So I know you made it safely? It would mean a lot to me."

"I won't forget," I assured her.

"Promise? It's important to me," she emphasized.

"I promise, cross my heart," I reassured her, wanting to ease any worries she had. In that moment, I longed to kiss her, to end the perfect date on an even sweeter note. However, I didn't want to overstep any boundaries or assume she was comfortable with it. Emily looked at me with anticipation, as if waiting for that very gesture, but I couldn't be certain. Instead, I leaned in and embraced her, surprising her momentarily. She returned the hug and held on to me a little longer. We savored the embrace before reluctantly parting. With gentle tenderness, I took her hand and gave it a quick kiss. "I'll message you the moment I arrive home," I whispered softly.

Emily seemed a bit disappointed as she opened her storm door, making quite a racket. "Sorry! We really need to fix this."

"It has its charm." I chuckled, eliciting a giggle from her. "Have a wonderful night, Emily."

"You, too, Wil. Be careful going home!"

"I will."

"... and text me!"

I couldn't contain my eagerness to be in her presence once more. The prospect of our next encounter brought a sense of joy and anticipation that would likely keep me awake, eagerly awaiting the new day and the moments we would share together.

As I readied myself to depart, Emily's phone emitted a soft buzz, prompting her to check it hastily. The broad smile that had adorned her face vanished in an instant, replaced by a troubled expression as her gaze fixated on the screen.

"What's wrong?" I inquired, my concern piqued.

Emily appeared to contemplate for a brief moment before responding with an apprehensive look. "It's Greg."

I arched an eyebrow in response. "Oh?"

"He … he's threatening me again, same old stuff," she replied, attempting to sound nonchalant about it.

"May I see?" I implored gently.

"It's nothing, Wil, just the same old nonsense," she hesitated but eventually relented, passing me her phone. As I read the text message, disbelief washed over me. It was difficult to fathom that someone would actually send such a message:

I know you were out with Wil tonight, bitch! You'll both pay for this, I swear!

I swiftly surveyed our surroundings, diligently searching for any signs of surveillance, yet nothing or no one appeared conspicuous. The familiar odor that had reached my nose earlier triggered memories of my time in the war.

"I need you to go inside immediately, Emily, and show your parents this text. Call the police right away—do you understand?" I asserted firmly, returning her phone and gently guiding her towards the storm door. She pushed open the main door, and the storm door closed with a resounding slam, her gaze locked onto me.

"What about you?" Her concern was palpable, and she questioned, "What's wrong?"

"Call the police, Emily, right now," I urged. The scent of gasoline was unmistakable, and there was no way she couldn't have noticed it; it was pungent. My suspicions were confirmed when, out of nowhere, her car suddenly burst into flames. The intense heat from the fiery inferno forced me to press my back against her house for protection. Emily's terrified scream cut through the air, echoing the shock and fear coursing through both of us. The blazing car sent plumes of black smoke billowing into the sky, making the situation all the more distressing.

It was apparent that I couldn't delay addressing Greg's latest threat any longer.

Acknowledgements

———⟨∘⟩———

I'd like to kick things off with heartfelt gratitude. First and foremost, my incredible, supportive, and loving wife, Emma. You've always been the wind beneath my wings, pushing me to chase my dreams no matter how far-fetched they seemed. Even on the toughest days when doubt crept in, you stood by me, reassuring me that my work was more than good enough. You've kept our little ones and our furry friends entertained, granting me the precious quiet time I needed to write. None of this would have been possible without your unwavering love and support. Thank you from the bottom of my heart, my sweet angel.

To my amazing children, Abigail Forloines and Mattie Bowman, who share the same roof with me: Your insights into the current teen lingo were invaluable, ensuring that I got the dialogue just right for the teens in the book. You were always there to bounce ideas off, and your eagerness to help touched my heart. I love you both more than words can express.

To my children who are away from home: Kelsey Forloines, Brooke Forloines, Gus Forloines, and Amber Vox—my love for all of you knows no bounds.

A heartfelt thank you to my mom and dad for bringing me into this world. I love you both deeply, and I wish dad were here to witness this moment.

My two incredible sisters, Patty Tucker and Cindy Forloines, you mean the world to me. I love you both immensely.

To my twin brother, Rob Forloines, or "Chip" as I fondly call you, thanks for your singular contribution to the book – "Jabsi Cola." One day, I'll unravel the mystery of that name for everyone! (Or at least what the "J-A-B" means.)

My dear friend, Lauren Novotny, a massive thank you for tackling the first draft, which was astonishingly lengthy at 210,110 words! Thank you for your unflagging support and encouragement to publish the book (even after my editor managed to trim it down significantly).

And a huge shout-out to my Copy Editor, Sara Kelly. Your support has been invaluable in dissecting the behemoth of a book it once was, now reshaped into two or three books. I eagerly look forward to our future collaborations!

For more information on upcoming books, please visit http:// jeffreyforloines.com